The Aviary Gate

The Aviary Gate

A Novel

KATIE HICKMAN

BLOOMSBURY

"Burnt Norton," from *Four Quartets* by T. S. Eliot, copyright 1936 by Houghton Mifflin Harcourt Publishing Company and renewed 1964 by T. S. Eliot, reprinted by permission of the publisher.

Published by Bloomsbury USA, New York
Distributed to the trade by Macmillan

All papers used by Bloomsbury USA are natural, recyclable products made from wood grown in well-managed forests. The manufacturing processes conform to the environmental regulations of the country of origin.

LIBRARY OF CONGRESS CATALOGING-IN-PUBLICATION DATA

Hickman, Katie.
The Aviary Gate : a novel / by Katie Hickman.
p. cm.
ISBN-13 978-1-59691-475-9 (alk. paper)
ISBN-10 1-59691-475-0 (alk paper)
1. Istanbul (Turkey)—Sociallife and customs—16th century—Fiction. 2. Istanbul (Turkey)—Court and courtiers—Fiction. 3. British—Turkey—Fiction. 4. Harems—Turkey—Fiction. I. Title.

PR6058.I27A95 2008
823'.914—dc22
2007050038

First U.S. Edition 2008

1 3 5 7 9 10 8 6 4 2

Typeset by Hewer Text UK Ltd., Edinburgh
Printed in the United States of America by Quebecor World Fairfield

This book is for my son
Luke
Nur 'Aynayya
Light of My Eyes

who was there at the very beginning

Footfalls echo in the memory
Down the passage which we did not take
Towards the door we never opened
Into the rose-garden. My words echo
Thus, in your mind.

T. S. Eliot – *Four Quartets*

Cast of Characters
(*indicates that they existed in real life)

English

*Paul Pindar – Levant Company merchant; secretary to the English ambassador
John Carew – his servant, a master cook
*Sir Henry Lello – the English ambassador
Lady Lello – his wife
*Thomas Dallam – organ maker
*Thomas Glover – Levant Company merchant, secretary to the English ambassador
*William and Jonas Aldridge – merchants, English consuls at Chios and Patras
*John Sanderson – Levant Company merchant
*John Hanger – his apprentice
*Mr Sharp and Mr Lambeth – Levant Company merchants based in Aleppo
*The Reverend May – parson to the English embassy in Constantinople
*Cuthbert Bull – cook to the English embassy
Thomas Lamprey – a sea captain
Celia Lamprey – his daughter
Annetta – her friend

Ottoman

*Safiye, the Valide Sultan – the mother of Sultan Mehmet III
*Esperanza Malchi – the Valide's *kira*
Gulbahar, Ayshe, Fatma and Turhan – the Valide's principal hand-maids

Gulay, the Sultan's Haseki – the Sultan's most favoured concubine
*Handan – the Sultan's concubine, and mother of Prince Ahmet
Hanza – a young woman in the harem
Hassan Aga, also known as Little Nightingale – Chief Black Eunuch
Hyacinth – a eunuch
Suleiman Aga – a senior eunuch
Cariye Lala – the Under-Mistress of the Harem Baths
Cariye Tata and Cariye Tusa – harem servants
*Sultan Mehmet III – Ottoman Sultan 1595–1603
*Nurbanu – his mother, the old Valide Sultan
*Janfreda Khatun – a former harem stewardess
Jamal al-Andalus – an astronomer

Others

*De Brèves – the French Ambassador
*The Venetian Bailo – the Venetian Ambassador

Glossary

Aga – Master, chief
cariye – The humblest ranking of the slave girls in the palace
gözde – 'Girl in the sultan's eye', a term indicating a possible relationship with the sultan
Haseki – 'Favourite', a sixteenth-century title given to the principal concubine of the sultan
kadın – An honorific meaning 'lady of rank'. This word replaced the earlier '*khatun*', also an honorific used by high-ranking women.
kira – Business agent working for the Valide Sultan, or any other lady in the harem
Padishah – 'God's Shadow upon Earth', the usual term used by the Ottomans to mean 'the sovereign'
Valide Sultan – 'Royal mother', the mother of the reigning sultan
yalı- A mansion beside the Bosphorous

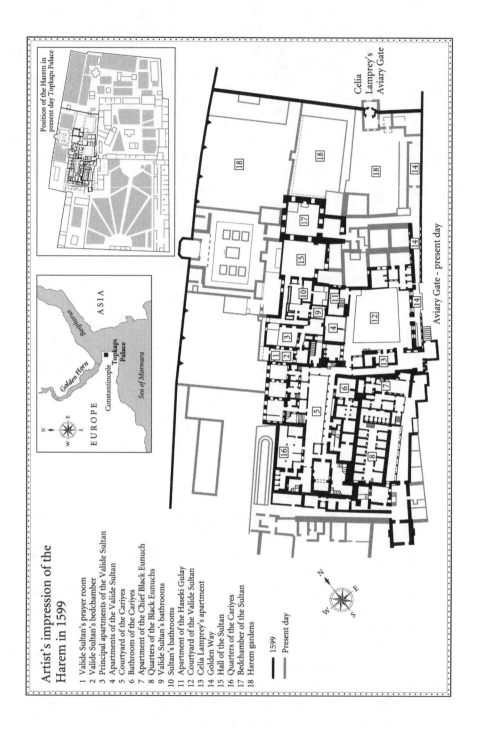

Artist's impression of the Harem in 1599

1 Valide Sultan's prayer room
2 Valide Sultan's bedchamber
3 Principal apartments of the Valide Sultan
4 Apartments of the Valide Sultan
5 Courtyard of the Cariyes
6 Bathroom of the Cariyes
7 Apartment of the Chief Black Eunuch
8 Quarters of the Black Eunuchs
9 Valide Sultan's bathrooms
10 Sultan's bathrooms
11 Apartment of the Haseki Gulay
12 Courtyard of the Valide Sultan
13 Celia Lamprey's apartment
14 Golden Way
15 Hall of the Sultan
16 Quarters of the Cariyes
17 Bedchamber of the Sultan
18 Harem gardens

—— 1599
—— Present day

Position of the Harem in present day Topkapı Palace

EUROPE

Golden Horn

Bosphorus

ASIA

Constantinople

Topkapı Palace

Sea of Marmara

Aviary Gate - present day

Celia Lamprey's Aviary Gate

Prologue

Oxford: the present day

The parchment, when Elizabeth found it, was the amber colour of old tea, frail as leaf mould.

A small folio sheet, it had been folded carefully three ways so that it fitted perfectly between the pages of the book. Along one of the folded sides was a watermark. Elizabeth looked back at the catalogue entry quickly – *opus astronomicus quaorum prima de sphaera planetarium* – and then at the folded sheet again.

I've found it.

Her throat felt tight. For a moment she sat quite still. The librarian had his back to her, was bending down over a trolley of books. She looked up at the clock on the wall opposite: five minutes to seven.

She had five minutes till the library closed, perhaps less. The bell had already rung, and most of the other readers were beginning to pack their things away. But still Elizabeth could not bring herself to unfold the paper. Instead she picked up the book and, holding it carefully ajar, the spine of the book cradled in her cupped hands, she raised it to her face. Carefully, very carefully now, she told herself.

Then, with both eyes closed, the sniff of a tentative cat. And at once: snuff and old dust, a faint whiff of camphor. And then the sea, definitely the sea. And something else, what was it? She breathed in again, very gently this time.

Roses. Sadness.

Elizabeth put the book down, her hands trembling.

Chapter 1

Constantinople, 31 August 1599

Night

'Are they dead?'
'The girl, yes.'

A slim figure, two thin gold chains just visible on delicate ankles, lay sprawled face down amongst the cushions on the floor.

'The other?'

The Valide Sultan's *kira*, the Jewess Esperanza Malchi, brought her lantern a little closer to the face of the second body, spreadeagled clumsily on the divan. From the pocket in her robe she brought out a small jewelled mirror and held it close to the nostrils. An almost imperceptible film clouded the surface of the glass. 'No, Majesty. Not yet.'

In the shadows by the doorway to the little bedchamber, Safiye, the Valide Sultan, the mother of God's Shadow Upon Earth, drew her veil a little closer round her shoulders, shivering despite the closeness of the night. On her finger an emerald the size of a pigeon's egg, briefly catching the light from Esperanza's lantern, glittered like a cat's eye. 'But it cannot be long. What do you think?'

'It won't be long, Majesty. Shall I send for the physician?'

'No!' the reply was sharp. 'No physician. Not yet.'

They turned towards the dying figure on the divan, a massive mound of soft black flesh. On the floor beside the divan was an upturned tray, its contents spewed across the floor. Thin stains of some dark liquid, food or vomit, glimmered like spiders' threads amongst the cushions. Another thin black stain trickled from one ear.

'Poison?'

'Yes, Majesty.' Esperanza gave a curt nod. 'Look . . .' she bent down and picked something up from amongst the broken porcelain.

'What?'

'I'm not sure. A child's toy, I think . . . a ship.'

'It doesn't look like a toy.'

Esperanza peered at the object in her hands more closely, and as she did so a piece came away in her fingers. 'No, not a toy,' she said, consideringly. 'A sweetmeat, made of sugar.' She made as if to bite off a piece.

'*Don't taste it*!' Safiye almost knocked the sugar toy from her hand. 'I'll take it, Esperanza. Give it to me . . .'

Behind the divan was an open window which gave on to a green and white tiled corridor where jasmine grew in pots. In the cloistered sweetness of the night, suddenly, there was a noise.

'Quick, the lamp.'

Esperanza damped down her lantern. For a few moments the women stood without moving.

'A cat, Majesty.' Safiye's handmaid, veiled like her mistress so that Esperanza could not see her face, now spoke softly from the darkness behind them.

'What time is it, Gulbahar?'

'Just a few hours till daybreak, Majesty.'

'So soon?'

Outside the window a sliver of night sky was visible in the space above the corridor's high walls. Now the clouds parted and a flood of moonlight, brighter by far than Esperanza's lantern, filled the room. On the walls of the little bedchamber the tiles seemed to shiver and tremble, silver-blue and silver-green, like water in a moon-viewing pool. Motionless beneath them the body, naked except for the thinnest wrapping of white muslin around the loins, was illuminated too. Safiye could now make out its contours. It was a woman's body, soft and almost hairless: the voluptuously naked hips, pendulous breasts, nipples the colour of molasses. A monumental sculpture of flesh. The skin, by day so shiny and black, now had a dusty matt look to it, as if the poison had sucked out all its light. And at the corners of the lips, which fanned out hideously fat and red as hibiscus flowers, bubbled flecks of foam.

3

'Majesty . . .' The Jewess's eyes flickered nervously towards Safiye. 'Tell us what to do, Majesty,' she urged.

But Safiye seemed not to hear her. She took a step forwards into the room. 'Little Nightingale, my old friend . . .' The words were no more than a whisper.

The heavy thighs were splayed out on the cushions, as unmindful of modesty as a woman in childbirth. The cat, which had been nosing around the fallen debris on the floor, now sprang up on to the divan. The movement caused some of the thin muslin covering to come awry, exposing the parts beneath. Esperanza made as if to cover them again, but the Valide Sultan, with a quick movement of her hand, stayed her. 'No. Let me look. I want to look.'

She took another step into the room. From her handmaid Gulbahar came a small muffled sound, an almost imperceptible sigh. Like the rest of the body, the groin was completely hairless. Between the plumpness of the thighs, where the parts should have been, there was nothing. In their place was an empty space: a single angry scar, sinewed and scorched as if by a burn, where a single slice of the knife had once, in some unimaginably far-distant moment of his unimaginably long life, sliced off the penis and testicles of Hassan Aga, chief of the Valide Sultan's black eunuchs.

Floating on a cloud of pain, Hassan Aga, Little Nightingale, acknowledged somewhere in his slipping consciousness that the Valide Sultan was near. The whispers of the women were confused, no more than a buzzing in his ears, but the smell of her – the myrrh and ambergris with which she perfumed her inner robes, the skin of her beautiful thighs, her belly and her forbidden sex – he could never mistake that scent, not even now, not even on his deathbed.

He drifted again. The pain that had torn like a demon at his guts and his bowels had subsided, as though his body had been tortured beyond sensation. Drifting, now, drifting. Was he awake or did he simply dream? Pain, he had known pain before. The picture of a boy came before his eyes. A small boy but sturdy, even then, with a furze of close-cropped hair like a black cap pulled down unusually low over his brow. Somewhere in this dream he could hear the sound of a woman's voice screaming, and then a man's voice – his father? But how could this be? Hassan Aga, Chief Black Eunuch, had no parents.

4

Or perhaps he had once, in that other life long ago, when he was still whole.

As he drifted, still on the edge of consciousness, other pictures came and went, spinning on the outgoing tide of his mind. In front of him now there was a horizon, a wide blue horizon. The boy with the close-cropped hair was walking, a journey that had no end, walking on and on. Sometimes, to keep his spirits up, he sang to himself, but mostly it was just walking and walking, through forests and jungles, across rivers and open plains. Once, in the night, a lion had roared. Another time there had been a flock of birds, bright blue and red, exploding like a burst of fireworks out of the forest depths.

Were there others with him? Yes, many others, most of them children like himself, all of them shackled together at the feet and the neck. They stumbled often, and some were left where they fell. He tried to put a hand to his throat, but there was no longer any sensation in his limbs at all. Where were his arms and legs? Where, after all, was his throat? A distant curiosity came upon him, and then a feeling of dislocation so vast and vertiginous, as if all the different parts of him were spread out, as far away from one another as the moon and the stars.

But he was not afraid. He had had that feeling before somewhere. Sand. Something to do with sand. The walking had stopped and there was a new horizon before him now, relentless and golden. It had made his eyes ache to look at it.

It was night-time when they came for him, and cool. There was a hut, and the men inside had given him something to drink which he had spat out at first, but they persisted. Had he sung for them? He remembered the distant glitter of their eyes as they squatted there beside the fire, and the way his head spun, and the bad taste in his mouth. He was glad when they laid him down beside the fire. Then there was a sound of metal on stone, and a sensation of great heat. A man's hand, quite gentle, had pulled his shift up to above his waist, exposing his genitals. They gave him a piece of wood to bite on, but still he did not understand what was happening to him.

'There are three ways.' There was a man speaking now who was different from the rest. His head was wound about with a turban of twisted cloth as was the custom of the men from the northern sand-lands. 'In the first two the testicles can either be crushed or removed completely. The penis remains, but the subject can never be fertile

5

after this. There is great pain, and some risk of infection, but most survive – especially the young ones.' The third way involves severing all the genitals.' Dimly the boy was aware of the man staring down into his face. 'There is far greater risk, of course – you may lose your cargo altogether – but the demand for such as these is very great. Especially if they are ugly . . . and, *hew*!' he laughed softly to himself, 'this one's as ugly as a hippopotamus.'

'What are the chances?' The man who had pulled up the boy's shift spoke.

'If the practitioner is careless, very few survive this third way. If the pain does not craze them, then the fever that comes after kills them. And if the fever does not kill them, then there is a danger that their parts will close up altogether as the wound heals. The practitioner must contrive to keep one tube open, the tube down which the patient's urine can pass. For if this is not well attended to, then there is no hope, and death will surely follow. The worst and most painful death of all. In my case however, for I am very skilled in this art, the odds are good: about half my patients survive. And in this case . . .' once again the boy was aware of a turbaned face peering down at him, 'well, he looks strong enough to me. You'll sell him to the harem of the Grand Signor himself, I am sure of it.'

There was some conferring amongst the men around the fire, and then the first one, who seemed to be the chief amongst them, spoke again.

'Our cargo is valuable. We have come too far – three thousand leagues or more from the forests of the great river itself – and we have already lost too many of our cargo on the journey to take such a risk. In Alexandria, where we are heading, we will easily sell the ones who remain as slaves, and our profit is assured. But it is as you say: a great fortune is to be had for one of this kind. Especially, in these days, for a boy from these lands. Just one good one, they say, will fetch as much again as all the others. The word in the markets, in Alexandria and Cairo, is that the Ottoman lords prefer them now to the white eunuchs who come from the easternmost mountains of the Great Turk's empire. These black eunuchs are affordable only by the very richest harems in the empire. Luxury goods, you might say, like the ostrich feathers, gold dust, saffron and ivory that many of the caravans crossing these sands bring with them. We will take a chance

6

on just one: let it be this boy, seeing, as you say, he looks strong and likely to survive. We will try your skill, Copt, this once.'

'The singing boy then. So be it.' The turbaned man nodded his approval. 'You are a true merchant, Massouf Bhai. I will need boiling oil to cauterise the wound,' he added matter-of-factly. 'And four of your strongest people to hold the boy down. The pain gives them the strength of ten men.'

Nearly forty years later, in the cool and scented Bosphorous night, the naked body of Hassan Aga stirred slightly, his fingers splaying and fluttering feebly against the cushions on the divan like monstrous moths. Slowly, his mind sank back into the past again.

It was still night. When it was over they had dug a hole, at the Copt's behest, in the sand just behind the hut. It was a narrow hole, but deep; just wide enough for the boy to be buried in it upright up to his neck, so that only his head was visible. Then the men went away and left him there. The boy had no memory of this, only of regaining consciousness some time afterwards with a great cool weight of sand all around him, and the sensation that his arms and legs had been bound as tightly to his body as if he had been trussed up by a giant spider.

How long had they left him, buried alive, in that hole? Five days . . . a week? The first few days, when the fever took hold of him, as it did almost immediately, he did not notice time passing. Despite the raging heat during the day, with a sun that seemed to make the very blood boil in his eardrums, his teeth chattered and rattled. And between his legs a pain so searing that bitter bile rose in his gorge. But worse than this was his thirst, a terrible, all-consuming thirst that obsessed and tormented him. When he cried out for water his voice, no stronger now than a kitten's, reached the ears of no one.

Once, he woke to find the turbaned man, the one they called the Copt, looking down at him. He had brought with him the chief of the slave masters, a man as black as night in a long, pale blue robe.

'The fever has broken?'

The Copt nodded. 'It is as I said: the boy is strong.'

'Then I can have my cargo?'

'Patience, Massouf Bhai, the fever has broken, but the wound must

7

heal, and heal well. If you want your cargo whole, you must allow the sand to do its work. He must not be moved yet.'

'*Water* . . .' Had he spoken? The boy's lips were so dry they cracked and bled at the slightest effort at speech. His tongue was so swollen it almost choked him. But the two men had already moved away.

It was that night that the girl came to him for the first time. He did not see her at first, but woke instead from a fitful half-sleep to feel a coolness against his brow and on his lips. At her touch a cry of pain, tinder dry, rose in his swollen gorge. But no sound came. The dampness of the cloth seared him like a knife.

A form, as insubstantial as a ghost, knelt beside him on the sand. '*Water* . . .' with an effort he moved his lips around the word.

'No, I cannot.' The boy blinked his eyes, and saw the broad smooth face of a small girl. 'You must not drink, not yet. Heal first, then drink.'

She was not one of the ones from his own journey here, of that he was reasonably sure, but the tones of her voice were familiar, and he thought that she, too, must be from the forests beyond the great river. The boy's eyes pricked, but they were too dry now even for tears.

The girl was now gently working around his face with a cloth. Carefully she brushed the sand from his eyelids, his nostrils, his ears, but when she tried to touch his lips again he drew back from her almost violently, and an inarticulate rasp, like the cawing of a crow, broke from him.

'Shh!' She held her finger to her lips, and in the darkness he saw the whites of her eyes gleam. Then she pressed her mouth to his ear. 'I will come back.'

She gathered the thin folds of her shift around her, and the boy watched as her small form disappeared again into the night. Her breath was still warm against his cheek.

When she came back she was carrying a small bottle in one hand. She crouched down beside him, and again put her lips to his ear. 'They use this oil for cooking. It will not hurt you.'

She dipped a small finger in the oil and dabbed it tentatively on his upper lip. Although the boy flinched, he did not cry out as before.

After that he waited for her every night, and every night she came to wash away the sand from his face with her cool cloth, and to anoint

8

his lips with oil. Although she steadfastly refused to give him water – saying that if she did so he would not heal – she brought him small slices of gourd and cucumber, hidden in the pockets of her robe. These she managed to slip between his lips, and he was able to hold them there, soothing and softening his swollen tongue. The two children did not speak to one another, but sometimes after she was finished the girl would sit beside him and sing. And since they had robbed him of his own voice, he would listen to her with rapture, looking up at the stars, vast and brilliant, turning above them in the desert sky.

As they had thought, the boy was strong and he survived. They treated him better after they pulled him from the sand. They gave him a new robe, green with a white stripe, and a cloth to wind around his head, and he was made to understand that he would no longer be shackled with the rest, but would ride up behind the slave master on his camel, as befitted the most valuable of their goods. His wound had healed neatly and, although it was very tender still, his tube had not scarred over. The Copt gave him a thin hollow silver quill and showed him how to insert it inside his own body. 'When you want to piss, you put it in like this, see?'

When the time came to leave, the boy saw another group of merchants assembling their cargo at the little caravanserai. A straggling group of men and women, shackled at the neck and ankles, stood sheltering against a wall, protecting themselves as best they could from the wind that blew across the sands whipping and stinging against their faces. At the end of the line the boy recognised a small figure, the girl who had helped him. 'What's your name?' he called.

She turned, and he knew that she could see him now, in his new green and white robe, mounted behind the camel master.

'What's your name?'

'Li . . .'

She was calling something back but her words swirled and broke against the whistling wind. With a creaking of leather and a jostling of bells, his caravan was moving now. The girl put her hands to her mouth and cupped them. She was calling to him again. 'Li . . .' she called into the wind. 'Lily.'

✴   ✴   ✴

9

Now, as Hassan Aga lingered still on the uncertain shores between memory and death, dawn broke at last over the Golden Horn. On the other side of the waters of the Horn in that part of the city they called Pera – the preserve of foreigners and infidels – John Carew, master cook, sat on the wall of the English ambassador's garden, cracking nuts.

The night had been heavy and warm. Sitting on the wall, which the ambassador had expressly forbidden, Carew had removed his shirt, which was also expressly forbidden, to get the benefit of the slight freshness of the dawn breeze. Below him the ground dropped away, giving him a fair view down over groves of almond and apricot trees. At the water's edge he could see the clustered wooden boathouses of the richer merchants and the foreign emissaries.

Although the first call to prayer of the Mohammedans had come more than half an hour ago, there was still little commerce visible that morning either on the waters or in the city beyond. A slight mist, tinged now with the very faintest wash of rose (a colour, Carew had learnt, that was not only peculiar to the Constantinople dawn, but also the very same colour as rose-petal preserve) still veiled the waters and the shores beyond. Presently a single small caique, the narrow rowing boat of the Bosphorous, pierced the mist, rowing slowly towards the Pera shore. Carew could hear the slap and dip of the oars, and then the cry of the seagulls as they circled above it, their bellies flashing white and gold in the dawn light.

And then, as he watched, the mist lifted from the opposite shore, and the Sultan's palace, with its cypress trees like black paper cut-outs, its domes and minarets and towers, was revealed suddenly: an enchanted city, rose and gold, trembling over the misty waters as if suspended by djinns.

'Up early, Carew,' a voice came from beneath him, on the garden side of the wall, 'or haven't you slept?'

'My master,' John Carew, lounging carelessly against the wall, saluted in the direction of the voice, and went on cracking nuts.

Paul Pindar, secretary to Sir Henry Lello, the English ambassador, considered briefly the rebuke, one of several, that rose to his lips, and then decided against it. If he had learnt one thing in all the years of his acquaintance with Carew it was that this was not the way to deal with him, a fact of which he had, as yet, not been able to persuade the

10

ambassador, nor was likely to. Instead, with a brief glance towards the still-sleeping house, he swung himself up on to the wall.

'Have a nut.' If Carew saw Paul's briefly raised eyebrow he gave no sign.

Paul regarded the lounging figure thoughtfully for a moment: the hair, curly and unkempt, hanging to his shoulders, the body, slight but taut and finely made, and as full of suppressed energy as the stretched string of a bow. He had often watched Carew at work, marvelling at the precision and grace with which he moved, even in the smallest and hottest space. A faint scar, the result of a kitchen brawl, ran down one cheekbone from his ear to the corner of his mouth. For a while the two men sat together in companionable silence, a silence honed by the many years of their unlikely friendship.

'And what nuts are these?' Paul said eventually.

'They call them "pistach". Look what a green, Paul!' Carew laughed suddenly. 'Have you ever seen such beauty in a mere nut?'

'If the ambassador sees you here, Carew, after he expressly . . .'

'Lello can go hang.'

'You'll hang first, my friend,' Paul replied evenly. 'I've always said so.'

'He says I'm not to cook any more, at least not in his household. I'm to leave the kitchens to that flat-footed lump of lard Cuthbert Bull, that great baboon who doesn't know enough to boil a Bosnian cabbage . . .'

'Well . . .' Paul took another nut, 'you've only yourself to blame.'

'Do you know what they are calling him?'

'No,' said Paul. 'But doubtless you are going to tell me.'

'"Fog."'

Paul made no answer.

'Do you want me to tell you why?'

'Thank you, I think I can guess.'

'You're smiling, Secretary Pindar.'

'Me? I am his esteemed Excellency's most humble servant.'

'His servant, Pindar, but there's nothing humble about you, had he the wit to see it.'

'And you know all about humble, I suppose.'

'On the contrary, on that subject, as you well know, I know nothing at all. Except for the humbles I bake in his pie. I know all about servants, though.'

'Not nearly enough, Carew. My father always used to say so in all those years when you were in his service, if "service" is the right word for your theatricals, which somehow I rather doubt.' The older man spoke mildly enough. 'Our esteemed ambassador is quite right on that at least.'

'Ah, but your father loved me.' Unperturbed, Carew cracked a nut open dextrously with one hand. 'Until he gives me a kitchen back, Lello can go hang. Did you see him on that morning when Thomas Dallam and his men opened up the great box at last, to find his precious gift broken and mouldy? Our Thomas – who for a Lancashire man has quite a way with words, by the by – said to me, and this is rare, this is, he said Sir Henry looked as if he were straining on a stool.'

'You know, sometimes you go too far, Carew.' Although Paul's tone was still mild, he threw the handful of nut shells he was holding away from him with an impatient movement. 'He is the ambassador and should command your respect.'

'He is a Levant Company merchant.'

'He is the Queen's Envoy.'

'But first and foremost he is a merchant. A fact that's only too well known amongst the other foreigners here in Constantinople, especially the other envoys, the Bailo of Venice and the ambassador of France, and they despise us for it.'

'Then they're fools,' Paul said shortly. 'We are all of us merchants now, since we are all in the service of the Honourable Company, and there is no shame in it. On the contrary, our fortunes, yours and mine – and the fortunes of our whole country, you mark my words – are riding on it. And that fact has never harmed our standing with the Turks. In fact, they hold us in greater esteem now than they ever have.'

'But only when it's politic for them to do so.'

'But so it is; very politic.' Paul said shrewdly. 'Not just for trade, which benefits them just as much as it does us, but because we have a common enemy: Spain. They might try to play us off against the Venetians and the French, but it's just a game. The fact is that they need us almost as much as we need them. Did you know that the Sultan's mother, the Valide Sultan Safiye, who they say is a powerful lady (although Lello, I fear, will never credit it) corresponds personally with our Queen? She has already sent her gifts, equal in value to the ones we brought to her from England, and will do so again, I am told. I'm to take them with me when I return.'

'How can anyone have power, incarcerated in that place?' Carew indicated the domes and spires on the far side of the shining waters below them. 'The Great Turk himself is all but a prisoner there, our janissaries say.'

The early-morning mist had dispersed completely now, and a dozen or so caiques, and some other bigger vessels, had begun to ply their trade along the shores.

'They say there are hundreds of women in there, all slaves and concubines of the Sultan, and that for as long as they live they may never show their face to any other man.' Carew continued.

'Their ways are not our ways to be sure – but perhaps it is not entirely as we think.'

'They are saying something else about the Valide Sultan,' Carew turned to Paul again, 'that she took a strong liking to the gentleman-like Secretary Pindar when he went to deliver the Queen's gifts to her. Dear God!' Carew's eyes glittered. 'Fog must have strained upon more than a stool when he heard that.'

Despite himself Paul laughed.

'Come on, Paul, what's she like? The Sultan's mother, the favourite of the old Turk, the Sultan Murad. They say that when she was young her beauty was such that he was faithful to her, and to her alone, for more than twenty years.'

'I didn't see see her. We spoke through a lattice. She spoke to me in Italian.'

'She's Italian?'

'No, I don't believe so.' Paul remembered the shadowy presence behind the screen, more felt than seen, like a priest in a confessional. He remembered a powerful perfume, mysterious as a night-scented garden, at once sweet and earthy; a vague impression of many jewels; and then that miraculous voice, low and rich and velvety. 'She doesn't speak like a native-born Italian,' he said, adding reflectively, 'but her voice is more beautiful, I think, than any I've ever heard.'

13

The two men, falling silent again, looked out across the waters of the Golden Horn once more, towards the distant black spears of the cypress trees and, beyond them, the half-hidden towers of the Sultan's palace. Suddenly it was no longer possible to avoid the real reason that had brought them together in the early-morning privacy of the ambassador's garden.

'The girl, Paul . . .'

'No.'

'She's in there, Paul.'

'No!'

'No? *I* know it.'

'How do you know it?'

'Because I saw her, Paul. I saw Celia with my own two eyes.'

'Impossible!' Paul grasped Carew's wrist, and twisted it hard. 'Celia Lamprey is dead.'

'I'm telling you I saw her.'

'You saw her with your own two eyes? I'll put out your eyes, Carew, if you're lying to me.'

'On my life, Pindar. It was her.' Silence. 'Ask Dallam. He was with me.'

'Oh, don't worry, I will.' He let Carew's wrist drop. 'But make no mistake, John, if any Turk comes to hear even a whisper of this adventure, it will be death to confess it.'

Chapter 2

Oxford: the present day

'What have you found?' Eve threw the shoulder bag in which she carried her books onto the chair next to her and sat down opposite Elizabeth's. They had arranged to meet in the café on the first floor of Blackwell's bookshop in Broad Street.

'The captivity narrative I was telling you about.'

'No kidding. Really?' Eve dragged off her woollen hat, making her short black hair stand up on end. 'Where?'

'In the Oriental Library Reading Room. At least I'm pretty sure I have. I haven't had a chance to read it yet. I came across it literally two minutes before the library closed, but I just had to tell someone.'

Elizabeth told her about the piece of paper she had found folded into the pages of the book.

'So how do you know that's what it is? It could be anything – a shopping list.'

'No, it couldn't. It's about Celia Lamprey. It has to be.'

'No shit, Sherlock.' Eve's eyes, framed by her thick black glasses, gazed at Elizabeth owlishly. 'One of those strange "intuitions" of yours,' she made inverted comma signs with her hands, 'I suppose?'

'Something like that.' Elizabeth put her cup down. 'Look, just hurry up and get yourself some coffee, will you? I want to tell you the rest.'

She watched Eve walk across to the counter, a small fierce figure, incongruously dressed in a 1950s red and white print dress and Doc Marten boots.

'Manuscript or printed?' Eve said when she came back.

'Manuscript.' Elizabeth did not hesitate. 'I'm guessing,' she added quickly.

There was a thoughtful pause.

'You do know there's no such thing as psychic, don't you?' Eve said after a while. 'Especially when it comes to research grants.' She spoke as if to a very small child.

'Oh, please.' Elizabeth rolled her eyes. 'What rubbish you talk sometimes.'

'Rubbish? You'd better watch what you say. Mind you, I've noticed that you *do* have a talent for the lucky guess. All right then, I'll bet you fifty quid you are right about the paper you've just found.'

'What! I've just told you that!'

'You said yourself you haven't even looked at it. So just how can you be so sure?'

'How?' Elizabeth shrugged. God only knows, she thought. But oh I can. Always have done. Elizabeth thought of that frail smell, and when she finally allowed her fingers to brush the paper at last, a sensation – like what? The puckering of a sea breeze on some smooth surface, a whisper against her skin. So . . . precise, really. 'Intuition. That's all.'

'Shame you don't have that kind of intuition about the present.'

'What is this, the Spanish Inquisition? Could we leave the present out of this, please?'

Another owlish look, then Eve softened.

'OK.'

The café was full of early Christmas shoppers sheltering from the cold. The air was muggy with the smell of wet wool and coffee beans.

'So. Do you want to tell me about it?'

'Well, it was just the most incredible piece of luck really . . .' Elizabeth pulled her chair in closer towards Eve. 'You know I've been looking for a possible DPhil thesis on captivity narratives?' For months Elizabeth had been researching accounts written by Europeans who survived being taken captive, mostly by Mediterranean corsairs. 'Well, the other day I found myself reading an account by this man, Francis Knight. Knight was a merchant who was taken captive off the Barbary coast by Algerian corsairs, and spent seven years in captivity in Algiers.'

16

'When was this?'

'In 1640. It was dedicated to a man called Sir Paul Pindar, a former ambassador to the Ottoman court. That seemed odd to me, why should Pindar have any particular interest in captives?' Elizabeth paused for a moment. 'And then I found something even more intriguing. Someone had pencilled in a note on the preface page, next to the name of the dedicatee: it said simply, "see also the narrative of Celia Lamprey".

'This stopped me cold because there are no known captivity narratives written by women before the eighteenth century, and even then they're pretty rare. But the other name – Pindar, Paul Pindar – did ring a vague bell.'

'So you found something about him?'

'He has a pretty long entry in the Dictionary of National Biography. Pindar was a merchant, and an incredibly successful one. He was apprenticed at seventeen to a London merchant called Parvish, who sent him the next year to Venice to act as his factor there. He seems to have stayed in Venice for about fifteen years, where he acquired what's described as "a very plentiful estate".'

'He was rich, then?'

'Very. In the late sixteenth century merchants were just beginning to make big money out of foreign trade – proper fortunes, like the later East India Company nabobs – and Pindar became hugely successful. So successful, in fact, that the Levant Company sent him to Constantinople to act as secretary to the new English ambassador there, another merchant, Sir Henry Lello. That was in 1599. From there he seems to have had various other diplomatic appointments, as consul in Aleppo, and then later back in Constantinople again, this time as James the First's ambassador . . . But none of those really seem to have mattered. The really critical moment for Pindar was this 1599 mission, when it seems that the whole of the British ability to trade in the Mediterranean hung on the presentation of a gift to the new Sultan, an extraordinary mechanical clock . . .'

'But what's all this got to do with Celia Lamprey?'

'Well, that's just it – I haven't been able to find out anything about her at all. It's the same old story: lots of information about the man, nothing at all about the woman – until now.'

'Go on then,' Eve said, impatient now, 'get to the point.'

'It turns out that Paul Pindar was a friend of Thomas Bodley, and when Bodley was founding the library here he famously went around collaring his friends and persuading them to collect books for him. With all his travelling in exotic lands, Pindar must have been a prime candidate. Anyway, to cut a long story short, Pindar did indeed make a bequest of books to the library, and today I went and looked at them. It was quite a small bequest, about twenty books mostly in Arabic and Syriac. From what I could make out they're mostly old medicinal and astrological texts. Anyway, it was just by chance, just by the most incredible chance, I was getting ready to go home when I opened one of the books at random, and there was this piece of paper inside, and I knew *at once* . . .' Stricken, Elizabeth stopped in mid-sentence.

'You knew at once . . .?' Eve repeated. Then she saw Elizabeth's face. 'What's wrong, you look as if you've seen—'

Eve made as if to turn around, but Elizabeth grabbed her hand.

'Don't look now, please. Just keep talking.'

'Marius?'

'Just keep talking to me, Eve. Please.' Elizabeth pressed the palm of her other hand to her solar plexus.

'Marius.' Eve's voice was sour. But she did not look round. Instead she took off her glasses and began to clean them on a fold of her dress in little staccato movements. Her eyes, without the glasses, were almond shaped, very black and bright. 'Who's he with this time?'

'Don't know.' Elizabeth said. 'Someone . . . else.'

She looked over to where Marius was now sitting on the other side of the café. She had not seen him for over a week.

The woman sitting with him had her back to them, all she could see was a blonde head. At the sight of her, something in Elizabeth's stomach lurched so violently she thought she might be physically sick.

In the King's Arms, Eve brought them both double vodkas, and found a corner seat for them as far away as possible from the other Friday drinkers.

'It's very noble of you not to say anything,' Elizabeth said after she had drunk some of the vodka. She could see that the effort to be tactful was about to make Eve explode. 'So go on then, spit it out.'

'No. I've said everything I want to say. Several times.' Eve fumbled in her bag and brought out a bandana in the same red and white print of her dress and tied it violently, washerwoman style, round her head.

'You mean how he uses me and I'm much too good for him and all men are bastards?'

Eve did not reply.

'Stop fumbling.'

'Why shouldn't I fumble?'

'You only fumble when you're angry.'

'Hmm.'

'Are you angry with me?'

'Oh for God's sake, Elizabeth!' Eve put her bag down. 'That man makes you miserable. He trifles with your heart. There is so much . . . so much negative energy around you when you're with him, or when you have anything to do with him, I can almost hear it crackling. Eventually it's going to make you ill. Actually ill.'

But I already am ill, Elizabeth felt like saying. This thing that I'm feeling, it *is* an illness. Instead she took another mouthful of vodka. *He trifles with your heart.* The sort of thing her grandmother might have said. Had Eve actually used those words, or had she just imagined them?

'Are you in love with him?' Eve looked at her intently.

'I suppose I must be.'

'But he treats you like shit.'

'Only sometimes.' Elizabeth managed a small laugh.

'Ah, you see,' Eve pounced on something else. 'You used to be always laughing. You don't laugh any more, Liz.'

'That's not true.' The vodka burned into her throat. 'I just did.'

'You know what I mean.'

'He's not my boyfriend, Eve. He never has been.' Elizabeth tried to stop herself from sounding bleak. 'Marius is my lover.'

'Oh, I *see*. Your lover. Is that what he tells you? How very glamorous. But shall I translate that for you, into Marius-speak? It means he can pick you up and then just drop you again whenever he damn well wants to. *Uh*!' she let out an exasperated cry, 'I don't understand why he *can't just let you go* . . .'

Elizabeth's phone buzzed. It was a text from Marius. Her heart lurched. *hello beautiful why you so sad?*

Elizabeth thought carefully for a moment before she texted back: *me? sad?*

After a moment the reply came: *u drinking vodka, baby.*

Her head jerked up, and then there he was, sliding into the seat next to her. 'Hello, beautiful,' Marius said, taking her hand proprietorially in his. Unkempt hair falling to his shoulders, the jacket he always wore smelling – improbably erotically – of cigarettes and damp leather. 'Hello, Eve. Off to a fancy dress party?'

'Hello.' Eve's almond-shaped eyes narrowed until they were two black slits. 'Marius.'

He laughed. 'Was that a smile, or did you actually just bare your teeth at me?'

He looked at Elizabeth, complicit; and despite herself, she laughed too. Marius could always make her laugh, could always charm her into feeling that she was at the centre of his universe. He picked up Elizabeth's glass and drained the last mouthful of vodka.

'Mmm, Grey Goose, very fancy. But don't worry girls, I'm not going to intrude on your little tête-à-tête, I just came over to say hello.'

He leant over and kissed Elizabeth on the neck. At his smell, his touch – his dangerous touch – she felt a shiver of pleasure.

'Is it just me, or is your friend completely bulletproof?' he whispered in her ear. Elizabeth suppressed another smile.

'Oh, don't go . . .' she began, 'stay and have a drink with us,' but he was already sliding away from her.

'Sorry, darling, can't stop. Departmental meeting in half an hour.'

'On a Friday night?' Eve said, acidly. 'That's very hard-working of you, Doctor.'

Marius ignored her. 'I'll call you soon, I promise,' he said to Elizabeth, and then with a wave he was gone through the thickening throng of people.

'He followed you here!' Eve glared at his receding figure. 'He must have done. Why can't he just let you get on with your life? He doesn't really want you, but he can't leave you alone either . . . oh, fuck it, I'll get us some more drinks.' She stood up. 'And I don't care what anyone says, someone really should point out to him that he's too old to be wearing leather trousers,' she added spitefully.

Elizabeth did not bother to protest. Suddenly she felt completely exhausted. The elation she had felt at seeing Marius so unexpectedly had plummeted away from her. Now, instead, somewhere inside her there was a hole.

Then her mobile buzzed again. *my place, half an hour?* She put the phone back in her bag. I know I shouldn't but I'm going to. Her face felt flushed. And her heart, her trifled-with heart? Soaring again.

'Sorry, darling. I've got to go.'

'I hope it's worth it,' Eve replied.

'Hope what is?'

'The sex.'

Elizabeth kissed her on the top of the head.

'Love you,' was all she said.

Later, Elizabeth watched Marius as he dressed. He seemed preoccupied. She did not mind. Still in the enchanted glow of his attentions, she was peaceful again. She had always loved to watch him as he dressed. For a man in his forties his body was still beautiful to her. She loved the slenderness of his hips, the way the hairs curled around his navel. He was putting on a pair of faded jeans. His legs, she thought, looked good in jeans. The leather of his belt made a sudden snapping sound.

She wanted to tell him about the captivity narrative. She wondered how to do it. I found something exciting today . . . she composed the sentence carefully in her head. At least I think I did . . . At the thought of her discovery her excitement flared, and then guttered again. No, she could just imagine what he would say. Better wait until she was sure.

'Where is it you have to go?'

'That departmental meeting I told you about.'

'Oh.'

'Well, it's not exactly a meeting. I just have to meet up to discuss some things.' He gave her a quick smile. 'Sorry.'

What did *that* mean? Marius was better than anyone she had ever met at not answering questions. Questions like who are you really going to meet? Is it another woman? Is it that woman I saw you with in Blackwell's today, and who the hell was she anyway? She knew instinctively how annoyed he would be if she asked any of them. Bit them back.

'What are your plans?' He sat down next to her on the bed.

She took his hand and held it to her lips, willing him not to go away from her just yet.

'Can I stay here?' she said, trying to sound casual.

'Well . . . you can if you want to,' he said.

If there was reluctance in his voice Elizabeth was determined not to hear it. 'I'll keep the bed warm for you.'

'Well, OK.' He drew his hand gently away from her. 'I might be late, though.'

'I don't mind.'

A few minutes later she heard the door slam and he was gone.

Elizabeth lay in Marius's bed looking up at the ceiling. It was a beautiful room, at least the architecture was. Tall windows with mullioned glass looking down over the college quadrangle. On summer mornings the whole room was flooded with sunlight. She remembered when they had first met, the previous June, and how the two of them would lie naked on his bed, the splintered light falling in rainbows over their naked bodies. Had he made her happy then? She supposed so.

Now she felt her peace of mind seep slowly from her again. It was still early, only half-past nine. A bitter rain sheeted against the window panes. Elizabeth looked around her forlornly. Without Marius in it, it occurred to her that the room was lonelier than anywhere she had ever known and had a curiously tawdry feel. For a man of such fastidious intellect, he was an untidy man. Piles of his old clothes lay on the floor. Dirty mugs full of old tea bags were piled on the dresser next to a little sink, a half-empty carton of milk next to them, which she knew from past experience was bound to be sour, even though the room was cold as the grave.

Her whole body ached. *I hope the sex is worth it*, Eve had said. Well, it might be for him, but not for me, she thought bitterly. Not even that. She pulled the duvet more closely round her, searching for his smell, trying to conjure the feeling of his arms around her. She felt utterly humiliated. Why do I do it? *He trifles with your heart.* Eve is right, this isn't love, this is torment. I can't stand it any more, Elizabeth thought. There was an emptiness in her so profound she felt she might drown in it.

*   *   *

22

Later, much later, she awoke to find that there was someone standing over the bed watching her.

'Marius?'

'You're still here.' Was it surprise she could hear in his voice? He sat down next to her, pulled the duvet down to uncover her naked shoulders. 'You look so sweet when you're asleep, like a little dormouse. Are you all right?'

'Yes.' She turned over sleepily, glad that in the darkness he would not be able to see her swollen eyelids. 'No, actually. What time is it?'

'Late. I didn't think you'd still be here.'

'Marius . . .' The fact that she could not see him properly made her brave. 'I don't think I can do this any more.'

'Why's that?' Thoughtfully he traced the warm curve of her shoulder with his fingers. 'I thought you liked doing it.'

'You know what I mean,' she turned over to face him.

'No, I don't.' He was undressing again, pulling off his shoes, his shirt. 'You've been talking to Rosa Klebb again, haven't you?'

'Don't say that, Eve's a good friend to me.' Normally the joke would have make her laugh, but not now. 'She says that you don't really want me, but that you can't let me go either,' Elizabeth said into the darkness.

'Uh—' Marius gave a non-committal grunt. She heard the buckle of his belt fall to the floor and then he was climbing into bed next to her. 'Come here,' he put his arms round her cold shoulders, cradling her so that her head was resting in the crook of his neck. She stretched out, fitting herself into the curve of his body so that every inch of her was touching him, warming herself against him.

'I'm sorry,' she said.

'Eve should get out more.' His breath, she noticed, smelt of whisky. 'You know I love you, don't you?' he said, brushing her forehead with his lips.

'Do I?' she said into the darkness again.

'Of course you do, woman,' he said, not unkindly. And then, turning over, 'Now can we please get some sleep?'

Chapter 3

Constantinople: 1 September 1599

Sunrise

The ambassador's residence was a large square edifice built, in the Ottoman style, of lime and stone, its windows shaded by elaborately latticed wooden shutters. Situated just a little way outside the walls of the district of Galata, the place had the air of a country house, with a large walled garden and adjoining vineyards. Freezing in winter, it was a pleasant place in summer, with a fountain of running water in the courtyard and waxy blooms of jasmine climbing up the inner pillars to the balconies above. A suite of the largest and most comfortable on the first storey was occupied by the ambassador, Sir Henry Lello and his wife. Those next in rank in the ambassador's entourage, including his secretary Paul Pindar, occupied smaller rooms on the second storey. The rest slept in dormitories on the ground floor.

The house was stirring now. Paul sent a servant to fetch Thomas Dallam, and then Paul and John Carew made their way to Paul's upstairs chamber, where they knew they would not be overheard. Soon they heard Dallam's solid tread on the wooden floorboards outside.

'Good day to you, Thomas.'

'Secretary Pindar.' Thomas Dallam, a stout Lancashireman in his middle years, nodded to them, but did not enter the room. He was dressed for the street, wearing a loose Turkish robe over his English clothes, a requirement of all foreigners living in Constantinople.

'Come in, Tom,' Paul said. 'I know you're anxious to be off to the palace, so I won't take much of your time. Tell me, how goes the marvellous device? Will the Grand Signor find it a gift worth waiting for, do you think?'

'Aye.' Dallam spoke shortly. 'The Honourable Company won't regret their choice.'

'I should hope not,' Paul smiled, 'the Honourable Company left us kicking our heels here for three years whilst they made up their minds what to send. They say the Great Turk has a rage for clocks and automata, and all kind of mechanical devices.'

'True.' Dallam grinned suddenly. 'He sends his man almost daily to see if my work is finished yet.'

'And . . . is it?'

'All in good time, Secretary Pindar.'

'It's quite all right, Thomas. I don't mean to press you.'

Dallam was known to be prickly on the subject, and jealous of any interference with himself or his men, no fewer than five of whom had accompanied him aboard the company's vessel the *Hector* on the six-month voyage to bring the Sultan's gift to Constantinople.

'I've heard that you've quite restored the damage that the organ sustained on the journey out here, although Sir Henry tells me it will take you and your men some time yet to reassemble in the palace. That's a job of work, my friend.'

'It is.' At the mention of the ambassador, Dallam, who had taken off his hat, now scratched his head impatiently and replaced it. 'Now, if it is all the same to you, Secretary Pindar, the caique's ready for us and our janissaries don't like to be kept waiting.'

'Of course, of course.' Paul held up his hand. 'But just one more thing.'

'Yes?'

'Carew tells me you took him with you yesterday.'

'Aye, sir.' He saw Dallam's gaze flicker briefly across to Carew. 'One of my men – Robin the joiner – fell sick. And after all that business in the kitchens, with Bull's finger and all—' he twisted his hat in his fingers. 'Well, we all know how good John is with his hands.'

'Tell him what we saw, Tom.' Carew, who was leaning up against the window, spoke now for the first time.

For a moment or two Dallam was silent.

'I thought we two had agreed?' he said at last, uncertain suddenly.

'We had, I know. I am sorry, Tom, but it can't be helped. I can vouch for Secretary Pindar,' Carew said. 'There is no danger with him, I swear it.'

'Well, I'm flattered to be spoken so highly of . . .' Impatiently, Paul walked three paces to the door. Grasping Thomas Dallam by the arm, he drew him into the room and shut the door. 'Enough now. Tell me what you saw,' he said, his face pale. 'Tell me everything, from the beginning, and it will be between the three of us.'

Thomas Dallam took one look at Paul, and this time he did not hesitate.

'Well, as you know, for the last month my men and I have been going to the palace every day to assemble the Honourable Company's gift to the Sultan. There are two guards assigned to us, and also a dragoman who interprets, and every day they escort us through the First and Second Courtyards, to a secret gate, behind which lies a garden in the Sultan's private quarters – that's where we're to assemble the clock. We're only able to do it because the Great Turk himself is not much there. It seems that at this time of year he comes and goes as he pleases between his various summer palaces, taking most of the court and his women with him. And because of this it happens that there's something of a holiday feeling about the place—' Dallam stopped, seeming a little abashed by what he was about to say.

Pindar was sitting with his arms folded. 'Go on, Thomas.'

'Our two guards are fine fellows, my particular acquaintances you might say, after all this time working at the palace – these two have sort of . . . shown us around, as it were.' Dallam coughed nervously. 'Sometimes they showed us other parts of the privy gardens, sometimes the little pleasure houses they call kiosks, once or twice they even ventured to show us the private chambers in the Sultan's own apartments. But yesterday – as chance would have it, on the day that Carew was there with me – they showed me something else.'

'What was that, Tom?'

Dallam hesitated again but Carew nodded to him to continue.

'While two of my carpenters were at work, one of them took us – Carew and I – across a little square courtyard paved with marble, and there, in the wall, he showed us a small grille. There was no one about, so our guard made signs with his hands – that's the custom of everyone who works in the palace – that we should approach, although he wouldn't go near himself.

'When we came to the grille we saw that the wall was very thick and grated on both sides with strong iron bars, and when we looked though the bars we saw a second, secret courtyard beyond, and in it some thirty of the Great Turk's concubines, playing with a ball.'

'At first we thought they were young men playing,' Carew added, 'for they were wearing what looked like breeches on their legs. But when we looked more closely we could see they had long hair hanging down their backs. They were all women, and beautiful ones, too.'

'John and I . . .' Dallam glanced across at Carew. 'We knew we shouldn't look. And even our guard grew angry with us for gazing too long, stamping his foot on the ground to make us come away. But we couldn't. We stood there amazed, like two men enchanted.'

'And could the women see you?'

'No. The grille was too small, but we looked at them for a long time. They were very young, just girls, most of them. I never saw a sight, Secretary Pindar, that pleased me so wonderfully well.'

'But what John wants me to tell you is this.' Thomas Dallam paused again, clearing his throat with a cough. 'There was one woman amongst them who was different from the rest. I noticed her because she was so fair, whereas the other women were dark. Her hair wasn't hanging down her back, but was fastened in a coil around her head and held with a rope of pearls. She seemed a little older than the others, and more richly dressed, with jewels at her ears and on her breast. But it was her skin that drew our eyes, the most beautiful skin, white and luminous as the moon. John took my arm, and I heard him say, "God help us, Tom. It's Celia. Celia Lamprey." And that is all I know.'

When Dallam had gone a long silence filled the room. From outside the latticed shutters came the throaty ruffling of pigeons in the eaves, the incongruous sound, it occurred to Pindar, of an English summer's afternoon. He had not been to England for – how many years was it now? Eighteen years in all since he had left, first to Venice as factor for the merchant Parvish, then as a merchant in his own right with the Honourable Company. He pushed open the window and looked out

27

towards the Golden Horn, and the seven hills of the ancient city rising beyond.

'That was quite a speech – for a Lancashire man.'

'I told you: he has a way with words.'

Paul sat down on the window ledge. Compared to Carew's generally maverick air, he cut an altogether more sober figure. Dressed in his customary black, he was at once slender and well built. He ran his hands through his dark hair, revealing his only ornament, a single gold ring pierced through the lobe of one ear.

'Celia is dead.' Paul spoke softly, his back still to Carew. From his pocket he took out a curious round object made from gilded brass, roughly the same size and shape as a pocket watch, and began to fiddle with it absently. 'Shipwrecked. Drowned, nearly two years ago now. You are mistaken, John. It is impossible that you saw her, do you hear me? Quite impossible.'

Carew did not reply.

Paul flicked at the catch of the metal compact with his thumb so that the lid opened out, revealing the metal discs inside. One of them, which was marked like a miniature sundial, he now held out in front of him as if to take a reading.

'You can discover most things with your compendium,' Carew noted drily, 'but you won't find Celia that way.'

With a sudden movement Paul got to his feet. When he stood up he was half a head taller than Carew.

'No man sees inside the Sultan's harem. No man – no Turk, let alone a Christian or a Jew – has ever seen inside it. And you, you who've only been here five minutes, you go in there once – just once – and expect me to believe that you did? No, John. Even by your standards, it's too much.'

'Things happen to me, you know how it is.' Carew shrugged, unperturbed. 'But I'm sorry, it must be a shock.' He ran a finger reflectively down his scar. 'After all this time. I know how you must feel—'

'No, you don't.' Paul interrupted him. 'You don't know how I feel. No one knows how I feel.' He snapped the instrument shut. 'Not even you.'

He sat down again, abruptly. 'We must be sure, absolutely sure. But even then, what's to be done, John?' He rubbed his hand over his face, pressing his fingers against his eyelids until lights danced before him. 'Even if we find out for sure she is there, how can we ever admit what we know? It will jeopardise everything. Four years kicking our heels here whilst the Honourable Company makes up its mind what gifts to send the new Sultan . . . and now this. But wait, wait: we're going too fast. First, I must have more proof, absolute positive proof.' Paul ran his hands through his hair again. He turned to Carew. 'You've been inside the palace. How difficult would it be to get some kind of message to her, do you think?'

Carew shrugged again, nonchalant. 'Not difficult.' He glanced at Paul.

Paul returned his gaze levelly. 'I don't like that smile, Carew,' he said after a while. 'I know it of old.' He put one hand on Carew's shoulder, and pressed his thumb thoughtfully against the man's throat. 'What have you done, Carew, you rat-catcher?'

'A subtlety, that's all.'

'A sugar subtlety?'

'My speciality. This one was a boat made entirely from spun sugar. The old Bull squeaked a bit because I used up all his supplies, but it couldn't be helped. A complete merchantman, one of my finest . . .'

Paul increased the pressure.

'. . . all right then, it was a figure of the *Celia*.'

'Let me get this straight: you sent a subtlety in the shape of the *Celia* – Lamprey's merchantman, the one that was wrecked – into the Great Turk's palace?' Paul said, letting Carew go at last.

'Not just into the palace, into the harem.' Carew rubbed his throat, and then added mildly, 'Fog wanted English sweetmeats sent to the Sultan's women. Apparently it's all the fashion with the French and the Venetian embassies, and we must follow them in all things, as you well know.'

'And so you thought you'd impress them?'

'That's why you brought me here, isn't it? To help impress the Turks. To add lustre to our friend Fog's lack-o-lustre. Ha, ha, I jest, of course.' He cocked his head to one side. 'Who would put up with me otherwise?'

'I have to hand it to you, Carew, you have the strangest ideas sometimes,' he sighed. 'But that—' he turned suddenly and pum-melled his fist into the top of Carew's arm, 'that was a damnably

29

good one. Brilliant, I might almost say. If it ever came anywhere near her, that is, which I doubt.'

'Have you got a better idea?' Carew said.

Paul did not answer him. He stood up and went across to the window. He took out the compendium again and turned it so that he could read the motto engraved around the outer rim. '"As Time and Hours Pass Away, So Does the Life of Man Decay,"' he read. '"As Time must be Redeemed with Cost, Bestow it Well and let no Hour be Lost."' Then he opened it again, and with his index finger carefully probed a second, hidden catch inside the base. A second secret lid opened, inside it a portrait.

The miniature of a girl. Reddish gold hair; pearls on milky skin. *Celia.* Was it possible?

'And I've lost enough time already,' he said, almost absently. Then, looking sharply at Carew again, 'but what we still need is more information.'

'What about the white eunuch in the palace school? The one they say is an Englishman turned Turk?'

'And there are several dragomen of his kind, too. They might be easier to get to. One's a Lancashire man, they tell me. Perhaps we should get Dallam to work on him . . . but no, you can never trust these turn-Turks. Besides, they say that it's only the black eunuchs who can enter the women's quarters. No. What we need is someone who has access to the palace, but doesn't live there. Someone who comes and goes freely.'

'Does anyone come and go freely from that place?'

'Of course, many, many people. Every day. It's just the small matter of finding the right one,' Paul said, lifting his head to look through the window.

Carew came and stood beside him. Although the sun was now high in the sky, the pale disc of an almost-full moon was just visible still, sinking slowly on the horizon. He rested his elbows on the window-sill, looked up at the sky. 'Perhaps the stars can tell us what to do. You should ask your friend, what's his name?'

'Do you mean Jamal?'

'If that's his name. The stargazer.'

'Yes, that's him. Jamal. Jamal al-Andalus.' Paul was already pulling on his Ottoman robe. 'Call the janissary, but be discreet. Come on; we've no time to lose.'

Chapter 4

Oxford: the present day

Loving Friend, I have received your letter, &ct. You desire to have the whole proceedings of the unfortunate Voyage and shipwreck of the good ship *Celia*, and still yet more unfortunate and tragical history of Celia Lamprey, daughter of the late Captayn of that ship, who on the eve of her marriage to a merchant of the Levant Company, later Sir Paul Pindar, the late Honourable Embassador from his Majestie at Constantinople, who was carryed as a Slave by the Turks and sold at Constantinople, and from there chosen to serve as *cariye* in the Seraglio of the Grand Signor, the which, as near as God shall enable me, I will make knowne unto you.

Elizabeth's heart was racing. *I knew it*. Although the ink was now faded to a thin sepia, it was still perfectly legible, the writing itself even and not too cramped: a good clear secretary hand, surprisingly easy to read. The paper, apart from the watermark along one of the folded sides, was in better condition than she had dared hope.

Elizabeth glanced up. It was just after nine on Saturday morning and she was one of only two or three people in the Oriental Reading Room at that early hour. She had managed to install herself at one of the corner tables, as far away as possible from the librarian's desk. Soon, she knew, she would have to show them her discovery, but she wanted a chance to be able to read it first, make her own copy of it, without anyone breathing down her neck.

She bent her head again over the paper and read.

The *Celia* set sail from Venice, with a fair wind, on the seventeenth, and a cargo of silkes, velvets and cloth of gold and tissue, Peasters, Chickines and Sultanies, in the hold, the last voyage the Captayn Lamprey would make before the winter storms.

The night of the nineteenth, ten leagues from Ragusa, on the barren, broken coast of Dalmatia, it pleased God to send dirty weather. There arose a great gust of wind out of the north, and soon the wind did increase so much that all on board were afeared of their lives . . .

Although the next few lines were made illegible by the watermark, Elizabeth read on.

And the *Celia* being something tender sided, and her Ports being all open, her Lee Ports were all under water and all the chests of silkes and velvets and cloth of gold and tissue, several of which were not the merchants wares but were to have been the bride's wedding portion, and all the other things that were betwixt the Deckes did swimme, and the Piece of Ordnance that was hald in, got loose and fell to Leeward, and like to carrie out the side.

Here, too, there followed several lines that were illegible.

At length they espied this Sayle coming out of the west, and gave thanks, thinking that their deliverance was at hand . . . of one hundred tunnes or thereabouts, and they knew then that hee was a Turkish man of Warre. And when Captayn Lamprey saw him, he knew that there was no hope of running away, but that they must either fight it out or runne ashore and be smashed on the rocks. So the Captayn he called up his Company, and asked them what they would doe, whether they would stand by him and shew themselves like men, and that it might never be said that they should runne away from him, being not much bigger than they, although hee had as many more Ordnance as they had.

. . . Captayn Lamprey bade all the women on board, nuns from the Convent at Santa Clara, shut themselves in the Steerage and hale the Steerage doore to and make it fast on the inside, and there guard the youngest nun who was with them, and also his daughter Celia, and cause them not to come out, not under any pretext, until he should give word.

32

Elizabeth now came to one of the folds in the paper, where the watermark had obliterated several lines of text.

But Captayn Lamprey, seeing what they were, told him that they were Dogges, scurvy cur-tailed skin-clipping Dogges, but that they should have all the silver plate, and all the Chickins and Piastres that they could carry if they would go away from them, that there was nothing more for them here. But one of the chiefs of these men, who was a Renegado, one that could speake very good English, said to him, Thou Dog, if I doe finde anything more then thou hast confest to me, I will give thee a hundred times as much, and when I have done, I will heave thee overboard. But still Captayn Lamprey he said nothing . . .

Now in the meantime the women were still locked in the Steerage, in terror of their lives, water lapping almost up to their waistes, the skirts of their gowns heavy as lead. As the Captayn had bid them, they made not a sound. Not daring to speke they beseeched God in their hearts to deliver them, for if the Turkes did not get them, they feared to drowne in the Sea . . .

And they caused three men to take him, and they laid him upon his belly upon the lower Decke, and two of them lay on his legges, and one sate on his neck and gave him so many blowes that his daughter, for all that the nuns entreated her nay, swiftly unbarred the Cabbin doore and ran out from her hiding place and cried out stop stop take me but spare my poor father I beseech you, and seeing that her father had six or seven bleeding wounds upon him she fell down on her knees, her face white as death, and did entreate the Turkes again that they would take her but save his life. Whereupon the Captayn of the Turkes did straight away pinyon her, and in the heat of bloud in front of her verie eyes did runne her father in the side with a Culaxee, and bore him up against the Steerage doore, cutting him cleane through his body—

*　*　*

'And there it ends, just like that?'

'Yes. In mid-sentence. What I thought was a whole narrative turns out to be just a fragment after all.'

The Reading Room closed at one o'clock on a Saturday and Elizabeth was having a late lunch with Eve at Alfie's in the covered

33

market. Although Christmas was still six weeks away the waitress was wearing a red and white pinafore and reindeer horns made from green tinsel.

'Oh, come on – it's an amazing find.' Eve was spreading butter on the last of her bread. 'And I believe that means you owe me fifty quid.'

'Yeah, right.'

'Ah well, at least I made you smile.' Eve looked pleased. 'You look almost cheerful this morning, my girl—' She seemed to be about to add something to this, but then thought better of it. *Shall I tell her about last night?* Elizabeth thought, still glowing inwardly – but Eve was in such a mellow mood it seemed a shame to spoil it by having another argument about Marius.

'So, what happens now? Will you be able to look at it again?'

'They've taken it off to show to their early manuscript expert, as you'd expect. But the librarian seemed to think that it'll come back to the Oriental Library – eventually.'

'Don't hold your breath,' Eve said cynically. 'In my experience, once you let the experts in, that's it – *pouf*. It'll never see the light of day again. You should have kept quiet about it.'

Elizabeth shrugged. 'Oh well, too late now.'

'Did you manage to copy any of it?'

'Most of it, although some of it's rather patchy.' Elizabeth explained about the watermark. 'But it's enough to be getting on with. The question of authorship, for instance—' the waitress came up, bringing them two cups of coffee, 'it's written in the third person, but the account is so incredibly vivid, I just can't believe the person who wrote it wasn't there.'

'And the letter, that didn't give you any indication?'

'None at all. Only that the account was written at someone's request, but it doesn't say who that someone was. It's a mystery.'

'How exciting, I love mysteries.' Eve took a sip of her coffee, her glasses misting up in the steam. 'Anything else?'

'Well, I did a lot of Googling yesterday. No prizes for guessing that there were no entries under Celia Lamprey.'

'And under Pindar?'

'What, an obscure Elizabethan merchant?' Elizabeth shook her head. 'You won't believe this, but there are hundreds, literally hundreds. Not all of them are about Pindar himself, of course. Quite a few turned out to be about this pub in Bishopsgate, it's built on the site where Pindar once had a house.' Elizabeth took a last mouthful of soup. 'A socking great pile, by the sounds of it, part of the country estate he built for himself when he retired; pulled down in the nineteenth century when they extended Liverpool Street Station. But that's really neither here nor there,' she waved her spoon in the air. 'The most interesting thing about him seems to have been the Levant Company mission, in which he took part in 1599.'

'I remember, you mentioned it before.'

'I seem to keep coming back to it. The company wanted to renew their trading rights in the Ottoman-controlled parts of the Mediterranean, and in order to do that the etiquette was that they had to give the Sultan a wonderful gift. Something that was better than anyone else's gift – most especially the French and the Venetians, who were their trading rivals. So after a great deal of wrangling they finally commissioned this man, an organ maker named Thomas Dallam, to create what seems to have been a wonderful mechanical toy.'

'I thought you said it was a clock?'

'More like a kind of automaton: part clock, part musical instrument. The clock was the main mechanism, but when it struck the hour all kinds of things began to happen: a chime of bells went off, two angels played on silver trumpets, the organ played a tune, and finally a holly bush full of mechanical birds – black birds and thrushes – shook their wings and sang.'

'So did it do the trick?'

'It was nearly a complete disaster. Thomas Dallam travelled all the way out to Constantinople with his amazing contraption – six months on the company's ship the *Hector* – only to find when he arrived there that it had been all but destroyed on the voyage. Sea water had seeped into the packing cases, and much of the wood was not only wet, but had completely rotted away. The merchants were dismayed, of course. They'd been waiting for four years to present the Sultan with their gift. Anyway, there was nothing else for it, Thomas Dallam had to rebuild the whole thing from scratch. He left his own account of his adventures,' she searched in her notes, 'yes, here it is, in Hakluyt apparently: *The Account of an Organ Carryed to the Grand Seignor and Other Curious Matter, 1599.*'

'I wonder what the other curious matter could be.'

'I'll let you know.' Elizabeth closed her notebook. 'I'm hoping to track it down this afternoon.'

Eve looked at her watch. 'Oh my God, is that the time? Sorry, sweetie, got to go.' She jumped up, pulling out a ten-pound note and putting it on the table. 'Will that be enough?'

'Yes, of course. Go, go.'

Elizabeth watched Eve pull on the bright pink mohair coat she was wearing that day. She was halfway to the door, when suddenly on impulse she came back to their table.

'Good girl!' she said softly. And leant in to kiss Elizabeth swiftly on the cheek.

Elizabeth was in no hurry. She ordered another cup of coffee and sat looking through her notes. The prospect of the work ahead of her filled her with sudden energy. She felt calmer and more focused, she realised, than she had for weeks.

From the table behind her she became aware of the voices of two women speaking together. Turning her head slightly, she recognised the older of the two women, a visiting American colleague of Marius's she had met once last summer at an English Faculty drinks party he had taken her to in the very early days of their affair. For reasons that she now found hard to recall, Elizabeth had not liked her much. 'There's something . . . phoney about her,' she had said to Marius, 'why should I think that?' But he had only laughed.

Now, although it was winter, the American wore open-toed white Birkenstocks on her feet. Her skin was heavily tanned, the exact colour, and, quite possibly, texture, Elizabeth mused with uncharacteristic spikiness, of some endangered tropical wood. She had patronised Elizabeth then as she was patronising the younger woman with her now – one of her students, Elizabeth guessed. Her voice had that quality peculiar to certain academics: not strident, exactly, but somehow . . . implacable. Its cadences, with their long flat vowels, rose and fell like the swell of the Pacific Ocean. They were taking of DPhil theses; the words 'gendered' and 'discourse' droned through their conversation.

Elizabeth turned back to her notes and tried to concentrate, but the two women were sitting so close to her that it was impossible to avoid hearing their conversation. She was looking round for the waitress when she heard Marius's name.

'In fact, a good friend of mine has just published a paper on exactly that. Dr Jones? Marius Jones? I expect you know him.'

The student made some giggling reply that Elizabeth could not catch.

'Oh well, I guess every female student knows Marius!'

Somehow his name on her lips seemed like an impertinence. You don't know him *that* well, lady, Elizabeth thought. Her irritation, she knew, was absurd.

'And on that subject, I must just tell you . . .' The woman's voice now lowered confidentially. 'I know I shouldn't but . . .' Something more was said; her tone serious, trying not to be. '. . . absolutely crazy about her. And the best thing? She doesn't give a *pin* about him. My dear, all his other floozies are absolutely in despair . . .'

Elizabeth did not wait to get the bill. She put down Eve's ten-pound note together with one of her own, and left the restaurant. In the doorway she passed a woman with blonde hair, who entered, not seeing her, with an enquiring look on her face. Through the glass restaurant front Elizabeth saw her greet the American and the student and pull up her own chair. That it was the blonde woman Elizabeth had seen in Blackwell's she had no doubt. She did not see her face, only the face of the American, upturned in greeting. A homely face, older than it looked, sun-stressed hair falling to her shoulders. And behind the smile, Elizabeth suddenly saw a look of such inner desolation that her hostility dissolved.

Oh, my God – not you too? No wonder then. Oh Marius!

Chapter 5

Constantinople: 1 September 1599

Sunrise

That same morning – while John Carew was cracking nuts on the wall of the English embassy, and Hassan Aga spiralling towards his own death – from her private chambers looking out over the waters of the Golden Horn, the Valide Sultan Safiye was watching the dawn.

Although she was attended by her four personal handmaids there was, as was customary, no sound at all in the room. The young women stood with their backs to the wall, still as glass, where they would wait, all day and all night if necessary, until she commanded or dismissed them at her will.

Outwardly composed, Safiye continued to look out through the window casement, her gaze apparently fixed on the rose-grey waters beneath her. Inwardly, through long habit and by employing that mysterious sixth sense which seemed to give her the ability to see without looking, she surveyed her women with a critical eye. The first, who had clearly risen in too much of a hurry that morning, had pinned her cap crookedly on to her dark curls; the second still had that bad habit of swaying slightly from heel to toe (could she not see it made her resemble an elephant in its stall?). And as for the third, Gulbahar – the one who had been with her when they discovered Little Nightingale – there were dark shadows under her eyes this morning.

'It is as if you have eyes in the back of your head,' Cariye Mihrimah used to whisper to her admiringly.

'Just a trick, something my father taught me,' Safiye would whisper back. 'In my country, in the mountains, we are all huntsmen, see?

You have to know how to stay ahead. I'll teach you, Cariye Mihrimah.'

But Cariye Mihrimah had not survived long enough, in the event, to learn anything much, other than to scent the lips of her pretty sex with ambergris, and to pinken her little girl's nipples with rose.

The Valide turned her thoughts back to the previous night. Of Esperanza's silence she was assured. But perhaps it had been a mistake to let Gulbahar see so much, after all? A slight breeze from the casement made Safiye shiver slightly. Although it was only the beginning of September already the morning air felt cooler, the leaves on the trees below her in the palace garden were flushed with the first hint of autumn. She felt the heavy pendulums of her earrings, pearls and cabochon rubies of improbable size and transparency, knocking at her throat. The lobes of her ears throbbed with their weight, and she would have liked to take them off, but long habit had taught her to ignore physical discomfort, or indeed any outward signs of weakness or fatigue.

'Ayshe,' Safiye turned her gaze away from the window slightly, 'my fur.'

But Ayshe, the fourth and newest handmaid, had already anticipated her command and even as she spoke was darting forwards to arrange her cloak, an embroidered shawl lined with sable, around her shoulders. Ayshe was doing well, Safiye thought, focusing quickly once again on the present and bestowing a smile upon the girl. She had quick wits, and the ability always to think a little ahead of what was required of her – a valuable talent to cultivate in the House of Felicity. She had been right to accept the favourite's gifts after all: the two slaves, Ayshe and that other girl, what was she called? Safiye watched Ayshe's fingers tuck the shawl deftly in around her feet. One so dark and the other so pale – such very pale skin that other girl had, miraculous almost. Not a blemish. Mehmet, her son the Sultan, with his unusual tastes, would have enjoyed her last night, she was sure. Anything to get him over his infatuation with the favourite, the one who was always known in the harem simply as the Haseki. He must be tempted away from her, and soon. She would see to that.

Outside her suite, in the corridor which ran past the women's courtyard to the quarters of the eunuchs, Safiye Sultan could hear the faint chink of china. The coffee mistress and her retinue were waiting outside. She would have known that there were women there, even without the noise: a faint feeling of apprehension, a thickening in the air. How could she ever describe how she knew these things? But despite the fact she had not slept at all that night Safiye had given the order that she was not to be disturbed. She did not need either refreshment or rest, a lifetime of vigils at the bedside of her master, the old Sultan Murad, had long ago accustomed her to do without. What she needed now was silence, and space in which to think.

There had been a time, when Safiye first came to the House of Felicity, when its silence oppressed and disturbed her. It was so different from the palace in Manisa. The three of them, the nightingales, had been together then. Those days, when she looked back on them, seemed filled with sunlight. But now, in the years since she had been Valide Sultan, at last she could recognise the silence for what it was: a tool to be used; a hunting trick, like all the others.

Pulling the furs closer around her Safiye turned back towards the familiar view of the Golden Horn. On the far side, at the water's edge, rose the warehouses of the foreign merchants, and behind them the familiar sight of the Galata Tower. To the right of the tower the walls of the foreign enclave gave out on to open countryside, and the houses of the ambassadors surrounded by vines. Behind them, the sun had well now risen. Beyond Galata, and to the right, flowed the Bosphorous, the shores of its eastern banks still in shadow, fringed with green forest. She remembered the Greek Lady, Nurbanu, who as Valide Sultan before her had sat on this very divan, wearing these very earrings of ruby and pearl, while Safiye herself had waited on her. 'They think I don't know that they are waiting outside,' she had once said to her. 'They think I cannot hear. They think that I cannot see. But in this silence, Safiye, there is nothing that I do not see. I can see through walls.'

The first rays of sun now struck the carved shutters of the windows, turning their mother-of-pearl inlay to points of shining light. Safiye drew her arm out of the furs and laid it along the casement. A faint aromatic smell of warm wood reached her. The skin on her arms and hands was milky and smooth, the skin of a concubine still, miraculously unscathed by the years. And on her finger, catching the sun's rays, was Nurbanu's emerald, its vertiginous depths smouldering with points of black fire.

'What would you do now,' Safiye wondered, 'if you were me?'

She closed her eyes briefly, feeling the sun at last strike the skin of her face. The image of Little Nightingale – swollen body, severed genitals – came again into her mind. And at last, 'Do nothing,' a sure voice inside her head replied. 'It is fate.'

It was not Nurbanu who had answered her, someone else: a voice from beyond the grave.

'Cariye? Cariye Mihrimah?'

'Do nothing. It is fate. After all these years. *Kismet*. The one thing you cannot outwit. Not even you.'

'Fatma!' Safiye's eyes snapped open so suddenly they made even Ayshe, the quick-witted, start at her post.

'Yes, Majesty?' Caught off guard, Fatma, the first handmaid, stammered and flushed.

'What, are you asleep, girl?' The Valide spoke softly, as she always did, but there was a note of steeliness in her voice that made the palms of the young woman's hands turn cold and clammy, and the blood drum in her ears.

'No, Majesty.'

'My coffee, then. If you would be so good.'

On soft and noiseless feet, Safiye's handmaids glided through the room to attend her.

Although the sun had now risen fully, its light never penetrated far into the Valide's quarters. These rooms, positioned as they were at the very centre of the House of Felicity, the Sultan's private quarters, were inward, not outward spaces. The women's rooms, and the larger quarters of the Sultan's favourite concubines, even the private chambers of the Sultan himself, all were connected to the Valide's rooms. No one, not even the Sultan's favourite concubine, the Haseki herself, could contrive to go in or out without passing through her domain.

With the exception of the Sultan's rooms, the Valide's suite was by far the biggest in the place. Their shadowy depths, dim with blue and green light, were cool in summer; heated with braziers and heaped with furs and sables in the winter. The women, moving in their familiar dance, seemed like a small shoal of silvery fish, gliding through its sub-aqueous depths.

Within moments a brass tray had been placed before Safiye, resting on a pair of folding wooden legs, and a tiny brazier, scented with cedar wood, was tucked beneath it. Kneeling before her, the first handmaid held out a bowl, while the second slowly poured rose water from a ewer of rock crystal, just wetting the tips of Safiye's fingers. Withdrawing soundlessly, they were replaced by the third handmaid who knelt also offering her a tiny embroidered napkin to dry her hands. Next they offered her the coffee. One held out a tiny jewelled cup; the second poured coffee; the third carefully placed a second brass tray on the table with pomegranates, apricots and figs arranged on a bed of crystallised sugar rose petals; whilst the fourth brought fresh napkins.

Safiye drank her coffee slowly and felt her body relax. There was, after all, no sign of nerves that she could detect from her women, usually a first and sure indicator that rumours in the harem were rife. It had been the greatest good fortune that most of the women and eunuchs were still at the summer palace. The Sultan had decided to return to the palace unexpectedly for one night, and she had come with him, together with a handful of her most trusted women. If the House of Felicity had been full there would have been no possibility at all of concealment of the night's business. The loyalty of Esperanza and Gulbahar, the only two who had been with her, was beyond question. All the same, it had been a good idea to keep them standing awhile – in her experience, always an excellent test of nerves. The first handmaid was jumpy, to be sure, but then she often was, especially since the Harem Stewardess had discovered her love letters from the eunuch Hyacinth, a misguided little *affaire* in which she still believed herself to be undetected.

'Never act in haste,' Nurbanu had once told her. 'And never forget: knowledge is power.'

You are wrong, Cariye Mihrimah, Safiye said to herself. This may be *kismet*, as you say – in her mind's eye she leant over and kissed Cariye Mihrimah on the cheek – but since when did that ever stop me knowing exactly what to do?

'Now listen to me, all of you,' Safiye drained her coffee cup and placed it on its saucer, 'I have sent Hassan Aga, our Chief Black Eunuch, to Edirne for a few days to see to some of my affairs,' she announced. It was more information than she would normally think fit, or necessary, to give out in front of her women: would they think it strange? A necessary risk, she decided. 'Gulbahar, stay with me, I need you to deliver some messages. The rest of you – go now.' She gave the sign of dismissal.

'And Ayshe.'

'Yes, Majesty?'

'Bring me your friend, the other new girl, I have forgotten her name . . .'

'Do you mean Kaya, Majesty?'

'Yes. Wait outside with her until Gulbahar comes for you. And until then, let no one in.'

Suddenly, Hassan Aga was awake. Short moments of lucidity punctuated the strange, phantasmagorical dreams, although how long he had been in this state he could not tell. As if through long habit, when the smallest noise, the tiniest diversion from the ordinary business of the harem would alert him, his eyes snapped open. He was no longer in his chamber, of that he was sure, but where had they taken him? It was dark here, darker than night. Darker, in fact, than it was when he closed his eyes, when streams and fountains of light seemed to cascade like shooting stars across the horizons of his eyelids.

Was he dead, then? The thought crossed his mind briefly, and he found that he was not afraid of the possibility. But a burning pain in his gut, and more strangely in his ears, made him think not. He tried to shift his weight, but the effort made a clammy sweat break out on his forehead; there was a strange metallic taste on his lips. His body heaved in a sudden, dry convulsion, but there was nothing left in his stomach to bring up. A lump like a stone seemed to be grinding into his neck, and the air around him smelt damp. Was he underground somewhere, and if so how did he get here?

Then, just as suddenly as he had awoken, Hassan Aga was slipping away again. How long he lay in this strange limbo of darkness he did not know. Did he dream or not dream, sleep or not sleep? Then suddenly, at the end of aeons, which might also only have been a few hours . . . a light.

At first he saw two thin lines, one horizontonal and the other vertical. They were very pale when he first became aware of them, as pale as the earliest dirty-grey light of dawn. As he watched them, they converged suddenly, vertiginously, into a single point of light. And behind the point of light were the unmistakable shadows of two people, two women, coming towards him.

A voice spoke: 'Little Nightingale . . .'

From a long, long way away he heard his own voice reply.

'Lily,' his voice said, '. . . is that you?'

Chapter 6

Istanbul: the present day

E lizabeth called Eve from the telephone in her room.
        'Where did you say you are?' Eve's voice sounded unusually
faint.

'Istanbul.' Elizabeth said again carefully, and then held the telephone receiver away from her ear.

'Istan*bul*?' There was a pause. 'What in God's name are you doing
there?'

'I caught a flight. Last night.'

'But we had lunch together. You never said anything.'

'It was a stand-by flight. I was lucky, that's all.'

Elizabeth wanted to tell her about the American, about what had
happened in Alfie's, but somehow she found that she could not, not
even to Eve.

'I need to . . .' she began, struggling against the ache in her throat,
'. . . stop all this.' There was a silence on the other end of the phone,
and she knew that Eve was listening. 'You know . . . all this,' she
managed eventually.

Cut it off. Tear it out. Bleed it from me. I'd rip out the still-beating
heart of this terrible thing with my own fingernails if only I knew
how . . . A feeling of hysteria gripped her.

'Just make it . . . stop. Please.'

'It's all right, it's all right.' She could hear Eve's voice catch. 'Don't
say anything, just breathe! OK, sweetie? Just breathe—'

Through her tears Elizabeth could not help but laugh. 'Dear Eve,
you're crying too.'

'I can't help it.' She heard Eve blowing her nose loudly. 'It's catching.' And then, crossly, 'You know, this would be *so* much easier in Oxford.'

'I know.' Elizabeth pressed the palm of one hand over her hot eyes. 'That's just the point. I need . . . to get a grip. I can't bear being like this.' Self-pity welled up inside her. 'Burdening you.'

'Darling Liz. You're not a burden, never . . .'

'I've decided to finish with Marius. No going back this time.' There, she'd said it. She'd said it, so it must be true. 'At least,' she added, knowing it was more truthful, 'I've told him I can't see him again.'

She could sense Eve trying to gauge the temperature from the other end of the telephone. But when she spoke, the relief in her voice was palpable.

'You've dumped him? Oh, well done. Well *done*, Lizzie.' And then: 'For good this time?'

'Oh yes, this time for good.'

'So, where are you anyway? Your hotel, I mean. I presume you are staying in a hotel?'

'Well actually . . .' Elizabeth looked round her. The truth was that she had no idea what the hotel was called. A taxi had brought her here late last night. There was a bed; it was clean. She had been beyond asking questions. 'I'm in room 312.' The number was on the base of an old-fashioned Bakelite telephone by her bed. 'And here's the number.' She read it out.

Eve seemed satisfied. 'How long are you going to stay?'

'Not sure.' Elizabeth shrugged. 'As long as it takes.'

'To delete Marius?'

'Yes.' Elizabeth laughed. 'But I'm going to do some work too. When I told my supervisor about the fragment she suggested I apply to look in the archives here, so I thought I might as well get on with it.' Anything not to be in Oxford, not to be tempted into forgiveness. 'Dr Alis agrees with me that the other half of Celia Lamprey's narrative must be somewhere, and I've a hunch it might be here. Do you remember Berin Metin?'

'From the exchange programme?'

'Yes. Well, I called her after . . . yesterday afternoon, and she's said she can fix me with a reader's ticket at the Bosphorous University here. They have an English library, so I can get on with my research while I wait for permission to come through to look in the archives.'

After she had put down the phone to Eve, Elizabeth lay back down on the bed. It was still early: seven o'clock in the morning Istanbul time, only five o'clock English time, she realised. Poor Eve.

Her room was large, but very plain. Twin beds with wrought iron bedsteads. An old-fashioned wardrobe. In the window there was a recessed area, like a little alcove, in which stood a plain deal table and chair. The floorboards, which listed slightly towards the front of the room, had been stained dark brown and were unadorned by rugs or kelims, even of the cheapest cotton kind. There was nothing whatever in the room to suggest that she was in Istanbul, or anywhere else for that matter.

Cautiously Elizabeth put her hand up to the wall. She shut her eyes and ran her fingers lightly along the plasterwork. But nothing. The place had the chaste, unadorned air of a convent dormitory. Or a ship.

Tomorrow I'll move, she thought to herself.

Elizabeth lay down on the bed again. From her shoulder bag she took out the notes she had made in the Oriental Reading Room:

> . . . his daughter, for all that the nuns entreated her nay, swiftly unbarred the Cabbin doore and ran out from her hiding place and cried out stop stop take me but spare my poor father I beseech you, and seeing that her father had six or seven bleeding wounds upon him she fell down on her knees, her face white as death, and did entreate the Turkes again that they would take her but save his life. Whereupon the Captayn of the Turkes did straight away pinyon her, and in the heat of bloud in front of her verie eyes did runne her father in the side with a Culaxee, and bore him up against the Steerage doore, cutting him cleane through his body—

Celia. Poor Celia.

Still holding the paper to her breast, Elizabeth fell into a dreamless sleep.

Chapter 7

Constantinople: 1 September 1599

Morning

Ayshe, the Valide's handmaid, found Kaya beside the fountain in the Courtyard of the Favourites.

'She wants to see you.'

In the House of Felicity, no one, not even the newest recruits, needed to be told who 'she' was.

'Now?'

'Yes, come with me. Quickly – but don't run.' Ayshe put a warning hand on the girl's arm. 'They don't like it if you run.'

'Don't fuss – there's no one to see us here.'

The general annual exodus to the Valide's summer palace on the Bosphorous, where everyone except a handful of the very youngest *kislar*, and the oldest servants, were still lodged, had given the outer reaches of the Sultan's harem an echoing, holiday feel.

'Haven't you learnt anything?' Ayshe said crossly. '*Someone* will see you. They always do.'

Ayshe led Kaya from the paved terrace with its fountain down a series of stone steps and through the palace garden: two small figures, scarlet and gold, flitting like dragonflies through the silent morning garden.

'Are you staying here? Or will you go back with her, do you think?' Trying to match her pace to Ayshe's quick footsteps, Kaya stumbled behind her, and once nearly fell. 'Don't walk so fast!'

'Keep up, can't you. And patience – I'll tell you when we are inside.'

'Patience! If you only knew . . . I swear to you, I'm sick to my stomach of being patient.'

At the garden walls they turned sharply to the left, making their way past the harem hospital and then through a second courtyard. Turning to the left once more they followed a steep flight of wooden steps which led into the rectangular paved courtyard at the heart of the women's quarters. There, in a small tiled vestibule at the end of the stone corridor which marked the entrance to the eunuchs' quarters, Ayshe came to a halt at last.

'What now?'

'We have to wait here.' Ayshe shrugged. 'When she is ready she will send Gulbahar to get you.'

'How long will that be?'

'How should I know, goose,' Ayshe frowned. 'An hour. Two hours.'

'Two hours!'

'Hush, will you!'

The two took up waiting positions, standing side by side with their backs against the wall. Kaya waited for the pounding in her heart to subside, clenched her now clammy hands, willing her jagged breath to return to normal.

There were few women around that morning. Two ancient black slaves, too decrepit and sleepy with age now to be included in any of the Valide's excursions, were sweeping the courtyard with bunches of old palm fronds.

'On your way now – go.' Impatiently, Ayshe waved her hand at the two women. 'The Valide is coming this way soon, and she does not want her eyes defiled by the sight of you hideous old crones.'

'Yes, *kadin* . . .' The two slaves were already backing away, bowing respectfully. 'Yes, my lady.'

Kaya glanced at her friend. 'What harm were they doing?'

'I just don't want us to be overheard, that's all. Not by anyone. And keep your voice down.' Ayshe spoke very softly. 'I swear, she can hear everything.'

'What does she want me for, do you know?' Kaya felt her stomach muscles tighten in apprehension.

'As if you didn't know! Probably wants to know if you've . . . you know . . .' Ayshe put her hand to her mouth to conceal her sudden smile. 'If you are still *gözde*. "In the Sultan's eye." ' She glanced slyly at her friend. 'Are you?'

49

'Oh, she'd know all right.'

'Indeed she would,' Ayshe agreed tartly, 'She probably watches it all herself . . .'

Kaya made an inarticulate sound.

'Really. I mean it. There is nothing she doesn't make it her business to know.'

'Yes, but no one actually *watches*,' Kaya glanced at her friend again. 'They . . . they write it down in a book. I know,' she added, 'Hassan Aga showed me.' There was a small silence. 'And no, they haven't written me in there yet.'

For a moment the two stood together, not speaking, suddenly shy of one another. In the courtyard where the old women had been sweeping sunlight shifted slowly. Servants' voices, and the sound of water flushing across stone, carried from the women's hammam which gave on to one side of the courtyard. The same half-empty holiday feel affected even this, the very heart of the harem. Kaya, unused to these long watches, swayed uncomfortably, lifting her little feet slightly one after another in their soft kid boots.

'How much longer? My back hurts.'

'Patience, goose . . .'

'You've said that before . . .'

'And don't sway, for pity's sake, she hates that. Stand still, can't you?'

Another silence.

'I miss you Annetta.'

'And I you, Celia.'

In the courtyard a trickle of water flowed slowly from the doorway of the hammam on to the hot stone.

'Don't cry, goose.'

'Me? I never cry.'

'You'll make your nose red.'

'He said that, do you remember? The day we were sold.'

'Yes. I remember.'

How could she not? Celia thought back to that day when they had first arrived at the House of Felicity. After the shipwreck – how long had it been? two summers now, by her reckoning – there had been a long journey, an even longer sojourn with the slave mistress in Constantinople, and then one day, just a few months ago, with no

50

warning at all a litter borne by eunuchs had arrived, and the two of them had been put in it, and brought here to the palace. A great lady had bought them as a gift for the Sultan's mother, they had been told. They were no longer Celia and Annetta, but Kaya and Ayshe; but beyond that no one thought to tell them anything of what lay ahead.

Celia remembered the sickening sway of the litter as they made their way through the city, and how at last they had passed through a brass-studded door, bigger and more doleful than any she had seen in her life. It was so dark inside that at first they could hardly see. She remembered instead her sense of dread as the eunuchs brought them down from the litter, and then her own voice crying out – *Paul, oh Paul!* – as the door ground shut behind them.

A sudden flurry and a clapping of wings as two pigeons came to roost on the sloping roof above them made both girls start.

'Annetta?'

'What?'

'Do you think we'll ever forget? Forget our real names, I mean. I asked Gulbahar once, and she said she couldn't remember hers.'

'But she was only six when she came here. Of course we'll remember. We'll remember everything.' Annetta's eyes narrowed. 'How could we forget?'

'And you do want to, don't you?'

'Of course I do, goose!' There was a short silence. 'But we're here now, and we must make what we can of it. You know, Celia, perhaps it would be better if . . .' Annetta stiffened suddenly, 'shh!'

'I can't hear anything.'

'Gulbahar's coming.'

'But how . . .?'

'I watch her, it's how she does it,' Annetta's voice was barely a breath in Celia's ear. 'But never mind that now: just listen. Whatever you do, try not to say too much. She'll use everything you tell her, *capito*? And I mean everything. But she doesn't want a milksop either. And whatever you do, don't try to play the fool.' Her dark eyes darted to the door and back. Celia stood beside her, deathly still now, a pulse, like the small quick beating of a frightened bird, in the skin behind her ear. 'Mark this, Celia: something has happened—'

'What kind of thing?' Celia turned to her in alarm. 'And how? How do you know?'

'I . . . don't really know. It's just a feeling I get.' Annetta pressed her hand against the pit of her stomach. 'Just remember what I've told you, it's the best I can do. Now – go!'

Celia had, of course, been in the presence of the Valide many times since she and Annetta had been taken into the House of Felicity.

There were many occasions in the life of the palace women – entertainments and dancing for the Sultan, alfresco picnics in the palace gardens and boating expeditions along the Bosphorous – when the Valide showed herself. At those times, when the music played and the sound of women's voices and laughter carried on the rose-scented air, when they were taken to watch the dolphins sporting in the Sea of Marmara or when the moonlight sparkled on the waters of the Bosphorous and the little boats of the women, lit up like fireflies, followed the Sultan in his mother Safiye's barge, its poop all inlaid with precious stones, shining with ivory and mother-of-pearl, sea-horse teeth and gold, at those times, Celia thought, it was sometimes possible to believe that the Valide was indeed the mother of them all. Those were times of grace; times when the palace women did indeed seem the most fortunate and blessed of all the women in the Sultan's empire. At those times no one watched and waited and spied. Formality and palace etiquette were forgotten. So, too, were pain and fear, and the strange, constricted feeling – almost a constant now – on her left side, beneath her ribs.

In their various capacities, the palace women saw the Valide Sultan often, many of them on a daily basis, but it was only a very few who were admitted into her private quarters. These included the four personal maidservants, hand-picked by the Valide herself, who always attended her; the Harem Stewardess, the Valide's right hand and the most powerful woman in the palace after the Valide herself; the Mistresses of the Laundry and of the Pantry, of the Coffee and the Ablutions Ewer; and some of the other high dignitaries who were responsible for the daily running of the women's quarters: the Treasurer, the Scribe, and the great mute Coiffeur Mistress.

Now, when Gulbahar ushered her into the Valide's presence, Celia stood, as she had been taught to do, with her eyes fixed on the floor, not daring to look up. Gulbahar had withdrawn, although Celia had neither seen nor heard her go. She stood for a long time, aware only of the deep silence that seemed to hang all around her in the Valide's chamber, its walls and high domed spaces slanting with cool green and golden light.

'You may look up now.'

So it was true what they said. The voice was light and low, a voice at once golden and mysterious; the voice, they said, of an angel.

'Come, *cariye*.' A hand raised, a flash of green emerald upon her fingers. 'Come, slave, and let me look at you.'

Celia took three small steps towards the voice. An upright figure, always smaller than she expected, was silhouetted against the window. A fur cloak was loosely folded across her shoulders. At her ears and throat jewels blazed, and her tunic, beneath the furred lining of the cloak, was made of pure gold thread. Strings of tiny pearls had been woven into her hair, which hung down in a rope, like a mermaid's tresses, over one shoulder.

'What is your name?'

'Kaya . . . Majesty.'

Half-fearful still, Celia looked up. To her surprise the Valide was smiling. The fur of her cloak moved slightly, and Celia saw that a large cat was curled on her lap. The cat had pure white fur, and one blue and one green eye.

'Ah.' The green emerald flashed once again in the sunlight. 'Then sit, little Kaya. Sit with me awhile.' She pointed to some cushions near her on the divan. 'This is Cat. Do you like cats? My son, the Sultan, gave him to me. It's not a very original name, I'm afraid, but it's what the eunuchs call her, and it suits her somehow.' The voice was kind, smiling even. 'Do you see her eyes?' The cat, knowing it was being spoken of, fixed Celia in its unblinking, lapidary gaze. 'They come from Van, these cats, in the east of our empire, near the mountains of the Caucasus. They are beautiful, no?'

'Yes,' Celia nodded stiffly. And then, remembering Annetta's words, added bravely, 'I've always liked cats.'

'Ah, is that really so?' Safiye sounded as if nothing could be more pleasing than this piece of information. 'Then we have something in common, you and I.' Jewelled fingers rubbed the sweet spot beneath the cat's chin. 'And you, Signorina Kaya? Where were you from, before you came to us here? *De dove viene*?' She laughed suddenly and delightfully. 'You see, I speak the language of Venice. Does that surprise you? You are from Venice, no?'

'No . . . I mean, yes, Majesty,' Celia said, anxious not to disappoint. 'That is, I travelled there very often with my father. He was a merchant; his trade was with Venice, before he . . . before he died.'

'*Poverina.*' The Valide's voice was soothing and kind.

'I am from England. It's Annetta who's from Venice.' Celia hoped she was not gabbling her words. 'We were on the same ship when we were . . .' Celia hesitated, uncertain of how to refer to that brutal and bloody episode which still haunted her sleep, 'That is,' she corrected herself, 'before we were brought here. To the House of Felicity.'

'Annetta? You mean Ayshe, your dark-haired friend?'

Celia nodded. She had started to relax a little; arranged herself more comfortably against the cushions.

'I believe your friend was born in Ragusa, which is where her mother is from,' the Valide said.

'Oh, you knew that?'

'But of course.' On the Valide's silken lap the cat yawned suddenly, showing its teeth, as sharp and white as razor-clams. 'There is very little about my women that I do not know, but then she has probably told you that, hasn't she?'

'No . . .' Celia bowed her head and flushed. 'Yes, Majesty.'

'You tell me the truth: that's very good. Ayshe is a clever girl. She sees things, but she is clever enough to conceal what she knows. Most of the time, anyway. She could go very far. But that is not the only reason why she is with me now, one of my chosen *cariye*. Do you know why I chose her?'

Celia shook her head.

'I chose her because she comes from very near where I was born – in the village of Rezi, near the mountains of Albania. Ragusa also belonged to the Venetians once; our mountains are in the Sultan's lands, but so close that many of our people still speak the Venetian tongue. Do you understand?'

Safiye turned and looked out of her window casement towards the grey waters, the Golden Horn now slashed with sunlight.

'Mountains!' She gave a small sigh. 'When I was your age, how I used to long and long to see them again. Let me tell you something, *cariye*, even I am lonely sometimes,' she said. 'Does that surprise you? Yes, even in the middle of all this,' jewelled fingers described the room in a graceful arc. 'My master the old Sultan is dead. All our companions from the days in Manisa, before we moved here to Constantinople, almost all of them are gone now, too.'

She turned to the dazzled girl.

'We come here as slaves, all of us: slaves of the Sultan. We give up everything, even our names. It is a strange fact – don't you think? – that not one of us was born Ottoman, or even a Muslim. Not one of us. There is nothing to unite us except the fact that we have the honour to be the Sultan's women. And do not forget this, *cariye*: there is no higher honour.' Safiye allowed a pause to fall. 'I chose to come here, you know, when I was just a child: chose this life of my own free will, as many of us do. But you must know that. Everyone talks, do they not? Every woman here has their story to tell. As you do, *poverina*. You have your story, and one day you shall tell it to me.'

Safiye allowed another, slightly longer pause, so that all this information should have time to sink in. Narrowing her eyes slightly, her gaze fell upon the English merchantman moored on the other side of the waters, its pennants fluttering, red and white, in the afternoon breeze. The *Hector*. A mighty vessel, by far the largest in the harbour, as no doubt the English had calculated: a symbol of their country's might. She remembered the stir it had made, only a few days ago, when it had made its formal entrance into the Golden Horn. The memory came to her of the Englishman who had been sent to deliver her gifts from the English Queen. A disquieting figure, all in black. Pale skin, hard eyes. For some reason, she could not quite think why, the thought of him still lingered at the corners of her mind. Was it possible, was it conceivable – it occurred to her suddenly – that the sugar ship she had found in Little Nightingale's room had been sent by him? It would be quite natural, after all, in their interests, indeed, to want to draw attention to themselves, not to lose their advantage. And there had been a name – hadn't there? – a name on the side of the ship. But it wasn't the *Hector* . . .

She turned back to Celia again, bestowed on her a brilliant smile. 'With all of us there is always something, something that reminds us of what we once were. And with me it is the mountains. The mountains in Rezi, where I was born. But for you, what is it I wonder? Come here, closer.' She beckoned to Celia. 'Look down there and tell me what you can see.'

Celia looked through the window casement. 'I see water.'

'And what else?'

'The tops of the trees in the palace gardens,' Celia added, conscious of the fact that the Valide was watching her carefully. 'Clouds?'

A pause.

'What about ships?'

'Ships. Of course, those too.'

Safiye Sultan fell silent, curling a strand of her pearl-braided hair between her fingertips. 'When I was young, I often used to watch the ships on the Bosphorous,' she said after a while. 'I used to wonder which of them came from my country; whether they would ever carry me back there. But I was wise, even as a child. I knew that even if I could, I would never go back.' All of a sudden the Valide seemed to snap out of her reverie. 'But come! I didn't bring you here to give you a history lesson.'

With an impatient movement the cat jumped from Safiye's lap, and stood shaking one paw fastidiously in front of her. A little bell on a golden chain around his neck chimed.

'That's right, Cat, away you go. Off with you,' the Valide made a play of shooing the cat away. She turned to Celia again, with a half-smile. 'As if Cat would ever do anything *I* told him to. Why, even the Sultan himself cannot tell a cat what to do. That's why we like them so much, isn't that so, *cariye*?'

'Quite so, Majesty.' Emboldened, Celia held out the tips of her fingers for the cat to sniff.

'Ah, look, he likes you. Ah no, he prefers you! Look: he's coming to sit on your lap now, so he is.'

The cat settled himself beside Celia, allowing her to trace her fingers through his coat. She could feel his bones, and his little ribcage, surprisingly fragile beneath the thick fur.

'And there is someone else I should like to prefer you, *cariye*.' The Valide's voice was caressing. 'Someone who I think will come to like you very much. But you did not play your part very well last night, am I right?'

The suddenness of her approach took Celia by surprise. She looked up, blushed, looked down again.

'The . . . His . . . I was not . . .'

What was the word? What word could she possibly use for the act that had not, in the end, taken place?

'I was not . . . honoured last night, no.'

'Hush! I have not brought you here to criticise. Come, aren't I your friend? Why, you're trembling. Here, foolish Kaya, give me your hand.' Taking the girl's wrist, the Valide laughed her golden laugh. 'Why, what have they been telling you? I am not really so frightening as all that, am I?' Celia felt light, soft fingers stroking the palm of her hand. 'It would not be very clever of me to criticise the one who could become the Sultan's new concubine; why, one day perhaps even his favourite, his Haseki. Now would it?'

Celia managed a weak smile.

'That's better. Now, you will tell me all about it. But first, little Kaya,' her hand closed around Celia's fingers. 'Tell me your name. I mean the name you were born with. The name your father gave you.'

'My name was Celia, Majesty.' And why was it when she replied that Celia thought she saw the shadow of a frown pass over the Valide's face? 'My name was Celia Lamprey.'

Chapter 8

Istanbul: the present day

E lizabeth woke so gently that for a moment or two she was not sure whether she had actually slept or not. Her watch said ten o'clock. She had been asleep for three hours. She dressed and went downstairs, and found breakfast still laid in a small windowless room in the basement. There was no one else around, so she helped herself to hard-boiled eggs, olives, cucumber and tomatoes, bread rolls and sticky pink jam, home-made from what looked like rose petals.

On her way back up to her room she saw an old woman sitting in the hall. The woman had positioned her chair – a curious object, which looked as if it had been fashioned out of string – in a commanding position, between two large potted palms in brass pots at the foot of the stairs. She was dressed entirely in black.

'Excuse me,' Elizabeth went up to her. 'I know this is going to sound like an odd question, but can you tell me the name of this hotel?'

The woman, who had been reading a Turkish newspaper, looked up at her over a pair of horn-rimmed reading glasses. Despite the shabby black clothes, a pair of exquisite golden earrings, Byzantine in design, hung from her earlobes.

'A hotel? My dear, this isn't a hotel.'

'It isn't?'

There must have been a note of alarm in Elizabeth's voice because the woman gave her a sudden amused smile. 'Don't look so worried. Please . . .' she indicated a second string chair next to her.

Elizabeth was so surprised she sat down.

'You slept well?'

'Yes,' Elizabeth stared at her. 'Thank you.'

'I'm so glad. You have slept, you have eaten, and in a moment you shall tell me your plans. But first, please take some tea with me. Have you ever tried our apple tea?'

'No . . .' Elizabeth realised that she must be staring almost rudely at the woman. She forced herself to glance away.

'No? Then you must try some. My name is Haddba, by the way. I am very pleased to make your acquaintance.'

'How do you do?' Elizabeth found herself shaking a proffered hand. 'Excuse me, but if this isn't a hotel . . .'

'One moment please – Rashid!'

A boy of about ten appeared, and was despatched to get the tea.

'Now.' Haddba gave Elizabeth an appraising look. Her eyes, Elizabeth saw, were exquisitely shaped, like teardrops; their lids, which had the thick creamy consistency of gardenia petals, drooped over them heavily, giving her a sleepy look, totally belied by a pair of piercing black eyes. 'I feel I should explain, we are a guest house, not a hotel.'

'Oh, I see!' Elizabeth said, relieved. 'So that's why you have no name?'

'Here in Beyoglu we are known simply as number 159.' The woman gave the name of the street. 'That's the address to give your people.' Her English, although heavily accented, had a clipped quality to it, as if it had been learnt from an Edwardian phrase book. 'Our guests usually stop here for some time: several weeks, sometimes even months.' The heavy eyelids blinked, once, twice, very slowly. 'One tries not to be in any of the guide books.'

'I wonder how the taxi knew to bring me here.'

'But you are planning a long stay.' A statement, not a question.

'Well, yes.' Elizabeth frowned. 'But I don't remember telling the taxi driver that.'

'It was late,' with exaggerated fastidiousness Haddba picked a piece of white fluff from the sleeve of her cardigan. 'And no doubt he saw the size of your suitcase.' She laughed, making the golden earrings dance.

Chapter 9

Constantinople: 31 August 1599

Day and Night

Except for the Valide herself, none of the senior palace women were present in the House of Felicity the day Celia was taken to the Sultan, an unusual occurrence which meant that the ritual ablutions – the scenting of her clothes and body, the careful choice of dress and jewels, and all the other preparations that it was customary for a new concubine to undergo – had been performed in the event by Cariye Lala, the Under-Mistress of the Baths.

No one could remember when Lala had first come to the House of Felicity. It was said amongst the other *cariye* that she had been there even before the Valide Sultan herself, as a still-young woman, had arrived, and was one of the very few to have served under the old Valide Nurbanu and her Harem Stewardess, the powerful Janfreda Khatun. At Sultan Murad's death most of the old guard, his women and his daughters, had moved, as was the custom, to the Eski Saray, the old palace. ' "The Palace of Tears", they call it,' Cariye Lala used to say when one or other of the younger women, curious about her life, asked her. 'I remember the day they all left. How we cried. And the little princes, dead, all dead, killed to keep the new Sultan safe.' Her rheumy eyes watered over. 'And some no more than babes. We cried until we thought we should go blind.'

Cariye Lala, her bones now bent and her skin beginning to weather, her face gradually subsiding into the featurelessness of age, had never been beautiful enough, even in her first youth, to catch the Sultan's eye. After she had been sold into the palace she had been trained, as was the custom for all women entering the Sultan's household, in each of the palace departments, ending up with the Mistress of the Baths, under whose supervision, all these years later, she still remained. Never clever or ambitious enough – or so it was always assumed – to rise to the top of that hierarchy herself, none the less she had become something of a feature in palace life, a last dusty link to the old ways, an expert on palace ritual and etiquette.

'It is not the only kind of etiquette she knows about,' the first handmaid had once told the two new slaves, Ayshe and Kaya.

'They say she knows all the tricks,' agreed the second handmaid.

'What kind of tricks?' Celia had asked.

But the others just stared at her and laughed.

'Then you must bribe her to tell you,' Annetta had said in her definite way that very morning, the morning Celia had first learnt the news she was *gözde*.

'Bribe her?' Celia was still bemused.

'With money, of course, you numbskull. You have got some saved?'

'Yes, like you said.' Celia showed her the purse.

'A hundred and fifty aspers! Good.' Annetta counted out the money quickly. 'And I've got another hundred. What did I tell you? No use spending it on fripperies like the others do. This is what our daily stipend is for. Here, take them.'

'Annetta, I couldn't—'

'Don't argue with me. Just take them.'

'But that's two hundred and fifty aspers!'

'Probably no more than a week's wages for our old Lala,' Annetta said shrewdly, 'not much for the experience of a lifetime. Or so we hope. All I can say is, she'd better be good! I remember a poem my mother used to recite – before she put me in the convent, that is. *Cosi dolce e gustevole divento/Quando mi trovo in letto . . .*' Annetta spoke the words mockingly, ' "So sweet and appetising do I become, When I find myself in bed, With him who loves and welcomes me, That our pleasure surpasses all delight." You are to find out how to make yourself sweet and appetising, that's all. Poor Celia!'

Bending over, Celia cupped her hands together under her left ribs and moaned softly to herself. 'Couldn't you go in my place?'

'Why?' Annetta said tartly. 'Because I was brought up in a brothel? *Santa Madonna*, I think not.'

'But you . . . you know about these things.'

'Not I, sweet Celia,' Annetta replied lightly. 'Not I.'

'But you do, you know about so many things. And I,' Celia shrugged her shoulders despairingly, 'I am all at sea.'

'*Tsh*! Are you mad?' Annetta gave Celia's arm a sharp pinch.

'Ow!'

'Can't you see? Haven't you noticed how they all look at you, now you are *gözde*? Spare us your maidenly blushes,' Annetta almost spat into her ear. 'We've been given a chance and you, my dear, are it. And this may be our only one.'

They came for Celia later that day, and took her without ceremony straight to the Valide's private hammam. Cariye Lala was there to meet her.

'Undress, undress, don't be shy,' Cariye Lala peered at Celia. The irises of her eyes, Celia saw, were still startlingly blue, the whites very white.

Her servant, a very young black girl, no more than twelve years old, helped Celia take off her overdress and her shift. She seemed so in awe, Celia noticed, that she barely raised her head, far less her eyes, or looked either of them in the face. Her hands, with their small pink undersides, were like the hands of some poor caged creature, probing softly and tremblingly at the long row of tiny, stiff pearl buttons down the front of Celia's dress.

I wonder where you have come from, Celia found herself thinking. Are you happy to be here, as many women here say they are, or do you wish yourself back home, as I do, every moment of the day? A sudden feeling of pity for the little girl swept over her. She tried to smile some encouragement, but her smile only seemed to make the girl's efforts all the more tremulous.

I must seem so far above her, Celia thought with a sudden insight. The Sultan's new concubine! Or perhaps I might be, she reminded herself, since I am not his choice after all, but I am to be a gift from his mother, the Valide. How different it would have been if Annetta had been chosen instead of me. Annetta – clever, restless, as sharp-witted as a monkey – would know just how to play the part. But how strange, how unreal, it feels to me.

Cariye Lala took Celia by the hand and helped her into a pair of high wooden pattens, their sides inlaid with chips of mother-of-pearl. From the disrobing chamber she led her into a second room. It was warmer in here, and almost dark except for a small brazier burning in a corner. Steam, scented faintly with eucalyptus, hung in the air like wisps of cloud. On three walls were marble niches from which water cascaded, filling the room with their sound.

'Lie down – over there.'

Cariye Lala pointed to an octagonal-shaped slab of marble in the middle of the room. Positioned in the ceiling above it was a small dome, its sides pierced to let in the natural light.

Cautiously, Celia walked across the room, the unfamiliar wooden pattens clacking on the floor. Although she was now four inches taller than normal, her nakedness made her feel somehow shrunken in size. For the first time she hesitated. Instead of lying down, she sat herself awkwardly on the slab, the small shock of cold white marble stinging her buttocks. She held the purse that Annetta had given her awkwardly in one hand.

'*Cariye?*'

Celia's heart beat faster now. She must delay no longer. In her palm the purse felt heavy, and strangely unreassuring. What if Cariye Lala did not understand? How could she possibly ever explain what she hoped to receive in exchange for this money, all two hundred and fifty aspers of it, a small fortune to Celia herself, who in spite of being *gözde* still carried the ranking of one of the lowliest members of the harem? The very thought made two spots of shame rise to Celia's cheeks. She thought of Annetta, and willed herself to have courage.

'Cariye Lala?'

But Cariye Lala was far away in a bathhouse world of lotions and depilatory creams, priceless vials of attar of roses, balm of Mecca, and jars of honeyed unguents, all set before her in gleaming rows like an apothecary's shopfront. As she worked, she sang to herself: her voice, surprisingly sweet and clear, echoed from the marble walls. Celia's mouth was dry; beads of sweat, like tiny seed pearls, pricked her brow. Desperately she rose to her feet on the teetering pattens.

'For you, Cariye Lala.' Celia touched her gently on the arm. Wordlessly, the old woman took the purse from her. Then it was gone, vanished. Had she secreted it away in some hidden fold of her robe? Celia blinked. Where did it go? Two hundred and fifty aspers! She tried not to think what Annetta would say. The whole transaction had been accomplished so quickly it was as if it never happened.

Celia blinked again, uncertain what to do, but now Cariye Lala was leading her back to the marble slab. The little room was hotter than ever. With a shiver she imagined the unseen hands behind the walls feeding the furnace beneath the floor with gargantuan logs brought specially on the Sultan's own timber boats all the way from the forests of the Black Sea. The women had often watched them coming up the Bosphorous from the palace gardens.

Washing Celia was wet work. In preparation Cariye Lala had stripped herself almost naked; a thin cloth was tied around her bony shanks, but her old dugs swung freely as she worked, their nipples long and shrivelled, the colour and texture of dried plums. Sometimes they knocked against Celia's back and legs as she lay face down on the marble.

What now? Poor Celia was tormented. What should I do now? Shall I say something to her, or just keep silent? The marble, burning to the touch now, stung her cheek and neck. For a woman who seemed so frail, Cariye Lala was full of surprising energy. She gripped Celia by the upper arm, and set to with a will.

As she worked the servant girl handed her water in silver pitchers, first hot, then gasping cold. Cariye Lala sluiced and scrubbed. On her hand was a rough hessian mitten with which she rubbed Celia all over. Celia's skin was so fair that soon that milky whiteness, which the Sultan would in a few hours be offered for his enjoyment, had flushed to a rosy glow, and finally, a stinging crimson blush. A small moan escaped from Celia's lips. She tried to pull herself away, but she found herself now in a vice-like grip. Cariye Lala was able to hold her down with as much ease as if she were a prize-fighter. Celia struggled briefly, then lay still.

Turning Celia over on to her back, the old woman began again, with renewed vigour this time. No part of Celia's body, it seemed, could escape this cleansing zeal: the tender skin of her breasts and belly, the soles and arches of her pretty feet. No part of her was too private. Celia blushed and flinched to feel Cariye Lala's hands spreading her buttocks, fingering the rose-coloured creases at the tops of her thighs.

From the brazier the girl now brought a small earthenware pot, its contents full of the clay that Celia had learnt was called *ot*. Since entering the House of Felicity, she had become accustomed to the bathing which took place constantly amongst the palace women, the ritual cleanliness that was a requirement of the new religion which they must all now espouse, and which normally took place in the cheerfully crowded and gossipy fug of the communal baths in the courtyard of the *cariyes*. This activity would have been regarded with amazement, and quite possibly dismay, by her distinctively muskier English and Italian friends who bathed rarely, if at all. Even when she was first brought to the palace, Celia had found herself enjoying those long scented hours in the bathhouse, some of the few in which she and Annetta could whisper freely with the other girls, unin-vigilated, and unrestrained. The appliance of *ot* was the one bath-house requirement, however, that Celia still regarded with both repulsion and dread.

Cariye Lala took a wooden implement like a flattened spoon and scooped up a small amount of paste from the proffered pot, smearing it deftly, here and there, on to Celia's skin. The *ot*, a sticky, clay-like substance, felt not unpleasing at first, smooth and scented and pleasantly hot to the touch. Celia lay back and tried to breathe slowly and calmly – a tip which Gulbahar had given her after her first time when she had not understood what was about to happen, and had brought both shame and disgrace on herself by slapping the Senior Bath Mistress smartly across the face. But it was no good. A searing pain, as if she had been branded by a red-hot flat-iron, spread across the whole of the sensitive flesh of her sex, making her sit violently upright with a cry.

'Child! Such fussing!' Cariye Lala was unrepentant. 'This is as it must be. See, how smooth and sweet you are to the touch.'

Celia looked down and saw tiny droplets of blood, no bigger than the minute prickings of a fine embroidery needle, on her sheared flesh. And where a few moments ago there had been a golden and womanly bush between her legs, she now found herself gazing, with a kind of fascinated horror, at the naked apricot-shaped bud of a little girl.

But Cariye Lala had not finished yet. Pushing Celia down once again, she busied herself with a pair of small golden pincers, pulling out any stray hairs left behind by the *ot*. The servant girl held a candle for her, so close that Celia was afraid that she would let fall some of its wax on to her skin. But even with the candle to help her, the old woman had to bend so low in her labours that Celia could feel her hot breath and the furzy tickle of hair against her still-smarting flesh.

How long she was in the ministering hands of Cariye Lala, Celia could not have said. After the Under-Mistress of the Baths had satisfied herself at last that not a single impious hair remained upon her body, Celia was allowed to sit up again. Scrubbed and plucked and rubbed all over with a succession of herbs and unguents, her fair skin glowed now with an unearthly translucence in the hammam's pearly gloom. Her nails were polished. Her hair, dried and waved so that it shone like tarnished sunlight, was braided with strings of freshwater pearls. More pearls, the size of hazelnuts, hung from her ears and were coiled discreetly at her throat.

Celia did not know whether it was the heat of the bathhouse, or the smell of myrrh from the little brazier which the girl kept stoked in the corner of the room, but little by little she had begun to relax. Cariye Lala's ministrations were rough sometimes, but she had not meant to hurt Celia in the way that some of the other senior mistresses sometimes did, with their sly pinches and hair-pullings at the smallest infringement of the rules. A kind of passive indifference to her fate had taken hold of her. Cariye Lala's slow but matter-of-fact ways had a soothing effect. It was restful not to have to think.

It was, then, with only a faint sense of unease that she allowed her lips and then her nipples to be coloured with rose-tinted powder, an unease that did not lessen when she felt Cariye Lala slide one of her hands deftly between the tops of her thighs. A finger parted the lips of her sex, probed expertly, and then pushed inside.

With a cry Celia leapt to her feet as if she had been bitten. The vessel of *ot* at their feet spun across the floor, shattering against the wall. 'Get away from me!'

Backing into the far corner of the room, she found herself in an unlit alcove, the third of the interconnecting rooms in the Valide's hammam. Except for the shadows there was nothing here with which to cover her nakedness. Somewhere above her came the sound of

66

running water. Celia crouched down with her back against the wall. A droplet of something warm and dark trickled down the inside of her thigh.

Cariye Lala made no attempt to follow her. Celia saw her laugh and shake her head. Then she turned to the servant and by hand-signing, the customary language of all the palace servants, issued a swift instruction.

'You can come out now.' For a moment Cariye Lala stood in the doorway to the little alcove, a small figure, hands on hips. 'Don't be afraid.'

In the darkness, Celia felt as if her heart was going to leap from her chest. But the old woman's voice was not angry.

'It was this, foolish child, look,' she held out a tiny cedar wood box traced with silver filigree. 'Perfume.' She sniffed the contents of the box. 'The Valide herself sent it for you.'

'Go away!' Celia felt her eyes beginning to smart.

'*Tsk!*' Cariye Lala clicked her tongue against her teeth impatiently. 'It's what you wanted, isn't it?' She cocked her head to one side; her eyes sparkled like a little old blackbird. 'Look – for you, I use only this finger.'

She held up her hands, and Celia saw that the nails of all her fingers were long and curved. Only the index finger of her right hand, which she was bending slowly backwards and forwards, was short and neat. 'Think yourself lucky. The others don't always trim theirs.'

Celia allowed herself to be coaxed back into the second room. There was no fight left in her now. A chemise of lawn-cambric, so fine it was almost transparent, was put on her. Cariye Lala talked away, sometimes to herself, sometimes to Celia, admonishing and soothing at the same time. 'What kind of a fuss is this, there is nothing to fear. He's only a man after all. And look how beautiful the skin is, just as they said, white as cream, without a flaw. Pleasure, what pleasure to be had here. But we mustn't be so afraid, no, no, not good, not good at all.'

For the moment she made no attempt to touch Celia again. Instead, from amongst the jars at her disposal, she picked out two more small boxes; one silver, the other gold. Taking them to where the diffused daylight fell most brightly in the centre of the room she opened them both, scrutinising their contents carefully.

'Hmm, hmm . . . Hot? Or warm?' Celia heard her say to herself. She watched as Cariye Lala held out both boxes in the palm of one hand, and then, spreading out the fingers of the other hand, moved them from side to side over the two boxes as if she were divining for water. 'Warm? Or hot?' She looked at Celia speculatively. 'No, not the itch,' she shook her head, her voice almost inaudible, 'not just yet.'

From the gold box she took what looked to Celia like a brightly coloured bead and handed it to her. 'Eat this.'

It was a small lozenge, covered in gold leaf. Obediently, Celia swallowed.

The servant girl came into the room again now, bringing a cup of something hot for Celia to drink and a plate of fruit. Cariye Lala took them from her and then waved the girl away. She selected a piece of fruit, a pear of the long, narrow variety, then she sat down next to her. 'Now, girl,' Cariye Lala patted her arm. 'You won't be afraid now?' It was half-question, half-admonishment.

'No, Cariye,' Celia replied. But even as she spoke, her heart bounded suddenly and painfully in her chest.

'Don't worry, there is still time.'

Cariye Lala held out the pear, as if offering Celia something to eat. Celia shook her head: the thought of food made her feel sick. But then she saw that the old woman had begun to eat the pear herself.

'Now watch,' Cariye Lala was saying, grasping the bulbous end of the pear firmly in one fist. 'See: first you hold it like this. Make sure to put your thumb here,' her thumb began to make a small circling motion on the green speckled skin at the base of the pear.

Celia's gaze flickered quickly from the pear to Cariye Lala, and then back again. The old woman raised the fruit to her lips as though to take a bite, but instead of opening her mouth, the tip of her tongue began to perform the same small circling motion against the base of the pear. A warm prickling feeling, beginning in her newly shorn armpits, slowly flooded up Celia's shoulders, into her neck and cheeks. Cariye Lala's still-circling tongue slid up the stem of the pear towards its tip, circled it briefly, and then descended again. A fleck of spittle glistened on her upper lip.

Celia wanted to look away but she could not. Outside the hammam some unseen hand, the servant girl's perhaps, had checked the flow of water into the fountains, and there was now absolute silence in the room. Cariye Lala's old pink tongue made its way busily up and down, up and down. And then her wrinkled lip hooked suddenly over the tip of the pear and she thrust it deep into her mouth.

A scream of laughter, high-pitched and shrill, rose in Celia's throat, only to die, still-born, against her lips. At the same time she became aware that something strange was happening to the rest of her body. A feeling of warmth, quite different from the sense of prickling shame which had consumed her just moments before, enveloped her: a feeling of lassitude, warmth and physical ease. With a small sigh, her shoulders drooped. Her fingers, which had been clenched into fists, unfurled. Her heartbeat slowed. Cariye Lala's display was not finished yet, but now, by some miracle, Celia found that she was no longer afraid to watch. Her face, which had been stretched tightly, absurdly, into a rictus smile, relaxed. A feeling of lightness, of buoyancy almost, took hold of her, while at the same time she had the sensation of being encased in velvet. Although she did not know it, the effects of the opium that Cariye Lala had given her had begun to take effect. She was flying now, fluttering like a caged bird, somewhere up near the domed and pierced ceiling.

At that moment there was a banging – the sound of staves on wood – in the corridor outside. 'They're ready for you,' Cariye Lala dried her lips sedately with a corner of cloth. 'Come: it's time.'

Celia rose weightlessly to her feet. The servant girl, who had appeared again discreetly, helped her into a floor-length, sleeveless gown in lightly padded silk. Cariye Lala took up a censer of smoking coals, and between them they bathed Celia in the smoke, wafting it amongst the folds of her gown, beneath the fine, transparent lawn-cambric of her chemise, between her legs, behind her hair.

Celia stood passively, watching them – and it was as if she could watch herself now, as well as Cariye Lala and the girl – with dream-like detachment. A shaft of late sunlight crept in through the dome in the ceiling, slanting through the steam. All her movements had become slow and dreamy. The eunuchs, it had been explained to her earlier, would escort her to the Sultan's rooms, but even this thought no longer had the power to make her heart hammer at her breastbone, and her mouth turn dry. Instead she lifted her hand to examine the small gold rings which Cariye Lala had placed there. She thought of Paul. What would he think if he could see her now? She smiled at her fingers, although they didn't seem to belong to her any more. They waved in front of her like the small pink and white fronds of a deep-sea anemone.

'*Kadin.*' Gradually, Celia became aware that the servant girl was trying to speak to her. With both hands she was holding out the drink that she had brought in earlier, which had stood untouched on the tray. But Celia had no desire either to eat or drink.

'No.' She shook her head.

'Yes, my lady, yes.' For the first time the girl dared to look up into Celia's face. Her face was small and pointed, but her eyes seemed wild, darting towards Cariye Lala who stood with her back to them, carefully locking her caskets. Even in her drugged state Celia could see the fear in the girl's face; smell it, almost, on her skin.

The servant girl's voice trembled. 'Please, *kadin*, drink.'

Slowly Celia lifted the little bowl to her lips. The liquid had cooled, and she drank it easily in three mouthfuls. The drink, she noticed, had a curious bitter aftertaste, just like Cariye Lala's golden lozenge.

With Cariye Lala and the girl behind her, Celia emerged from the hammam and crossed the Valide's courtyard. At the gateway she hesitated; and then, for the first time since she had been brought to the palace, found herself stepping over the threshold of the House of Felicity. A small, false, note of freedom sang down her spine.

But she was not free. Hassan Aga, the Chief Black Eunuch himself (whose fate, although he did not know it yet, was almost as close at hand as Celia's), and four of his eunuchs, were waiting at the gateway to escort her to the Sultan's rooms.

Eunuchs: Celia regarded them with a little shudder of revulsion. Even after several months in the harem she was still not accustomed to these amphibious creatures, with their flabby bellies, their eerie, high-pitched voices. She remembered seeing one once with her father, in the Piazza San Marco in Venice. The eunuch was part of a delegation of merchants sent by the Great Turk. He was a white man, although he wore the flamboyant robes of his adopted com-patriots, and had become, for a day or so, a marvel in that city of marvels, a wonder to rival the gypsy mountebanks and the Circassian wrestlers, and even the miraculous speaking image of the Madonna situated above the doorway of the church of San Bernardo, which were the Serenissima's newest and most popular sideshows that summer.

She had been a little girl then, small enough for her father to lift on to his shoulders. 'Look, the *castrato*, the gelded man,' he had told her, although she had only a dim notion then of what this meant. She remembered the rough silkiness of her father's beard as she clasped her fingers round his neck, and her first fascinated sight of that strange hairless creature, his soft woman's face blinking mildly back beneath the folds of his turban.

There was nothing mild about the eunuchs who guarded the House of Felicity. From the beginning they had always seemed to Celia like creatures from another world with their heavy bodies and their bloodshot eyes, their skins so black it was as if all the light had been sucked out of them: creatures who moved, half-seen, on noiseless feet about the dimly lit corridors encircling the women's quarters, hardly more real, and no less terrifying, than the *efrits* that the old black serving maids said lurked in the shadows of the palace at night.

Annetta, of course, who for a few weeks in their very early days in the palace had been sent to work in the eunuchs' quarters, was dismissive of Celia's timidity.

'Men without *cogliones*!' she would say, a hand on an indignant hip. 'And with those names? Hyacinth, Marigold, Rosebud and I don't know what. *Faugh!* why should we be afraid of them?'

But even she was afraid of Hassan Aga.

'He looks like the dancing bear I once saw in Ragusa,' Celia remembered her whispering the first time they set eyes on him. 'And those cheeks! Like two great puddings. Why, my old Mother Superior had more hair on her chin than he has. And those little red eyes. *Santa Madonna*, they chose that one well! He's as ugly as the Pope's rhinoceros.'

But at his glance – a glance that would have been enough to have made any of the other *cariye* faint dead away – she fell silent soon enough, and quickly lowered her gaze.

But now Celia was no longer afraid. Hassan Aga looked at her without speaking and then turned on his heel and walked ahead of her, leading the way along a dark corridor.

It was evening now and each of the four eunuchs accompanying him carried a flaming torch in one hand. Celia watched the figure of the Chief Black Eunuch recede, his tall white hat of office now no more than a ghostly silhouette sailing ahead of her into the darkness. For a big man, it struck her, he was strangely nimble on his feet.

Flanked by the four more junior eunuchs, she too began to walk along the corridor. There was no sensation in her legs now. Instead she was able to observe how she seemed to be gliding, floating almost, her golden slippers barely touching the floor. A delicious languor filled her body. Celia put her hand to her neck, feeling the heavy pearls clustered at her throat, and smiled. It was so quiet she could hear the sound of her robe pooling behind her, the soft rasping of silk on stone. It was all so much like a dream – and there was really no reason to be afraid.

The figure of Hassan Aga blurred, and then jerked suddenly back into focus again. One of the eunuchs put out a hand to steady her but she recoiled from him in disgust. Ahead of her the corridor stretched out, never-ending. Strange shadows, orange and black and formless, reared up along the stone walls. This was her wedding night, wasn't it? Were they taking her to Paul? At the thought of him, Celia felt her heart leap in her breast. But her eyelids felt as if they were made of lead.

'Hold her, can't you! The girl can hardly stand.'

Two hands, one on either side of her, grasped her beneath the elbows, and this time she did not resist.

The next thing she was aware of was being carried into the vast, vaulted emptiness of the Sultan's bedchamber. She had no memory of getting there, only a shadowy recollection of Hassan Aga, the rolls of his fat neck glistening with sweat, placing her in the centre of an enormous divan in one corner of the room, its jewelled canopy held up by four columns, twisted like sticks of gilded barley sugar. Paul? But no, she remembered now, she wasn't going to Paul. She was looking up instead at a domed space the size of a church basilica.

'What have you done to her?'

Celia had never got over her sense of strangeness at the sound of Hassan Aga's voice, a high-pitched reedy sound. It was forbidden to speak at all in the Sultan's quarters, and here was the great Hassan Aga, whispering like a boy. He did not sound like the master of the House of Felicity now.

Cariye Lala, on the other hand, sounded savage.

'I've done nothing!' Her fingers, so sure and nimble in the Valide's hammam, fumbled with the buttons on Celia's robe. 'She must have got hold of more opium somehow; someone's given her a double dose . . .'

'Who?' Hassan Aga again.

'Who do you think it was?' She spat the words out. 'Who else could it have been?'

Celia's head nodded forwards on to her chest. From somewhere nearby came a low moaning sound of distress. She tried to look round, but now her eyes were rolling up into their sockets and sleep was sucking her down – down, down, down – into the abyss. Hands, more of them, were undressing her. She made no protest. Her body was as limp and weak as an infant's. They removed her robe, but left her with the white chemise still demurely covering her shoulders and breasts. The moaning sound was closer now.

'Help her, can't you?'

That strange fluting voice again, sounding from somewhere close. Celia was aware of more hands, small ones this time, fluttering near her, propping her up with an assortment of silken bolsters and coverlets, coiling them round her, up to the waist. The face of the young servant girl, shiny and swollen with tears, appeared beside her for a few moments and then receded. The girl's cheek, and Hassan Aga's, were almost touching. And it was from the girl, Celia now saw, that the moaning was coming: an inarticulate animal sound of terror.

Celia sank into blackness again.

She was at home, in England. At a window casement sat her mother. She was sewing, in her red dress. Her back was turned to Celia, so she could not see her face, only her hair, brown and sleek as an otter's, caught at the nape of her neck in a golden net. The late afternoon sun glanced off the diamond-shaped panes. Celia tried to call out to her, tried to run, but she found that she could not. No sound came from her mouth; and her legs would not move, held fast as if they were buried in quicksand.

When she woke again she was lying stretched out on her stomach on the divan. A small splashing sound came from the far wall of the room, where a recess contained a fountain, but apart from this there was no other sound in the room. Amongst the bolsters and cushions surrounding her was a tiger skin, its tawny stripes glimmering in the candlelight. She put out her hand to stroke the fur, and as she did so a small movement caught her eye: the hem of a man's robe.

For several moments Celia lay quite still, her eyes closed. Although her mouth felt dry, and there was a strange bitter taste on her tongue, a warm and sleepy lassitude paralysed her limbs. Cautiously she opened one eye. The hem of the robe was in the same place, but there were no feet protruding from beneath it. He must be standing with his back to her. The robe twitched again, and Celia heard a faint chink of porcelain, a drinking cup or a plate being set down, followed by a soft cough. Dreamily her eyes closed again. Her body floated gently on top of the silken coverlets as if she were in a warm sea.

'Awake at last, little sleepyhead?'

With an effort, Celia swam up to the surface again. Somehow she managed to kneel up on the divan: her arms were crossed over her breasts, and her head was bowed so low that she could see nothing at all of the man now approaching her.

'Don't be afraid,' he was standing in front of her now. 'Ayshe, isn't it?'

Celia thought of Annetta; remembered how they had clung together, right until the moment when the ship went down. We survived that, Annetta had said to her, and we'll survive this.

'No, Majesty . . .' with an effort, Celia rolled her tongue around the words. 'It is Kaya.' Her voice sounded thick.

'Kaya, then.'

He was sitting beside her now. He reached out and pulled the thin shirt from one shoulder. She saw his hand: the skin was fair, slightly freckled, the nails polished until they shone like moons. On his thumb he wore a ring of carved jade. Did he expect her to look up at him? She did not know, and it did not seem to matter much. He was stroking her shoulder, and as he did so his robe fell open and she saw that beneath it he was naked too, and so close now that she could smell him. A big man. A sweet musky smell came from the folds of his robe, but mixed with this perfume was another unmistakable scent: a rich male odour of sweat and skin, armpit and groin.

'How fair you are . . .' he drew his fingers gently down her neck and along her back, making her shiver. 'May I look at you?'

It was some moments before Celia realised what he was asking her. Then, still kneeling, she raised her arms to pull off the chemise. Although it was a warm night the air in the room felt cool. She shivered a little, but she was quite calm. Submissive. Will it hurt, she wondered? Look: I am not afraid, she told Annetta in her mind, not afraid after all.

'Lie back for me.'

His voice, when he spoke to her, was gentle. With a small sigh Celia lay back amongst the peacock-coloured cushions. Her limbs felt supple and warm and strangely boneless. When he parted her legs, she turned her head to one side and looked away. But it was so pleasant lying there, after all, and his touch was so soft against her skin, that she did not try to pull away, even when he fingered between her legs, stroking the soft milky skin of her thighs. All sensations were magnified: the fur of the tiger's tawny pelt against her cheek, the heaviness of the jewels at her neck and in the lobes of her ears. Wearing only jewels, she realised, made her feel doubly naked, and yet she felt no shame. She felt him cup one breast with his hand, pinching and sucking the nipple until it hardened. She arched her back, wriggled down still further into the bed.

For how long she lay like this, Celia did not know. For long trance-like moments she could almost forget that he was there at all. He did not seem to want to kiss her, so she kept her head turned to one side, and found herself looking round the chamber instead. A folding table in the centre of the room contained a tray of fruit and flowers, and a flask of some cooling drink, water or iced sherbet.

Next to them a curious object now caught her eye. It was a ship. The figure of a ship in miniature. And not just any ship: the vessel was the distinctive size and shape of a merchantman. Celia blinked. She was looking at an exact replica of her father's boat. It looked as if it were made of something fine and brittle; something caramel-coloured. It's a subtlety, a sugar subtlety! Just like the ones John Carew used to make! But it can't be, she thought, what could such a thing possibly be doing here?

It was a dream, of course. But the little ship seemed so real that for a moment its sails seemed to billow, its pennants fluttered in the breeze, and sailors, tiny men no bigger than her little finger, swarmed the decks. And a feeling of such pain came over her she almost cried out loud.

Then suddenly there was a commotion outside: a loud banging on the door, a woman's slippered feet running across the room towards them. Eunuchs, the same four who had escorted Celia to the Sultan's chamber earlier that evening, ran in after her.

'Gulay!' He sat up. 'What's this?'

'My lord . . . my lion . . .' A young woman, whom Celia recognised as the Haseki, the Sultan's favourite, was weeping, crouching at his feet and kissing them; wiping them with her long black hair. 'Don't let her . . . don't let her take me away from you.'

'Gulay!' He tried to pull her up, but she clung, still weeping, to his feet. 'What nonsense in this, Gulay?'

She did not reply, but shook her head incoherently.

'Take the girl,' he signalled brusquely to the eunuchs. 'Take all this, and get out.'

And so, bowing low, they raised Celia up and escorted her swiftly from the room.

Chapter 10

Istanbul: the present day

Elizabeth's application for a reader's pass at the university would take several days to be approved. While she was waiting she spent the days trying, alternately, to sleep, and not to think about Marius. She failed in both.

Her nights were fitful. Sometimes she dreamt she had found Marius again, other times that she had lost him, and she woke each morning with a feeling of such desolation in her heart that she wondered how much longer she could stand it.

It was cold and she did not feel like going out. Misery seemed to have sapped her energy for even the most basic sight-seeing. Instead she took to sitting with Haddba in the hall. Elizabeth found her company soothing. She accepted Elizabeth's need just to sit still, and asked no questions.

They did not talk much. Instead the boy, Rashid, would bring them tea. He brought it on a tray in two tiny little glasses like perfume phials. The liquid tasted very sweet, more like sugar than apples.

'If there is anything you need – a newspaper, cigarettes, whatever – you simply send Rashid out for it,' Haddba said.

But I shall be gone by tomorrow, Elizabeth would think, but somehow she never was.

Dearest Eve

It seems strange to be writing you a letter, but certainly in keeping with the spirit of this place which doesn't seem to have changed at all for the last fifty years, and still doesn't have computer connections of any kind. (I should think this notepaper has been in the same drawer for at least that long. Can you see the old telegram address on the bottom of this page? I wonder, when was the last time anyone sent one of those?)

Elizabeth took off her shoes, and tucked her feet up under her on the sofa to get warm. She sucked the end of her pen. 'The weather is cold and grey . . .' she wrote after a while, but a voice inside her head kept saying: *and I'm cold and grey and I want to come home, and it's only pride that's keeping me here.* Elizabeth glanced down at her mobile to check for messages. *And Marius hasn't texted me, not once, since I've been here . . . No. No. No!* She scratched out the words about the weather, and then looked around the room for something else to write about.

Oh, and did I tell you? [she wrote with an animation that she did not feel] It turns out that this isn't a hotel at all, but a sort of guest house. There's a film director who has taken a room here for three months; a French professor ditto; and some sinister-looking Russians who don't talk to anyone and who I'm sure must be something to do with the white-slave trade. Oh, and a mysterious old American woman, who wears amber beads and a turban, and looks as if she has read too many Agatha Christie novels . . .

There was a faint sound on the other side of the hall. Elizabeth looked up and saw that she was no longer alone. She had been joined there by a man. He sat behind the newspaper that Rashid had brought for him.

The other guests are mostly Turks, if you can call them guests. They don't seem to stay here, but come to drink tea with the owner, Haddba, if she's here, or just sit around doing crossword puzzles or playing draughts.

She looked up again. The Turk was still there, reading his newspaper. The rustle of his paper made a peaceful sound in the otherwise silent room.

I meet the other lodgers over breakfast every morning, and sometimes in the drawing room, which is the most amazing place full of palms in brass pots and stiff Edwardian furniture, and an old record player, like the one my parents once had (strange to think it's more or less a museum piece now). You can stack all these old LPs on to it, one on top of another, and they play for hours, very crackly scratchy music for the most part. Occasionally one of the records gets stuck, and then we all play a kind of game waiting to see who will be the first to crack and get up to unstick it . . .

As soon as I can I'll look for somewhere else . . .

Later on, lured by watery sunlight, Elizabeth went for a walk. In her hand, in the pocket of her coat, she felt the smoothness of her phone, like a talisman. Still no messages. She walked through the narrow streets, with their innumerable little *pasajs*, where intellectual-looking men in fedoras sat playing dominoes or reading the papers; past the spectres of the old embassies in the main street, Istiklal Caddesi, past the pudding shops and *büfes*.

Any other time she would have enjoyed the ordinariness of it. But now it was all Elizabeth could do to bow her head against the cold and walk on. Although it was only November, she could smell snow; the air was brittle against her face.

Everything is grey, I am grey, she thought again, dragging herself listlessly across the Galata Bridge. Men with fishing rods lined the balustrades. Beyond them, on the other side, the minarets of the mosques and their curious squat domes seemed sinister, looming over the horizon like fantastic insects.

On the Karaköy docks on the other side of the bridge, Elizabeth stopped. She hovered briefly on the steps of the Yeni Cammi, the 'new' mosque built by a sixteenth-century Valide Sultan, but did not have the energy to go in. Instead she walked down to where the ferries docked.

So this is Constantinople, she said to herself. And this, the watery inlet that divides it from Galata, is the Golden Horn. Elizabeth shivered. Hardly very golden, she thought, staring into the water moodily. The water was dark, almost black, and clouded by a faint oily iridescence. Men with charcoal burners roasted chestnuts at the water's edge, others carried trays of snacks: bread rings covered with sesame seeds, pistachio nuts, strange-looking rubbery tubers which turned out to be fried mussels.

Elizabeth bought a bag of pistachios for Rashid and a fish sandwich for herself. She stood eating the sandwich, looking back across the water to where she had just come from, and tried to find the street with Haddba's guest house in it, but at this distance all she could make out was the Galata Tower, and beneath it a tangle of telegraph wires, billboards and buildings, glinting yellow and pink, running down to the water's edge.

The smoke from the roasting chestnuts swirled. Elizabeth gazed across the water. The vanished place known as the Vines of Pera had once been there, where Paul Pindar had lived. She tried to imagine how it must once have looked, the district on the other side of the Golden Horn where the houses of the foreign merchants had once stood, their waterfront wharves filled with bolts of cloth with jewel-like names: cambrics and calamancoes, damasks and galloons, tiffanies, taffetas and cobweb lawn.

The Genoese had been the first to start trading with the Ottomans in Constantinople, then the Venetians, followed by the French. The English merchants were relative newcomers, muscling in with all the energy and brashness of youth, to claim their place amongst the established trading powers. Upsetting the apple cart, I shouldn't wonder, Elizabeth smiled to herself. Is that how they were seen? Upstarts, *nouveaux*. She imagined them: City barrow boys, improbably dressed in doublets and hose.

In her pocket, Elizabeth felt her phone vibrate. She snatched at it, her cold fingers nearly dropping it on the pavement in her eagerness to answer it.

Oh, Marius, Marius my . . . But it was not Marius.

'Hello, Elizabeth,' A woman's voice. 'It's Berin.'

'Berin!' Elizabeth tried to sound enthusiastic.

'I have some good news for you. At least I hope you will be pleased.'

'You've got my reader's pass?'

'Well, not yet, but don't worry, it won't be long now. No, something else. Do you remember I told you that I'd been interpreting for that English production company that's making a film here?'

80

'Yes, I remember.'

'Well, I spoke to the director's assistant. I told her about your project, and she was really interested. She says that if you want you can come in with us to the palace when they film there on Monday. The place is usually closed to visitors on that day but they've been given special permission to film inside the old harem. They'll just put you on the list as one of their researchers, and then you can have a really good look around.'

'That's fantastic, Berin.'

'Usually you can only get in on a timed ticket, and even then they only allow you to stay in there for about fifteen minutes with a guard breathing down your neck. Somebody up there . . .'

Berin was still speaking when one of the ferries sounded its horn. 'What was that?'

'I said, somebody up there must love you.'

'Thanks Berin,' Elizabeth managed a wintry smile. 'I'm glad someone does.'

Chapter 11

Constantinople: 1 September 1599

Morning

T he house of the astronomer Jamal al-Andalus was at the top of a
narrow street in the network of steeply winding alleyways
which ran from the Galata Tower down towards the merchants'
wharves on the waterfront. Paul and Carew were escorted there by
two of the embassy janissaries. It was early still and there were not
many people about. The houses leant together, their wooden walls
buffed to a rich brown patina. Vines grew on trellises between them,
throwing a dappled shade on to the ground.

'So, who is this fellow, then, this astronomer?' Carew asked him as
they walked.

'Jamal? I've known him since I first came to Constantinople. You
know how long I've been here, waiting while the Honourable
Company quibbled over what gifts were to be sent to the new
Sultan. I heard of Jamal al-Andalus, one-time protégé of the astronomer Takiuddin, quite early on. I tracked him down and asked him to
teach me astronomy.'

'Takiuddin?'

'The master is dead now, but he was a great man in his day. He
built a famous observatory here in Constantinople, in the time of the
old Sultan, Murad III. Jamal was one of his pupils, the most brilliant
of them all, so they say.'

'Is that where we're going, to the observatory?'

'Not exactly. It is an observatory of a kind, but not Takiuddin's.
His was destroyed years ago.'

'What happened to it?'

'The Sultan was persuaded by some of the religious leaders that it was against the will of God to pry into the secrets of nature. They sent a wrecking squad of soldiers who destroyed the entire observatory. Books, instruments, everything,' Paul shook his head. 'They say that the instruments Takiuddin had built here were the finest the world has ever seen – more accurate even than Tycho Brahe's in Uraniborg.'

They had now reached a house that looked like a small tower. One of the janissaries knocked on the door with his stave.

'That's all very well,' Carew said looking round him, 'but what's his business at the palace? That's what we've come for isn't it, to see if he can help us?'

'Jamal goes to the palace school where he teaches the little princes their numbers.'

'Do you know how often he goes there?'

'I'm not sure. Often enough. People talk – he'd be bound to pick something up if he knew what to listen out for.'

'And you really think he'd do that for you?' Carew was sceptical. 'Why would he? Won't it be dangerous for him, spying for a foreigner, a Christian at that?'

'I'm not going to ask him to spy, just to help us find something out.'

'Fog wouldn't like it.'

'Fog will never know.'

Jamal's servant, a boy of about twelve, opened the door and admitted them. Carew waited with the janissaries while Paul, as befitted his superior status, was shown into an antechamber. After a few minutes, a small man of middle years, wearing a long tunic of snow-white cotton cloth, entered the room.

'Paul, my friend!'

'Jamal!'

The two embraced.

'It's early for us to call on you. I hope you weren't sleeping?'

'Not at all, not at all. You know me, I never sleep. What matters is that you're here. Why, it's been weeks – I thought you'd forgotten me.'

'Forget you, Jamal? You know I'd never do that.'

'You've been busy, of course, with the affairs of your embassy.'

'So I have. Our company's ship, the *Hector*, arrived at last, two weeks ago now.'

'Indeed, my friend, it would have been hard to miss.' The astronomer's eyes gleamed. 'The *Hector* is the talk of the town. And they say she has brought our Sultan and our Valide Sultan – blessings be upon them – the most wonderful gifts. An English horse-drawn carriage for our Sultan's mother. And for His Majesty a mechanical clock that plays tunes – can this really be so?'

'The company is giving the Sultan an organ as a gift. But I believe that it also incorporates a clock, angels that blow trumpets, a bush full of songbirds that sing and I don't know what else. As many marvellous automata as our ingenious organ maker could devise. It's to be the most wonderful device the Sultan has ever seen, or so it will be as soon as our organ maker has repaired it. Six months in the bowels of the *Hector* took their toll, alas, but mark my words, it will be worth the wait. So you see,' Paul smiled, 'for once, the rumours are true.'

'Rumour and truth? I would be careful before I put those two together. All the same, I congratulate you.' The astronomer made a small bow. 'And now your ambassador, the esteemed Sir Henry, can present his credentials at last,' he said. 'You see, I am a palace spy! I know everything.' He caught sight of Carew, still standing outside the antechamber. 'But who is your friend? You have brought someone to meet me, I see. Bring him in, by all means.'

'I've brought John Carew with me.'

'The famous Carew? The one who is always in trouble – whom has he broiled now?'

'My esteemed ambassador's cook, I'm afraid, but that's a long story. You mustn't mind him, Jamal. His manners are – how shall I put it? – a little rough sometimes. He was with my father's household for many years, and now I have brought him into mine, but if the truth is to be told he is more like a brother to me than a servant.'

'Then he shall be as a brother to me also.'

Paul beckoned to Carew to come forwards. 'Jamal says are you the one who is always in trouble? What shall I tell him, John?'

'Tell him I am the one who's gone halfway round the world in a leaky tub to do my master's bidding,' Carew returned the astronomer's steady gaze. 'Tell him how I've helped get you out of trouble as many times as I've been in it. Tell him to mind his own . . .'

'Greetings, John Carew. *Al-Salam alaykum.*' The astronomer bowed, putting his right hand to his heart.

'Greetings, Jamal al-Andalus, *Wa alaykum al-Salam.*' Carew returned the customary greeting. He turned to Paul. 'From what you told me, I thought he'd be older.'

'Well, I am sorry to disappoint,' Jamal gave a slow but brilliant smile. 'You, on the other hand, John Carew,' he said gracefully, 'are exactly as your master describes.'

'My apologies, Jamal, for my servant's bad manners,' Paul said 'Jamal al-Andalus is a famed scholar, and a very wise man; wise beyond his years, it is true. Wise enough, happily, not to pay any attention to a numbskull like you.'

'D'you know,' Carew flashed a quick smile at the astronomer, 'there are times when my master sounds just like his father.'

Jamal al-Andalus gazed from one to the other of them. His eyes, which were startlingly black and bright, gleamed with amusement.

'Come, gentlemen! Come, please, let me offer you some refreshment.'

Jamal led them up some stairs to the first floor of the house through to a second small antechamber. Cushions had been placed along a raised platform, and latticed windows gave out over the street below. Over the rooftops the distant grey shimmer of the Bosphorous was just visible. The same servant boy who had opened the door to them brought a pot and some tiny cups on a tray.

'This is our *kahveh*, an arab drink from the Yemen. Would you like to try it, John Carew? Paul has quite a taste for it already.'

Carew sipped at the aromatic liquid, which tasted thick and bittersweet on his tongue.

'It has many interesting properties,' Jamal said, draining his cup. 'One of them is that it helps to keep me awake at night, so I can work for longer,' he turned to Paul, 'but you are a little early in the day for stargazing, my friend.'

'I didn't come for that. I came to bring you a gift, a small token of my esteem. I had Carew bring it out with him on the *Hector*.' Paul took out a small leather-bound volume and gave it to the astronomer.

'*De revolutionibus orbium coelestium libri sex*, Six Books on the Revolution of the Heavenly Spheres.'

'Ah, your Nicolaus Copernicus.' The astronomer smiled. 'My master, Takiuddin – may he be granted grace – often spoke to me of him. How can I thank you? They destroyed all my books you know. Almost all of them anyway.'

'After everything you have taught me – please, no thanks,' Paul said.

'Expensive things, books.' Carew said without rancour. 'But Secretary Pindar is rich; I've heard it said that his years in Venice have made him richer even than our own ambassador.' He glanced at Paul, suddenly cheerful again. 'He can afford it.'

'It's a beautiful thing,' Jamal examined the book, stroking the leather binding with his fingers. He opened the book carefully and glanced at the title page. 'In Latin, of course.'

'I had it bound for you in London, I knew you would want the original,' Paul said. 'The embassy has a scribe here, a Spanish Jew,' he added. 'I've arranged for him to transcribe it for you.'

'Mendoza? Yes, I know him,' Jamal nodded. 'He'll do a good job. This Copernicus, his ideas are still very controversial in your country, I think?'

'Our churchmen don't love him, that's for sure. He's been dead many years, of course, and its only now that his ideas are starting to gain support. A heliocentric view of the heavens, some call it,' Paul said. 'And others call it plain heresy.'

'You Europeans,' Jamal smiled, 'so set in your ways.'

'When I was a boy they told me the moon was made of blue cheese,' Carew put in cheerfully, 'but I wouldn't go to the stake over it.'

'In our tradition there is no such conflict,' Jamal was turning the pages of the book thoughtfully. 'The Qu'ran simply says: "It is He who made the sun a shining radiance and the moon a light, determining phases for it so that you might know the number of years and how to calculate them; he explains his signs to those who understand."' With his eyes closed, he repeated the suras. '"In the succession of night and day, and in what God created in the heavens and earth, there are truly signs for those who are aware of him."' Jamal put the book down. 'What it means is this: that the movements of the stars and the planets must be studied seriously, in order to discover the true nature of the universe.'

'That is not what the *ulema* said when they destroyed your observatory.'

'Ah, that, yes. But that was a long time ago,' the astronomer sighed. 'I believe that we do God's work.'

As if anxious to bring the conversation to a close, he rose to his feet. 'Would you care to see my observatory? It is not much, but I have a new instrument, Paul, which I know would interest you.'

The astronomer led them through a curtain to the right of the room where they had been sitting and up a spiral staircase. At the top they found themselves in a small octagonal room. Windows opened out on all eight sides, covered by louvred shutters, each of which could be separately opened or closed at will.

'You see, wherever the moon rises, I can find her,' Jamal explained. 'The tower isn't very high, but it is surprising what a clear view you get from here, not just of the skies.'

Leaning on the window Paul could see the roofs of the Galata houses spread out before him: the shingles of their roofs, worn to a patina of soft grey, gleamed in the sunlight. The distant cry of a water-carrier came to him faintly, and in the muddy alleyway below he watched the robed forms of two women walking past, their faces veiled so that only their eyes were visible through a slit of cloth.

He turned back into the room, marvelling, as he did every time he came here, at its chaste beauty. Beneath each window was a simple whitewashed niche on which Jamal had arranged his instruments. Paul went over to them, picking each one up in turn.

'This is an astrolabe.' He showed Carew a brass disc covered in an elaborate grid of lines and overlaid with several movable dials, each one minutely engraved with Arabic numerals.

Jamal took it from him. 'Astronomers use this for many purposes,' he explained, 'but principally it is an instrument for finding and interpreting information from the stars.' Dangling the disc between two fingers, he held it up to one eye. 'You can find the time by the position of the stars; and the position of the stars from the time.'

Jamal picked up another instrument, a smaller brass tablet engraved with a similar web of lines and inscriptions. 'This is what we call a quadrant. It's just like an astrolabe, but folded into quarters. We use it to find the times for our daily prayers. See here,' he pointed to the Arabic inscriptions, 'this one is made for the latitude of Cairo, this one for Damascus, this other for Granada, where my family once came from.'

He passed it to Carew, who took it and held it up between his fingers.

'Now I know why Paul's been coming here. Instruments! You're as mad for them as he is. It's quite a collection you've got here.'

Carew picked up another device about the same size as the astrolabe and scrutinised the workmanship.

'That one is an altitude sundial,' Jamal told him.

'*Carolus Whitwell Sculpsit*,' Carew read out. 'Well, well, I know Charlie Whitwell – the mapmaker, his shop's near St Clements. If I could have a penny for every pound Pindar has spent there I'd be a rich man.'

He examined the sundial again. The signs of the zodiac, separated by scrolls and flowers, were engraved around the edges.

'You find them beautiful too, I can tell,' Jamal said. 'And you are quite right, it was a love of instruments such as these that first brought Paul and I together. In fact, it was Paul who found many of them for me. Had them sent to me, mostly from Europe, but as your quick eyes have noticed, quite a few of them are from London, some of the best ones, in fact.'

'It was Jamal who taught me how to use the compendium,' Paul said. 'Especially the nocturnal; I always had trouble with that.'

'And you can read the time by the stars now quite as well as any astronomer.' Jamal turned to Carew again. 'These are the basic instruments that I work with. But here are some other things, look.'

He pointed to a little brass case containing a lodestone, a pair of globe dividers, a pair of bronze globes and a miniature armillary sphere.

'I haven't seen one of these before,' Paul said. He picked up a circular brass box and showed it to Jamal.

'Ah, yes, this is what I wanted to show you. This is a *qibla* indicator,' he turned to Carew to explain, 'with this we can always discover the direction of Mecca. It includes a compass, and look,' he opened the box and showed them a list of inscriptions on the inside of the lid, 'here is a list of places, together with the compass directions to Mecca.' He turned to Paul again. 'A thing of beauty, is it not?'

Just then there was a sound of knocking on the outside door below. A few moments later the boy came in, and whispered something discreetly to his master.

'Just a few moments, please gentlemen,' Jamal excused himself. 'It seems I have another visitor, but this won't take long.'

When he was gone, Carew turned to Paul. 'This is all very well, but when are you going to ask him?'

'All in good time – you can't rush these things, you Barbary Ape.'

'Well, all right, but I hope you know what you're doing.'

Carew picked up one of the brass astrolabes. Holding it up to one eye he positioned the alidade, squinting through the tiny aperture, as he had seen Jamal do. On a table were various parchments covered in grids of strange-looking figures and symbols, various sectors, rules and pens for drawing were scattered in amongst calligraphy brushes and pots of ink, some sheets of gold leaf, pots of finely ground minerals, red and blue and green.

'A regular wizard, your friend Jamal.' Carew's quick gaze took it all in. 'Are you sure it's just mathematics he teaches?' He picked up one of the pots and sniffed it. 'You know, I still can't see why he should help us.' Putting the pot down he picked up a piece of parchment, a chart covered in figures, and held it this way and that, trying to make sense of it.

'It's an ephemeris. Jamal calls them *zij*. Paul said. 'They're tables by which astronomers predict the movement of the stars. And I'd put it down before you tear it.'

But Carew was in no mood to be deflected. 'You haven't answered my question. Is he part of your intelligencing? Does he have a code number – like the Sultan, and the Grand Vizier – for Fog to put in his letters?'

'Not exactly.' Paul gave Carew an appraising look. 'It's as I've already told you, I've known Jamal since I first came to Constantinople. We had an arrangement: he taught me astronomy—'

'and in return you helped him make a new collection of instruments.'

'You're so sharp, Carew, you'll cut yourself one day.'

'Oh come on, Paul. Charlie Whitwell's sundial? I was with you when you bought it, remember? And I know what it cost – more than an astronomy lesson, that's for sure.'

'It was a fair exchange. *Quid pro quo.*'

'Don't think you can fob me off with fancy Latin. Sounds like intelligencing to me.'

'When you know Jamal better, you'll understand. Call it . . . a meeting of minds. If anything, I consider myself to be the gainer.'

'If you say so, Secretary Pindar.' Carew picked up one of the astrolabes again, putting his finger through the ring at the top and testing its weight. 'But these are expensive gifts.'

'They weren't all gifts,' Paul said. 'I gave him Whitwell's sundial, and one of the astrolabes. But the others he paid for himself.'

Carew looked around the simple room. 'Then he really must be a wizard.'

'Jamal?' Paul laughed. 'I don't think so.'

Carew gave Paul a sharp look. 'But he'll help us, all the same.'

At that moment both Jamal and his servant came back in. The astronomer was dressed for the street, wearing a travelling robe over his indoor clothes.

'My friends,' he looked apologetically at them, 'I'm afraid I have been called away. Something . . . unexpected.' He seemed tired suddenly. 'But please, stay. Look at anything you like. My boy here,' he put his hand tenderly on the child's head, 'my boy will take care of you.'

Just as he was about to go, Jamal turned back to them briefly. 'You are quite well, Paul?'

'Of course. Why do you ask?'

'You seem . . . restless. But I see that I am wrong.' And with that he smiled, and was gone.

After Jamal had left the room there was a pause.

'Well, don't say I didn't tell you so.'

'Don't worry, he'll come back.'

Paul moved over to one of the latticed windows, where he stood, staring thoughtfully down over the rooftops. As he watched, in the alleyway below he caught sight of Jamal emerging from the house. With him was a woman, unveiled, but wearing the characteristic black robes of a Jewess.

'Wait a moment, I'm sure I know that woman from somewhere.' Carew, who had come to stand next to him, had seen her too.

'Yes, you do,' Paul said, 'everyone knows her.'

'The Malchi woman?'

'Esperanza Malchi,' Paul drew back from the window slightly so that he would not be seen, 'the Valide's *kira*, a sort of agent or messenger woman. Now there's someone with access to the Sultan's harem . . .' He rubbed his chin thoughtfully. 'She was with the Valide the day I went to present her with the Queen's gifts.'

'What d'you think she wants with Jamal?'

Paul did not answer. He watched as the Jewess walked on ahead of Jamal, making her way with a strange undulating walk down the narrow street. She had the air, it occurred to him, of one who is accustomed to being followed. From his pocket he took out his compendium, weighing it nervously in his palm.

Behind him he heard Carew say, 'And supposing Jamal does find out for you that an English woman – that Celia – is really there. What's your plan then, Pindar?'

'If Celia is alive?' With a trembling hand Paul brought the compendium to his lips. 'We get her out, of course.'

'I had a feeling you might say that.' Carew watched Esperanza and Jamal as they disappeared from sight. 'This,' he said with satisfaction, 'is going to be more interesting than I thought.'

Later that same morning

Hassan Aga awoke to the sound of voices.

'Does he speak? What does he say?'

He knew at once that it was Safiye who spoke. What was she doing in this dark place? But before he could discover an answer, something happened to amaze Hassan Aga still further: a man's voice answered her. A man, inside the harem? It wasn't possible . . .

'I can't . . . it is not clear.' He was aware of the second figure bending, as if listening, towards him. 'A dream. Or a hallucination. Quite natural under the circumstances.'

'He is still alive then.' Safiye again. 'Can he hear us?'

'It is very hard to say. It is his body that is paralysed. But his spirit . . .' The man placed the tips of his fingers softly beneath Hassan Aga's nostrils, feeling for his breath. 'Yes,' he confirmed, 'his spirit lives.'

'Is there anything that can be done?'

The man hesitated. 'I am not a physician—'

'I know that,' she said impatiently. 'I have brought you here because you have . . . other powers. We – I – want to know if he will live. I must know what his fate is to be.'

'I cannot tell you that without preparing the charts, and that will take time. But perhaps—' there was a short pause, then the man said softly, 'perhaps if I examined him?'

'Do what is necessary, and without fear. Anything at all, you understand. You know you always have my blessing.'

Hassan Aga could hear the sound of a lamp being lit, and the light was brought close. There was a sharp intake of breath.

'In the name of God, the merciful, the compassionate,' in his soft voice the man stammered out a *besmele*. 'Who could do such a thing?'

'Is it poison?' Safiye spoke from outside the pool of light now illuminating the room. Her figure, heavily veiled, cast long shadows against the wall.

'Yes, poison,' the words seemed to catch in the man's throat, 'without a doubt.'

Hands, dry and warm, felt along the hairless and once smooth skin of Hassan's face and upper body. A faint smell of sandalwood.

'Lesions. See, there are lesions everywhere. Poor devil.' There was a gentle pressure on the side of his head. 'And he has bled – from his ears. *Tsssh* . . .' another involuntary intake of breath, 'and from his eyes. Who could do such a thing? Who would want to inflict such suffering?'

'Never mind that. Will he live?'

The man passed his hands, palpating gently, over Hassan Aga's monstrously distended stomach. 'His internal organs are swollen, swollen to many times their usual size.' He picked up Hassan Aga's wrist and held it between his fingers for a long time. 'But – by some miracle – his pulse is steady.'

'Tell me,' she could only repeat, impatient now, 'will he live?'

'The Chief Black Eunuch has the strength of many men,' the man sat back upon his heels, 'with the right care, it is possible that he will live.'

'Then you must help him – you have the powers . . .'

'Alas, I fear that my powers, as you call them, can do little to help him now. As you can see, the damage is already done.' The man looked around the damp, windowless room. 'What he needs is proper care. Not here. He needs light, air . . .'

'He will get all those things,' Safiye said shortly. 'Even I can't keep the Chief Black Eunuch hidden indefinitely. But I needed you to see him first, before anyone else. There is something else that he needs. Make him a talisman – for protection – the most powerful that you can. And if he lives, you will be rewarded, richly rewarded, I swear it. I have been generous enough to you in the past, haven't I?'

For a while the man did not answer her. Then eventually, with a bowed head, he said, 'I will do as you wish, but first there is something I need to know: who are his enemies? And how do you know that they will not try this again?'

'There is no need to fear.' Safiye Sultan stepped out of the shadows into the pool of light cast by the man's lamp. 'You are under my protection.'

'You know I don't fear for myself,' the man said. He spoke so softly his voice was barely more than a whisper. 'Do you know who did this? Indeed, Majesty, you must tell me.'

There was a long pause.

'I do.'

'Then you must tell me their names. The talisman won't work without them.'

Hassan Aga strained to hear Safiye's reply, but all he caught was the sound of blood drumming in his ears.

Later, much later, Hassan woke again. There was a pressure in his bladder and he knew he needed to urinate. They must have given him water to drink or liquid of some kind to replace the fluids he had lost.

The pressure grew more insistent, but he knew he could not urinate without his quill. He put a hand to his head, but the tall white cap of office inside which it was normally pinned was not there. Gathering all his strength, Hassan Aga rolled himself over on to one side. The effort set his heart hammering. From this position he reached out with one arm, blindly sweeping the cold stone floor – but there was nothing. Beads of sweat broke out on his forehead, and between the thick fleshy folds on the back of his neck.

They had tried to poison him, his mind was quite clear now. They had tried to kill him, but they had not succeeded. He knew what they did not, that Hassan Aga had the strength of ten men. But without his quill, without the ability to urinate, not even the strength of a hundred men could save him.

Hassan Aga, Little Nightingale, lay back on the straw mattress, his swollen bladder screaming. His eyes began to close again, and as they did so so his gaze caught a line of daylight seeping into the room. There was a doorway, then. His mind wandered again. He remembered how they had put him in the hole up to his neck in sand, and how the girl would come to him and press the pieces of gourd to his mouth to soothe his swollen lips.

Lily. Poor Lily. They had been just children then.

Gathering all his strength, he rolled over on to his side again, and this time found that he could push himself up into a squatting position. He waited like that for the pounding in his heart to subside. A memory came to him, startling in its clarity, of how Lily and he had sat together and watched the sky turning above them through the long desert nights. He felt a stab of something he could not put a name to, in a place which might have been his heart; could it be remorse that he was feeling?

Hassan Aga stood up and began to walk towards the light.

Chapter 12

Constantinople: 2 September 1599

Morning

'Annetta!'

'Celia.'

'You're back.'

'As you can see.'

'I wondered . . . where have you . . .?'

'Shh!' Annetta put her finger to her lips. Two damp tendrils of hair clung to the sides of her neck. 'She'll hear you.'

She jerked her chin in the direction of the Chief Mistress of the Girls, a sour-faced Macedonian with a big nose, who was patrolling the courtyard outside the *cariyes'* communal bathhouse. She carried a hazelwood switch in her hand which she was not afraid to use with zeal on those who indulged in too much chatter.

'Something's happened,' Celia whispered, kneeling down beside Annetta at one of the stone basins.

'What sort of thing?'

'I don't know. But I thought you might – didn't you say yesterday that you had a strange feeling about something? Early this morning there was a commotion. People shouting. Didn't you hear it?'

'Actually shouting?'

Both Celia and Annetta had been in the House of Felicity long enough to appreciate the seriousness of any untoward noise penetrating the usually monastic silence of the Valide Sultan's quarters. A group of senior mistresses stood in the courtyard, speaking together in low tones. From the upper chambers came the sound of running feet, the distant echo of muffled voices.

'Actually, I do know something.' Annetta glanced quickly behind her at the Mistress, who was now giving orders to one of her servant women, 'but you must *swear* not to say anything.' She gave an anxious shiver. 'They've put *cariyes* in a sack and drowned them for less.'

'What are you talking about?' Celia looked about her uneasily.

'They've found him, that's what.'

'Found who?'

'*Him*. The Chief Black Eunuch.'

Celia looked at Annetta blankly. A vision came to her of that terrifying form, a black giant in his tall white cap of office, almost mincing with his absurd swaying gait down the passageway ahead of her. She remembered how his black skin had glistened; the way the thick flesh rippled at the base of his neck.

'Was he missing?' she asked tentatively.

'Don't you know anything, goose?' Annetta looked at her in exasperation, but for once had no sharp retort. 'They said he had gone away to do business for the Valide in Edirne. That was yesterday. Then some of the Chief Gardener's guards found him, collapsed somewhere in the palace gardens. They've no idea how he got there.' She pressed her lips to Celia's ear. 'I made the eunuch Hyacinth tell me, you know, the one who is in love with Fatma, the Valide's first handmaid. They say he is horribly disfigured – poisoned—' The words seemed to catch in her throat. 'It is not certain yet whether he will live or die!'

To Celia's amazement tears had sprung into Annetta's eyes.

The Macedonian had been replaced by one of her under-mistresses, a Georgian woman, who now approached them. Her pattens clattered against the marble floor.

'Enough of this, *cariyes*.' She brought her switch down against the basin, but without as much malice as the Chief Mistress, who was fond of creeping up on the unsuspecting, inflicting bleeding welts on the backs of their hands. 'Everyone to their rooms now, by order of the Valide.'

At once the other girls in the bathhouse rose to their feet obediently and filed out. Celia saw them signing to one another, the language used by everyone in the palace when the rule of silence was enforced.

Celia stood up, shielding Annetta as best she could. From the expression on the Georgian's face, she knew that she had been recognised; felt, for the first time, the power of her new status. Although she was not yet an official concubine, none the less the woman's face clearly told her she was still *gözde*. She would be worth breaking a rule for – for the time being, anyway.

The knowledge made her strong. 'Madam . . .' She bowed low to the Georgian, thankful, for the first time, for the formal manners that the harem had taught her. 'I find . . . I find that I am unwell. Yes.' She put her hand to her stomach, then said with all the authority she could muster. 'I have asked Ayshe, the Valide's handmaid, to escort me to my room.'

'Well . . .' The under-mistress took a step back, and looked doubtfully between them. Seeing her hesitate, Annetta put her hand under Celia's arm.

'Her Majesty the Valide Sultan recommends a cold compress on these occasions.' Before the woman could make any objection, she had steered Celia to the door. 'I will see to it immediately, Under-Mistress of the Girls.'

'A cold compress! I had my hand on my *stomach*, not my head . . . what must she have thought?'

'Luckily it doesn't matter what she thought; we didn't give her time to think.' Annetta shook her head at Celia, half-laughing. 'Well, well! So this is where they put the Sultan's new *culo* is it?' Looking round the tiny room to which, as palace etiquette required, they had moved Celia the day before her encounter with the Sultan, Annetta traced her hand along the cool green tiles, then put her eyes to the lattice work at the top of the door, which gave out on to the Valide's courtyard.

'Why, you can see everything from here,' she observed.

'And everything can see you.'

'Well, what do you expect?'

Although Annetta still looked a little pale, she seemed to have recovered her usual wits. Celia saw her sharp gaze sweep quickly over the room, taking in the silk cushions, the richness of the tiled niches in the walls, the mother-of-pearl-inlaid doors. In an open chest lay the cambric shirt that they had dressed her in when they took her to the Sultan; the cloak lined with sable they had folded round her afterwards. The room was very small, and apart from these few things quite bare, but in the ordinary *cariyes*' quarters, as Celia well knew, half a dozen girls shared a spartan space not much bigger than this.

Annetta was not one to waste time on small jealousies. Already she was opening the door into the courtyard a crack, testing its hinges. They creaked.

'Hmm. Might have known. She never leaves anything to chance.'

'How much longer will they keep me here, d'you think?'

'Has he asked for you again yet? Taken your precious cherry and written it down in his great big book?'

'Not yet.' Celia did not know whether she felt more shame or relief at this confession.

'Then who knows?' Annetta shrugged. 'A day, a week.' Her expression was one of feigned indifference. Then, nonchalant, 'So, did he give you anything?'

'Just these earrings.' Celia took a small box from a niche in the wall. 'Pearls, and gold, I think. You're allowed to take anything that he leaves behind. Here,' she held them out with both hands. 'You have them. I owe you. For Cariye Lala, remember.'

'Much good it did you. My!' Squatting down on the floor, Annetta held the earrings up to the light. Her black eyes gleamed. Then she put one of the pearls between her teeth and bit into it experimentally. 'Freshwater,' she pronounced, half-accusingly, as though Celia had been trying to pass them off as something else. 'Not such good quality as sea pearls, but quite as big as pigeon eggs.' She dropped them carelessly back on the bed. 'Want my advice? Ask for emeralds next time.'

Celia put the earrings carefully back into the box. There was a short silence. Then she said, 'I didn't want it to be me, Annetta. In fact, I wish with all my heart it had been you.'

'Nice fresh *culo* for that fat old man?' Annetta pulled a face. 'No thanks. You still don't understand, do you? I grew up in one brothel, and that was enough for me. Because that's all this place is, just a brothel with one fat old client. And then everyone pretends it's some extraordinary honour to be chosen by him. *Madonna!*' She turned on Celia, furious suddenly. 'Well, they got a bad bargain when they brought me here. Did you ever wonder why I ended up in a convent? My mother once tried to sell me to an old man like that, and I bit him so hard I swear he'll never touch *culo* ever again. I was only ten, just a little child. If they ever try to put me with that old cockerel,' she jerked her head towards the Sultan's quarters, 'I swear I'll bite him too, so I will.'

'Enough!' Two spots of colour appeared in Celia's cheeks. 'One day you'll get us both killed with that tongue of yours, I swear it.'

'I know, I know, I'm sorry, I'm sorry—' Feverishly, Annetta began to pace the tiny room. 'There's something strange going on today – can't you feel it?'

She pushed the door into the courtyard open and put her eye to the crack, but there was no one there. She turned to Celia again, her hand plucking nervously at her throat. 'Why is everything so quiet? I thought you said you heard shouting?'

'I did. Early this morning, from the Haseki's room.'

'From Gulay Haseki's room?'

'Yes, her doorway is opposite mine,' Celia pointed across to the other side of the courtyard. 'Just over there.'

'Is that so?' With her eye still to the crack in the door, Annetta grew very still. 'There's a small dome just over her room, so it must be on two floors . . .' She craned her neck, trying to see further into the courtyard. 'Very clever: it must have at least three entrances. Her rooms must connect with the Valide's bathhouse as well . . .'

'Yes, they do.' Celia came and stood behind her. 'At night, I can see the stars from here,' she said. 'It reminds me of being with Paul, on my father's boat. Paul knew all the stars.'

'Oh, forget about the stars, you stupid girl,' Annetta snapped. 'Forget everything from the past.'

'I can't.'

'You must.'

'How? How can I?' Celia demanded, stricken. 'I am nothing without the past—'

'Of course you are, you feather-head,' Annetta countered fiercely. 'You'll be a person with a future.'

'Don't you understand?' Celia sat down, clutching her stomach. 'I dream about him every night, about Paul . . . why, I even thought I almost thought I saw him the other day, saw them all,' she said sadly, remembering the sugar ship, and the little figures in the rigging, certain now that they could not have been real.

'Better not to sleep in that case,' Annetta turned to Celia, her face hard. 'How many times do I have to tell you? The past is no good to you here, *capito*? Your dreaming will get you nowhere.'

Celia looked at Annetta thoughtfully. How she had clung to her during those first days and weeks of their captivity. The temper of a devil, the Ottoman corsairs had said, and had considered throwing her overboard, as they had the only other women on board, the two nuns from Annetta's convent with whom she had been travelling and who were too old to sell even for a minimal profit in the slave markets of Constantinople. But it was precisely Annetta's temper, Celia knew, her temper and her dangerous, fiery wits, that had saved them. Annetta always seemed to know what to do: when to fight, and when to cajole; when to sparkle and be noticed; when to make herself invisible. Somehow she had managed to play off every person they met against every other, even the woman slave dealer, from whose house in Constantinople they had been sold at last, nearly two years later, as a gift for the Valide from the Sultan's favourite.

The dark and the fair together, mistress. Celia remembered how Annetta had twined her arm lasciviously around Celia's waist, pressed her cheek against Celia's cheek. *Look, we could be twins.* Against overwhelming odds, it had been she who had kept the two of them together.

But now? Watching her, Celia felt her own sense of disquiet grow. She had never seen Annetta so on edge. She had actually wept, she recalled with astonishment, at the news of the Chief Black Eunuch. Celia had never seen Annetta weep before. If Hassan Aga died, what of it? He was feared equally by almost all the *cariyes*. Who in the harem, she wondered, would mourn his passing? Not Annetta, surely?

'Do you ever see her? The Haseki, I mean.' Annetta was peering curiously through the crack in the doorway.

'Gulay Haseki? Well, they only moved me here two days ago, so no, not yet – not here anyway. But I expect I will. When the Sultan sends for us – for her – the Mistress of the Girls has to escort her across the courtyard, and hand her over to the eunuchs,' Celia shrugged. 'Mostly she keeps to her room. We're not really supposed to go anywhere. There's nothing else to do.'

In the courtyard it was unnaturally quiet. Even Celia began to feel it now. A pair of doves sitting on the rooftops called to one another, their ruffling call breaking the still air.

Annetta shivered suddenly, her face looked pinched. 'They say she's not well. The Haseki, I mean.'

'Do they?' Celia answered her sadly. 'They say lots of things in this place.' A memory came to her of the candlelit room, and the concubine, Gulay, weeping at his feet. She shook her head slowly. 'The Sultan loves her, that's all I know.'

'Love? What does *he* know about love?' Annetta said in a disgusted tone. 'What does anyone in this place know about love? You don't think that *you* – tempting little morsel that you are – are being offered up so that he can fall in love with you, do you?'

'No.' Celia sighed again. 'I am not such a fool as to think that.' A blade of sunlight came through the crack in the doorway, slicing through the dim interior of the little room, to where she sat on the edge of the divan. She put her hand out, watching as it illuminated the paleness of her skin, the fine reddish-gold hairs. 'But I was in love once.'

'Love? I tell you there's no such thing.'

'Yes,' Celia insisted. 'There is.'

Annetta looked at her. 'You think you were in love with your merchant, I suppose?'

Celia ignored her taunt. 'My father wanted us to marry.'

'Lucky goose, most fathers don't consider such fine feelings when they choose a daughter's husband. So why didn't you marry him then?'

'You know why not,' Celia answered her. 'We were to marry in England. I was on my way back there from Venice in my father's ship when . . . Well, you know what happened.'

'It's just as well you didn't marry before,' Annetta added heartlessly, 'or you might have been thrown overboard with the nuns.' And then, sensing that she might have gone too far this time, she added in a softer tone. 'Well then? Tell me about him, although it isn't as though I haven't heard it all before,' she put one hand on her hip, 'just don't go getting all green-sick on me, that's all. He was a merchant, no?'

'A friend of my father's.'

101

'An old man then? *Faugh!*' Annetta wrinkled her nose in disgust. 'But very rich, you said?' she added hopefully. 'I tell you, I'd never marry a man who wasn't rich.'

'No, no, he wasn't old at all,' Celia said.

'But he *was* rich?'

'And clever, a scholar. And kind.'

And he loved me, her heart cried out. He loved me, and I loved him, right from the beginning. She remembered the time when they had met in the merchant Parvish's garden in Bishopsgate. It was on the eve of her voyage to Venice, two years before the shipwreck. She was eighteen. He had not recognised her, she had grown so much.

'Don't you know me, Paul?' she had laughed, giving him a curtsey.

'Celia? Celia Lamprey?' he said, frowning into the sun. 'Why, look at you. Have I really been gone so long?' He held her at arm's length. 'Why, look at you—' he said again, his eyes dancing at her, and then he stopped, as if he did not know what to say.

'Shall we go in?' she said at last, hoping her reluctance would not show.

'Well,' he seemed to consider this carefully, 'your father's still in with Parvish.' Paul looked back towards the house. And then, offering her his arm, 'I hope you're not grown too fine a lady to take a turn with me first?'

Celia remembered the startling blue of the lavender beds; the silvery-green leaves of pleached hornbeams in the walled garden. The way he had looked at her, as if he were seeing her for the first time. What had they talked about? Venice, his travels, Parvish's box of curiosities . . . He was going to show her the curiosities – there was a unicorn's horn and a lock of mermaid's hair amongst them, she remembered – but somehow there had been too much else to talk about . . .

When Celia came out of her reverie, Annetta was still standing at the door.

'A clever, rich merchant – now that's something,' Annetta was saying. 'And not old! *Madonna*, no wonder you still believe in love. So would I, if I ever met such a paragon. And don't tell me, he was handsome as well?' Annetta's eyes sparkled. 'Did he have nice legs? You know, I've often thought even I could marry a man if he had nice legs.'

With an effort Celia composed herself. 'Yes, he had nice legs,' she smiled.

'And did he speak sweetly to you? Ah, don't say it – I can tell by your face that he did.' She shook her head pityingly. 'My poor goose.'

Celia was silent. 'He had to go on a voyage, just a few weeks before we set sail,' she volunteered after a while. 'In fact, I believe he came here, to Constantinople. With the Queen's embassy. He was to have joined us back in England.'

'He came here?' Something in Annetta's voice made Celia glance up. 'You never told me that before. Here to Constantinople? Are you sure?'

'Yes, but it was a long time ago; two years at least, and it was only to have been for a short time. He must be back in Venice now. Why?'

'Nothing, nothing.' Annetta suddenly seemed struck by a thought. 'Celia . . .?'

'What now?'

'Does he know you are dead?'

'Does he know I am dead!' Celia almost laughed. 'But I'm not dead, in case you hadn't noticed. What a thing to say! You mean, would he have heard about my father's boat? I should think so,' she said drily, 'half of it was his merchandise.'

'But what about us?' Annetta's eyes glittered. 'Celia, have you ever wondered if anyone knows what really became of us?'

'There was a time when I never thought about anything else.' Celia looked at her sadly. 'But you cured me of that, remember? No looking back, you said. If we're going to survive this, there must be no looking back.'

'Yes, yes, you're right of course.'

That nervous gesture again, the plucking at her throat.

'What is it, Annetta?' Celia looked at her curiously. 'You seem so strange today.' She tried to put her arm around her, but Annetta shrugged her away.

'Celia, there's something I've been meaning to tell you . . . but I don't know how to . . .' She seemed to struggle over the words, speaking as if to herself. 'But no, no, not now. I'm sorry, but it's too late, too late . . .'

Then suddenly she stopped. She drew away from the doorway, her body tense. 'Look out! Someone's coming.'

From the gateway that connected the Valide's courtyard to the eunuchs' quarters a woman now came walking. Despite being unveiled she was dressed for the street: a short stout figure, with a long black robe over her dress.

'Esperanza!' Annetta whispered. 'Esperanza Malchi.'

There were many *kiras* connected to the palace – women, mostly Jewesses, who earnt their living by carrying out small commissions for the harem women, and who by virtue of their non-Muslim status, passed with relative freedom between the palace and the city – but Esperanza, it was well known, worked only for the Valide.

'I don't like her. She has all the eunuchs in her pocket, and no one seems to know exactly what she does,' Annetta said, frowning, 'and if you ask me it's probably better not to ask.'

The woman made her way slowly across the courtyard. She had a stick in one hand, a cane topped with silver, as she walked she swayed a little, listing from side to side.

'Look at her, hideous old trubkin,' Annetta scowled. 'Bunions, I expect. They all get them. Haven't you noticed that all old women here walk like that, like geese treading on egg shells?'

Although she could hardly have said why, a knot of fear rose suddenly in Celia's throat. 'Quiet, she'll hear you!'

Halfway across the courtyard, the woman stopped and looked around her, and then, apparently satisfied that there was no one in view, she hobbled with surprising speed straight for Celia's door.

Instinctively, the two shrank back into the shadows. Annetta flattened herself against the wall, whilst Celia found herself pressed up awkwardly behind the back of the door.

Outside there was a small shuffling sound and then silence. Celia closed her eyes. Nothing. The woman must have her hand on the open door. Then, at last, a soft creak. The door opened tentatively another few inches and then stopped. Celia could feel the blood racing in her head. She felt as if she were suffocating. Finally she could bear it no longer. She opened her eyes again, and nearly screamed.

An eye was staring at her through a hole in the lattice work. In terror, Celia stared back. Her heart was hammering so loudly in her breast the woman must surely hear it. And yet her head was saying: what madness is this? Why are we hiding? I have every right to be here. I must open the door, Celia thought, confront the woman herself. But somehow she could not. Every instinct screamed at her to remain still. But it was no good; slowly she felt the backs of her knees begin to give way beneath her.

And just then, evidently satisfied with what she had seen, Esperanza suddenly retreated. She pulled the door close-to, adjusting it carefully so that it was exactly as it had been before, and in her strange listing gait made her way across to the other side of the courtyard. At the entrance to the Haseki's apartment she stopped again, and without looking round this time, scratched softly at the door.

At once the door opened. From beneath the folds of her billowing black robes Celia saw the woman draw out a lumpy-looking package. An unseen hand took it from her and the door closed again, as silently as it had opened. Esperanza Malchi continued on her way, her stick tapping against the stone.

For a few minutes after she had disappeared from sight, there was silence. Then Annetta began to laugh. 'Your face! Dear Lord, what a goose you are! You look as if you've seen a ghost.'

'She looked at me.' Trembling, Celia sunk to the floor. 'I swear she looked right at me.'

'You looked so funny!' Annetta sprawled against the cushions on the divan, one fist crammed into her mouth.

'Do you think she saw me?'

'Of course not, it's so bright out there she wouldn't have been able to see a thing. It would have seemed as black as the grave in here.'

'But she was only this far away . . .' Celia held out two fingers and saw that her hand was still trembling.

'I know . . . your face!'

A kind of hysteria seemed to take hold of Annetta. She rolled from side to side, knocking off the golden cap that she wore pinned to the back of her head.

'Stop it! Please stop . . .' Celia shook her by the shoulder. 'You're beginning to frighten me.'

' . . . *can't.*'

'You must.' Another thought now occurred to Celia. 'Besides, you're not supposed to be here. You must go back. Won't the Valide be wondering where you are?'

'No. She sent us all away for a few hours. She usually does when the Malchi woman comes.'

The mere mention of the Valide, however, had an instantly sobering effect. Annetta sat up and dabbed at her eyes, suddenly businesslike again. '*Madonna*, I'm hungry, I swear I could eat a horse.'

'Hungry?' Celia looked at her in amazement. A faint feeling of nausea at the thought of food came over her. But Annetta was smoothing down her hair and pinning her cap back on as if nothing at all had happened, as if the tension she had felt earlier had simply evaporated.

'In the convent,' she began, cheerful again now, 'they always said I laughed too much, and ate too much . . .' She stopped suddenly. 'What's that?'

'What's what?'

'That, look, on the doorstep.'

Celia stood up to look.

'How strange.'

'Why so?'

'It looks like . . . it looks like sand,' Celia said. 'Blue and white sand. In a pattern,' she peered at it, 'like a sort of eye.'

'An eye?' Annetta scrambled off the bed, and made as if to pull Celia back bodily from the threshold. 'Don't touch it!'

'Don't be silly, of course I'm not going to touch it.'

But, unsteady still on her feet, when Annetta took hold of her she lost her balance, lurching over to one side. As she did so she pushed against Annetta, who stepped over the sand. There was a short uncomfortable silence.

'What have I done?' Stricken, Annetta looked down at her foot.

'Nothing, nothing. Come inside now.'

Speaking to her as soothingly as she could, Celia pulled her back into the room and shut the door. The two stared at one another.

'Well, we know something about Esperanza Malchi that we didn't know before.' Annetta's pale face stared back at Celia through the shadows. 'I swear to God, that woman is a witch.'

Chapter 13

Constantinople: 2 September 1599

Midday

'Where did they find him?'
'By the north kiosk, Majesty. Just inside the palace walls.'
Safiye Sultan surveyed Hassan Aga's bloated body which lay before her on a bed of cushions.

'What's that in his hand?'

'A piece of reed, Majesty.' The eunuch lowered his eyes. 'He used it to empty his—'

'I know what he needed it for,' Safiye interrupted impatiently. 'Is the physician here?'

'Yes, Majesty. He is waiting in the pages' quarters. Shall I call him in?'

'At once.'

At her signal another of the eunuchs positioned a stool for her, two more brought in a folding screen behind which she would sit while the physician made his examination. Safiye Sultan sat down and looked around her. They had not yet managed to carry Hassan Aga into the main infirmary, and had placed him instead in a large room, nearest the harem gates. It was a sunless place, bare except for its tiled walls. The Valide's appearance in this part of the harem was so rare that she could feel the cluster of eunuchs huddling together in the corridor outside, their black faces mute with wonder at the events of the past few hours. The mere thought of them – open mouths, slack jaws, their hands signalling to one another in the silent language of the palace – all of it made her suddenly furious. What fools! They think I can't hear them when they speak with their hands, she thought, when their presence alone, their fear, deafens me. Fools, all of them. Any one of my women has more sense than they do. All except for Hassan Aga, of course. What had he been thinking of, breaking out like that? Did he not trust her to keep him safe? Well, whether she liked it or not, it was all out in the open now; and besides, even she could not have kept the poisoning secret for much longer. As it was, it had given her vital time to plan, to manoeuvre. Safiye glanced again towards the prone figure. Found in the gardens . . . well, I can guess who you were looking for. Something of that old familiar feeling – was it excitement or was it fear? – shivered down her spine. He would not betray her, surely? Not now, not after all these years.

At her signal the physician was ushered in. How different the official palace physician was from the other one. Safiye Sultan watched him as he shuffled by: a white eunuch from the palace school. His face had an unearthly pallor, greenish-white, the colour of a spider in an old garden.

Bowing reverently in the direction of the screen, the physician made his way towards the makeshift bed on which Hassan Aga lay. A group of senior black eunuchs drew back a little to allow him to approach. There was complete silence as the physician put his ear to Hassan Aga's chest, at the same time feeling tentatively with two fingers for the pulse on his throat.

'In the name of God, the merciful, the compassionate,' he pronounced in a quavering high-pitched voice, 'he lives!'

A collective exhalation of breath, like the sigh of wind through autumn leaves, rustled through the room.

Encouraged, the physician took Hassan Aga's arm, and examined the palm of his hand carefully. The nails on his hand were thick and curved, yellowing like old elephant bone. For a long time there was silence again. With a stillness imposed by years of rigid discipline the eunuchs stood motionless. Then at last a single voice spoke out, 'Tell us, what has happened to our chief?'

It was the youngest of the senior eunuchs who spoke. Taller and broader-shouldered than the others, his voice – gentle and fluting as a girl's – was strangely at odds with his powerful physique. Emboldened by this display of independence, other voices now spoke up.

'Yes, tell us, tell us!'

At once, as if some spell had been broken, there was movement in the darkened room. From behind her screen, the Valide could see their white hats nodding together

'Was he poisoned?'

Through the lattice, Safiye saw that it was the same creature who spoke, the eunuch Hyacinth.

'Ahhh, no . . .!' She heard their sharp intake of breath. 'Not poison!'

Some of the younger eunuchs, who had been standing silently out of sight in the corridor outside, now began pressing into the room. 'Who has done this, who?' The sound of their voices trilled eerily around the room.

'Silence!' It was one of the senior eunuchs, the Keeper of the Gate, who spoke now. 'Let the physician examine him. Stand back!'

But if they heard him they paid no heed, jostling together to get a view of their chief.

Holding up his hand for silence again, the physician drew back Hassan Aga's robe. All at once, with a flash of panic he covered him up again, but not before a terrible stench, a charnel-house gust of pus and putrefying flesh, filled the room.

'Ahhh . . . he's dying.'

'Rotting, rotting from the feet up.'

The eunuchs moaned together in their shrill voices.

'Whoever did this will pay for it. We'll turn them into heads and trotters.'

'Wait!' The young eunuch Hyacinth was now kneeling down on the floor beside Hassan Aga's body. 'See! He moves!'

And it was true. Before them all the immense bloated body had begun to stir. His lips moved silently.

'In the name of Allah he speaks!' the gate keeper said. 'What does he say?'

The eunuch Hyacinth leant down and put his ear to Hassan Aga's lips.

'His voice is too weak, I can't hear him.'

Hassan Aga's lips moved again, beads of sweat stood out on his forehead.

'He says . . . he says . . .' The eunuch Hyacinth's soft forehead puckered as he strained again to hear Hassan Aga's words. Then he stood up, a perplexed expression on his face. 'He says it was the sugar ship that the English sent. It was their sugar ship that poisoned him.'

Less than than a mile away, Paul Pindar, secretary to the English embassy at Constantinople, stood on the deck of the *Hector*.

A whole day had passed since the interrupted visit to Jamal al-Andalus in his tower, but he had had no chance to return. The affairs of the embassy – preparations for the long-delayed delivery of Queen Elizabeth's gifts to the Sultan, and to the ambassador's long-awaited presentation of credentials – had taken every waking moment. Today would in all probability be the same. Only that morning one of the most senior palace officials, the Chief Aga of the Janissaries, had sent a request to come on board and inspect the *Hector*, and the ambassador had ordered all hands on deck to receive him.

Now, despite the preparations going on around him for the arrival of the janissary chief, Paul cut a solitary figure as he stood listening to the familiar creak and groan of the ship's timbers, feeling the rising swell beneath his feet.

The sun beat down dazzlingly upon the navy-blue waters of the Golden Horn which was now full of the usual midday traffic: fishermen's caiques and little swift-moving skiffs, the long narrow barges used by palace officials going about their daily business; the unwieldy rafts that plied their way up and down the Bosphorous from the silent forests of the Black Sea with their supplies of firewood and furs and ice. On the Galata shore, a dozen or so tall ships lay at anchor. An Ottoman man-o'-war rowed past on its way to the Sultan's naval shipyards.

If Paul saw any of this, he gave no sign. His gaze was focused on one thing alone: the golden roofs and spires of the palace. Was it possible that Carew had not been mistaken and he really had seen Celia that day? He strained his eyes towards its now familiar contours: the Tower of Justice, the long pepper-pot row of kitchen chimneys. In the distance, between the tips of the cypress trees, he saw a sudden flash of sunlight catching on the glass of a shutting window. Might that have been her, he thought wildly, looking down on them from some hidden casement? In all his years as a merchant he had heard far stranger travellers' tales: stories of honest Englishmen who had turned Turk and were now doing very well for themselves in the kingdoms of the East. There were several of them, to his certain knowledge, right here in the Sultan's palace.

But Celia? Everyone knew Celia Lamprey had died two years ago, shipwrecked and drowned alongside her father and every man on board her father's merchantman. He remembered how, on the long voyage to Venice all those years ago, he had loved to watch her sitting at the bow of the boat looking out to sea; how gentle she was, and how fearless too. Remembered how he would make excuses to go and sit with her, how they would talk for hours. How she had ravished him, and every man on board, with her pearly white skin, and her hair like spun gold. His Celia, food for the fishes now, at the bottom of the Adriatic Sea. Paul shivered. Was it possible that she really had come back from the dead? She still came to him in his dreams sometimes, calling to him like a dying mermaid, her long hair wrapped around her neck, dragging her down, down, into the green abyss.

And what if it were true? What if Carew really had seen her, and by some miracle she were still alive, a prisoner now in the Sultan's harem, what then? He could not sleep, could not eat for thinking about it.

'A penny for them, Pindar.' Thomas Glover, his fellow secretary at the embassy, a great red boar of a man, came over to where he stood.

'Hello, Glover.'

With an effort Paul turned to greet him. Glover was accompanied by three other embassy men, the two Aldridge brothers, William and Jonas, English consuls at Chios and Patras respectively, and John Sanderson, one of the Levant Company's merchants who also acted as the embassy treasurer. All four were dressed as though for a high holiday. Compared to Paul's sober black form, they made an outlandish group.

'What's this, not brooding again? Come on, Paul. You know the Turks have never loved a sad man,' Thomas Glover said.

'As if anyone could be sad to look at you, my friends,' Paul forced himself to smile. 'Thomas, you shine like a comet. What's this . . . new sleeves?' He put his hand out to feel Glover's elaborately slashed and pinked sleeves of crimson silk tied to an embroidered doublet of fine, blond suede. 'And quite as many jewels as a Sultana. I believe there's a law against it somewhere.'

'I knew you'd like 'em.' Thomas Glover grinned down at him, the sun flashing against the heavy gold hoops in his earlobes. Two large rose-cut amethysts gleamed against the blackness of his high-brimmed hat; precious gems, topaz, garnet and moonstone, glittered on the fingers and thumbs of each hand.

'So, what news, gentlemen?'

'As a matter of fact, we bring great news. They say the Sultan himself is coming by boat to inspect the *Hector* this morning.'

'Well, well, that'll be one in the eye for the French ambassador.' Paul felt his spirits begin to lift.

'Not only de Brèves, but the Venetian Bailo, too,' Jonas, the second Aldridge brother, added. 'We all know how those two stand on their diplomatic etiquette.'

The two brothers were nearly as richly dressed as Glover. Instead of gemstones, they wore knots of iridescent birds' feathers in their caps.

'We do indeed,' Paul said. 'What do you say, Glover? You know the ways of the palace better than any of us. Will the Great Man really come?'

'It's always hard to second-guess the Porte, but on this occasion I think it's very likely.' Thomas Glover fingered his bearded chin, his rings glittering.

'Does it really matter that much, whether the Sultan comes to inspect the boat or not?' John Sanderson, the eldest of the group, said to Paul.

'Does it matter?' Paul levered himself on to the balustrade of the ship. 'John, you think too much like a merchant. This isn't about currants, or cloth, or tin; or not for the moment anyway. The business of the embassy is all about theatre, about prestige. About being noticed. And the Sultan has noticed us all right. With the arrival of the *Hector* we've trumped them all. De Brèves and the rest may mock us for being a band of merchants, but the truth is, this is a simple enough game. And they hate us because we're better at it than they are.'

'Paul's right,' Thomas Glover added. 'All eyes are on the *Hector*, and that means on us. To my knowledge there hasn't been a ship yet to rival her in these waters.'

'To rival a three-hundred-ton merchantman? I should think not,' William Aldridge said with pride.

112

'And if we're to be their allies against Spain, what better symbol could there be of our Queen's strength, and the strength of England?' Glover said. 'Now gentlemen, excuse us please. Paul, a word in your ear.'

Turning to Paul he drew him a little to one side, and the two men conferred together quickly.

'Whatever happens, Paul, if the Sultan does comes to inspect the *Hector* today, we mustn't risk losing our advantage.'

'My thoughts exactly. De Brèves and the Bailo will do anything they can to interfere with our cause, and prevent us trading freely.'

'And that means the ambassador must present his credentials as soon as possible now – neither the Sultan nor the Grand Vizier will negotiate with us otherwise. What news of Dallam?'

'His repairs to the Company's gift are nearly finished, or so he tells me.'

'Then it must be impressed upon him that it is a matter of the utmost urgency to get it finished. Today, or failing that tomorrow if possible. Our Queen's gifts to the Sultan must be presented at the same time as the ambassador's credentials.'

'Leave it to me, I'll talk to him again,' Paul said. 'And here's another thought, Thomas. Until then we must make sure that Sir Henry lies as low as possible—'

'You mean, the less mischief he is allowed to do between now and then, the better?' Glover said bluntly. 'My thoughts exactly . . . oh, and speaking of which, I nearly forgot. He wants to see you right away. He's waiting down below in Captain Parson's cabin. It's about the Valide Sultan.'

'The Valide?'

'Yes,' Glover looked at Paul curiously, 'it seems she has asked to see you again.'

'Carew?' The ambassador, Sir Henry Lello, sounded as if he had just sucked on a lemon. 'I don't think it will be necessary for him to accompany you, Pindar; most certainly not.'

'No, sir, of course not. You are quite right.'

Paul and Sir Henry were talking together in the *Hector*'s tiny captain's cabin at the rear of the ship. Sir Henry was pulling at his beard, a trick he had adopted, Paul noticed, whenever he was nervous or upset.

'Most irregular.'

'Yes, sir. It'll be best to go quietly, I see that.'

'Eh?'

'Irregular. Sir. As you so rightly say.' Paul bowed respectfully. 'And perhaps it is best to do these things quietly.'

He allowed a small pause whilst Lello digested this, then added carefully, 'After all, the French ambassador's not going to be very happy about the fact that the Valide has asked for a private meeting with someone from your embassy.'

The seed took immediate root.

'De Brèves?' Sir Henry Lello's eyes narrowed. 'No, he certainly won't.' He brightened. 'There's a thought, eh Pindar? Do things quietly you say, but I am not so sure. Perhaps we should make more of an . . . occasion . . . of it, what do you think?'

'And risk annoying de Brèves?' Paul shook his head. 'Let alone the Venetian Bailo. You know the Venetians think they've always had a special relationship with the Porte. Our informants tell us that they send gifts to the Valide and her women almost daily, thinking that it keeps up their influence with the Sultan. De Brèves might think we were trying something similar . . .'

'But that's just it!' Lello said. 'It's the very thing, don't you see, to make him think that!'

Paul gave a good impression of suddenly seeing the light.

'But of course!' he said. 'De Brèves will think this visit a deliberate strategy of yours. And that might distract them from our real strategy: to win over the Vizier, and renew the Capitulations.' He gave a small bow, whose tincture of irony was in no danger of being recognised by the ambassador. 'A brilliant idea! Congratulations, sir.'

'Hmm, hmm!' Lello gave vent to a little neigh which Paul recognised as the ambassador's infrequently aired laugh. 'And what's more, Pindar, it won't cost us a penny! No bribes to the Vizier for this!'

'A most statesmanlike thought,' Paul laughed in turn. 'You were not made Her Majesty's ambassador for nothing, Excellency.'

'Take care, Mr Pindar,' Sir Henry frowned at the mention of the Queen. 'Her Majesty is munificence itself. She's only asked the

Company to pay for our gifts to the new Sultan – quite right too, in my opinion.'

And the cost of this entire embassy, my old friend Fog, Paul thought to himself, the very considerable expense of which must somehow now be dunned out of a company of London merchants even more parsimonious than the Queen herself. And who, if we don't succeed in this mission, are quite capable of making us pay for the whole enterprise ourselves.

'What's this? Well, Henry, my love, what won't cost a penny?'

Without ceremony Lady Lello, the ambassador's wife, inserted herself into the tiny cabin. A stout woman, she wore an enormous goffered ruff, on which her small and apparently neckless visage rested uncertainly, for all the world (as Carew was fond of remarking) like a pig's head on a platter. When she saw Paul her small eyes widened, and her face crinkled into a benevolent smile. 'And Secretary Pindar, too! Good morning to you.'

'My Lady.' Paul made room for her as best he could in that tiny space.

'Well, what news, Sir Henry?' Any physical movement more rapid than that of the stateliest pavane deprived Lady Lello of oxygen, and now she sat herself down, breathing heavily, and nestling the wheel of her farthingale more comfortably against her hips. 'What will not cost us a penny?'

'Pindar has been summoned to see the Valide again.'

'Well!' Lady Lello's eyes widened again.

'The Valide herself has sent for him,' Sir Henry added.

'Well!' Lady Lello took out a piece of cambric which she kept tucked inside her sleeve and dabbed at her forehead. 'Well!'

'The news makes my wife quite speechless, Pindar,' the ambassador pointed out.

'Shame, my Lady. Am I such a poor choice of emissary?' Pindar turned to her with a smile.

'Indeed no, Mr Pindar!' The fleshy folds gathered on the top of Lady Lello's ruff quivered a little, like a pink syllabub. 'But twice in as many days! Well, I say, isn't that very unusual? Mr Glover tells me that the Frankish envoys to the Porte must often wait many weeks before they are received by the Great Turk, and that the Vally Sultana is scarcely ever seen.'

'That's just the point! It's a sign of great favour,' the ambassador said, rubbing his hands together. Tall, thin and unprepossessing, he did indeed merit his nickname 'Fog'. His fingers were long and etiolated, like strange-looking tubers deprived of sunlight. 'Pindar and I were just saying,' Lello leant towards his wife confidingly, 'the French ambassador won't like this at all.'

'Well, I say . . .' Lady Lello looked from one to the other.

'It seems that the gift our Queen sent the Valide—'

'—You mean the coach that Mr Pindar presented to her?'

'The coach, yes,' Lello rubbed his hands again, and the skin of his fingers made a faint rasping noise, 'well, quite simply, she is delighted with it. I'm told that she has already been seen riding in it. They say that the Sultan himself accompanied her. And the upshot of it all is she wants to see Secretary Pindar again. To send her thanks to the Queen, I shouldn't wonder.'

'And she has asked for him in person – to thank him, I suppose. Well, Paul,' Lady Lello beamed at him, her little eyes all but disappearing into the soft fleshy folds of her face, 'this is great news. We must hope the company's great box of whistles – when Dallam has mended it –' she gave a sceptical sniff, 'will find similar favour. Now, Sir Henry, you must think of a suitable escort for Mr Pindar, you know. We cannot have them, de Brèves and the Bailly, I mean, making remarks.' She lowered her voice and leant towards Paul. 'They speak slightingly of Sir Henry, I'm told, and of his being but a merchant, you know.'

'The Bail-o, my love. The Venetian ambassador is called the Bail-o . . .'

But Lady Lello was not listening. 'Perhaps Mr Consul Aldridge and Mr Secretary Glover should go with you, what do you think?'

'Not so fast, my love,' Sir Henry interposed, glancing round at Paul who took up the ambassador's cue.

'But as you know, my Lady, Secretary Glover and Consul Aldridge are needed here; there's much important business to attend to,' Paul said.

'Then we must send you with someone who is not needed here, someone who is not important. Let's see: Ned Hall the coachman? No, too much of a yokel. Or our parson, the Reverend May? No, too timid.' Lady Lello widened her eyes suddenly, a small fleshy tree

116

stump struck by the lightning of inspiration. 'Good Lord . . . Carew, of course! Your cook, John Carew. Mr Pindar, he must go with you. Isn't that right, Sir Henry?' Dimpling, she put up one small hand to pat her coiffed head, only to be impeded by the enormous ruff. 'He does not have to say anything, only look the part,' his wife went on serenely. 'He has a set of livery, I take it? And he's a good enough leg, I'll say that, even if he is more new-fangled than an ape in those Venetian fashions of his. What's wrong with good honest English cloth, that's what I always say, don't I, Sir Henry? Sir Henry—?'

She tried, despite her ruff, to look round at her husband, but he had already left the cabin.

'He's gone to have a word with the men, I dare say,' she said comfortably. 'They've sent word that the Great Man himself is coming to inspect the *Hector*. We must go up there ourselves, to pay our respects.'

She began to heave herself up, and Paul took her arm to help her. 'Well,' she said, panting a little from the exertion, 'it's a great day, it is indeed. And so pleasant to be back on board a ship. We were always quite comfortable aboard ships, you know.' She shook out her skirts, which gave off a strong odour of the camphor they had been wrapped in to preserve their stuff during long sea voyages. 'Between ourselves, I prefer it here to that draughty great house, with all those plaguey janissaries cluttering up the place.'

Looking round the tiny cabin, Lady Lello gave a small nostalgic sigh. 'A place for everything, and everything in its place, is what we always used to say. I sailed a great deal with Sir Henry when we were first married – and then later, too, you know, after my babes were taken.' She gazed out of the cabin window for a moment. 'Well, well,' she patted Paul softly on the arm, 'no good dwelling on the past. I know that you, of all people, understand that.'

'Let me help you up the steps, Lady Lello,' Paul put his hand out to her gently. 'The ambassador is waiting for us.'

'Thank you.' She took his proffered arm. 'That's a pretty bit of cloth, Mr Pindar, for all it is so very black.' She fingered the stuff of his cloak. 'You look quite the Venetian noble, if I may say so,' she dimpled at him kindly, 'but I can forgive that in you, Paul. I won't have them plague you about wearing sad colours. Sir Henry was to speak to you about it – the Turks don't like it, he says – but I said to him, you leave that young man alone. He lost his lady love, drowned, they say.' She looked up at him, her old eyes as pale and blue as a distant horizon. 'I told him, you leave that young man alone.'

'Shall we go up, my lady?'

'With your kind help, Mr Pindar, I think I shall manage these steps very well.' She took his arm. 'I wanted to show you my new gown. What colour would you call it?'

'We're calling this one "Drake's colour", I believe.' Paul steered her up the wooden steps towards the poop deck. 'Or sometimes "dragon's blood".'

'The names they think of these days: "lady blush" and "lion-tawny" and "popinjay-blue". The Lord knows I've been around cloth long enough, but even I can't keep up.' Lady Lello struggled briefly to get her ruff through the narrow opening. 'And how about "pimpillo", I like that one, don't you? Pim-pillo . . .' Her voice faded a little, borne away on the snapping sea breeze, as she popped out finally on to the deck. 'A kind of reddish-yellow, I'm told. I asked your Carew what colour his new cloak was,' she turned, puffing a little from her climb, to call back down the steps to Paul, 'and you know how he answered me?'

'No.'

'Goose-turd-green! What next, Mr Pindar?'

'What next indeed,' Paul echoed her faintly.

'Apparently it is similar to "Dead Spaniard". Was he jossing me, d'you think?'

'He'll be a Dead Spaniard if he was doing anything of the sort,' Paul replied in his most jovial voice. 'I'll make sure of that myself.'

On deck there was a sudden commotion.

'The Grand Signor!'

'Look sharp, the Great Man!'

'Here comes the Grand Signor!'

Excusing himself from Lady Lello, Paul made his way to the side of the merchantman where Thomas Glover and the other Company merchants were standing together.

'There he comes now, Paul,' Glover made a space beside him. 'By God! Here he comes, gentlemen, here he comes.'

Paul followed his gaze and saw the Sultan's barge pulling out smoothly from the royal boathouse at the water's edge. On board the

English ship the men in the rigging, the assembled company of merchants, even Lady Lello in all her holiday finery, were silent now, watching as the barge approached. And in that silence a strange sound, like the barking of so many dogs, could be heard, carrying faintly across the waters,

'Listen!' Glover said. 'Can you hear them? The oarsmen barking like dogs. They say they do it so that none of them can overhear the Sultan if he speaks.'

The barge was now nearly level with the *Hector*. As it grew closer Paul could see that twenty oarsmen dressed in red caps and white shirts rowed the great barge, at one end of which was a small raised poop, painted scarlet and gold, in which the Sultan rode, his presence carefully screened from prying eyes. The eerie sound of the barking oarsmen – *bough, bouhwah, bough, bough, boughwah* – sounded louder and louder. Behind the imperial barge came another, less finely decorated, in which Paul could make out a company of the Sultan's court attendants, dwarves and mutes dressed in brilliant silk robes. Each of them wore a curved sword at his hip, and several of them had hunting dogs, as finely dressed as their masters, in purple coats figured with gold and silver threads. Skimming swiftly over the waters, the barges circled the *Hector* once, and then were gone again, skimming away across the waters as suddenly as they had come.

On board the *Hector* the little knot of merchants clapped one another on the back and talked amongst themselves. Only Paul did not share their sense of elation. He felt weary to his bones, suddenly: managing Sir Henry, dealing with the other merchants, even his discussions with Glover had become a strain, as though he were playing a part, an actor on the stage.

Paul ran a hand over his eyes. There were times since his first conversation with Carew about Celia when he had thought he was going mad. At first his reaction had been sheer disbelief, followed by rage, but in his calmer moments he knew Carew would not lie. Gradually he had allowed himself to hope, and then to believe in the impossible. Celia, alive! Celia, living and breathing, flesh and blood. Then exultation had turned to despair. Celia alive, but incarcerated in a place where he could never hope to reach her. Or could he? At Jamal's house he had begun to hope again. At night he lay staring into darkness, sleepless, dreamless, wrestling with his thoughts. Two years as a slave at the hands of the Turks. What had they done to her? He tried not to imagine, but it was impossible. With the slave master, the Sultan? With eunuchs? The thought made him feel as though his head might explode.

On the shore, a sudden flurry of movement caught his eye and he saw that another barge was now leaving the imperial boathouse. This one was smaller than the Sultan's, but more richly decorated. The screened cabin on the poop deck was inlaid with ivory and ebony; gold leaf and mother-of-pearl and carbuncles of precious stones glinted in the sun. The oarsmen rowed silently this time. Droplets of water from the ends of their wooden paddles described arcs of shining brilliants as the barge skimmed towards the English ship. Then, just a few feet short of her, it stopped.

Shading his eyes, Paul looked towards the screened cabin. Something green flashed in the sunlight. And then he knew: Safiye, the Valide Sultan herself, had also come to inspect the *Hector*. She did not stay long. At some hidden signal, the men took up their oars and the barge began to move again, only this time it did not return to the imperial boathouse, but set off swiftly in the opposite direction, towards the deep green waters, the steeply wooded and shadowed hills of the Bosphorous.

Paul stood alone once more, thinking hard. What could the Valide Sultan want? The ambassador seemed satisfied that it was to thank him again for the Queen's gift, which Paul had been deputed to deliver on the ambassador's behalf immediately after the *Hector*'s arrival, but he was not so sure.

Not for the first time he thought back to that day, still the strangest of all the strange days that had passed since his arrival in Constantinople. Surrounded by her black eunuchs, and guarded by a battalion of Tressed Halberdiers, the Valide had been brought, in a carefully screened palanquin, into the courtyard where the coach waited for her. Of course Paul had not seen her – palace etiquette had proscribed even raising his eyes to the screen – but if anyone had thought to ask him he could have told them that there were many others ways of perceiving; that the presence behind the screen was so powerful that eyes had not been necessary to see this miraculous woman. Her voice alone was enough.

'*Venite, inglesi.* Come closer, Englishman.'

120

He remembered how when he first heard it, the hairs rose on the back of his neck. Company intelligence suggested that the Valide was an old woman, fifty at least. This was the voice of a woman who was still young.

'Come closer, Englishman,' she had said to him once more. And seeing him eye the eunuchs, their hands at the ready upon their curved scimitars, she had laughed. *'No aver paura.* Don't be afraid.'

And so he had approached the palanquin, and they had talked. How long had they talked for? Afterwards, Paul could not have said. He remembered only a certain perfume, like a night-scented garden, and when she moved, the distant glimmer of jewels.

The sight of the Valide's barge seemed to clear Paul's mind. He pushed his other thoughts away, and tried to concentrate instead on the other matter at hand. Here, almost miraculously, was another chance to enter the palace and, as if in answer to a prayer, with Carew, too. Carew could be a liability sometimes, but he had qualities that his detractors would never even guess at: eyes that missed nothing, nerves of steel and a quickness of wit in a tight situation that had sometimes struck Paul as a kind of devilry. There was no one Paul would rather have had with him than Carew, if you could find him, that was.

Paul looked around the *Hector* and cursed. Where was that good-for-nothing rat-catcher when you needed him? Disobeying orders as usual. It was only then that the thought struck him that he had not seen Carew at all that day. Impatiently, he looked round the decks, and even up in the rigging, but could see no sign of him.

Instead, Paul became aware of yet another vessel approaching the *Hector*. No imperial barge this time, but a small skiff which was being hurriedly and somewhat inexpertly rowed towards them, this time from the Galata shore. Paul watched. Two janissaries were holding the oars, their headdresses slipping with the exertion. Their strokes were so jagged that twice the little vessel nearly collided with passing water traffic. As the skiff drew closer, Paul could see the figures of some of the other embassy members crammed together in the back: the Reverend May and next to him two Company merchants recently arrived from Aleppo, Mr Sharp and Mr Lambeth. As the little vessel drew closer he saw that John Sanderson's apprentice, John Hanger, and the coachman, Ned Hall, were also rowing.

121

'Well, they can row as hard as they like, they've missed the Great Man's inspection,' Thomas Glover had come to stand next to Paul, his broad arms akimbo.

'No,' Paul shook his head slowly, straining his eyes towards the little group, 'there's something wrong, look.'

When they saw Paul and Glover watching them, the two merchants started waving their hands in the air. The parson stood up and seemed to be shouting something through his cupped hands, although the wind bore his words soundlessly away.

'That fool of a parson . . .' Glover said impatiently. 'I don't like the look of this at all.'

'Nor do I.'

At last the skiff drew up alongside the *Hector*. Now that they were within earshot, the men seemed unsure how to proceed.

'Well, what news, gentlemen?' Paul called to them.

Lambeth, one of the merchants from Aleppo, got to his feet unsteadily.

'It's your man Carew, Secretary Pindar.'

'What about him, Mr Lambeth?' Paul's mouth felt dry.

'Some janissaries came to arrest him.'

'That scoundrel,' Paul felt Glover put a hand on his shoulder, 'he'll be the death of us all.' Then: 'On what grounds? What's he done?'

'We don't know, they wouldn't say.'

Paul gripped the balustrade. 'Where did they take him?'

'Take him?' Lambeth took his cap off, and mopped his sweating forehead. 'Oh no, they didn't take him. He wasn't there. We came to warn him. We thought he was with you.'

Glover looked at Paul. 'Well?'

'No, he's not here,' Paul answered grimly. 'But I think I know where I might find him.'

Chapter 14

Constantinople: 2 September 1599

Afternoon

A t the house of Jamal al-Andalus the servant who had been in attendance the day before opened the door to Paul. At first the boy seemed reluctant to announce him, but eventually he was persuaded, and Paul went in only to find, to his discomfiture, that there had been some confusion at his unexpected arrival. In the antechamber in which he was usually asked to wait there was a good deal of moving and talking: the sound of Jamal's voice, the bang of a door closing abruptly, footsteps treading in an upper chamber. Then, as he waited, he could hear in the room above him what sounded like two people talking together, a man – Jamal, presumably – and, if Paul was not mistaken, a woman; their voices now soft, now loud, disputing together. After a few more minutes Jamal came out. He looked uncharacteristically harried. Was Paul imagining it, or did he catch a glimpse of a woman's black robes inside? He noticed that the astronomer made sure to shut the door carefully behind him.

'I can wait, Jamal, if you have other business.'

'No, no, you are most welcome, my friend. It's nothing of importance,' Jamal waved Paul's objections aside with his usual courtesy. 'As a matter of fact there is something I want to discuss with you. Go to the tower,' he said, 'we can talk there in a moment, no one can overhear us.'

'It's about Carew,' Paul began when Jamal joined him in the tower a few minutes later. 'He's disappeared, and I don't know why but I had an idea that you might . . .'

Jamal put a hand on Paul shoulder. 'Carew is safe.'

For a moment Paul was stunned into silence. He stared at Jamal. 'Where is he?' he said at last.

'It is probably better if you don't know that. Not just yet.'

'What are you talking about?' Paul ran a hand through his hair in exasperation. 'It's absolutely vital that I find him. Some janissaries were sent to arrest him today—'

'I know.'

'—and I have to find him before they do . . .' Paul checked himself. 'You know about the janissaries?'

'Sit down, Paul, please.'

'I don't think so,' Paul felt a sudden unexpected stab of anger towards the calm figure in white robes standing before him. 'Forgive me, Jamal, but I don't have time for pleasantries. For God's sake, will you just tell me what's happened?'

If Jamal felt surprise at Paul's tone he did not show it. 'Someone at the palace has been poisoned and they think it might have something to do with Carew.'

At Jamal's words, Paul felt a wave of nausea come over him. 'But you say he's safe?'

'He's being kept somewhere safe until the whole business can be sorted out.'

'Where exactly is "somewhere safe"?'

'I just told you, I can't tell you.'

There was a short, uncomfortable silence.

'Who was poisoned?'

'Hassan Aga, the Chief Black Eunuch.'

'I see.' Paul wiped a hand quickly over his face.

'He was found yesterday, collapsed somewhere in the palace gardens. No one knows how he got there, or what had happened to him.'

'Is he dead?'

'No, he's still alive. Very sick, but alive.'

'And what could this possibly have to do with Carew?'

Jamal did not answer Paul immediately. He picked up a piece of polished glass from amongst the articles on the tabletop near him, weighing it carefully in his hands.

'Did John make some figures out of spun sugar, including one in the shape of a ship? I believe you told me once that he is highly skilled in these things.'

124

'We call them subtleties. And, yes, Carew is a master of them.' Paul felt himself go cold; there was a prickling sensation on the back of his neck. 'Don't tell me,' he put his head in his hands, 'please, don't tell me they are saying that it was Carew's sugar ship that poisoned the Chief Black Eunuch.'

'Poor John,' Jamal's expression was almost apologetic, 'he is rather accident prone, isn't he?'

'I'll say.' In his mind's eye Paul slid his hands around Carew's neck, pressing with both thumbs against that scrawny windpipe until his face turned purple and his eyeballs bulged. But then a thought struck him. 'But this is absurd! What possible motive could Carew have to put poison into a subtlety? We're trying to impress the Sultan, for God's sake, not poison him! No, no, I'll bet my life I know who's behind this, either the Baillo, or de Brèves. Probably both for all we know.'

'The Venetian and the French ambassadors?' Jamal raised his eyebrows. 'Surely not.'

'Oh, don't look so surprised. They've been intriguing against us ever since we got here, trying to stop us renewing our trading rights with the Porte—'

'Wait, Paul, you go too fast,' Jamal held up his hands. 'At the moment I think it may be the case that no one knows *what* to think. Hassan Aga is still too ill to give any proper account of what happened, but the unfortunate fact is that "the English ship", as they are calling it, is the only thing that he has said since he was found.'

'Just that: "the English ship"?'

'Just that.'

'How do you know?'

'I was there this morning when they found him. I often use a room in the eunuchs' quarters in which to teach some of the little princes. Hassan Aga was delirious, wandering around the gardens; no one knows how he got there, or why. The whole place was in an uproar. I tell you, Paul, it would have been impossible *not* to know what was going on.'

'So, are you going to tell me where John is?'

'No, I can't. I don't know myself.' Jamal shrugged. 'He's safe, that's all I know.'

'But how did they know to go after Carew?' Paul said, perplexed.

'Apparently, it was he who delivered the sweetmeats himself. One of the halberdiers at the harem gates recognised him. It seems he'd been there once already that day, on some other business.'

'But surely as far as the palace is concerned he's just a servant?' Paul sat down again heavily. 'Why bother with him? Why not come after the ambassador? Or me, for that matter? Carew is not an embassy retainer: he is here because he is my servant.'

At this Jamal did not reply.

'Why Carew, Jamal?' Paul insisted. 'None of this makes the least sense.'

'I think you've already answered that question, my friend: because he is not important. The palace does not want a big scandal any more than your embassy does. That's my conclusion, anyway. But, until Hassan Aga recovers enough to say what really happened, they must be seen to be doing something.' He gave Paul a quick glance. 'For internal reasons, let's say.'

Paul walked over to the other side of the octagonal room. A breeze was blowing through one of the windows. He looked around him. Everything was the same as it had always been, ever since he had first met Jamal, two years ago. The austere space, with its plain white-washed walls, more reminiscent to European eyes of a monastic cell than an astronomer's observatory. The collection of instruments that Jamal had showed them yesterday – the quadrant, his collections of astrolabes and sundials, the *qibla* indicator – were all here. And yet it all felt somehow . . . different. The paints and pots of gold leaf, the parchments and pens with which the astronomer recorded his observations and that they had seen on his work bench only the day before were no longer there. In their place were pieces of ground glass, similar in shape and size to the piece that Jamal was still holding in his hand. Some were flat and round, like large coins; others were almost spherical, like crystal balls. Under any other circumstances Paul's curiosity would have drawn him to them immediately. He would have picked up the pieces of glass and examined them, besieging Jamal with questions as to their exact manufacture and function. Now he hardly noticed them.

Instead, he was aware of the astronomer watching him from the other side of the room. Jamal's face was in shadow. His white gown fell in gleaming folds to the ground like an alchemist's robes. His expression, it seemed to Paul, was no longer playful. He seemed taller suddenly; taller and graver.

Paul's head was spinning. The feeling of nausea returned, stronger now. This was the moment for which he had been waiting. If he were going to ask Jamal for help this was surely the right time – and yet now that it was here, somehow he could not speak. So much was in the balance, so much was at stake – Celia, and now Carew – that his courage almost failed him.

Perhaps Carew had been right after all: why should Jamal help him? Why did he suddenly have the feeling that the astrologer knew a great deal more than he was telling him? Paul put his hand in his pocket, his fingers closed around the smooth form of his compendium. He was aware that Jamal was watching him from the other side of the room, intently now, and felt a shiver down his spine.

'I know you must have many questions, Paul,' Jamal was saying. 'If there are any I can answer, I will do so gladly.'

'Will you?'

'But of course. For example, you ask: why Carew?'

'No,' Paul met Jamal's gaze steadily. 'Why you, Jamal?'

With his hand still inside his pocket, he flicked the catch on his compendium: open and shut, open and shut.

'Why me?'

'You are privy to a great deal in the affairs of the palace suddenly.'

To Paul's surprise, Jamal threw back his head and laughed. 'And I thought that was what you wanted from me?' His eyes glittered, the old Jamal again. 'Someone with an insider's knowledge of the palace.'

'Carew told you that?'

'But of course. That's what he told me when he came to visit me again this morning.'

In his mind's eye Paul slid his hands around Carew's neck again, shaking him like a rat so that his teeth rattled.

'What else did he say?'

'Only that you wanted to speak to me again urgently about something, and that you needed someone with such knowledge. He wouldn't say anything more. I must say I am curious: what was it about?'

'It's not important now.'

'Really?' Jamal had come to stand in front of him. 'Why are you so strange today, Paul? Look at you, clothes, hair – dishevelled, all of it. This isn't to do with Carew at all, is it?'

Before Paul could stop him, Jamal reached out and caught at his wrist, pulling his hand, compendium and all, from his pocket and holding it between his fingers.

'Are you ill?'

'No, of course not—'

'But your pulse is racing.' Still holding his wrist, Jamal stared intently into his face. 'Pupils, dilated. Skin, cold and clammy.' He shook his head wonderingly. 'You look – forgive me for saying so – but you look as though you've seen a ghost.'

With a click the loosened catch sprung free, the compendium glided open on Paul's outstretched palm.

'That's just it, Jamal,' he heard himself say. 'I have. I think I have seen a ghost.'

Chapter 15

Istanbul: the present day

On Monday morning Elizabeth presented herself at the Topkapı Palace. She had arranged to meet Berin, her contact at the Bosphorous University, at the gateway of the second courtyard. There were no tourists that day. Two sulky guards at the entrance-way took Elizabeth's passport, and after examining it for what seemed like an unnecessarily long time, checked her name off their list and with obvious reluctance let her through.

Berin, a small mild-mannered Turkish woman in her early forties who was wearing a neat brown coat and headscarf, was waiting for Elizabeth on the other side. 'This is Suzie.' Berin introduced Elizabeth to the English production assistant. They shook hands. Suzie wore black jeans and a leather biker's jacket. A walkie-talkie buzzed and crackled in a belt at her waist.

'Thanks so much for this, I really appreciate it,' Elizabeth said.

'I just thought your project sounded so cool. If anyone asks just say you're a researcher. Which is exactly what you are,' she smiled at Elizabeth, 'just not one of ours, that's all.'

'Berin told me about the work you're doing here,' Suzie added as they walked across a formal garden of grass and cypress trees. A few late-flowering roses shivered in the chilly wind. 'And that you think there might once have been an English slave here in this harem.'

'I'm pretty sure of it, yes. A young woman called Celia Lamprey.' Elizabeth explained about the fragment of narrative she had discovered. 'She was the daughter of a sea captain, shipwrecked in the Adriatic, probably some time in the late 1590s, then taken captive by

129

Ottoman corsairs. The part of the narrative that has survived claims that she ended up here, in the Sultan's harem.'

'And what would she have been: a wife or a concubine or a servant, or what?'

'It's hard to say at this stage. The narrative says she was sold as a *cariye*, which in Turkish simply means slave woman. In the palace hierarchy the term was generally used to describe the lowest-ranking women, but since every woman here was technically a slave – oh, except for the Sultan's daughters and his mother, of course, the Valide Sultan, who would automatically have been freed on the death of her master – it might not mean that at all. My guess is that she was sold to the palace as a potential concubine. With one or two exceptions, the Sultans never took wives. It's one of the strangest things about the Ottoman system, the fact that every one of the Sultan's women was from somewhere else: Georgia, Circassia, Armenia, various parts of the Balkans, Albania even. But never Turkey itself.'

'There was a French woman, I seem to remember, in the early nineteenth century.' Suzie said. 'What was she called?'

'You're probably thinking of Aimée Dubucq de Rivery.' Elizabeth said. 'A cousin of Josephine Bonaparte. Yes, that's right, but until now, no Englishwoman, or not that we know of anyway.'

They reached the entrance to the harem. A large quantity of filming equipment, rolls of flex and large black and silver crates, was piled up nearby, but apart from that the place was deserted. An empty crisp packet swirled at their feet. In the window of a ticket office a hand-written sign, left over from the day before, said 'Last tour 15.10 hours'.

Elizabeth followed Suzie though one of the now unguarded turnstiles. Berin followed after them.

'But what you're forgetting is that it wasn't just the women who were slaves,' Berin said. 'The whole Ottoman empire was based on it. But it wasn't slavery in the way people usually think of it today. There was no stigma attached to being a slave. And it wasn't a particularly cruel system – not at all like what you might call "plantation slavery". More of a career opportunity, really.' She smiled. 'Most of our Grand Viziers started out as slaves.'

'You think that was what the women thought about it?' Suzie said sceptically. 'I doubt it.'

'Don't be so sure.' In her quiet way, Berin was insistent. 'I think that's exactly what most of them thought. Even your Celia Lamprey might have come to think that way eventually.' She put her hand on Elizabeth's arm. 'Don't dismiss that as an idea, it's not impossible, you know. Plenty of European men did very well for themselves under the Ottomans – so why not a woman?'

An immense wooden door stood before them, studded with brass nails. Over the door was some lettering in gilded Arabic script. Elizabeth looked up at it and shivered. What had Celia Lamprey thought when she entered these doors for the first time? Had it been a haven for her, or a hell? Was it ever possible to see clearly into the past?

'The fact is, no one has ever really known who these women were.' Berin pulled up the collar of her coat, as though she too felt a sudden chill. 'And for the most part we never will. Of all the hundreds of women who passed through these doors, we can only put names to a handful of them, let alone any other details. That's the meaning of the word "harem" after all. It means "forbidden". We're not *supposed* to know.' She gave Elizabeth a teasing smile. 'Still, I hope you find her – your Celia Lamprey, I mean. Come—' She too looked up at the vast door in front of her. 'Shall we go in?'

The first thing Elizabeth noticed was how dark it was inside. She left Berin, Suzie and the rest of the film crew setting up their equipment in the Sultan's Imperial Chamber and began to look around on her own. At first one of the guards followed her, but he soon grew bored and went back to his guard room where he could read the newspaper in peace. Elizabeth found that she could wander at liberty through the deserted rooms.

From the entrance hall, the Dome with the Cupboard, she made her way slowly down the corridor of the eunuchs. No furniture, few windows; tiny rooms no bigger than cubby holes. Iznik tiles of extraordinary antiquity and beauty lined the crooked walls, giving off a curious pale green light.

At the end of this corridor was a high domed vestibule from which three other corridors led off at angles. She looked at her map and read their names. The first, leading to the Sultan's quarters, was marked on her map as the Golden Road, the corridor down which concubines

131

were taken to see their master. The second, leading into the heart of the harem, was marked prosaically as 'the food corridor'; while the third, which led out of the harem altogether and into the innermost courtyard and the men's quarters, was marked as the Aviary Gate. Elizabeth decided to follow the second corridor, and found herself in a small two-storeyed courtyard, cordoned off with ropes. A sign said 'Courtyard of the Cariyes'.

She looked around her. There was no sign of the guard, so cautiously she stepped over the ropes. A number of rooms led off the courtyard. Most of the doors had been bolted shut. Through a crack in one door she could just make out the marble remains of an old bathhouse. The rooms beyond it were empty, their plasterwork cracked and stained. There was a feeling of decay and a slight fustiness about the place, which even the insolent gaze of the modern tour groups had somehow been unable to dispel. Opposite the bathhouse, she found a staircase which led steeply down into some dormitory-like rooms, and from there out into the gardens. But in these rooms, so small and cramped that they could only have been occupied by rank and file women, the planks were so rotten that she nearly put her foot through one of them.

Returning to the courtyard she found herself at the entrance to the Valide Sultan's apartments. A series of interconnected rooms, still surprisingly small, but decorated as the eunuchs' corridor had been with the same turquoise, blue and green tiles; the same curious pale green light. Elizabeth half thought that the guard might have followed her in here, but he had not. She listened, but there was not a sound.

When she was sure that she was entirely alone, Elizabeth sat down on a raised divan next to a window and waited. She closed her eyes and tried to concentrate, but nothing came. No connections at all. She trailed her hand along the tiles, tracing their patterns of peacock feathers, carnations, tulips – but still nothing. She got up again and made a thorough search of the apartment, but it was the same everywhere. Even the discovery of a series of hidden but interconnecting wooden passageways behind the Valide's main rooms, bedroom, prayer room and sitting room, did nothing to decrease her sense of detachment from the place.

These rooms are simply – empty, she thought. And then, half-laughing at herself: well, what did you expect?

Elizabeth was about to leave the Valide's apartments altogether when, in the tiny entrance vestibule, she caught sight of a closed door. She put her hand to it, expecting it to be locked as the others had been, but to her surprise it opened easily and she found herself standing on the threshold of a disused apartment.

It was quite a large room; by far the largest in the harem, apart from the Valide's own suite, to which it was connected, but not, as far as Elizabeth could make out, a part of it. For a moment or two, she hesitated on the threshold. Then quickly she took two paces into the room.

More fustiness. Winter light filtering through small holes in an overhead cupola. Carpets, their edges frayed and rotting, lined the floor. Beyond, another door and a courtyard she had not seen before. A room filled with the breath of the past, like the distant roar of the sea.

For a moment or two Elizabeth stood quite still. *Careful. Careful now*. Not breathing this time, but listening. *You're listening. What are you listening for?* But in the now deserted harem there was not a sound, not a footfall.

Cautiously, Elizabeth took a few more steps into the room; stood there, feeling like a trespasser this time, her heart hammering in her chest. Still silence. With the toe of her boot she lifted up the corner of one of the carpets. Pieces of decomposing raffia matting lay beneath. A raised platform took up most of the centre of the room. When she looked more carefully she saw that it was still covered in old coverlets and cushions. They seemed to her to be lying exactly as the last occupant must have left them. Was it her imagination, or could she actually make out the imprint of a woman's body?

Don't be a fool! Elizabeth shook herself, found she was shivering suddenly. She recalled an old black and white photograph she had once seen, taken after slavery had been officially abolished and the last Sultan's harem disbanded in 1924. It showed six of his ex-concubines, unfortunates who had remained unclaimed by their relatives, on their way 'to exhibit themselves', so the caption had read, in Vienna. Their faces, stripped naked, stared palely out from beneath black shrouds. Incurious, a little grumpy even, they returned the camera's gaze, looking more like novice nuns, Elizabeth thought, than the well-fleshed odalisques of Western imagination.

She looked around her. The walls here too were lined with green and blue tiles. In places there were cupboards, their doors hanging off the hinges; in others small alcoves for storing things. Just then there was a movement in the corner of her eye. Startled, she turned, but it was just a pair of pigeons whirling into flight in the courtyard beyond. Their wings made a tearing sound in the cold air.

Elizabeth turned back into the room. She sat down gingerly on the edge of the platform and opened her notebook, but somehow she could not concentrate. Perhaps it was the atmosphere of the place, the sense that she was violating some private space, that made her nervous. Despite the cold the palms of her hands were clammy and the pen kept slipping in her fingers. In one of the little alcoves she saw a glint of blue. Elizabeth leant over and picked it up carefully. It lay in her palm, a tiny chip of blue and white glass.

It was then that she heard it.

Not pigeons' wings this time but the sound of laughter, and a woman running past the door on little slippered feet.

Chapter 16

Constantinople: 2 September 1599

Afternoon

'Y ou sent for me, Safiye Sultan.'
      'Is it done?'
'It is done, Majesty, just as you said.'
The Valide's *kira*, the Jewess Esperanza Malchi, stood in the shadows. Her eyesight was no longer good; through long practice, she felt, rather than saw, the shadowy outline of the Queen where she lay in the darkness. There were no windows at all in the innermost sanctum, the most private chamber in the Queen's withdrawing chambers. Even in the oppressive heat of summer the room was always fresh, made so by the thickness of the walls, the coolness of their tiles, with their soaring arabesques of blue and milky green, like so many fronds of seaweed in an underwater cavern. In the middle of the floor, lumps of some sweet-smelling resin burned on a small brazier.

'And so, Malchi?' The figure stirred in the darkness. 'The Haseki's parcel has been delivered?'

'Cariye Lala was there as you said; I handed it to her myself.' The Jewess addressed herself to the shadows. She hesitated, then added, 'I don't like it, Majesty. Cariye Lala is—' she checked herself, aware of the need to choose the word with care, 'forgetful these days. How do we know she'll hide it safely?'

There was a pause.

'Cariye Lala can be trusted, that's all you need to know. She will hide the parcel in the Haseki's room until we need it.' There was a faint smile in the beautiful voice. 'When it's found, Gulay Haseki will be implicated completely. Not even the Sultan himself will be able to save her then.'

'The physician didn't like it.' Esperanza shifted uneasily. 'I'm not sure he'll be persuaded to do it again.'

There was another short silence while Safiye digested this information.

'Well, I can't say I'm altogether surprised,' she sighed. 'Although it's not as if he hasn't done it before.'

'But that was years ago,' Esperanza said. 'I told him we may not need it. There are signs that the other plan may be working.'

'True.' Safiye Sultan considered this. 'The Haseki must be . . . put aside, that's all. I don't really care how. She has too great a hold on the Sultan; he doesn't even look at any of the other *cariyes*. This is not a good state of affairs. He must be helped to do so, that's all. For the good of us all.'

A smouldering lump of resin flared briefly into a small red flame. It illuminated the clusters of diamonds on Safiye Sultan's girdle, at her ears and buttoned down her bodice, a king's ransom of jewels, making them glitter briefly. On her finger, Nurbanu's emerald winked like a green eye.

'And the other business?' Esperanza ventured.

The velvety figure stirred slightly, and then was still again. 'They found him, as I'm sure you've heard. Wandering about just inside the palace walls.'

'Impossible!' The Valide's *kira* wrung her hands. 'He was as good as dead.'

'Oh?' Once again there was a faint smile in the beautiful voice. 'If you think that, then you don't know Hassan Aga as I do. Little Nightingale may not be a man, but he has the strength of ten of them.'

'But how did he escape? He was right here, in the cell, right beneath our very feet. There was no way out except through this room . . .'

'There is a way. The harem is full of ways. But that's not for you to know, Malchi.'

Esperanza bowed her head in acquiescence. 'They're saying that it's the English ship.'

'Who says that it's the English ship?'

'But I thought that Hassan Aga himself said . . .'

'Hassan Aga said no such thing.' Safiye gave a short laugh. 'It was the eunuch Hyacinth who said it, because I told him to.'

'But – why?' Esperanza was bemused.

'Why?' Safiye regarded her *kira* thoughtfully. 'I always forget with you, Malchi. You know so much about us, but you have never lived as one of us.' She shrugged. 'Call it a hunting trick, if you like.' She saw Esperanza's look of bewilderment. 'If your prey feels safe, it gets careless,' she explained slowly, as if to a child. 'Don't you see: if whoever really poisoned Little Nightingale thinks we've all been fooled by that sugar toy, they'll show their hand eventually. This way we'll flush them out into the open.'

'And the English?'

'I had one of their cooks arrested, the man who made the sweet-meat. Someone who is entirely expendable,' Safiye said carelessly. 'If they have any sense – which I think they do – they won't squeal too much. They want their Capitulations too badly for that. Then later we'll just quietly let him go.'

'And when Little Nightingale recovers?'

'He won't betray us because those were the rules. The Nightingales. We were all agreed.'

At the Valide's signal, Esperanza made as if to leave. Then at the door, she hesitated. 'There is one other thing, Majesty.'

'Speak then.'

'Your girl. The new one. The one they used to call Annetta.'

'Ayshe?'

'Yes.'

'She was in the room with the Sultan's new concubine.'

Safiye Sultan considered this for a moment. 'Did they see you?'

'Yes. But they believe that I did not see them.'

'They hid from you?'

'Yes.' A thoughtful silence. 'Is it possible that she knows something?'

'Ayshe?' Slowly Safiye Sultan pulled one of the fur wraps around her shoulders. 'No, I don't think so.' Another small lump of resin was dislodged in the brazier. A small flame hissed, illuminating the room briefly. 'It's the other girl, the one they call Kaya. Celia. She's the one, Malchi. She's the one we have to watch.'

✻ ✻ ✻

When Esperanza had gone, Safiye lay back amongst her cushions again, drawing her solitude luxuriously around her like a cloak. It was not often she indulged herself in such moments.

Most of the women Safiye had known retained only shadowy memories of where they came from, of whom they had been before they entered the harem's domain. But Safiye Sultan, the Mother of God's Shadow Upon Earth, remembered her former life very well: the sharp spines of the Albanian mountains; the colour of the sky, as blue as gentians; the cruel sharpness of stones against her bare feet.

Her father, Petko, like almost all the men in those parts, lived in their village only in the winter months. In the summer, he and the other men made their way up into the fastness of the mountains, where they camped in caves, or in the open air, living by their wits, with only their dogs and their lutes for company. Safiye remembered the strange sight of them, barbarous figures they had seemed to her even then, with tattoos inked across their broad cheekbones and along their forearms, their shaggy sheep pelt coats reaching down to their ankles.

The women stayed down below, and seemed lighter-hearted somehow, without their men-folk. Safiye's mother, a pale-skinned beauty from the Dalmatian sea-coast near Scutari, had been bought by her father-in-law for a bride price of ten sheep. She was just twelve when she was married to Safiye's father, and had never been into the mountains before. Although it was often said that the Albanian mountain men did not have much use for their females, preferring the company of their male clansmen, she gave birth to eight children in as many years, all of whom died except for Safiye and her brother, Mihal. The harsh mountain sun soon weathered Safiye's mother's beautiful cheeks; her belly and breasts sagged like an old woman's. By the age of thirty she was worn out. Her husband often beat her, smashing her face so badly one time that he broke both her front teeth, and dislocated her jaw. She rarely spoke after that, except to whisper to her daughter the stories and lullabies that she had learnt as a child from her Venetian grandmother, snatches of songs in the dialect of the Veneto, the tongue of their ancient overlords, which she had thought long forgotten, but which now, since that blow, ran round and around, word perfect, inside her head.

138

Safiye grew up to be as pale skinned as her mother had been, but with the strength and agility of a boy. Headstrong and unafraid, she was always her father's favourite. Her brother, a snivelling sickly child who had been born with a limp, cringed whenever his father came near him, and so it was Safiye, his small daughter, he took with him to the mountains.

Safiye went everywhere with her father, like a mascot. In the summer when he took her up to live in the high pastures with the other clansmen, she wore leather chaps and a piece of sheepskin slung over one shoulder like a boy. From her father she learnt how to trap the wild mountain hares and skin them, how to lay fires, and even how to whittle arrows for her own small bow. She learnt how to leap between the crags of rock, surefooted as a goat, and how to keep cover when they hunted, lying next to her father silently for hours, crouched behind rocks or hidden beneath piles of leaves. She was so proud to be with him, and with the other men, that she would have cut out her own tongue rather than complain. No matter if thorns tore at her bare feet, or if her mouth was so dry with thirst that it stuck to the roof of her mouth, or if the stone floor of the cave bit into her shoulders at night.

Hunting tricks, my little maid, her father would say. And her first lesson, she would realise many years later, in survival.

She was twelve when the slave collectors came to their village: strange men sent by their Ottoman overlords, they rode on horses with jingling harnesses, their saddlebags and turbans and silk robes a blaze of such textures and jewelled colours that it made Safiye and her brother gasp and stare. Their village, Rezi, was small, and so collecting the boy tribute – one boy to be given up by each Christian family living within the Ottoman Sultan's dominions – did not take long.

'Will they take Mihal, too?' Safiye asked, observing her brother dispassionately.

'Mihal? What good would he be? A boy must have either brains or brawn to serve the Sultan.' Her father's voice was sour. 'And besides, they would never take an only son.'

Standing at the front of the ragged little group of villagers who had gathered to see the caravan leave, Safiye observed the five boys, aged between seven and ten, who had been selected by the tribute-takers.

They wore garlands crudely woven from wild flowers and grasses on their heads. Their families seemed to be rejoicing rather than grieving at this sudden turn in their fortunes. As the caravan moved off some of the young men from the village ran alongside the horses, whooping and banging drums. Others scrambled on to the overhanging branches of the trees, and threw petals before the horses' feet. In a cloud of gunpowder, the tribute-takers let off their muskets in a farewell salute.

Throughout all this the boys stared back impassively at the knot of villagers. Already, it seemed to Safiye, they looked taller and somehow older, possessed of an instinctive knowledge that these first few jingling steps down along the valley pathway had in fact taken them across a far greater divide, wider and deeper than any mountain crevasse, which had already separated them for ever from their families, and was never again to be breached.

She pulled at her father's sleeve. 'If they won't take Mihal, let them take me.'

'You?' he laughed. 'You are just a girl. Why would they take you?'

An old man who had been standing behind them wiped his cheek, but his eyes were bright. 'They are *kul* – the slaves of the Sultan, now.'

'But what slaves!' others put in. 'Our sons will rule the Sultan's lands. They will become soldiers and janissaries . . .'

'They will be pashas . . .!'

'My grandson will be the next Grand Vizier!'

Talking amongst themselves the villagers made their way back into their houses. Only Safiye stayed staring after the caravan, the boys no more than dots now on the mountain path below them. The silver stirrups of the horsemen flashed in the sun.

'Don't worry, my maid: when little girls become slaves of the Sultan, it is quite another thing,' her father laughed, pinching her cheek. 'We'll find you a good husband soon enough – right here.'

A husband! At the very word something sharp and hard lodged in Safiye's breast like a stone.

'So they've found you a husband, sister, have you heard?'

Mihal lay beside her on the mattress they shared, the greasy felt coverlet pulled up round his bony shoulders.

'Who?'

'Todor.'

'Todor, our father's friend?'

'He has offered twenty sheep for you.'

Safiye did not doubt Mihal. Although they had never been close, a certain uneasy alliance had always existed between them. Mihal, who with his withered leg would never be a huntsman or a *banditto* like the other clansmen of the Dukagjin mountains, none the less had an ability, which she admired very much: the ability to watch and listen, to move about almost unseen in the village and the surrounding pastures. He did not seem to resent his sister's pre-eminence in their father's affections; she, in turn, often found his information useful.

Through a crack in the wall Safiye could just make out the silhouettes of the village houses, bathed in silent moonlight. In the mountains a wolf bayed at the stars. After a while she said, 'But Todor is old.' Her voice, in her own ears, sounded very small.

'But he can still do it.' Mihal sniggered, thrusting his hips up against the back of her thighs. 'He'll mount you like an old bull.'

Safiye dug her elbow as hard as she could into her brother's bony rib cage. 'Get off me. You're disgusting.'

'Not half as disgusting as Todor.' Mihal sniggered again, louder this time, and a piece of snot flew out of one of his nostrils. He wiped it away with a corner of the thin coverlet. 'I've heard him boasting. A young wife always gets the old ones going again.' Safiye could smell Mihal's breath, rank against her neck. If a boy smelt this bad, how much worse would be the smell of an old man?

'Get away from me!' She wriggled away from him, wrenching as much of the coverlet as she could with her. Then, trying not to sound hopeful. 'Anyway, I know you're making it up.' But she knew he was not. There was one thing about Mihal that could be relied on: he never lied. He did not have to.

'And you won't be able to go to the mountains any more, because he won't let you.'

At first Safiye did not reply. A feeling of such dread gripped her throat she could hardly breathe. 'Our father would stop him ever doing that . . .'

'You think so?' Mihal paused again, his last and most poisoned barb poised for the kill. 'Why, you fool, can't you see? It's all his idea in the first place. You can't go on being his little toy for ever, you know.'

At first her father did not believe that she would dare to disobey him. Later, he beat her, and when that did no good he locked her in the sheep corral. For six days they brought her no food, only water to drink, until she was so hungry she was reduced to scraping moss and lichen from the stones, sucking the flakes from beneath her blackened fingernails. The hut was too low for her to stand up in, and the smell of her own filth made her retch, but still she would not relent. At first, she was surprised at her own strength of mind. But after a few days she realised that if you wanted something badly enough, it was not all that hard.

'I would rather die,' she shouted at them when they came to talk to her, 'than be sold like a sheep to that old man.'

When the hunger visions came she thought she saw her mother's grandmother. Sometimes she was dressed like a Venetian lady with pearls at her throat; at other times she was in blue, like the painting of the Madonna in the church at Scutari, which her mother had once told her about. Almost always she was riding a horse, her silver stirrups flashing in the sun.

When they brought her out on the seventh day they had to carry her into the house. It was Mihal, of course, who told her what had been decided. 'If you won't be married,' he shrugged, 'you'll have to be sold.'

It was then that she knew she had won.

Two weeks later Safiye was sold to Esther Nasi, the Jewess of Scutari. Esther conducted her business from her own house, an elegant mansion built in the Ottoman style, which looked out on one side over the lake and on the other towards the ancient Venetian fortress. Rumoured to have once been a slave herself, the concubine of a rich provincial governor from the Balkans, Esther retained, despite her great size, the face and haughty demeanour of a Byzantine princess.

When Safiye was brought to her she showed no surprise. It was not unusual for families to sell a pretty daughter into slavery, hoping to secure for her a life of luxury in the protective confines of some rich man's harem. Sometimes, indeed, it was the girls themselves who desired it, taking their fate into their own hands. But with this group it was hard to tell.

'What have you brought her to me for? She's skin and bones.' The Jewess pinched Safiye's arm just below her shoulder and then the inside flesh of her upper thigh. 'What have you been doing to the child? She looks half starved.'

'She'll soon fatten.' The father, whose facial tattoos identified him immediately as a mountain dweller, spoke awkwardly, shuffling his feet. Esther Nasi saw the girl glance towards him, her face inscrutable, and then quickly back again.

'To be frank, I'm not so sure . . .'

Sunlight caught the planes and sharp angles of the girl's half-starved face. She had something, Esther thought, there was no doubt of it. Unlike so many of the peasant girls who came to the Scutari establishment, she did not shrink or cringe away from Esther's gaze, but held her head up, examining with a level gaze the rich carpets, the milky green and blue tiles from Iznik, the marble floors and carved casements. All the same, Esther reminded herself, it was the flesh that counted. The girl's skin was already burnt – ruined, very probably – by exposure to the mountain sun. How tiresome it all was: Esther sighed, and rolled her kohl-darkened eyes so that the whites showed very white. Perhaps she was getting too old to be running a business.

'All right, then. Let me look at her, but be quick, I haven't got all day.'

With her strong old woman's fingers she grasped Safiye's shoulder, turning her arm out, and running an expert thumb along the tender inside skin. Where the sun had not burnt her, it was quite white and fine-grained; so were the broad lids of her eyes. The space between her lids and brow bones, Esther noticed, was high and beautifully moulded. She slipped her finger quickly inside the girl's mouth, counting her teeth, inspecting their whiteness. Her fingers, Safiye would always remember, tasted sweet, like powdered sugar.

'Does she snore? Have bad breath? Has she ever been with a man?' She might have been talking about a farm animal. 'A brother, uncle? You, her father?'

'No Signora.'

'You'd be surprised how often it happens,' Esther sniffed. 'Well, I

143

can check that soon enough. And be assured I always do. There is a market in second-hand goods, but not with me.'

She clapped her hands together and a king's ransom of golden bangles, thin as paper, cascaded down her wrists.

'Walk!' she commanded.

Safiye walked slowly over to the window and back again.

'Here, put these on.' Esther handed the girl a pair of pattens, four inches high, the wood inlaid with ivory flowers. 'Let's see if you can walk in these.'

Safiye walked again, less certainly this time, and teetering with the unexpected height. The wooden heels clacked loudly on the floor.

'No good.' Esther clicked her tongue against her teeth. 'No good at all – thin *and* clumsy,' she added plaintively. 'Why do you come here, wasting my time?'

The three men turned to go, but the girl did not follow them. Instead, she remained standing calmly in front of Esther Nasi.

'I can sing and I can speak the Venetian language.' It was the first time that she had spoken in front of Esther. 'My mother taught me.'

Esther's black eyebrows, painted together, Ottoman style, in a single black line, shot up quizzically. 'Is that so?'

Safiye handed the little pattens back. 'And I can soon learn to walk in these.'

For a moment Esther did not say anything. Then her eyes narrowed shrewdly. 'Sing something for me then.'

So Safiye sang one of the lullabies that her mother had taught her. Her voice was not strong, but it was low and pure: a voice which, once heard, was never to be forgotten, and which, although she could not then know it, was to change her life for ever.

In the early days of her business there were those who said that Esther Nasi's establishment was too far from the great slave trading centres of Constantinople and Alexandria to be feasible. But with her woman's instincts and her sharp business head, Esther had always known what she was about, and her establishment on the lakeside in Scutari quickly become famous as a halfway house. Traders not wishing to make the long and arduous sea journey all the way to Constantinople brought her the finest of their crop, for which she always paid generously, knowing that by the time she had finished with them, these raw mountain girls, these ignorant fishermen's daughters, would fetch more than fifty times their price in *bedestens* throughout the Ottoman empire. Soon, some of the shrewder traders from the capital, those who specialised in supplying high-quality slaves and concubines to imperial harems, found it more than worth their while to make the journey to Scutari once or twice a year, where they could pick up Esther's exquisite handiwork for less than half the price they would pay in Constantinople.

Esther Nasi kept Safiye with her for a year. About a dozen other girls aged between six and thirteen – whom Esther both bought and sold, as she had done for several decades now, through a succession of dealers who plied their trade along the scented and pine-fringed shores of the Adriatic Sea – came and went during that time.

Many of the girls were Albanians, like Safiye herself, or from other parts of the Balkan interior, brought down from the mountains to be sold by their own parents in the hope of a better life for their daughters; others were captives, taken by Uskok and Ottoman corsairs in raids along the coast, or in attacks against unprotected ships sailing on the Adriatic Sea. There were two Greeks, a Serb, two little sisters from Venice, no more than eight years old, and one poor Circassian girl; no one seemed quite sure how she had come there, far, far from home.

As for Safiye, she watched and she waited. She did not mix with the other girls, who regarded her as aloof. Instead, she concentrated on what Esther Nasi could teach her. It was from Esther that she learnt not only how to refine her singing voice, but also to accompany herself on the lute. She learnt how to walk, how to eat, how to enter and leave a room, how to embroider and sew. She learnt something of the refined manners and etiquette of the Ottoman court: how to pour coffee and sherbet, how to stand for hours behind her mistress, hands clasped demurely at her back.

On the special milk diet that Esther devised for her, and deprived now of the physical exercise she had always been used to, her skinny twelve-year-old body soon filled out. Her breasts, which had been no bigger than unripened figs, swelled. For six months she was forbidden to go outside and, with the help of Esther's preparations, the skin of her face and hands became as white and smooth as a child's; her arms and cheeks plump and pink.

A few months after Safiye was taken into Esther Nasi's establishment, a commotion in the courtyard announced the arrival of a trader. Half an hour later, Esther herself came to the girls' quarters.

'You, you – and you.' She pointed peremptorily to the Serb and two of the older Albanians. 'Come with me. One of you will pour the coffee, the other two will bring the basin and napkins for him to wash his hands. Then you will come and stand behind me, and wait for my instructions. Prepare yourselves, quickly now.' She clapped her hands. 'And you –' swinging round suddenly, she let her sharp gaze fall upon Safiye, 'you come with me.'

'But shan't I dress first?'

'No need.'

Safiye followed Esther to a small room which led off from the large first-storey reception room where Esther showed off her wares to visiting traders. It was separated from the main room by a screen, through which Safiye could see, but not be seen.

'I want you to sit here. And when I tell you to, you will sing for me. But no matter what is said, you must not come out, you must not show yourself. Do you understand?'

'Yes, Signora.'

Through the screen Safiye could see the trader reclining upon Esther's embroidered cushions. He was a wiry little man with a seafarer's weather-beaten face, but his cloak, Safiye noticed, was lined with the most sumptuous fur she had ever seen.

'I hear that you may have something for me – something special,' the trader said.

'Indeed I do.'

Esther raised her hand and signalled to the Serb girl to step forwards. She sang two songs, accompanying herself on a lute.

'Very pretty,' the man remarked without enthusiasm when she had finished. 'I congratulate you, Signora Esther. But are you sure you have nothing else?' His eyes roamed around the room, to the other two girls now standing demurely behind their mistress.

'Well . . .' Esther seemed to hesitate. 'As a matter of fact, since it is you, Yusuf Bey,' she said with exaggerated politeness, 'there *is* something else that I think may interest you.'

She clicked her fingers and, as she had been bidden, Safiye began to sing. When she had finished there was a long silence.

The trader, when he spoke at last, was blunt. 'May I see her?'

Esther Nasi smiled at him and took a sip of coffee, replacing the cup, so tiny she could have used it as a thimble, carefully on its saucer. On her wrists the golden bangles whispered softly. 'No.'

The man was visibly taken aback. 'Why ever not?'

'Because she is not for sale.'

'Not for sale?'

'I have my reasons.'

'She has some defect? A harelip, or a birthmark?'

'A defect in one of my girls?' Esther smiled complacently, sinking her teeth into one of her favourite rose-petal-flavoured sweets. 'You know me better than that, I think.'

'She is too old then?'

'Ha, ha!' Esther sucked the fine white sugar dust from her fingers. Her black Byzantine eyes flashed witheringly.

'May I see her at least?'

'No.'

And no matter what arguments he used, Esther refused to allow him to see Safiye, or even to hear her sing again, insisting that she was not for sale.

After that, whenever the traders came Esther followed the same strategy. She hid Safiye behind a screen so that she could be heard but not seen, and insisted that she was not for sale. As the mystery spread, so Safiye's fame grew. Rumours abounded: she was said to be a Venetian princess, the illegitimate daughter of the Pope, even Esther Nasi's own child.

Six months went by, and Yusuf Bey arrived for his summer visit. He found Esther Nasi fatter than ever, strands of grey peppering her once pure onyx locks.

'So, Signora Esther *effendi*, are you ready to sell to me yet?'

Popping a honeyed pastry between her lips, Esther settled her huge bulk comfortably into the cushions of her divan. 'No, not yet.'

The trader considered her for some moments in silence.

'If I might be permitted an observation,' he said after a while, 'you have so cleverly arranged things that any one of us will buy her from you, sight unseen, probably for more than ten times what you paid for her. In our business you are held in the highest possible esteem, Signora. But don't you think we might all get a little bored with this game?'

Selecting another pastry for herself, Esther seemed unperturbed. 'Believe me, Yusuf Bey, I know what I am doing.' She licked the flakes from her fingers. 'You'll see. It'll be worth the wait.'

'So you will sell her then?' Esther regarded him consideringly for a moment. 'This is a prize worth waiting for. What can you offer me in return?'

'The new young prince at Manisa.'

'What of him?'

'The Sultan Suleiman is getting old, he can't last many more years. His son Selim, who is his heir, they say is a drunkard, but Suleiman has a grandson by Selim who is said to be a more likely prince. Although the grandson is very young still, he has recently been appointed provincial governor of Manisa. In Constantinople this is taken as a sign not just of great favour, but of great political importance, for in all likelihood it will be this prince, Murad, who will be chosen to succeed his father.

Murad is still young, but not too young to have his own household in Manisa. His cousin, Princess Humashah, sent her *kira* to me, with the request that I find suitable slave girls – concubines of the highest possible quality – whom she can bestow on her cousin as a gift.' He paused. 'I think the princess would be very grateful indeed for a prize like this.' He took a small sip of coffee. 'How old is she?'

'Thirteen.'

'The prince is sixteen.'

Esther Nasi considered Yusuf Bey's proposal for what he thought to be an unnecessarily long amount of time.

'I have to confess, the girl is getting restless,' she said eventually. 'And between ourselves I doubt there is much more I can teach her.'

'She has had her courses?'

'Six months ago now.'

'And you have taught her *everything* . . .'

'She knows how to please a man, if that's what you mean.' Esther brushed away the question impatiently. 'I taught her myself. You traders – if *I* might now be permitted an observation – have such crude ideas about all that.'

'She is beautiful, then?'

'Beautiful? Ah, Yusuf Bey, my friend,' she leant towards him, and as she did so, the trader saw two tears, the size and translucency of pearls, fall from Esther Nasi's eyes, 'as beautiful as a witch.'

As she always knew she would, Esther sold Safiye of the beautiful voice to Yusuf Bey for three hundred ducats, more than ten times what she paid for her. And in Constantinople, Yusuf Bey sold her for nearly ten times that again to the Princess Humashah, who thought it money well spent.

As for Safiye, she made the journey to Constantinople, and from there to Manisa, a gift to the sixteen-year-old future Sultan. With her were two other gifts of slaves, the finest that the Princess Humashah's imperial purse could buy.

One, whom the girl Safiye would learn to call Cariye Mihrimah, was a child about the same age as Safiye herself. The other was a young black eunuch called Hassan.

'But the princess has given you all another name,' Safiye could remember the slave traders saying to her. 'From now on you will be called the Nightingales. The Nightingales of Manisa.'

Chapter 17

Constantinople: 2 September 1599

Late afternoon

L ate that afternoon there came a knock at Celia's door. A black servant girl, elegantly dressed, and wearing many gold chains around her neck and ankles, stood before her. She said nothing when she saw Celia, but smiled and beckoned her to follow. When Celia asked where she was taking her, or who had sent her, she merely shook her head and refused to speak.

They passed through the courtyard, and then some antechambers which flanked the Valide's bathrooms, and along several corridors though which Celia had never ventured before. After some time they came to a small door in a wall. The girl opened it, and Celia saw that it led to a flight of steps. Although they passed several people – some of them merely servants, but one or two high-ranking harem officials – they showed no surprise when they saw the girl. No one questioned her, or asked where she was going. They merely bowed respectfully to Celia, and with lowered eyes allowed the two girls to pass silently by.

At the bottom of the stairs they emerged from another doorway into the palace gardens. The girl took a pathway that led first down a series of terraces, and then turned sharply to the right, skirting along the periphery of the palace walls. Eventually they came out in a small clearing.

'Oh!' Suddenly Celia saw where they were. In the middle of the clearing was a marble pavilion. Beyond it, on one side, the city of Constantinople lay stretched out before them; on the other, like a distant blue dream, the sea.

For the first time now, the girl gave a signal to Celia in the silent language of the palace: a signal instructing her that she should now go forwards on her own. *Who?* Celia signed back to her, but the girl gave her one last shy smile, turned and walked swiftly away.

Celia looked around her. It was so quiet in the garden that at first she thought she was alone. The pavilion, its white marble walls decorated with golden lettering, glowed in the sun. Somewhere, out of sight amongst the cypress trees, water played into a stone basin. Then suddenly a small movement caught her eye, and she saw that, after all, she was not alone.

There was a person waiting in the kiosk. She had her back to Celia, and had been sitting very still, looking out over the waters of the Bosphorous: the very last person that Celia had ever expected to see.

'Dear lady, it's kind of you to come so quickly. I am honoured, *kadin.*'

'Haseki Sultan,' Celia bowed very low to the little figure in the pavilion, 'the honour is all mine.'

Gulay Haseki held out her hand to Celia. 'Forgive me for not standing up – I mean no discourtesy. It's just, well, as you can see,' she pointed to her legs, which were tucked up under her, 'it's not one of my strong days today.'

The Haseki, the Sultan's official favourite, wore a robe of pale blue, embroidered with a delicate gold motif of scrolls and flowers. On her head was a tiny cap, to which was pinned a veil of almost transparent gold tissue. Beneath the hem of her robe, Celia saw, were two small slippers, embroidered with silver and gold thread. Many jewels, as befitted her status as the second most high-ranking woman in the harem after the Valide, shone at her neck and on her fingers. But when she smiled she seemed to Celia to be almost as shy as her little mute serving maid.

'It is true then, what they say . . .' Before she could stop herself, the words were out of Celia's mouth.

'What do they say?'

'That you are not well – but forgive me,' Celia said, ashamed by how crude her words sounded, 'it was I who meant no discourtesy.'

'I know that.' When she spoke the Haseki's voice was very gentle and low. 'It's always the same, isn't it? Everything here is rumour and

151

surmise, whispers.' She looked out to sea, where the little boats floated like children's cut-outs on the horizon. 'But for once it's really true. I'm not well. I shall be glad not to be part of it any more.'

'Are you . . . are you going somewhere?' Celia asked.

When the Haseki turned to Celia again her eyes were very bright. 'In a manner of speaking, *kadin*, yes; I suppose you could say that. I have asked if they will send me to the Eski Saray, the old palace. After all, that's where we will all be sent after the Sultan's death anyway.'

Although Celia had often seen Gulay Haseki before, it had almost always been on formal occasions. Then she had appeared as a distant figure, solitary and bejewelled, at the Sultan's side; an object of intense speculation amongst the other women in the harem. Now, for the first time, Celia studied her closely. Although she was older than Celia had expected, and slender to the point of thinness, her skin was still fine and very pale. It was always said there were many more beautiful girls in the harem, but Celia could now see that her face had a softness about it, and a sweetness of expression which could never have been detected from a distance. There was something about her mere presence that was restful. Her eyes were both dark and blue, the exact colour, Celia thought, of deep sea.

Then, as if bestirring herself from her daydreams, she gave the signal for Celia to sit.

'*Kadin* – for that is what we must all call you now, is that not so? – dear lady, please, let's have no formalities here, we don't have all that much time. I have brought you here because I wanted to tell you something.'

Instinctively Celia glanced around to see who might be listening.

'Don't worry,' the Haseki saw her look, 'there is no one to hear us, I've made quite sure of that. I wanted you to know that I bear you no ill will.'

'Please, Haseki Sultan . . .' Celia began, but before she could say any more the favourite had quickly put her finger to Celia's lips.

'Shh, we both know what I mean.'

'But I don't want . . . I've never wanted . . .'

'It's not about what you want. It's about what *she* wants. We both know that. I have tried fighting her, but it's no good. She's set everyone against me, and she'll do the same to you – no, no, please, hear what I have to say,' she said when she saw that Celia was about to protest. 'No one – none of us – can stay close to the Sultan for long while she is Valide. It is my fate. I must accept it. Besides, look at me,' she looked down at herself with a wistful smile, 'I've grown so thin. Why should the Sultan want to be saddled with such a bag of bones? And anyway,' she glanced up at Celia and then away again quickly, 'I don't want to end up like Handan.'

'Handan?'

'Surely you have heard of Handan?'

'No, Haseki Sultan.'

'She was the Sultan's chief concubine before me. He has other bedfellows, of course, but she was more than that to him: she was his companion. As I am. The Sultan – the Padishah—' she stopped, and searched the horizon again, as if it were an effort for her to speak of these things, 'he is a lonely man sometimes. You must remember that.'

'What happened to her? To Handan.'

'She has a son, Prince Ahmet, who still lives in the palace with the other princes, but Handan herself, well, no one sees her now, she who was once raised so high above us all.' Gulay looked sadly out to sea. 'They say she stays in her room. That she has lost the will to live.'

'But why?'

Gulay turned to Celia again, and for a moment her expression changed into something more. 'What's your name, *kadin*?'

'My name is Kaya.'

'No, no, dear lady, I know that of course! I mean your real name, the name you had before you came here.'

'It was – it is – Celia.'

'Well then, Celia,' the Haseki took Celia's hand between her own, 'I am forgetting that you have not been here as long as most of us have. The Valide hates Handan because she became too powerful. Not only was she the Sultan's favourite, but she had given birth to a son. A son who might be – who still could be – the next sultan.' She stroked Celia's hand softly. 'As both the mother of a son and a favourite, her stipend became very great, second only to that of the Valide herself. The Sultan also gave her many gifts – jewels and gold. Soon she began to notice the power these things gave her. Handan had grown powerful, but not wise.

153

'With her considerable wealth she could now afford to give many gifts, but she grew careless about who saw her do it. Many women in the harem, even senior ones loyal to the Valide, began to court her. If the Sultan were to name Handan's son as his successor, you could see them thinking, then she would be the next Valide. And you could see Handan thinking the same thing too. Gradually a palace faction grew up about her, everyone felt it.' As if the subject still made her nervous, Gulay glanced over her shoulder, towards the palace. 'You don't need me to tell you what it can be like here. It became a very dangerous situation.'

'For Safiye Sultan?'

'For the Valide?' The Haseki laughed, squeezing Celia's hand. The little golden discs sewn into her cap made a glassy sound in the breeze. 'No, dear lady. Not for the Valide, for Handan of course. Safiye Sultan doesn't mind who sleeps in her son's bed, but she'll never give up her power, not ever. When she was Haseki, in the days of the old Sultan, they say she fought tooth and nail with the Valide Nurbanu. But it's the Valide who always holds the trump cards,' she lowered her eyes, 'so they say.'

There was a pause, and then Celia said, 'But you have a son, too, Haseki Sultan.'

'Yes, I do. He has an equal claim to be the next sultan. And I must do everything I can to protect him. You see, I saw what they did to Handan . . .' She bent forwards until her lips were just inches away from Celia's own. Celia could smell her skin and hair, perfumed with jasmine and myrrh. 'Remember this, *kadin*: to be the Haseki is no protection from *them*.'

'What do you mean, them?' Celia put her hand to her stomach; the familiar pain had returned in her side, just below her ribs.

'The Valide has spies everywhere, both in and outside the palace, even in the most unexpected places. She has spent a whole lifetime accumulating them. A web – a web of loyalties, of people who will do her business for her. Like that old jewess, her *kira*—'

'You mean Esperanza Malchi?'

'That's right: Malchi. You know her?'

'She came to my room only this morning.' Celia shifted nervously on the cushions. 'I don't think she realised I was there.'

Should she confide to the Haseki what had happened? Surely she was the last person in the harem who would ever help her, and yet she seemed so earnest, so vulnerable. Surely she could trust her?

In the end it was Gulay herself who spoke. 'And she left some coloured sand?'

'Yes,' Celia whispered, staring at her, 'but how did you know? What does it mean?'

'Don't look so anxious; it's unlikely to be anything that can harm you – not yet anyway.'

Not yet? Celia's heart bounded in her chest.

'My friend Annetta was there too. She thinks it's some kind of spell.'

'A spell!' the Haseki exclaimed. Then she smiled charmingly. 'I know she looks like a witch, but no. Probably just a charm against the Evil Eye – look, like this one.' She lifted up her wrist to show Celia a fine silver bracelet, from which hung several little discs of blue glass. 'We wear these for good luck. For protection. Don't you see, they need you – for the moment. Malchi is the creature of the Valide, she wouldn't dare do anything to harm you. But one thing's for sure,' she gave Celia another of her searching looks, 'you must be very careful. They're watching you already.'

The Haseki drew back against her cushions again, as though the effort of talking had tired her out.

'Is that what you wanted to tell me?'

Gulay shook her head. 'Esperanza's not the one you need to watch out for,' she went on, speaking quickly now, 'there are others, others who are far more dangerous. Handan knew it, too. Have you ever heard talk of the Nightingales?'

Celia shook her head.

'The Nightingales of Manisa. Three slaves, with beautiful singing voices, who were given to the old Sultan Murad by his cousin, Princess Humashah. They were famous in their day. One became his Haseki—'

'The Valide.'

'Another became the Chief Black Eunuch.'

'Hassan Aga? But they say he's going to die . . .'

'And the third—' The Haseki leant towards Celia as if to whisper in her ear, but then, just as suddenly, she drew away again in alarm. 'What's that?' She turned to look behind her.

Celia listened, but all she could hear, from a distant part of the gardens, was the sound of workmen, the sound of their hammers carrying faintly on the afternoon breeze. 'It was nothing. Just those workmen, perhaps.'

'Yes, look, they're coming.' Gulay picked up her fan and began to wave it in front of her, shielding her face from view. 'My servants – they are returning.' She seemed very nervous suddenly, smoothing down her robe with anxious fingers. 'I thought we would have longer,' she whispered to Celia from behind her fan, 'but the Valide doesn't allow them to leave me for too long.'

And as she spoke Celia saw that the Haseki's servants were indeed now coming towards them. They brought trays of fruit arranged in frosted pyramids and cups of iced sherbet which they placed on a low table inside the kiosk. Although they served the Haseki with all the deference that was owed to her, the atmosphere, Celia thought, seemed tense. One servant girl in particular kept glancing at Gulay with an expression Celia could not read. To their evident reluctance, at the Haseki's insistence they served Celia first. Only afterwards did she eat herself, Celia noticed, and then only sparsely, and from the same foods that Celia had first taken.

The presence of the other women made further conversation impossible. The two sat silently whilst their attendants moved around them. The shadows in the garden had begun to lengthen, and the cypress trees sent cool shadows over the little pavilion.

Celia looked at the woman sitting next to her, and realised what it was that the Valide must fear in her: beneath that gentle exterior was something else, some other quality that, despite her fear, made Celia's heart soar. From time to time she detected an expression that was neither soft nor shy, an expression of pure intelligence. If you are my friend, my guide, she thought, then perhaps, after all, I can survive.

But under the watchful eye of the servants, all ease was gone now. Soon the Haseki gave the signal for Celia to take her leave.

'Until we meet again, Kaya Kadin,' she said. 'There is much that we have to talk about still.' A look of understanding passed between them.

As the attendants backed away, Celia seized her chance.

'But why me, Haseki Sultan?' she murmured, in a voice she hoped could not be overheard. 'I don't understand why they are watching me.'

'Because of the sugar ship, of course,' came the reply. 'Didn't you know? It was sent by the English.'

In the silence that followed, Celia could see the waters of the Sea of Marmara sparkle like beaten silver in the distance

'Ask your friend Annetta, she knows,' the Haseki said, 'she was here, in this kiosk, with the Valide, on the day the English ship arrived, two weeks ago now.'

'The English ship?' Celia whispered.

'Yes, indeed. The English embassy ship. The one that has brought the great gift for the Sultan. The one they have been waiting for these last four years. Listen!' And there came again, still more faintly now, the sound of the workmen hammering. 'There they are now at the gate.'

'The gate?'

'But of course. They're setting the gift up at the Aviary Gate.'

'You knew!'

'Yes.'

'You *knew*! And you didn't think to tell me?'

'You know why not.'

Annetta stood before Celia in the Courtyard of the Favourites. Now that Celia was considered a *kadin*, a lady in the palace hierarchy, it was against etiquette for Annetta to sit unless asked to do so; and Celia, in her anger, kept her standing. It was nearly dusk now. In the fading light she could see that Annetta did not look well; her skin had a greasy pallor to it, like old cheese.

'You know we agreed, no looking back. Please, Celia, give me the sign to sit.'

'No – I think I'd like you to remain as you are.'

An expression of surprise flitted across Annetta's face, but she remained standing. 'What good would it have done?'

'And after everything I told you?' Celia's lips were white, fear almost forgotten in the heat of her anger. 'Don't you think I might have been the judge of that?'

Annetta lowered her eyes and did not reply.

'An English ship arrived here two weeks ago. An English *embassy* ship. Paul might have been on it. He might be here, right now. Don't you see – how that changes everything?'

Annetta looked up with dull eyes. 'But don't you see, it doesn't change a thing.' The words came out slowly, almost thickly. 'We agreed, remember? No going back.'

But anger had made Celia bold. 'That's what you always told me, but I don't remember ever agreeing to it. Even if I had, this would have changed everything. It *does* change everything.'

'Don't be a fool, if anyone ever finds out it will ruin us, can't you see?' Annetta was pleading with her now. 'There's no way out of here. You are our best chance of survival – perhaps our only chance. You could become one of the Sultan's concubines, perhaps even the Haseki . . .'

'You're not thinking about me at all, are you? All you've ever really cared about is yourself – how to save your own miserable skin.'

'Very well, if it makes you happy I'll admit it.' Annetta put her hand to her throat, as if to loosen the buttons there. 'My star is linked with yours, of course it is. But I've helped you too, you know, or have you forgotten? Two is better than one. How many times . . . oh, never mind!' She shook her head wearily. 'Have you stopped to ask yourself *why* the Haseki is telling you all these things?' She looked at Celia, beseeching now. 'Why is she trying to drive us apart?'

'Oh, stuff and nonsense,' Celia said sharply, 'you've done that very successfully all by yourself. She was trying to help me, that's all. She's got no idea of the significance of any of this, why should she?'

'If you say so. But believe me,' she gave a tired shrug, 'you don't want to draw attention to your connection with the English ship, not now, not after what's happened to Hassan Aga.'

'I think I've worked that out for myself, thank you,' Celia said bitterly.

'Please, I was trying to protect you, that's all.'

Although the evening was cool, Celia could see that Annetta was sweating; tiny droplets stood out on her brow and the top of her lip.

'Please, goose, I need to sit down.' Annetta swayed slightly to one side.

'Sit then.' Softening, Celia gave her the signal. 'But don't call me goose.'

Holding one hand to her side, just beneath her ribs, Annetta sat down. Celia regarded her friend. 'You aren't well.'

Not a question, a statement.

'No. I have a pain, just here, since this morning.' Annetta pressed her hand to her ribs.

'Me too,' Celia said, unsympathetically. 'Probably just indigestion, that's all.'

'Indigestion!' Annetta moaned. 'It's that witch, Malchi, she's put the Evil Eye on us, I know it.'

'She's not a witch.' Celia said calmly. 'The sand was a charm, for good luck.'

Annetta looked at her sceptically. 'Who told you that?'

'The Haseki.'

'Not her again.' Annetta's voice was sour. 'And have you asked yourself why she wants to ingratiate herself with you all of a sudden?'

'You wouldn't understand.'

The two sat crossly together side by side, not speaking.

It was nearly dark now. Small groups of girls, some merry, some silent, were making their way back inside. Their figures, Celia thought to herself, were like the black paper silhouettes the pedlars in London used to sell in fairgrounds and on feast days. In the gardens only the white roses in the flower beds could be seen now, their heads glowing with an eerie phosphorescence. High overhead the bats swooped, threading their way though the dying light.

Soon they must go in, but not just yet. Her anger with Annetta was spent. In its place the terrible question came to her again: does he know I'm dead? But I'm not dead. I'm alive. And if he knew I were alive, would he still love me? If he knew I were here, would he try to find me?

'If he's here, you know I'll have to try to reach him somehow,' she said to Annetta slowly, 'you know that, don't you? Annetta?'

But Annetta did not reply. Celia turned, and what she saw made her jump from her seat in alarm. 'Quick, quick, someone come quickly.' She began to hurry towards the palace, and almost at once a group of senior women were coming out to meet her. Their way was lit by servants carrying flaming torches. Forgetting the harem rules, Celia ran up to them.

'It's Annetta – I mean, Ayshe – she's not well. Please, someone help her . . .'

The little procession stopped short. At the head of it were two of the harem's most senior officials, the Mistress of the Robes and the

Mistress of the Bathhouse. Despite Celia's pleas for help they seemed not to register what she was saying at all, did not even look towards Annetta.

'Greetings, Kaya Kadin, you who are *gözde*,' they intoned.

The women bowed low, so low that the sleeves of their robes dragged in the dust before her.

'The Sultan, the most glorious Padishah, God's Shadow Upon Earth, will honour you again tonight.'

Chapter 18

Istanbul: the present day

It was early in the afternoon when Elizabeth finally left the palace. She found a taxi easily outside the First Courtyard and gave the address of Haddba's guest house. But halfway across the Galata Bridge she realised she felt too restless to return to her room just yet. On impulse she leant forwards to speak to the driver.

'Can you take me to Yıldız?' she asked him in English. 'Yıldız Park?'

A few days ago she remembered that Haddba had told her about a little café in this park overlooking the Bosphorous, a pavilion known as the Malta Kiosk where all the Istanbullus went to take tea on Sunday afternoons, only then she had felt too lethargic still, and too cold, to take up the suggestion.

The ride took longer than she expected, and by the time Elizabeth reached Yildiz the clouds had cleared. The taxi driver dropped her at the walls of the park, at the bottom of a hill, leaving her to walk up to the kiosk itself.

Inside, Yildiz turned out to be more of a forest than the metropolitan shrubbery of Haddba's description. Immense trees, their few remaining leaves as yellow as golden guineas, stretched up through deep glades on either side of the path. Elizabeth walked quickly up the road, enjoying the sweet damp smell of the forest air. Jackdaws chattered in the branches. Perhaps it was the sight of blue sky after days of grey or the feel of the sun against her face, she could not tell which, but she was surprised by the sudden energy she felt, as if, after days of lassitude, something inside her, some hard and bitter place, had begun to thaw.

The kiosk turned out to be a nineteenth-century baroque building surrounded by trees. Elizabeth ordered coffee and some baklava in the café, and found a table outside on the terrace, a semi-circle of white marble shaded by a pergola, which looked down over the park and the Bosphorous below. A few leaves blew fitfully across the flagstones. Even in the sunshine the pavilion had the melancholy feel of an out of season attraction. Yesterday, it would have suited her mood exactly; but today, after her visit to the palace, and the strange deserted rooms of the harem, today was different. As Elizabeth drank her coffee, a surge of optimism flowed through her. She would find the remaining fragment, she felt sure, if not here then back in England; she would find out what really became of Celia Lamprey.

More than anything at this moment she found that she wanted to tell someone about her experience at the harem but there was no one to tell. Should she ring Eve? Better wait until she could use the telephone in her room, her mobile bill must be astronomical by now. Haddba? But, no, she didn't want to leave the kiosk just yet. She could tell Haddba about it later. On the terrace, where until now she had been sitting alone, she was joined by a Turkish couple. They sat a little way away from her at the end of the terrace. For one anarchic moment Elizabeth wondered what they would do if she went up to them and just started talking, telling them about a lost story, the tale of an Elizabethan slave girl.

But no, perhaps not. Tilting her head backwards she smiled to herself and closed her eyes, feeling the sun warm her skin. With her eyes still closed she half expected a likeness of Celia Lamprey to come into her head, but instead, in her mind's eye she saw again the deserted room inside the harem. She saw the rotting raffia beneath the carpet, the coverlets on the divan, with their faint suggestion of having been recently slept on.

Elizabeth put her hand in her pocket. The chip of blue and white glass glinted in her palm. A talisman against the 'Evil Eye', that's what Berin had said when she had shown it to her. They were supposed to ward away bad spirits. You saw them everywhere in Istanbul, hadn't she noticed?

'Should I show it to someone?' Elizabeth had asked.

'Of course not,' Berin had said, 'keep it. It's just a cheap thing, a trinket from the bazaar. You can get them anywhere. One of the caretakers probably dropped it.' She gave Elizabeth a quizzical look. 'Are you all right?'

'Why do you say that?'

'You look a little pale, that's all.'

'It's nothing.' Elizabeth's fingers had closed around the smooth glass. 'I'm fine.'

Now, sitting on the pavilion terrace, Elizabeth dropped the charm carefully back into her pocket. She took a pen and notebook from her bag, and started to write ideas down at random: thoughts, questions, anything, in fact, that came into her head, allowing her mind to slide. Freefalling, down and down.

'Celia Lamprey,' she wrote at the top of the page. 'Paul Pindar. A shipwreck. 1590s.' There's four hundred years separating me from their story, she thought, although it might as well be four thousand. 'And in the heat of bloud in front of her verie eyes did runne her father in the side with a Culaxee . . .' Elizabeth's hand flew across the page '. . . cutting him clene through his body.'

She stopped; put down her pen. Then picked it up again and began to make a doodle around the 'C' of Culaxee. A double trauma then. Not only had Celia been taken captive – dowry and all – on the eve of her marriage, but she had seen her own father struck down, murdered, in front of her eyes. She stared, unseeing, at the page. And what about Paul Pindar: had she loved him, too? Had she mourned her lost love, as I do . . .?

Elizabeth shook the thought away, forced herself back on to neutral ground.

The question was: how had Celia's story survived in the first place? Was it at all possible that she had lived to tell her *own* tale? Had lived to be reunited with Paul Pindar, perhaps married him after all, travelled with him to Aleppo, had children . . .

The *Oxford Dictionary of National Biography*, which contained a long entry for Paul Pindar himself, made no mention of a wife, but that didn't prove that he hadn't had one. There had been nothing under 'Lamprey', of course. The fact remained: someone had known Celia's story, and known it well enough to write it down.

Idly, she carried on doodling, cross-hatching the circles of the 9s in the date, 1599. The same year as Thomas Dallam, the organ maker, presented his wonderful device to the Sultan. Well, at least his story had survived.

Elizabeth had found the passage in Hakluyt easily enough. She took out a well-thumbed photocopy of Thomas Dallam's diary. *In this Book is the Account of an Organ Carryed to the Grand Seignor and Other Curious Matter.* The diary described his journey to Constantinople in the Levant Company's ship, the *Hector*; it told of how, after a six-month voyage, the marvellous gift, on which so many of the merchants' hopes had depended, had arrived half-rotted by sea water; of how Dallam and his men went every day to the palace to rebuild it. It described his growing friendship with the guards, and how one day when the Sultan was at his summer palace, one of them had allowed him a forbidden glimpse into the women's quarters:

When he had showed me many other things which I wondered at, than crossinge throughe a litle squar courte paved with marble, he poyneted me to go to a graite in a wale, but made me a sine that he myghte not go thether him selfe. When I came to the grait the wale was verrie thicke and graited on bothe the sides with iron verrie strongly: but through that graite I did se thirtie of the Grand Sinyor's Concobines that weare playinge with a bale in another courte. At the first sighte of them I thoughte they had bene yonge men, but when I saw the hare of their heades hange doone on their backes, platted together with a tasle of smale pearle hanginge in the lower end of it, and by other plaine tokens. I did know them to be women, and verrie prettie ones in deede . . . I stood so longe loukinge upon them that he which had showed me all this kindes began to be verrie angrie with me. He made a wrye mouthe, and stamped with his foute to meke me give over looking; the which I was verrie lothe to do, for that sighte did please me wondrous well.

Than I wente awaye with this Jemoglane to the place where we lefte my drugaman or intarpreter, and I tould my intarpreter that I had sene thirtie of the Grand Sinyores Conconbines; but my intarpreter advised me that by no means I should speake of it, whearby any Turke mythte hear of it; for if it were knowne to som Turks, it would presente deathe to him that showed me them. He durste not louke upon them him selfe. Although I louked so longe upon them, theie saw not me,

nether all that whyle louked towards that place. Yf they had sene me,
they would all have come presently thether to louke upon me, and
have wondred as moche at me, or how I cam thether, as I did to se
them.

Elizabeth put down the page and tried to order her thoughts. Everyone always assumed that it would have been impossible to have any contact with the women in the Sultan's harem. But Thomas Dallam's diary proved that the women's quarters were more accessible than most foreigners would ever guess. It might have spelt death for the organ maker and his guard if any Turk had come to hear of his escapade, but the temptation to tell his English friends about it must have been overwhelming. Whom had he told? Tilting up her face to the sunlight again, Elizabeth pressed her fingers over her eyelids. In her mind's eye she could see the soaring tiled corridors of the harem; the room where she had found the lucky charm. What was it that had been so puzzling about it? Carefully she added more curlicues and cross-hatchings to the doodle. I know, it should have been a sad place, she thought with sudden clarity. But it wasn't. I heard footsteps running. Laughter.

Sitting back in her chair Elizabeth pushed the notebook to one side, stretching her arms luxuriously over her head. Her thoughts were still a jumble, but somehow it did not seem to matter. Live with the mess: who had said that? This was how projects always began. She had a good feeling, a good instinct about this. Things would become clear soon enough, when she was in possession of more facts. How Marius would deplore her methods so far, if you could call them methods – so messy, so *emotional* – but, do you know what, she said to herself with a small inward shrug, so what?

It was still warm out on the terrace, and Elizabeth lingered. She had finished the coffee but not the baklava, and she ate it now, breaking off small pieces and then carefully licking the flakes from her fingers.

She was not sure what made her turn round, but when she glanced up at the couple sitting at the other end of the terrace, something about them, a certain stillness, told her that they must have been watching her for some time, and that it had been their gaze that had made her turn. Only it was not the couple after all, she saw now, but a man sitting on his own.

165

Elizabeth met the man's eyes briefly; and then turned away again quickly, so that he should not see that she had seen him. But of course he had.

Feeling foolish she sat staring resolutely ahead of her. She had thought herself alone here, had felt energised by the combination of sun and solitude, but now, beneath this stranger's gaze, the charm of the discovered pavilion, of the whole afternoon, was altered subtly. It was time to leave.

But for some reason she did not go. Elizabeth waited, half afraid that the stranger would make some attempt to approach her. But he did not. Why should I go just yet? she told herself, I still have one piece of baklava left.

Elizabeth ate the remaining piece of pastry slowly. The honeyed flakes stuck to her lips. Perhaps I should use a spoon, she thought; but somehow her fingers seemed best. She ran a thumb over her bottom lip, licked the tips of her fingers, sucking them slowly and carefully, one by one. She knew that he was still watching her. What are you *doing*? one part of her whispered to the other. But she did not stop, not because she was able to ignore him, but because there was, she realised, a quality to his gaze which robbed it of any insolence. He merely sat watching her, with an air of . . . what? Elizabeth searched for the word. Appreciation? Yes, something like that. Balm to her bruised soul. Sunlight after days of cold and rain.

But that's ridiculous – that whispered voice again – he's a complete stranger. The other part of her merely shrugged: who cares? I'll never see him again.

For one long surreal moment she knew that he knew that she knew he was watching him. And then, all of a sudden, Elizabeth had had enough. She took one last bite, and without a backward glance, picked up her bag and began to walk back down the hill.

Chapter 19

Constantinople: 2 September 1599

Night

The second time Celia was prepared to greet the Sultan there was no Cariye Lala to help her; no drug to blur the edges of her mind, to blot out memory, or to help her sweet flesh – on display like one of Carew's subtleties – forget the indignities heaped upon it.

Was it a consolation, the fact that she was not alone?

As before she was taken with all ceremony to the Sultan's chamber. Only this time there was another with her: another who was also *gözde*. The two of them, with their scented thighs and their unripe breasts, made their way with their attendants across the Valide's courtyard, to join the waiting band of eunuchs.

Celia followed the procession down the Golden Corridor to the Sultan's chamber, but here there was yet another surprise. This time they did not stay in the chamber itself, but were led beyond it to a small anteroom which gave out on to what Celia imagined must be the Sultan's private courtyard. Two eunuchs struggled ahead with a large object, a low table or dais, which they placed in the centre of the room, and then covered carefully with a carpet.

At the head of the main procession was the Chief Black Eunuch's deputy, Suleiman Aga. Whereas last time, in her drugged state, Celia saw almost nothing, and afterwards could remember still less, this time she was in a state of heightened awareness. Even by the standards of the palace eunuchs, Suleiman Aga – with his gargoyle face and his pendulous pudding of a stomach – was grotesque. She saw how, as he took the chemise from her shoulders, Suleiman Aga's eyes ran over her naked breasts; felt his hands, soft and damp as uncooked dough, on her arms. His cheeks were somehow both plump and sunken, hairless as a baby's; his mouth hung slackly, revealing unnaturally pink gums and tongue. He was so close to her now that she could actually smell him; the rankness of old skin and the odour of recently eaten meat clung to his person. Celia felt her mouth fill with bile.

The two girls were arranged together on the dais, and then with one bald instruction not to move from that position, Suleiman Aga and the eunuchs were gone, and they were left alone.

At first Celia did not recognise the creature sitting naked beside her. She was thin, positively skinny compared to Celia's well-nourished body, with a small pointed face and the high sliding cheekbones of a Circassian, but – Celia saw with some surprise – she was not beautiful at all. Her face was aggressively plain, her skin coarse and of such paleness that she seemed sapped of colour, like a plant that had grown in a cellar or beneath stones. But it was her eyes that were the most striking thing about her. They were the very palest brown, so pale they were almost golden, fringed with sandy lashes.

When she saw Celia gazing at her, her eyes narrowed suspiciously. 'What are you looking at?' Her tone was so insolent that Celia felt as if she had been slapped. Then she remembered.

'Wait a minute, I know where I've see you before,' Celia said, 'this afternoon, with the Haseki. You're one of Gulay Haseki's servants, one of the ones that brought us fruit.' How could she have forgotten that face? There was something about the girl, something unformed, almost feral, that had made Celia recoil even then.

'Well, I'm not her servant any more.'

'You mean you are not one of *Haseki Sultan's* servants any more,' Celia corrected her coldly.

For a long moment the girl stared back at Celia with her steady insolent gaze. She gave a shrug. 'That fool,' was all she said.

Celia was too amazed to speak. The harem insisted on such decorum of behaviour and language that even in the few months she had been here, Celia had learnt to regard any departure from its extravagant habits of *politesse*, even in the most informal of situations, as a shocking breach of etiquette.

Although the evening had seemed warm enough earlier, now it was very cool, almost cold, in the little antechamber. She felt herself shiver. She looked through the archway, back into the Sultan's chamber, but everything was as before and the candlelit room was silent, the ceiling full of empty shadows.

'You look different.' Celia turned to the girl again.

'Oh?' The girl gave a sarcastic snort. 'So do you.'

This time she did not even bother to look at Celia, but arched her back luxuriously, seeming quite at home in her nakedness.

'What's your name?'

'You'll learn that soon enough.'

'I am Kaya. Kaya *Kadin*, to you,' Celia went on evenly, not taking her eyes off the girl. Then she said curiously, 'How old are you? Thirteen? Fourteen?'

'How should I know?' The girl shrugged. 'Younger than the Haseki – but she's old now, more than twenty. Younger than you too. That's what he likes isn't it? Young flesh.'

'Maybe.' Celia was still gazing at her thoughtfully. 'And maybe not.'

She was hugging herself now, trying to get warm. Her buttocks and the tops of her legs stung with cold. 'Why's it so freezing in here?' She slapped at the tops of her arms, which were mottled blue.

'You mean to say you haven't noticed?' The girl went on arching her spine, back and forth, back and forth, like a circus tumbler waiting for her act.

'Noticed what?'

'What we're sitting on.'

Celia put her hand down to feel beneath the carpet, and brought her fingers away quickly, as if she had been burnt.

'Ice! My God, we're sitting on a block of ice.'

Seeing the look on Celia's face, the girl smiled for the first time, bringing some animation to her hard little face.

'Well, Miss High and Mighty, you really don't know, do you? I may not be pretty like you, but he's not going to be looking at my face, is he?' She gave Celia a look of pure malevolence. 'Look at me, see, skin: white skin.' She leant towards Celia and her words came out like a hiss. 'The colder the whiter. Because that's what he likes.'

Of course, Celia thought, how can I have missed it? In the candlelight the girl's skin now shone dazzlingly, the blue-white of snow. Celia looked down at her own naked body. She was so cold now that her skin was almost transparent. She could see the blue veins running along her breasts, along the insides of her thighs, all the way to her feet. Of course!

'It's why I was chosen,' she said aloud, 'and the Haseki, too.'

'Oh yes, the Valide tried with you – but you were no good. We all heard about the opium.' The girl gave a strange hoarse laugh.

'How did you hear about that?'

The girl shrugged. 'We all heard about it, that's all.'

'We? I don't think so.' Celia met the girl's gaze steadily. Perhaps because of the cold she found that she was thinking very clearly now. 'I think you mean you. *You* know something you shouldn't know.'

Another laugh, but this time Celia saw the sandy eyelashes flicker. 'Who says I shouldn't know?'

'How could a servant possibly know? Tell me at once, *cariye*.' Celia spoke sharply.

'Work it out for yourself.'

'Don't worry, I will.' Celia looked down at her hands. She was trembling, but more with anger than with cold.

'You're cold now, Kaya *Kadin*.'

'Yes, but not as cold as you.'

Celia saw with satisfaction that the girl's lips were almost blue. She had stopped rocking, and was hugging her knees to her chest, her whole body tensed to stop herself from shivering.

'But he will come soon – and when he does, he will prefer me.' The girl answered.

'What makes you so sure?' Celia was clenching her jaw now to stop her teeth from chattering.

'Because I know what to do. I've watched him with that fool Gulay.' The girl flashed her a triumphant look. 'Listen, there they are at the door now.'

Then, as Celia watched, the girl spread her legs, shamelessly opening the lips of her carefully plucked sex, and slipped her fingers inside. Slowly and deliberately, she pulled out a small object. The object was round and black, the same size and shape as the opium tablets that Celia had taken.

'What's that?'

'You'll see.' She gave another hoarse laugh. 'You're not the only one who knows how to get tips out of Cariye Lala.'

170

The girl did not swallow the tablet, but placed it carefully under her tongue. Then she pushed her two middle fingers into her sex again, and smeared the juices from her body behind her ears and over her lips. All the time she was watching Celia avidly, a small smile hovering at the corners of her mouth.

'Disgusting things, men, don't you think?' was all she said.

When the Sultan entered his chamber at last, the two of them climbed down from the freezing dais and prostrated themselves in front of him. Afterwards Celia would remember how stiff and slow her limbs had felt, and the burning rush in her toes and fingers as the blood began to flow through her veins again. She had not dared look up and so had heard, rather than seen, his displeasure.

'What's this? I didn't ask for you.'

There was an uneasy silence.

Then: 'Where is Gulay?'

Another silence, and then Celia heard the girl say in a steady voice. 'Gulay Haseki is indisposed, my Sultan. She begs your forbearance. Her Majesty the Valide Sultan, who thinks ceaselessly of your pleasure and repose, has sent us to you instead.'

The hard cold floor dug into Celia's forehead and knees. She had not been given the signal to rise and so she remained as she was, her naked buttocks in the air. Long moments passed. From the corner of one eye she could see a chip in one of the tiles just beneath her nose. She watched the chipped tile for what felt like a long time. Then, when still nothing happened, she tilted her head very slightly, and saw that the girl had risen up, unbidden, and was now kneeling in front of the Sultan.

As though to cover her nakedness the girl had flung one arm across her chest, cupping her left breast in her right hand: a gesture that was both submissive and inviting. Her breasts were large for her thin body, the broad and flat nipples now stiffened into two hard points by the cold. The Sultan said nothing, but as Celia watched he took a step towards her. As he did so the girl's lips parted slightly. 'Ah.'

It was barely a sigh. She swayed towards him, as though unsteady on her knees, and then drew away again shyly. Her eyelids fluttered against her cheeks.

171

'Don't I know you?' When the Sultan spoke at last Celia was struck by how strange it was to hear a man's voice again after all this time. 'It's Hanza, isn't it? Little Hanza . . .'

The girl said nothing, but Celia could see her strange eyes glittering, dark as gold in the candlelight.

But how can he even look at you – you are so ugly, was all she could think. Yet even as she thought it, the Sultan took another step towards her.

'Haa . . .' The girl breathed out, and as she did so Celia saw her draw her tongue slowly across her lips, wetting them so they glistened in the candlelight.

The room became very still suddenly. All Celia could hear was the sound of Hanza's breath and her own heart.

Still prostrated on the floor, Celia could hardly breathe, but no one spoke to her, and she did not dare to sit up unasked, so cautiously she tilted her head a little more to the side. She could see the other girl, Hanza, more closely now, see how she held her body – a body that had seemed so insubstantial, so skinny beside her own – like the most delicate bud, and the way her skin, still half blue with cold, glowed like the white roses in the dusky garden.

If she were cold, she gave no sign of it. The Sultan was gazing at her, and as he did so Hanza dared to gaze up at him at last. Their eyes met.

'Ahh . . .' With a strange little sob, she twisted her head away again as if she had been struck.

'Don't be afraid,' he said. But the idea, Celia noticed, did not seem displeasing to him. He was standing close to Hanza now, his robe hanging open and falling loosely to his sides. The more he gazed down at the girl, the more she tried to draw back from him, twisting first to the left, then to the right, like an insect on a pin.

'Let me look at you.'

Hanza twisted away again slightly, as if to shield her nakedness from his gaze; as she did so thrusting forwards one perfectly white shoulder, stretching out her snowy neck and throat. Like a dancer, Celia thought, or a bitch submitting to a dog.

Torn between fascination and fear she closed her eyes and then quickly opened them again. What should she do now? Was she expected to go or stay? She saw him take Hanza's hand away from her cupped breast. The girl tried to stop him, slapping and scratching at him with a flailing arm, but he caught her wrist and gripped it hard, pinning her to him, whilst with the moistened tip of a finger he slowly began to trace the outline of her nipple.

With a sigh Hanza sank towards him, lay her head submissively against his chest. He bent to kiss her neck, hesitated, snuffled at her ear.

'Come now, into the other chamber.' His voice was thick. 'You too, Sleepyhead.' He motioned to Celia. 'Cover yourself, or you'll get cold.'

So he had remembered her, after all. She felt his hand touch her lightly on the cheek; the fingers soft-skinned, a cloying odour of myrrh.

The Sultan's bed was just as Celia remembered it, a canopied divan covered with drapes, damasks and cut velvets, cloths embroidered with silver and gold tulips, many of them lined with fur. In the lamplight their colours glittered like the carapaces of insects. The rest of the room, including the vast basilica-sized dome above them, lay in darkness.

Celia put one of the fur wraps around her shoulders and knelt down at the bottom of the bed. Hanza, without being asked, stretched herself out in the middle of the divan. She too found one of the fur wraps, and draped it luxuriously round her shoulders, rubbing her cheeks against the fur. She seemed completely at ease now, completely unafraid.

'So, little Hanza, are you ready for me?'

He was kneeling on the bed in front of her now. The girl pulled the fur more closely around her shoulders and looked at him through narrowed eyes. Then, slowly and deliberately, she shook her head.

'No, my Sultan.'

'You dare say no to your Sultan?' And to Celia's astonishment he laughed again, as though delighted by her reply. With an impatient movement he dashed the robe from his shoulders. 'Well, we'll see about that.' He made as if to move towards her, but she drew back from him as before. He lunged, and as she twisted away from him he caught her ankle and jerked her roughly back towards him.

'Not so fast.' She heard him grunt with the effort. The sound of a big man. A wild pig after a truffle.

She watched as he turned Hanza over on to her back, pinning one arm down over her head. She struggled, lashed out at him with her other hand, scratching at his face with her nails before he caught and held her other arm. Trapped, she arched her white neck away from him and then lay perfectly still. Both of them were panting now, and as he bent to graze on her face Celia saw him pause, his face hovering over her neck and mouth, as if breathing in her perfume once more, and the secret juices that had dried there.

'Have they given you something?'

She shook her head.

'Have they?' Celia watched as he traced a finger over her throat. Hanza did not reply, but instead reached up suddenly and licked his mouth with her tongue.

He laughed again softly. 'You are ready for me then?' His voice was low. 'It won't hurt . . . not much.'

'No . . .' With a last display of reluctance, Hanza pulled feebly at her arm, trying to get it away from him, but he was too strong for her. She rolled back towards him with a sigh.

Celia braced herself, felt her stomach curdle at the thought of what was to come.

'So, shall I take her instead?' He nodded towards Celia who was still kneeling at the foot of the bed.

'No, my Sultan.' She shook her head again. Was it a sob or a smile that Celia could hear in her voice? 'Take me,' she said.

Then she took his hand and drew it between her legs, guiding his fingers towards her sex, where he stroked her, making her gasp and squirm.

With a grunt, he entered her. It was over very quickly. Celia heard Hanza cry out, and only a few moments later the Sultan climbed off her.

He put his robe on.

'Wait here,' he told them both, 'the eunuchs will escort you back shortly.' He patted Hanza almost absently on the shoulder. 'You have pleased me, little Hanza; the Aga will write you in the book.'

Then, without a backward glance, he was gone.

Celia was still kneeling at the bottom of the bed. For a moment there was complete silence. Then Hanza turned to her. 'Well, aren't you going to congratulate me?' She hugged her knees to her chest. 'You must call me *kadin* now.'

'My congratulations, Hanza Kadin.' There was a pause and then Celia added slowly. 'Have you no shame at all?'

'Shame? Why should I?' By the light of the guttering candles the girl's eyes were huge. All of a sudden she seemed very young, a small pale child in the middle of the vast bed. 'He chose *me*. You'll never be the Haseki now.'

'The Sultan can have many favourites, but he only ever has one Haseki – and that position, as you know, is already taken.' Celia spoke carefully, as if she were explaining to a child.

Hanza flashed one of her thin, feral smiles. 'Not for much longer.'

'What do you mean?'

'You'll find out soon enough.'

She scrambled out of the bed, and walked over to where a plate of small honeyed pastries had been left. She seemed quite unconcerned about her nakedness. 'Aren't you hungry now?' She crammed a pastry in her mouth, licked the sugary syrup from her lips. 'They call these ones Ladies' Nipples,' she giggled. 'Here, have one.'

Celia ignored her. 'Who taught you?'

'Taught me?'

'To do all that . . . to please the Sultan in that way.'

'I told you, I've watched.' Hanza licked her fingers.

'I don't believe you. Nobody learns all that just by watching.'

'You mean all that ooh and ahh.' Giggling, Hanza parodied herself. She was spinning around the room now, on the tips of her toes, intoxicated by her experience. 'All right then, I'll tell you, Kaya Kadin,' she said to Celia over her shoulder. 'It was the slave mistress in Ragusa.'

'Ragusa?'

'Yes. Why sound surprised? The Valide likes people from Ragusa.'

Celia gazed across at her in silence.

'With a little help from Cariye Lala, of course.' Hanza stopped her spinning and took another sweetmeat. Two spots of colour had appeared on her pallid cheeks. 'Oh yes, Lala will be the first one I'll reward when I'm Haseki.'

Celia felt very weary suddenly. 'So that's what she's been telling you, is it?'

'Cariye Lala didn't tell me anything. She just gave me the medicine, same as she did you,' she giggled. 'The "itch", she called my one—'

'I don't mean her,' Celia interrupted. 'I mean the Valide. Is that what the Valide's been telling you? That you could be the next Haseki?'

'I don't know what you're talking about.'

'I think you do . . .' Celia started to say, then a thought occurred to her. 'The eunuchs will be here in a moment to take us back. Did they tell you what to do? About the blood, I mean.'

'Blood?'

'Yes, blood. You know – after your first time with the . . . surely there must be blood? You must show it to them. Didn't Hassan Aga tell you? Oh, but he's not here is he?' Celia put her hand to her mouth. 'Don't tell me they forgot?'

There was an uncomfortable silence.

'Blood?' Hanza repeated in a small voice.

Another silence.

'There is no blood, is there?'

'No.'

The girl's manner, so full of feverish energy a moment ago, suddenly changed. 'What shall I do, *kadin*?' She sat down, a poor skinny sparrow on the edge of the bed, and looked at Celia. 'What will they do to me? Help me, *kadin*,' she fell to her knees, 'please!'

Celia thought quickly. 'Hurry, find me a cloth.' Amongst the coverlets she seized upon a piece of embroidered linen, Hanza's discarded napkin. 'Now you must cut yourself somewhere. With this – look.'

On the floor next to the bed where he had left it was the Sultan's belt. Attached to it was a dagger. Its curved sheath was made from beaten gold inlaid with brilliants, the handle fashioned from three solid emeralds. Celia drew the blade; felt the tip carefully. Although the dagger was a ceremonial one, it seemed sharp enough to do the job.

'Here,' she held it out to the girl, 'use this.'

But Hanza shrank from her. 'No, I can't.'

'You must,' Celia urged her. 'Quick now, we haven't much time.'

'I can't.'

'Don't be a fool.'

'Please,' Hanza looked at Celia in terror, 'you do it.'

'*Me?*'

'Yes, don't you see?' She was crying now. I can't hide a cut. They'll find it on me. They'll know what I did.' There was a sound of movement outside the door, footsteps. 'Please – I'll never forget that you helped me, never. I promise.'

There was no time to think. Celia took the dagger and placed the blade over her wrist.

'No, not there. Under your arm,' Hanza urged her. 'Where it won't show so much.'

Celia lifted her arm and positioned the blade again. Then she paused.

'Why should I, Hanza? Give me one good reason: why should I protect you?'

'Please – I'll never forget you helped me, never, I promise.' The whites of Hanza's eyes rolled in terror. 'You don't understand. They'll cut off my hands and feet – they'll gouge out my eyes – they'll put me in a sack and drown me in the Bosphorous . . .'

'Yes, they will, won't they?' Thoughtfully, Celia tested the point of the dagger against her finger. But why should she help Hanza? Had the experience of the last few days taught her nothing? Hanza would stab her in the back at the first opportunity, that much was crystal clear.

Sensing her hesitation, Hanza made as if to snatch the dagger away, but Celia was too quick for her. She held the dagger up, just out of reach.

'Give it to me!' Hanza let out a sob. 'I'll tell you about the opium . . .'

'Not good enough.' The eunuchs were at the door now. 'Like you said, I think I can work that one out for myself . . .' but before she could finish the sentence, Hanza blurted something out that made Celia stop short.

'What did you say?'

'The Aviary Gate. I said I'll get you the key to the Aviary Gate.'

Their eyes met as if for the first time. No time for questions. Celia could hear a roaring sound, the sound of blood drumming in her ears.

'Promise?'

Beads of sweat stood out on Hanza's brow. 'On my life.'

In the pause that followed there was a creaking sound as the doors to the Sultan's chamber swung open. Quickly Celia made a cut. The girl held out the napkin, and together they watched as three drops of blood fell on to the white linen.

Chapter 20

Constantinople: 3 September 1599

Morning

'I still can't believe that you knew they were here.'
   'Yes.'

'All along, you knew! That after all this time the English embassy is still here!'

'Am I imagining it, or have we had this conversation before? I've said I'm sorry.'

Annetta lay on her bed, a mattress rolled out on to the floor, in the dormitory she shared with twelve other *kislar*. Although she sounded more like her old self, she still looked pale, and made no attempt to sit up.

Celia knelt down on the hard wooden floorboards beside her.

'But not only did you know that an English ship had arrived here, with the Levant Company's gift for the Sultan, but that they had sent some sort of replica of it – made of sugar, they tell me – right here, to the palace.' So as not to arouse the curiosity of the servants who were waiting for her in the corridor outside, Celia kept her voice low. 'And that they are now saying that this same sugar ship is what poisoned Hassan Aga.'

'Why are you still tormenting me about this?' Annetta said weakly. 'I tried to tell you. Several times, I thought of telling you, really I did. I just thought it was better if—'

'Better if I didn't know?'

'Yes, you numbskull! Much better if you didn't know,' Annetta hissed out the words, 'look at you now.'

'But now I do know.' Celia sat back on her heels. 'You know what this means, don't you?'

'Don't say it.'

'It means Paul might be here.'

'Don't even think it!'

'But I do think it.' Celia, hiding her face in her hands, did not see the look of pity on Annetta's face. 'How can I help it? Day and night, waking and sleeping, everywhere I go he's there, at my shoulder, in my dreams.' She pressed her fingers to her eyes, feeling their cool tips against her hot lids. 'You say that I torment you – but I tell you, Annetta, *I* am the one who is tormented.' Celia pressed her hand to her side, the pain had returned, tenfold. 'Only yesterday you asked me: 'Does he know you're dead?' And I laughed, because it seemed such a strange thing to say – but now, now all I can think is: I have to find a way to tell him that I'm not dead. I'm here. I'm alive. Somehow, Annetta, I must—'

'I know what you're thinking.'

Celia shook her head. 'No you don't.'

'You're thinking that if only he knew you were here he'd come for you.'

At first Celia did not answer her. Her gaze flickered nervously towards the door. Then she began, speaking very rapidly, 'Actually, Annetta, I think there might be a way—'

'No!' Annetta interrupted furiously. 'I'm not listening to this.' She put her fingers in her ears. 'D'you want to get us both drowned?'

'If I could just *see* him, Annetta.' Celia looked up, her face piteous. 'That's all I ask. My father's dead, I'll never see him again. But if I could just see Paul, just one more time, I could bear this. I could bear anything.'

She looked around the room that she had once shared with Annetta, a windowless second-storey chamber in the newest part of the harem overlooking the bathhouse courtyard. Although it was bare of furniture, with only painted cupboards at either end in which the girls' mattresses and coverlets were stored during the day, the room gave off the clean smell of freshly sawn wood.

'And you'd better prepare yourself,' she sighed. 'I don't expect it will be too long before I'm back in here with you.'

'Poor Celia.' Annetta lay back on her cushions. She looked very pale.

'Oh, don't feel sorry for me. Believe me, I'd much rather be back here with you. I am too watched, too waited on – you've no idea what it's like.' Celia put her hand to her throat. 'It's as though they suck away all the air from me. Even when I wanted to come and visit you here, they sent three serving women with me.' She glanced round again. From the corridor outside came the sound of her women's voices drifting together. 'I'm never alone. Everything I do – the smallest thing – is reported to the Valide,' she whispered, pressing her hand to her side. 'They're spying on me – even now.'

Annetta frowned. 'Why do you think that? Who's spying on you?'

'The Valide's spies. The Haseki told me. She called them the Nightingales.'

'The Nightingales? What nonsense – she's just trying to frighten you, that's all.' Annetta put her hand weakly on Celia's arm. 'What's she done to you? You were never like this before she got her hands on you.'

'No, no,' Celia shook her head, making her earrings shake. 'You must understand. She was trying to help me.' She blinked her eyes rapidly several times. 'If you really want to know, the person who really scares me is Hanza.'

'Who's Hanza?'

'She used to be one of the Haseki's servants,' Celia said. 'But last night she became one of the Sultan's concubines.'

'You mean he . . .' Looking suddenly interested, Annetta struggled to sit up. 'With *both* of you?'

'Yes, both of us. But he only did it to her.'

'Oh, goose!' There was a sympathetic pause. 'I'm so sorry.'

'Well don't be. "Nice fresh *culo* for that fat old man", remember when you said that to me? Well, that's exactly what it was like. I know, I had to watch.'

'You watched!' A ripple of laughter escaped from Annetta's throat. 'I'm sorry!' She put her hand to her mouth. 'What's she like, this Hanza?'

'Don't laugh. She's about as bad as the Haseki is good. But fortunately not nearly as clever as she thinks she is.'

Celia told her about the blood and the napkin.

'*Madonna!*' Annetta looked up at her in amazement. 'How on earth did you know about all that?'

'I didn't, I made it up.' When she saw the expression on Annetta's face Celia allowed herself a wintry smile. 'Don't look at me like that. Something the Haseki said made me think: here we are, right at the very heart of things, but no one ever tells us anything. Not the rank and file girls, the *kislar*. It's all whispers and surmise; rumours and counter-rumours, most of them false. And the further up the ladder you go, the worse it gets. After a while, you don't know what to think any more. I realised that I was going to have to find things out for myself. You were always good at that, Annetta, but not me. It's as though I've been in a dream all this time.' She pressed her fingers wearily over her eyes again. 'Lord, I'm so tired.'

'So what did Hanza tell you then? It must have been good for you to save her miserable skin.'

'It was.' Celia sat back. 'Can you keep a secret?'

'You know I can.'

'It wasn't anything she said.'

'What then? That look on your face – it's making me nervous.'

'She gave me this.' From her pocket Celia produced a key.

Annetta stirred uncomfortably. 'What's it for?'

'The Aviary Gate. One of the old gates leading from the harem quarters into the Third Courtyard. It's hardly ever used these days. The Haseki told me that the English merchants have been told to set up their gift to the Sultan just behind it – I've heard them at work on it myself. So don't you see, if I can just . . .'

'How did she know?' Annetta interrupted her again.

'The Haseki?'

'No, not the Haseki! *Hanza*, of course. Have you asked yourself *how* Hanza knew that you might be interested in the Aviary Gate?'

'I don't know, I suppose she overheard Gulay telling me about the English merchants.' Celia shrugged. 'I don't know and I don't care.'

'Well, you should care.' Annetta's forehead was damp. 'Don't you see, it means they're on to you – on to us.'

Celia stared at her. 'What do you mean: "on to us"?'

'I mean that they've guessed at your connection with the sugar ship.'

'That's nonsense. If they thought I had anything to do with it someone would have said something by now.'

'But that's just it, don't you see?' Annetta's eyes were hollow, smudged with tired shadows. 'That's not how they do things here.' Her eyes flickered nervously towards the door. 'They watch. They watch and they wait.'

'For what?'

'For you – for us – to make a mistake.'

'Well, I don't care!' Celia said, reckless now. 'This is my chance, and I'll never get another one. Don't you see?' Tears sprang to her eyes. 'They're there; every day; just the other side of the gate!'

'No!' Annetta's voice was sharp. 'You mustn't!'

'But why ever not?'

'You just mustn't, that's all. Please! They'll kill us! You mustn't do anything that will associate us with the English merchants.'

For a long moment the two girls looked at one another.

A feeling of dread came over Celia.

'What's wrong, Annetta?' Her words came out thickly.

'I'm not well.' Annetta almost whimpered. She turned on to her side and closed her eyes. 'That woman, that witch – she's put the Evil Eye on me, I know it.'

'Don't be an idiot, you know that's not true.' Impatiently Celia shook her by the shoulder. 'She gave you a fright, that's all. If you go on like this, Annetta, you're going to make yourself really ill.'

'Can't you see?' There were specks of foam at the corners of her mouth. 'I *am* ill.'

Perhaps it was true. Her skin was drained of colour, and had a greasy sheen to it. Looking at Annetta, Celia had been reminded of something; now she knew what it was.

'I've seen you like this before, haven't I? Just after they found the Chief Black Eunuch,' she said. 'You wept when they found him – I couldn't understand it. You're not ill, Annetta, you're frightened.'

'No!'

'What are you frightened of?'

'I can't tell you.'

'Yes, you can—' Celia was pleading with her now, 'you *must* tell me.'

'I can't! You'll hate me!'

'Don't be a fool, we haven't got much time. They'll be coming for me in a moment.'

'I'm so sorry! It's my own fault.' Tears were seeping now from Annetta's eyes. 'And it *is* an Evil Eye . . . you don't understand.' There was a note of hysteria in her voice now. 'They're punishing me!'

'You're right, I don't understand.' Celia shook her again, more roughly this time. 'What punishment? It's me they're spying on. Why should anyone want to do that to you?'

'Because I was there!'

Outside two pigeons who had been pecking in the courtyard started up in alarm.

'You were there?'

'Yes! I was there when the Chief Black Eunuch was poisoned.' Annetta's voice was barely a whisper. 'They didn't see me. They thought it was the cat. *They* didn't see me,' she swallowed nervously, 'but he did.'

Celia's head was spinning. So *that* was why Annetta had been so upset when they found him. That at least made some kind of sense. But what in God's name had she been doing there? It was not Annetta's body that was ill, but her mind. Her terror of Hassan Aga was so great she seemed almost unhinged.

'So Hassan Aga knows you were there? You're sure of it?'

'I think so. I thought he was dead. But then . . . then . . . he wasn't. And he isn't. And, oh Celia,' she was crying harder now, 'then they found him, and now it looks as if he will live after all. Suppose he did see me there, he's going to think I had something to do with it.' She stared up, her eyes dry now, burning in her sallow face. 'They know we came here together.'

'What's that got to do with it?' Celia said, perplexed.

'It's the other thing I should have told you. The sugar ship, the one they think poisoned Hassan Aga – it wasn't a figure of the English merchantman at all. It was a replica of your father's boat, goose. An exact replica of the *Celia*.'

Chapter 21

Istanbul: the present day

The next day dawned cold and grey. Elizabeth awoke with a sense of well-being, surprised to find that she had slept through the night. Half a sleeping pill lay untouched on her bedside table. Her body felt warm, soft and pink with sleep. She lay back amongst the pillows, contemplating the sky outside. Something was different, something had changed. Sleepily she put her hand out to turn on her mobile, checking the screen for messages; but as usual there were none from Marius. Only a short text from Eve, which must have been sent the previous evening: *sleep tight darling speak 2morrow xx.*

Marius had not rung in the night, was not thinking of her, was not pleading with her to change her mind; but this morning, for some reason, the feeling of bleakness she was so used to feeling every day when she woke up did not materialise.

She had not dreamt of Marius, she realised, but of the Turk she had seen the day before in the Malta Kiosk. The thought of him still lingered, an erotic whisper at the edges of her mind.

That morning Elizabeth was the last down to breakfast. The other guests – the old American woman in the turban, the French professor, the film director – had almost finished by the time she emerged. She took her coffee and a bread roll with rose-petal jam and went to sit upstairs in the sitting room beneath one of the potted palms. The antique gramophone was playing Russian marching songs. From her bag Elizabeth took out a pen and paper, and as she ate, she began to write another letter to Eve.

185

Hello again, Eve darling, so sorry about my last gloomy missive. You're right, I probably am the last person in the world who actually writes letters, but without you here I need someone to talk to, don't you see? Who else is going to listen to me moaning on about Marius. Heigh-ho: it's cheaper than therapy I suppose (and who knows, perhaps some historian or DPhil student down the years will thank us some day: thank me anyway; they say that no email ever really disappears, but I've never believed it myself. Where do they go? Where are they stored? On a microchip; or do they just float about in the ether somewhere? God knows, paper manuscripts can be hard enough to track down – don't I know it – let alone something the size of a nanobite).

On that subject, nothing to report about the Lamprey captivity narrative. My reader's ticket for the the Bosphorous University has come through, but I'm still waiting for permission to look in the State archives – so far, *nada*. Now, if Celia Lamprey had written a letter or two, think what a help that would have been . . .

Elizabeth licked the sticky traces of rose-petal jam from her left hand, and turned the page. What should she tell Eve about? Her morning in the harem's deserted labyrinth, of Thomas Dallam's 'other curious matter'? Or, better still, the stranger at the Malta Kiosk. For a moment or two her hand wavered over the page.

The other guests here get odder and odder. Two of the Russians I thought looked like white slave traders turn out to be a pair of opera singers invited here by a congress of the Turkish Communist Party. The American in the turban – the Angela Lansbury look-alike – is a writer, or so she claims. Haddba, the guest house owner told me. Now *she* is the strangest of the lot: always wears black and has a face like nun, while somehow contriving to be exactly like a madame in an old Parisian brothel (pure Brassaï – you'd love her), and for some reason has taken me under her wing. Perhaps she's thinking of selling me to the white slave traders . . .

She could imagine Eve's reply via text: *u got 2 b joking we 2 old 4 that worst luck*. Elizabeth smiled. Past it at twenty-eight . . . So how old were you supposed to be? Thirteen, fourteen, that's how young some of those slave girls had been. Celia Lamprey had probably been older than that if she was already betrothed to someone when she was captured, but the others? They were no more than children. Could Berin have been right about them being willing participants in the system? What could they possibly have known about love, about sex? Well, that was the point, wasn't it? They weren't supposed to know; weren't supposed to have needs and desires of their own, just be moulded by what others wanted them to be. It sounded almost restful . . . Elizabeth thought of Marius and sighed.

The old gramophone creaked to a halt, and an unaccustomed silence descended on the room. Elizabeth's mind wandered. She kept waiting for that familiar feeling of dread in the pit of her stomach to return, but to her surprise it did not. And last night she had dreamt, not of Marius, but of another man, a stranger. How odd: she tried to remember exactly what it was that she had dreamt, but as soon as she tried to grasp it in her conscious mind it dissolved like smoke. All that was left was a vague feeling of – what?

Warmth. No. Disquiet.

'Elizabeth?' It was Haddba. 'You're not going to the library today, I see? May I sit?'

Without waiting for a reply she sat down next to her and fitted one of her cigarettes into the ivory holder with her elegant fingers. 'I'll send the boy down for some more coffee.'

She snapped her fingers at Rashid and said something in Turkish. Then she turned her beautiful kohl-lined eyes on Elizabeth again. 'This weather – simply perishing.' She gave a little shiver, pulling a gold-embroidered pashmina a little more closely around her shoulders. 'Today is a good day for you to be going to the hammam, I think.'

'Well, I was thinking of writing up my notes . . .' Elizabeth began, then saw a determined flicker in Haddba's eyes.

'No, Elizabeth.' Haddba had a way of saying her name, which made her sound as if she were singing it. E-*li*-za-beth. She gave the cigarette holder two impatient little taps against the arm of her chair. Ash fluttered around her, making little pools on the floor. 'You must look after yourself. You do not, why is this? Look at you, always so melancholy.' She regarded Elizabeth from beneath her curious thick eyelids. The boy arrived with the coffee. Haddba did not so much take the cup from him as accept it from him, like a tribute.

'Thank you, but really – I've so much to do.' Again Elizabeth began to make her excuses.

'But E-*li*-za-beth, do not say no. This building is by Sinan. So beautiful, you really must see it; you will enjoy.' Haddba's tiny coffee cup, no bigger than a thimble, rapped against the saucer. 'Rashid will take you,' was all she said.

With the boy to escort her, Elizabeth took the bus over the Galata Bridge to the district of Sultanahmet; then the tram up to the Burnt Column near the Grand Bazaar. When they got out Rashid pointed to a door in an anonymous-looking building, hung about on the outside with telephone wires and shop signs.

'In here?' Elizabeth looked dubious.

'*Evet* . . . yes,' the boy nodded, 'hammam.' He gave her one of his luminous smiles.

There were two sides to the hammam, the men's on the left-hand side of the building, a smaller women's side on the right. Elizabeth was taken into a narrow changing room and given a locker containing two threadbare blue towels and a pair of stained plastic slippers. It did not look promising. Several women in long skirts, their hair tied up on their heads with coloured scarves, were in charge of the proceedings. They paid no attention whatever to the handful of tourists who had come in behind Elizabeth – a group of lumpen European students, wrapped up against the cold in jeans and ugly grey cagoules – but sat around chattering volubly. There was an air of cheerful slovenliness about the place; a faint smell of mould.

After the unpromising locker room Elizabeth was completely unprepared for the beauty of the room she now stepped into. A single dome soared above her, supported by four smaller domes; beneath them, on twelve sides, were a series of marble niches, each one containing a small fountain in the shape of a scallop shell. Not so much a room as an architecture of pure space, perfect in its simplicity.

Holding the tiny towel awkwardly at her waist, Elizabeth stepped into the room. In the centre was a slab of white marble on which four women were already lying face down. The light was diffuse, pearly with steam. Elizabeth could not see their faces, only their bodies. One still wore a towel around her hips, but the other three had discarded theirs. They lay very still; some spoke together quietly.

188

Elizabeth sat down on the edge of the slab, and almost jumped off again; the marble was hot to the touch, almost scalding. She took off her towel and, arranging it under her, lay down quickly.

After the noise of the city, it was very peaceful inside. Others entered: the girls – German or Dutch – who had been undressing at the same time as Elizabeth in the locker room. They giggled as they came in, trying to cover themselves with their too-small towels, but soon a kind of languor overtook them, too.

How beautiful they are. Elizabeth was absolutely struck by the thought. These women are absolutely beautiful. In the locker room they had seemed so plain and pasty-faced, their bodies ungainly in their ugly jeans and ill-fitting jumpers. In the street no one would look at these girls twice, but their nakedness, she thought, has transformed them.

A dark-haired girl whom Elizabeth had noticed standing directly behind her in the queue came and took up a place on the marble slab next to her. In the locker room she had appeared short and dumpy, with her hair dragged into a greasy ponytail on the nape of her neck. Now, lying naked in the misty warmth, her hair around her shoulders, she looked quite different. Elizabeth saw how perfect and unblemished her skin was, the pleasingly erotic plumpness of her uncovered buttocks. Not wanting to embarrass her, Elizabeth turned her head away.

There were about twenty women in the hammam now. As she lay there Elizabeth became aware of other details, too. The symmetry of a shoulder blade; a pair of upturned breasts; the sculptured bones of the neck and upper back. A pair of perfect narrow feet.

God, look at you – stop it at once! Laughing at herself, Elizabeth turned on to her back and gazed up at the domed ceiling. It was pierced with small slits in the shape of suns and moons through which the daylight – even the dull grey daylight of that early winter's day – shone. A feeling of intense pleasure came over her. Sinan, hadn't Haddba said?

She closed her eyes, trying to remember the dates, but instead the memory of the stranger she had seen at the Malta Kiosk came to her again. Almost irritably she opened her eyes, as if to push the thought away. Don't be ridiculous, he's not at all your type. She remembered him: a big man; not fat, but well fleshed. A man with presence. And at the thought of him another altogether more powerful thought inserted itself in her mind – what if he could see me now? – closely followed by an erotic charge so powerful it made her catch her breath.

One of the gypsy women now came up. She shook Elizabeth by the shoulder, and without speaking took her hand and led her over to one of the scallop-shaped basins. Elizabeth, her cheeks burning, followed her meekly. The woman made a signal for her to sit down on the step next to the basin. First she scooped ladlefuls of water all over her, then began to scrub her rapidly all over with a thick hessian glove.

The woman worked quickly, her movements brusque to the point of roughness. She picked up Elizabeth's arms and held them over her head, one by one, washing her armpits, her sides, her breasts and belly. When Elizabeth tried to help her, she slapped her hands down by her sides and shook her head as if annoyed, until Elizabeth satisfied her by obeying her unspoken commands, sitting quite still, submissively accepting her ministrations.

What if he could see me now? This time Elizabeth allowed herself a little longer to linger on this pleasing thought. She imagined his eyes on her, that extraordinary, erotic gaze . . . And once again, to her confusion, that intense *frisson* of desire. My God, what's got into you? She nearly laughed out loud at the sheer absurdity of it, at this other, wanton self.

The woman had now begun to wash Elizabeth's hair. Water sluiced over her in shining arcs. It ran over her eyes and in her ears, sticking her hair to her back in long streaming black tendrils. She felt the woman's fingers at her scalp, and then her head being pulled back so sharply she winced. Sharp nails were scraping her head, scratching into her scalp so hard it was almost painful. And then, after a few more shining arcs of water, she was done.

Trembling, Elizabeth stepped back into the room.

Chapter 22

Constantinople: 3 September 1599

Evening

Hassan Aga, the Chief Black Eunuch, would live. The news was all around the House of Felicity. The palace physicians – not only the white eunuch from the palace school, but the Sultan's personal physician, Moses Hamon, had pronounced him out of danger at last. Some talked of a miracle, others of the dreams the Valide Sultan was said to have had presaging his recovery, and of the talismanic shirt she had caused to be made for him: a great wonder, everyone was agreed, covered not only with holy verses from the Qu'ran, but with strange numerals and symbols, close-written in pure gold leaf.

Celia's servants brought word to her that there was to be a celebration in the Great Chamber. An all-women troupe of acrobats and tumblers – gypsy women from Salonica, the eunuchs said – had recently arrived in the city, and had rapidly become the latest fashion amongst the harems, big and small, along the Bosphorous and the Golden Horn. The Valide Sultan herself had sent for them.

That evening as Celia made her way with the other women into the hall which divided the women's quarters from the Sultan's bedchamber, she sensed the atmosphere immediately. Something was different, something had changed. The sense of foreboding that had permeated every courtyard and corridor over the last few days had lifted; in its place was a feeling of energy, of lightness almost. If only I could feel it too, Celia thought. Looking neither left nor right, she walked along the corridors, followed by her attendants. But although her eyes were fixed demurely on the ground, inside her heart and mind were ablaze.

Paul *was* here in Constantinople, she was certain of that now. Who else, other than Carew, could possibly have made a sugar subtlety of the *Celia*? And wherever Carew was, she knew, Paul would not be far behind. But why? The thought tormented her. What could it possibly mean? Was it a sign? Was it conceivable that they knew she was here? She dismissed the thought instantly. They couldn't possibly know, not possibly. Paul thought she was dead. Shipwrecked, drowned.

But now she knew she had no choice: whatever Annetta said, she must *make* them know. Round her neck, hidden beneath her clothes, Celia could feel the key to the Aviary Gate hanging safely on its chain. At the thought of it – the thought of what she must do – she felt a stab in her side so sharp she gasped, almost stumbled against the wall.

'Careful, Kaya Kadin.' One of the women put out her hand to steady her.

'It's nothing; my slipper, that's all.'

Celia composed herself quickly. She mustn't let them see, mustn't let them guess what she was feeling, what she knew. An unguarded word, or even a look, might give her away. They were watching you – always. She knew that now.

They arrived at the Great Chamber.

Since she had received no formal announcement of any change in her circumstances, Celia took up a position on the long cushioned dais close to the Valide's divan on the left-hand side of the room: the place of honour reserved for the highest-ranking women in the harem. Next to her were the Valide Sultan's four handmaids, Gulbahar, Turhan, Fatma, and another girl whose name she did not know, who was standing in until Annetta was well again. Next to them there were spaces for the older officials, in strict order of precedence. After the Valide herself came the Harem Stewardess, followed by the Mistresses of the Girls and of the Bathhouse, the Coffee Mistress and the Coiffeur Mistress. Some of the Sultan's children, the princesses and even some of the little princes who were still young enough to live in the women's quarters, were guided by their attendants to places on the other side of the Safiye Sultan's divan. One of the Valide's own daughters, the princess Fatma, had arrived earlier that day for the occasion, with her children and her own retinue of slaves.

At each end of the chamber silver censers had been lit, and the room was filled with perfume. Fresh flowers – roses, tulips and sprays of orange blossom and jasmine – had been arranged in blue and white vases in each of the room's four corners. Fountains bubbled from marble niches in the wall. Beside the Valide's divan was a small pool on the surface of which the petals of musk roses had been scattered, mingling with candles that had been made to float in tiny boats, their flames reflecting in the pale green water.

The younger girls, the novices and the rank and file *kislar*, were allowed in now, directed in well-ordered rows by the Mistress of the Girls and her deputies to take up their positions opposite the Valide's divan, on the far side of the room.

On holidays like today, the strict rules that governed every aspect of harem life were relaxed, even the rule of silence. The unaccustomed sound of their own voices (rarer in the harem, Annetta was fond of saying, than a man still in possession of his own *cogliones*) acted on the roomful of women like a drug. A flush of excitement was spread across every cheek. Everyone was talking to her neighbour. And everyone, even the youngest, some no more than eight or nine years old, was dressed in gala. Silks, picked out in circles, stripes and crescent moons, brocades embroidered with gold and silver threads, cut velvets patterned with tulips and cascades of fluttering leaves glistened in the candlelight. Sashes and caps and veils of golden gauze were pinned with aigrettes of precious stones, blue and yellow topazes, the reds of garnets and carnelian, the greens of malachite and jade and emerald; opals and moonstones and strings of pearls, softened and warmed by the skin. Everyone, it seemed to Celia – even Cariye Lala, the humblest and oldest under-mistress who came to take up her place just in front of her on one of the bottom steps of the Valide's dais – had some precious gem to wear.

The first few times that Celia had seen all the women together like this she had been so dazzled by the spectacle that it had been enough just to sit and gaze. Now she was almost indifferent to the display. Was anyone watching her, anyone unusual? She scanned the crowd. The Macedonian from the Bathhouse; her assistant, the Georgian.

193

The great mute Coiffeur Mistress, her face as broad as it was long, with her enormous teeth that shone as white as tombstones. There was a little stir in the room as the eunuchs brought in Hassan Aga on his litter. At the sight of him, his great mound of black flesh apparently undiminished by his ordeal, her heart gave a lurch. How had Hanza acquired the key that now hung secretly around her neck? She had been too afraid to ask . . . Celia felt it, like a red-hot coal, burning into her flesh.

When Gulbahar put a hand on her shoulder she jumped as if she had been struck.

'Do you think she'll come?' she was whispering into her ear.

'Who?' Celia asked.

'Gulay, of course.'

Gulbahar pointed to the gilded canopy at the far end of the chamber. Beneath it stood the throne on which the Sultan would sit; at its foot a small cushion had been placed: the Haseki's seat of honour.

'Why shouldn't she?' Celia replied.

'They're saying Hanza has replaced her.' Gulbahar gave Celia an enquiring look.

'What?' Celia said, dismayed. 'So soon?'

'He called for her again, you know – this afternoon.'

'I see.' Celia looked round, but could see no sign of Hanza. 'Where is she anyway?'

But before they could say any more the great doors on the Sultan's side of the hall were opened and a hush descended on the chamber. Escorted by Suleiman Aga and three other eunuchs, Gulay Haseki entered the room. She wore a dress of cut blue velvet figured with silver circles, beneath which was a bodice and trousers made of gold tissue. And fastened to her cap, to her bodice, and even pinned to her sash, were more brilliants than Celia had ever seen in her life. In silence the Haseki walked very slowly through the doorway, crossing the Great Chamber to take up her position beneath the golden canopy. She turned to face the room full of women, and then carefully took her place on the cushion at the foot of the Sultan's throne.

As if breathing a collective sigh of relief the women erupted into chatter again. Celia looked round at the crowd of excited faces, and then back at Gulay again. But if the Haseki had seen Celia in the crowd, she gave no sign.

The Haseki was right: whispers, rumours, surmise. We thrive on it because there's nothing else, Celia thought. Earlier the atmosphere in the Great Chamber had been like an audience waiting for a play to begin, at the Curtain or even the new Rose theatre in London where her father had taken her sometimes. But this – Celia shivered, glancing across at the glittering mannequin, remote and motionless beneath the Sultan's gilded canopy – this was more like bear-baiting than a play.

A thought occurred to her. She turned to Gulbahar.

'Where does the Sultan's old favourite sit? I'm not sure I've ever seen her.'

'Do you mean Handan Kadin? The mother of Prince Ahmet?'

'Yes, Handan. I think that's her name.'

'She never comes here.' Gulbahar shrugged. 'Not now. I don't think anyone sees her, except for the Valide.'

Somewhere out of sight now came the sound of the acrobat troupe warming up: a distant roll of drums, the plaintive sound of a reed-pipe. At that moment another hush, a silence deeper and more profound than before, descended on the room. Everyone rose to their feet. Not another murmur was heard as the doors at either end of the chamber were flung open. From the harem entrance on one side of the chamber came the Valide Sultan, while from the opposite side the Sultan himself now entered. They met in the middle of the chamber for the Sultan to greet his mother, then they took their respective seats.

It was then that Celia saw Hanza. She had slipped in almost unnoticed behind the Valide and came to take up her place beside Celia. Around her thin neck was a jewelled necklace and a pair of matching pear-shaped diamonds glittered in her ears: the spoils – Celia guessed – of her afternoon's work. Against Hanza's pale little face they took on an improbable, almost tawdry look, like so many trinkets bought at the bazaar. Her expression was so venomous that Celia's greeting curdled on her tongue.

Now that everyone had taken their final places, with a drum roll the entertainment began. The musicians came in first and settled themselves on a piece of matting on the floor; one woman struck a pair of cymbals, another rattled a tambourine, a third played the reed-pipe, while the fourth carried two small drums. Following immediately behind them, shouting and ululating, the troupe of tumblers came leaping into the room, strange, barbarous-looking creatures, with oily black hair hanging loose to their shoulders. They wore short brightly coloured fitted jackets which left their shoulders and arms bare, and a strange trouser-like garment made from fine lawn cotton on their legs, voluminous around the buttocks and thighs, close fitting from the ankles to the knees. Some walked on their hands, others threw themselves backwards, arching their spines into strange crab-like shapes; yet others spun round in cartwheels.

The youngest of the tumblers were two little girls no more than six or seven years old. The eldest, who was also the leader of the troupe, was a stout barrel-chested woman who wore a red bandana across her forehead. At a signal from the drums she squared her shoulders, and on to her, one by one, leapt the other women, until six of them were balanced astride her in a pyramid. The cymbals crashed. The legs of the woman in the red bandana trembled, but somehow she walked three steps across the room. The drums sounded again and the two little girls flew to her, leaping up the pyramid, climbing like monkeys to the very top of the human tree. The cymbals crashed again; the acrobats held out their arms, and at this signal, their leader took three more steps towards the Sultan's throne. Her skin glistened, the veins in her great bull's neck bulged with the exertion, but she held her ground. Another drum roll, and one by one the women leapt from her again as effortlessly as they had climbed up, landing soundlessly on their feet as if they were no heavier than rose petals. From nowhere the two little girls produced two red roses which on bended knees they laid at the Sultan's feet.

The evening wore on. The acrobatics were followed in quick succession by feats of balancing, juggling and contortionism. The women, young and old, sat spellbound by the spectacle. Even Hassan Aga, slack-mouthed with concentration, lay quite still on his cushions. Only Celia could not concentrate. With so many women crammed together and the heat of the candles, the chamber had become so airless that Celia felt as if she were suffocating; but she dared not get up, dared not draw attention to herself by such a blatant breach of etiquette, by anything that might hint at her inner anguish. She put her hand to her chest, felt the comforting outline of the key on its chain against her breast. Willed herself to act the part of the unseeing, unknowing *cariye* she had been just a few days previously. *Not much longer, sweetheart, I promise*, feverishly she tried to conjure the sound of Paul's voice, *not much longer now*.

Other than herself there was only one other person that Celia could see who was not utterly absorbed by the acrobat troupe. Hanza had eyes only for the Sultan. Or at least that was what Celia thought at first. Then she realised that it was not the Sultan Hanza was staring at. It was the Haseki.

Hanza was staring at Gulay Haseki with such intensity that Celia was amazed the favourite did not feel the force of those strange pale eyes upon her. If she did she gave no sign. Gulay was watching the performance as intently as everyone else, or so it seemed. After some moments of watching her closely Celia noticed that every so often her gaze would dart towards the Valide's divan, and then back again, as if she were looking for someone.

'She looks well, don't you think?' Celia could not resist whispering to Hanza. 'The Haseki, I mean.'

'What's she still doing there?' Hanza gave a small cat-like sneeze. She seemed consumed by some intense emotion: rage, disappointment? It was hard to tell.

'And where else should she be?' Celia was enjoying the girl's discomfiture. She had the key now, she thought with triumph; Hanza couldn't touch her. 'Do you think it should be you sitting there? You're a fool – worse than a fool – if you think that.'

But Hanza gave no reply.

The strongwoman in the red bandana now took to the floor on her own. Various props were lined up in front of her: a large pot of the kind used for storing oil, some logs of wood, a row of cannonballs of various sizes, some of them attached to chains. Tying leather straps around her wrists and then a thick leather harness around her waist, she began to juggle with the logs of wood, balancing them on her head, then on her forehead, then on her chin, and even on her teeth.

The Sultan bent down to say something in the Haseki's ear, making her turn to him with a smile. How can she bear it, Celia thought? At a distance he seemed so very ordinary, for all his jewels and finery, with his speckled skin and his fat paunch, and large blond beard. Beside her Celia felt Hanza shiver.

The strongwoman was now juggling with two of the cannonballs, heaving them up into the air with hands calloused like old leather. Droplets of sweat from her brow flew into the air; Celia could see them glisten as they caught the candlelight. The Sultan turned to the Haseki again, and this time he offered her one of the red roses that had been laid at his feet. The other he sent over to the Valide Sultan. Celia waited for Hanza's reaction, but none came. It was some minutes before she realised that the place next to her was empty. Hanza had gone.

Where did she go? Celia signalled to Gulbahar.

'Hanza? I don't know.' Gulbahar whispered. 'She went out a few minutes ago. Good riddance to her. I only hope, for her sake, the Valide didn't see her.'

Celia put her hand to her throat; she could hardly breathe.

'Are you all right, *kadin*?' Gulbahar put a hand on Celia's arm. 'You look strange.'

'I'm all right. Just . . . it's a little hot in here, that's all.' Celia tried to steady her breath. Then, before she could stop herself, she said, 'I have a bad feeling about that one, Gulbahar.'

'That little snake in the grass?' Gulbahar's lip curled. 'Don't worry, we all have a bad feeling about *her*.'

'It's more than just a feeling.' Celia glanced around, trying to see which way Hanza might have gone. 'She means mischief, Gulbahar, I know she does.'

'Oh, what can she do?' Gulbahar shrugged dismissively. 'Mark my words, she'll be in trouble enough already for going off without permission. She's terrified of the Valide – I know, I've seen them together,' Gulbahar gave a dry laugh, 'like a rabbit and a snake. Don't worry, she wouldn't dare try anything. Just enjoy the entertainment, Kaya.'

The Valide, of course! Surely she must be the key to all this? Someone had certainly given Hanza ideas about how easy it would be for her to replace the Haseki in the Sultan's attentions, ideas that would have seemed completely absurd to anyone else. Who else could have been that persuasive? And I should know, Celia thought. After all, she tried the same thing on me only a few days ago.

198

She looked towards the Valide and was surprised, once again, by how small she was in the flesh. Safiye Sultan was seated on her divan, her slender body curled against the cushions, one foot tucked beneath her, chin propped on a delicate wrist. The robe she wore that evening was of the richest red damask with a gold embroidered bodice, and she wore many jewels; her long hair was twisted and plaited through with gold chains strung with pearls. How dazzling she was, and how dangerous. More than a match for Hanza.

In her hand Safiye Sultan held the rose that the Sultan had sent her – a musk rose, of a red so dark it was almost black – twisting it absently between her fingers. Like everyone else she was watching the acrobat troupe, occasionally turning to address a remark to her daughter, Princess Fatma, sitting next to her. From time to time she bent down to smell the rose. Her air was carefree, but there was something about her that was – Celia searched for the right description – what? Concentrated. Watchful. You are still watching us, it occurred to Celia. Every one of us, even now. What was it that Annetta had said? *They watch and they wait, that's what they do in here.* She knew then that the Valide must have been expecting Hanza to leave.

The strongwoman had finished now and her place in the centre of the room had been taken by another member from the troupe whom Celia had not seen before: a grave-faced woman, her face whitened with chalk like a Pierrot's. Unlike the others she was not wearing trousers, but a curious robe made from brightly coloured striped material with a voluminous skirt and sleeves. Every inch was stitched over with silver spangles. When she walked she seemed to glide over the floor as if on wheels.

It was completely dark outside now and the lamps had been lit. The holiday atmosphere created by the tumblers and the strong-woman was replaced by a hush of suspense. In silence the white-faced Pierrot woman circled slowly round the room. Her robe glittered as she moved, as if it were made of ice. And as she moved objects materialised mysteriously in her wake. Feathers, flowers and pieces of fruit – pomegranates, figs and apples – were produced from the folds of robes, from behind ears and up sleeves. From each of the Valide's handmaids she took an embroidered handkerchief, pushing each one after another into her clenched fist, then pulling them out again, magically knotted into a streaming silk rainbow. From behind the ears of one of the little princesses she found two eggs which she then threw into the air, making them vanish, then materialise again in the lap of the smallest child, in the form of two softly cheeping chicks. Bowing low before the Sultan, the magician now turned her sights upon Gulay Haseki, still sitting next to him on her cushion. The Sultan signalled his permission and the Haseki rose to her feet and stepped into the middle of the room. The musicians, who had been sitting silently all this time, now played a burst of music. There was a roll of drums and they all saw that the doors on the Valide's side of the harem were opening. Everyone turned expectantly towards them, but no, it seemed that this was not part of the act. For through the doors, who should come flying towards them all but Hanza.

Hanza, her cap awry, her face as pale as death. In her hands she held a package.

'See!' She held it out with trembling arms. 'It was Gulay Haseki. She did it.'

A deathly hush descended on the room. The Haseki turned pale, but she remained standing motionless next to the white-faced magician. Celia saw her reach for her bracelet of blue glass charms, as if these might somehow have the power to protect her. Safiye Sultan was sitting up now, but even she made no move.

When Hanza realised that everyone was looking at her, she suddenly appeared completely panic-stricken. She shook the package and something fell out. It landed softly on the floor. She held it up: a piece of paper with symbols and figures written all over it in blue and gold ink.

'See! A horoscope. I found it. It was hidden in her room.'

Still no one spoke.

'Don't you want to know who it's for? It's for *him*,' she pointed towards Hassan Aga, 'for the Chief Black Eunuch. It's sorcery, the Devil's work! The Haseki wanted to know when he was going to die . . .' Hanza's voice, unnaturally shrill, echoed through the silent room. Flecks of spittle had appeared at the corners of her mouth. 'Don't you understand? It was she who tried to kill him!'

And then, as if from nowhere, there came the sound of running feet; the metallic scrape of metal on stone. The eunuchs came flying in, their swords drawn. But who were they coming for, Hanza or

Gulay? The room erupted into noise and confusion. Everyone was shouting all at once; the children and some of the younger *kislar* cried and wailed. At the centre of the chaos, Celia saw Hanza fall to the ground. At first she thought that she had merely fainted, but then she saw that the girl had fallen into some kind of fit. Her lips had turned blue; her eyes rolled so that only the whites showed; her thin body was jerking and twitching on the tiled floor.

Even the senior mistresses, normally so careful of their dignity, were on their feet now.

'Look!' voices were crying out, 'look at her, a demon has taken her!'

The great mute Coiffeur Mistress, a giant of a negress, taller and broader than the Sultan's own halberdiers, was screaming and pointing, incoherent sounds coming from her tongueless mouth. Everyone was standing now, moving, pointing, running; the room, to Celia's dazed eyes, a whirling mêlée of fur and silk.

The elite of the eunuch guard surrounded the Sultan immediately and escorted him from the room. The others closed in around Hanza, picking her up bodily as if to remove her from the room, but it was only with difficulty that they could hold her, and several times she slipped back on to the tiled floor. Her head struck the marble floor with a sickening crack. Blood now mixed with the spittle at the corners of her mouth.

The panic in the chamber was infectious. Celia felt it grip her too. She could see the Harem Stewardess on her feet and shouting for order, but no one could hear her above the noise. Celia wanted to run, but she found that her legs would not move. Don't run, think, said a voice inside her head. And suddenly she was calm. In the storm of frenzied women Celia stood still, and saw that there were only two others who, like her, were neither running nor shouting.

In the centre of the room the Haseki was still standing beside the magician. Watching her from one side of the room, vast and unblinking on his litter, was the figure of Hassan Aga, while on the other side, sitting absolutely still on her divan, was the Valide. Two eunuch mutes, amongst the most trusted of the Valide's personal servants, had taken up positions on either side of her. When she was sure that she had the Haseki's attention, the Valide slowly lifted the rose which she was still holding between her fingers, and snapped it violently in two.

201

Immediately the mutes moved towards Gulay, seizing her by the shoulders. She did not cry out, and she did not struggle, but before they could take her away, Celia saw her pluck quickly at her wrist. Suddenly something blue and shining flew through the air towards her. It was the bracelet, the bracelet with the blue glass talismans. Celia watched it describe a shining arc through the air. She put her hand out to catch it, but the bracelet fell short, landing instead just below her, on the hem of Cariye Lala's robe. She leant down to retrieve it but Cariye Lala was too quick for her. The old woman, with surprising agility, bent down and scooped up the bracelet.

'Cariye!' Celia's voice was sharp. 'Cariye Lala – I believe that's for me.'

The under-mistress looked up at her, an expression of surprise in her blue eyes. A memory came to Celia of that night in the Valide's hammam: the feel of cool marble against her thighs, the smell of *ot*, Cariye Lala's old head working up and down over the pear. She remembered, too, the exact sensation, the needle-fine scrape, of Cariye Lala's finger as it pushed hard into her sex. The same finger from which the Haseki's blue glass bracelet was now dangling.

'If you please . . .' Celia stood tall, 'the bracelet.'

But Cariye Lala showed no sign of handing it over. She merely stood there looking at Celia, her little head cocked to one side, her eyes very bright. In her holiday finery, Celia thought unkindly, she had the look of a trumpery old parrot.

'The bracelet,' Celia summoned as much authority as she could, 'if you please, *cariye.*'

She held out her hand.

But still Cariye Lala showed no sign of handing over her treasure.

Then, without warning, as if she had suddenly tired of some childish game, or as if she had satisfied herself about something, she reached across and dropped the bracelet into Celia's outstretched palm.

Celia's fingers closed over it at last. When she looked up the Haseki had gone.

No one sees the sacks when they are dropped at night into the inky black waters of the Bosphorous. But you can always hear the guns which signal some nameless harem woman's demise.

On board the *Hector*, a sleepless Paul Pindar heard them.

Lying awake in her room in the palace harem, Celia Lamprey heard them.

And on his silken litter, still wrapped in his talismanic shirt, Little Nightingale turned and stirred, his eyes two black slits in the darkness.

Chapter 23

Istanbul: the present day

Elizabeth's research at the Bosphorous University now began in earnest. She travelled there on the bus. The first few days Haddba insisted on sending Rashid with her to show her the way, but soon she was confident enough to negotiate the route herself. She found that she enjoyed the ride. Until now, it occurred to her, she had felt like a ghost in this ancient city; but the bus rides, repeated every day, seemed to flesh out her bones, gave her a sense of belonging, a sense, however temporary, of being part of this place, rattling and bumping her way with the other commuters along the cobbled Istanbul streets.

In the evenings she came home by the same route. As she grew to know the city better she would stop off sometimes at one or another of the old villages along the Bosphorous: at Ermigan, famous for the excellence of its water, to drink tea and to buy pastries for Haddba at her favourite shop, the Citir Pastahane; or one of the cafés in the old village square at Ortakoy, much frequented by students, where she would eat mezes – garlicky yoghurt flavoured with mint and dill, stuffed mussels, quince cheese – and watch the world go by.

They were solitary days, but Elizabeth was not lonely. Late autumn deepened into winter, and the melancholy of the city still suited her mood. In the long dark evenings she would play cards with Haddba, old-fashioned games like cribbage and rummy, or write letters to Eve. It was restful, she found, not to have to talk.

The first few weeks working in the library were very slow. But although there turned out to be no archival material, there were other unexpected breakthroughs.

One day she came across a book on the Levant Company, and opening it quite at random, found herself staring at a portrait of Paul Pindar. There was no date; no provenance. Just a name: Sir Paul Pindar.

Her first impression was how very dark he was: black eyes – intelligent and quizzical – looking out beneath close-cropped hair, beard trimmed into a neat point, not a trace of grey. Apart from a small white ruff at his neck he was dressed entirely in black. When she looked more carefully she saw that the portrait was of a man of later years, but his figure was still slim, not a hint of flesh on him, none of the tell-tale signs of wealth, of indolence or excess. Instead a feeling of restless energy emanated from the picture. Every inch, in other words, the merchant-adventurer. In one hand he held an object that Elizabeth could not quite see, proffering it to the viewer on an open palm. She turned on the reading lamp at her desk, but the book was old, published in the 1960s, and the reproduction of such poor quality that even in the brightest light the object was impossible to discern.

Elizabeth took a photocopy of the portrait. When she got back to her room that evening she laid it out on the table next to her handwritten copy of Celia Lamprey's narrative, and the photocopy of Thomas Dallam's diary. She picked up the latter and read the words again:

> *. . . than crossinge throughe a litle squar courte paved with marble, he poyneted me to go to a graite in a wale, but made me a sine that he myghte not go thether him selfe. When I cam to the grait the wale was verrie thicke and graited on bothe the sides with iron verrie strongly: but through that graite I did se thirtie of the Grand Sinyor's Concobines that weare playinge with a bale in another courte . . . that sighte did please me wondrous well.*

She arranged the pages carefully on the table again. Who else had known about the grate in the wall? If one junior palace guard had been aware of its existence – even if he didn't dare approach it himself – then there must have been others who knew the secret. And as Thomas Dallam had realised, if he could see in, then a woman, if she had been made aware of it, could just as easily see out. 'Yf they had sene me, they would all have come presently thether to louke upon me, and have wondred as moche at me, or how I cam thether, as I did to se them.'

As she read the words Elizabeth thought of the deserted rooms and corridors in the harem, of the dim blue and green light. Of the sound – so puzzling to her at first – of laugher; the echo of running feet.

It's no good, she passed a hand over her eyes, I must stick to the facts. I know, I'll ask Eve what she thinks, and as if on cue, she heard the bleep of an incoming message from her mobile phone. But it was not Eve. It was a text from Marius.

Elizabeth stared at it, almost dispassionately, like a starving person who has been given a crust of bread too hard to eat. *where u been baby?* Insouciant, she said to herself. How can a text be insouciant? But from Marius, somehow, it could. Where have I been? I'll tell you where I've been, hell and back, she felt like replying. But she did not. She deleted the message, felt euphoric for about five minutes, and then wept for half an hour as if her heart would break.

November turned into December. The days passed, saved from pleasant monotony by Haddba, who from time to time would issue her with an instruction – thinly veiled in the form of a courteous suggestion – to go to this restaurant or that café, to the Egyptian spice market to buy camomile flowers for her *tissanes*, to this shop, where she must try out a glass of *boza*, the winter drink made famous by the janissaries, and where a glass once used by Atatürk was enshrined in a cabinet on the wall.

But for the most part Elizabeth worked and read, immersing herself so deeply in her work that she had not time or energy to think about England. Her dreams, when she could remember them, were neither about Marius, nor about the man in the Malta Kiosk, but about the sea, and a shipwreck, and Celia Lamprey, the lost love of the merchant Pindar.

One morning as she was walking down to breakfast she heard the familiar sing-song voice call after her in the hall. 'E-*li*-za-beth?'

'Haddba! Good morning.'

'I have something very nice for you to do today.' Haddba was dressed in her usual dusty black shift; in the gloomy light of the hallway her golden earrings danced at her throat. 'Should, that is, you not be too busy today my dear?'

She gave Elizabeth one of her beady stares. Elizabeth, whose mind that morning had been far away on the niceties of Elizabethan trading missions, gave an inward smile. Haddba, she thought to herself, had a distinctly laissez-faire approach to the life–work balance.

'What have you got up your sleeve?'

'Well, I have been thinking about it for some time: I think it's high time you made a little trip on the Bosphorous. You know, on a boat.'

'On a boat? Today?'

Elizabeth hoped that she did not look as though her heart was sinking.

'But of course today. You work too hard. Look at you, so pale.' Haddba pinched Elizabeth's cheek between her fingers. 'You young people, you young girls, you don't know how to look after yourselves any more. Some pure air is what you need, so good for the complexion . . .' She patted Elizabeth's cheek.

'Will it take me to the university?'

'The *university*?' Haddba made it sound as if she had never heard of anything so preposterous. 'Not everything can be learnt from books, you know. No, no, I have asked my nephew to arrange a visit to one of the *yalis*. One of our Bosphorous summer houses. I think you will like it.'

'A *yali*?' Elizabeth repeated. In December? And then, 'I didn't know you had a nephew.'

'You haven't met Mehmet?' Haddba sounded as if this were the greatest possible surprise to her. 'Ah well . . .' She made a gesture, uncharacteristically vague, towards the drawing room door. 'He's here now.'

Elizabeth now saw that a man was standing in the doorway. Now he came forwards to greet them. Elizabeth looked at him. Oh God! was all she could think, not you!

'Mehmet, I want you to meet my friend Elizabeth. Elizabeth, Mehmet.'

They shook hands.

'I'm surprised you two haven't met before.' Haddba looked innocently from one to the other.

'Ah, well, you'd better go into the sitting room. I'll find Rashid.'

They sat down opposite one another on one of the stiff horsehair sofas. There were no Russian marching songs, no other residents in there that morning. For once the room was silent.

'You're Haddba's nephew?' Elizabeth said after a while, cringing inwardly at the banality of the statement.

'Actually, "nephew" is more a figure of speech. I am not really Haddba's nephew,' he smiled. 'At least not in the way that you might understand it.' She noticed that he spoke English very correctly, with a slight French accent that surprised her. 'My uncle was her friend.' He used the word carefully. 'But a very dear friend, I believe. He left her this house when he died.'

'Oh.'

They lapsed into silence again. Elizabeth tried to think of something else to say but she could not. Does he recognise me? was all she could think.

'Actually, I think we have met before.' Mehmet was the first to break the silence.

'Mm?'

'Well, not exactly met. It was here in this room. I came in to read the paper one afternoon and you were in here doing something, writing a letter, I think. You changed the records on the record player.'

'Of course!' Elizabeth had to stop herself from laughing out loud. 'Yes, I think I do remember now.'

But not the time at the Malta Kiosk! Oh thank God! She felt light-headed with relief.

Rashid came in with two cups of coffee on a tray.

'Shall we wait for Haddba?' Elizabeth said, trying to see into the hall. She was conscious of the fact that she was sitting up very stiffly on the formal sofa. 'Where do you think she's got to?'

'I think she thought she would be . . . *de trop*,' he said. And then, watching Rashid serve her the coffee, 'I think this boy's in love with you.'

'Ah . . . no,' Elizabeth said. He started to say something teasing to the boy in Turkish, but she put her hand out to stop him. 'No, you mustn't, please don't embarrass him.' And then, 'He's a sweet boy, and he works hard. I bring him things sometimes, that's all.'

'You are fond of children?'

From anyone else the question would have sounded patronising; but from him somehow it did not.

'Yes,' Elizabeth considered the question seriously. 'I suppose I always have been.'

'Well then, that's why they like you.'

Silence fell again between them. Elizabeth looked around again, but there was still no sign of anyone in the hallway. Where was Haddba when you wanted her? She saw him looking at her and quickly dropped her gaze, but not before he had intercepted her look.

'Haddba is a very remarkable woman.'

'She is certainly that.' And more bordello mistress than nun today, Elizabeth thought drily to herself. What's she playing at?

Now that she had recovered something of her composure she saw that Mehmet was a man somewhat older than herself, in his forties she guessed, well fleshed, without being heavy. The pure profile of a figure in a Persian miniature. Not good-looking exactly, but . . . she searched for the word . . . *soigné*. And rather charming, actually.

'You know her well, then?'

'No!' he laughed. 'I don't think anyone knows Haddba *well* . . .' He leant forwards, suddenly complicit. 'Did no one tell you? Haddba is one of the great mysteries of Istanbul.'

'What a shame, and there was I thinking that I would be able to ask you all sorts of things about her.'

'Ah, but you still can. Ask me, for example, if she is Turkish.'

'All right then.' Elizabeth looked directly at him. 'Is she Turkish?'

'No, although she speaks the language better than I do; not what you might call demotic Turkish, but the old Ottoman of the imperial court, very elaborate, very courteous.'

'Really?'

'Yes, really.' He held her gaze. His eyes, when he smiled, crinkled at the corners. 'The only person I ever heard speak like that, years ago now, was a friend of my grandmother's who as a young girl had been in the Sultan's harem.'

'But Haddba is not that old, surely?'

'Isn't she?' He gave her a quizzical look. 'But no, you're right. She's probably not. All the same, someone must have taught her.'

'So if she's not Turkish?'

'My uncle's theory was she is an Armenian Jew, but she denies it. Others claim that she is Persian, or even Greek.'

'And you, what do you think?'

'My favourite theory is that she is the daughter of a Russian dancer, one of three famously exotic sisters who came to Istanbul in the thirties,' smiling, he gave a small shrug, 'but who knows?'

'Hasn't anyone just come out with it and asked her?'

He raised an eyebrow. 'Would you?'

A look of understanding passed between them. He's absolutely right, Elizabeth thought. She would think it an impertinence. How interesting that he sees that . . .

'Well, aren't you going to ask me something else?'

Something about his manner made Elizabeth relax.

'No, actually,' she sat back, resting her head against the hard chair, and smiled at him, 'but I have a feeling you are going to tell me anyway.'

'Ask me about her jewels.'

'Her jewels?'

'Ah, you see! I had a feeling that might interest you.'

'All right,' despite herself, she was enjoying their conversation very much, 'tell me about her jewels.'

'But surely you have noticed them?'

'I've seen that she has some amazing earrings.'

'Museum pieces.'

'Really?'

'Yes, really.' He was completely serious now. 'All of them. A priceless collection – necklaces, bracelets, rings – exquisite things. She keeps them in an old tin box beneath her bed.'

'Under her bed? Isn't she afraid that someone will steal them?'

'Steal from Haddba? No one would dare.'

'And where did they all come from?'

'Ah well, that's another question. Some say old King Farouk of Egypt . . .' He spread his fingers. 'But again, no one really knows. In any case, I like mysteries,' he said, standing up. 'Don't you?'

Elizabeth watched him pick up his things.

'Are you going?' she asked, then realised, too late, that there was disappointment in her voice.

'Forgive me, I have taken up too much of your time already.'

'Oh no, not at all.'

'You see, Haddba told me that I must take you for a trip up the Bosphorous, you know how she gets these enthusiasms,' he pointed to Elizabeth's laptop and briefcase, 'but I can see that this isn't a good day for you.'

'Oh no, really.'

'But you were hoping to go to the university today, weren't you?'

'I was, yes.' She was at a loss to know what else to say.

'Ah, well, in that case it would most definitely be an intrusion. Another time perhaps?'

'Yes, another time.'

There was a silence between them, and to stop it she put her hand out quickly to shake his, but instead he took it and raised it swiftly to his lips.

'Goodbye, Elizabeth.'

'Goodbye.'

From the window Elizabeth watched as Mehmet's upright figure receded down the street. She heard the bleep of a car unlocking automatically, and on the street corner saw him get into a white Mercedes. He had not turned round, but she had the odd feeling that he knew she was watching him; was perhaps even half expecting her to go after him. And why didn't she? What, after all, was to stop her?

The day, all of a sudden, seemed to lack savour.

'So, Elizabeth.' It was Haddba beside her. She had entered silently, and was now looking over Elizabeth's shoulder to where Mehmet's car was just pulling out. 'I see you decided to keep him waiting.'

'I'm sorry, Haddba.' Elizabeth turned round, but to her surprise Haddba had a look of deep satisfaction on her face. Her Mother Superior eyes glittered.

'It's quite all right, my dear.' She patted Elizabeth's cheek approvingly. 'You are a clever girl after all.' She gave a low laugh. 'Now don't tell me they teach you *that* at your university.'

Chapter 24

Constantinople: 3 September 1599

Night

Celia woke with a cry. At first she did not know what it was that startled her out of sleep. The realisation – that it was the guns sounding over the Bosphorous to signal the demise of Gulay Haseki – brought with it a terror that Celia could only remember feeling once before. In that split second between sleep and wakefulness she had experienced again the roar and smash of the waves against rock and wooden deck; the sickening crack of the mast; the leaden weight of her sodden skirts; eyes blinded by wind and salt; the flash of a blade as it came down; her father left bleeding on the deck of the sinking ship.

Gasping for breath, she sat up. Even amongst the coverlets, her skin felt cold and clammy. It was so dark in her room – like all the rooms allocated to the *kislar*, it had no external windows – that she could not even see her own hands when she held them up to her face. Was this what it would be like to be blind? For a moment Celia thought she could hear footsteps – the sound of an unknown intruder padding softly round her room? – and it was only after some moments that she realised it was the sound of her own heart beating.

Gradually, as her eyes adjusted, shapes and forms began to come into focus. Against the far wall were the still-sleeping figures of her two servant women, curled up beneath their quilts on the floor. In a niche in the wall behind her a single candle was guttering, its flame like a small blue firefly. Celia put her hand into the niche and pulled out the Haseki's bracelet. Then she lay back against the cushions again to think. Who was it, she wondered, who had really been behind the Haseki's betrayal? Hanza was ambitious, but, Celia was convinced now more than ever, there was something about her that was simply too green for her to have been working entirely on her own. Gulay Haseki had been about to tell her who the third Nightingale was – could it be something to do with that? *Too late for her to tell me now*, she thought sadly.

After the eunuchs had taken Hanza and Gulay away, the Valide and the senior harem mistresses had lost no time in restoring order again. As a means of keeping the *kislar* calm the rule of silence had been imposed for the rest of the evening. No one knew for sure what had happened to Hanza; but – if the shocked and pale faces that Celia saw everywhere around her were anything to go by – in their hearts everybody knew the fate of Gulay Haseki.

They say that there are some fates worse than death. Although she tried not to, Celia imagined what it would be like to be sewn up into a sack; she imagined rough hands lifting her up; the sound of a voice begging, screaming – *no, no, kill me first, anything, anything but this* – a frenzy of tearing, biting – then the terror of water penetrating the sack, water roaring into her ears and eyes, exploding in her throat and into her nose.

And then cold, cold, cold.

A feeling of panic, thicker than bile, rose in Celia's throat. Fighting for breath, she sprang up from her bed and ran to the door, shivering and breathing in great lungfuls of air. After a few minutes the sweet night air, the solid ground beneath her feet, soothed her. She put her hand to her throat – willing her breathing to return to normal – and felt the solid shape of the key to the Aviary Gate still hanging on its chain around her neck.

It would be madness, wouldn't it . . .? Celia took a few exploratory steps across the courtyard. How quiet the courtyard was. There was not a sound. Moonlight poured down, so bright she could see the red of her dress. There was no one to see her, no one to hear. The key was already in her hand . . .

But no, she couldn't. *They watch. They watch and they wait.* Annetta's words came back to her. And it was true – whoever 'they' were. The Nightingales? She hardly knew any more. Annetta's fear, and the Haseki's, had infected her. She could feel spying eyes on her whatever she did, wherever she went, perhaps even now. To attempt

213

to open the Aviary Gate – and for what? – would be worse than madness, it would be death.

At the thought of it, the feeling of breathlessness started to come over her again, only this time she realised that it was not the fear of the sack. Celia put her hand to her throat. *It's this place, this life, this is worse than drowning.* A feeling of desperation, almost of madness, rose in her.

Before she could change her mind, Celia started to run.

Afterwards she had no memory of how she got to the Aviary Gate. Without looking once behind her, Celia ran fast and silently, along corridors and passageways, down steps and across paths, towards that part of the harem gardens where, after she was declared *gözde*, and when the rest of the harem had been at the Valide's summer palace, she had once been permitted to come and watch the novice *cariyes* play their ball games. She did not stop running until she came to the furthest wall of the garden, and there, sure enough, just as Hanza said there would be, in between two myrtle bushes in ornamental pots, she could just make out the outline of a metal grille, part of an old gateway in the wall that was now completely concealed by ivy. The grille was so small, and so hidden by vegetation, that unless she had known exactly where to look for it, she would never have been able to find it. Celia put the key in the lock and the door opened smoothly towards her.

At first, like a caged bird that has forgotten it knows how to fly, Celia stood on the threshold, uncertain how to proceed. She turned, listening carefully, but behind her the harem gardens, silvered by the moon, were absolutely silent. There was not so much as a breath of wind. Then, on the other side of the gateway, she saw it: the English gift. It was far bigger than she had imagined: a huge box-like object, three times her height, standing on its own about thirty yards away. As though in a dream, she watched her own moonlit form flit silently towards it.

Celia examined the strange object carefully. The lower part consisted of a keyboard with ivory and ebony keys like a spinet. Here and there small scraps of paper had been pushed between them, as if the keys had been only recently glued in place. Above them, set into a headboard, were the organ's pipes, in ascending order of size. Set into

214

the middle of this strange contraption was a clock telling the hours, and on either side of the clock two angels, silver trumpets at their lips, sounded a silent tantara. On the topmost part of the structure was what appeared to be a bush made from wires, and in amongst the wires were the figures of birds of different kinds, their beaks open as though they were singing, only no sound came from them. Frozen in the moonlight, their little glittering eyes seemed to follow Celia as she walked round and round them, marvelling at the delicacy and artistry of the workmanship.

Paul, oh Paul! Celia put one her hand to her cheek. It's a thing of beauty, so it is! Did you have something to do with this? At once she felt her eyes begin to smart with tears, and yet when she put her other hand up to her mouth, she knew that she was smiling too. As if I didn't know! With an expression of absolute anguish Celia laid her trembling fingers against the keys, feeling them against her skin. Oh God! Paul, my sweet love! She was half-laughing and half-crying. It's a box of curiosities, so it is! I'll bet my life this was your idea. Celia laid her forehead against the wooden casing, and then, her cheeks damp and salty now, stretched out her arms as far as they would go, as if she were melting into the wood, feeling for each grain and whorl, stroking it with her fingertips, breathing in its pungent, new-cut smell.

Just then there was a sound. Celia froze. It was a small cracking sound that had come from somewhere beneath her feet. She bent down, and her fingers closed around something small and hard: the stub of a workman's pencil.

She tore a fragment from one of the pieces of paper sticking from the keyboard, and then stood with the pencil poised. Whatever I write it must be something that can never betray either of us – fear tore at her insides – not words, Paul, but – that's it! – a curiosity of my own.

Swiftly Celia drew three lines on the paper. Then she was away and gone, running, running, back through the Aviary Gate, through the gardens, up stairs and down the dark and deserted harem corridors, silent as the wind.

When she reached her own courtyard Celia's overwhelming feeling was of incredulity at how easy it had all been. So much for Annetta's warnings: she had been through the Aviary Gate and no one had seen her! She had not been watched, had not been found out! The shadows in the courtyard had scarcely moved; she must have run there and back, she estimated, in not much more than ten minutes.

Intoxicated by her success, Celia felt reluctant to go back to her own room straight away. Instead, curiosity now brought her to the entranceway of Gulay Haseki's apartment, something she had not dared to do before. One of its doors hung open on a broken hinge. She peered in cautiously. The room had the forlorn look of a place vacated in a hurry: a broken cup lay on the floor; a tiny embroidered napkin, crumpled and thrown to one side; a dead bluebottle. She felt something against her bare foot and bent down to pick it up. She recognised it at once, and felt an ache in her throat: a single tiny slipper, embroidered with gold and silver thread.

She was already halfway back to her own room when she glanced up and saw, or thought she saw, a faint movement in the corner of one eye. She waited. There it was again, more distinctly now: the gleam of a lamp coming from the rooftops somewhere, just above the doorway. Someone, it seemed, was in the Haseki's apartments after all.

Celia hesitated. Hadn't she taken enough risks for one night? But no – rather it had shown her just how easy it was to move about the palace, unseen, if you had the courage. A few more minutes wouldn't make any difference. She crept back towards her own room, and it was just as she thought, there was no sign of any movement from her servants. She turned and made her way quickly back to the empty room.

Stepping over the threshold, Celia looked around. Nothing – the place was silent as a tomb. Then she remembered the conversation that she had had with Annetta that day; the same day the Chief Black Eunuch had been found, and when Esperanza Malchi had left the coloured sand outside her door. What was it that Annetta had noticed then that she, Celia, had failed to see? What was it she had said?

'All very clever,' she could hear Annetta's familiar tones, 'it must have at least three entrances. Her rooms must connect with the Valide's hammam as well.'

Annetta had noticed that the Haseki's rooms were not what they at first seemed; that they were spread over two storeys, and that there was more than one entranceway.

Celia looked around again, more carefully this time. Opposite her she saw one of the other doors almost immediately, the door which, as Annetta had suspected, must lead to the Valide's hammam, but she could see no sign of any other exit, nor any visible means of reaching an upper storey. Only wooden cupboards. Celia went over to one of the cupboards and looked inside. Nothing. Except for a rolled-up mattress, it was empty. Then she tried the other. The door would not open as easily as the first, but eventually she managed it. Nothing: that one was empty too.

Annetta had been wrong, then. If there was another floor on top of this apartment, there did not seem to be any way of getting there from here. Celia shivered. She felt weary now, and cold, but then just as she was about to leave the room she heard a noise, small but distinct: the creak of a footstep on an overhead floorboard. It was coming from just above the first cupboard. Celia ran swiftly over to it and looked inside again, more carefully this time. She took out the rolled-up quilt. Behind it there was a second door.

She opened it. And there, sure enough, was a flight of stairs.

The stairway was both crooked and extremely narrow, barely big enough for her to climb up without knocking her head on the rafters. She wished she had had the foresight to bring the candle from her room. Luckily, a splinter of moonlight was shining at the top of the stairs. Celia climbed on up, and when she emerged it was to find herself in a small circular space, a rickety attic room with a domed ceiling. She realised then that she was inside the cupola that Annetta had pointed out on the roof of the Haseki's apartment. And it was from here, Celia felt certain, that the lamplight had come.

She looked around her, but there was nothing in the little space except for a few cobwebs. A strong frowsty smell of rotting raffia matting came from underfoot. This place, at least, had never been used by anyone, she thought, except perhaps as a secret look-out post. The base of the cupola was pierced all the way around with holes where the moonlight filtered through. Anyone standing here, Celia saw immediately when she put her eye to one of the openings, had a clear view of the courtyard below; they would be able to see not only everyone who came and went across it, but also anyone going in or out of the two apartments.

It was then that Celia saw the second door, very low down in the wall. It too had looked like a cupboard at first, but when she stooped to open it she saw that it was in fact the entranceway to another corridor. And there, receding into the distance, she could just see the faint glow of a lamp.

Celia now found herself in another extremely small and narrow space, a corridor that seemed both older and more makeshift than the rest of the harem buildings. She remembered hearing that there had been an extensive rebuilding of these quarters just before the new Sultan had moved in. Perhaps this corridor was part of the old structure, and had just been built over instead of dismantled.

Bent almost double, she kept walking, feeling her way along with the tips of her fingers. The corridor twisted and turned, to the left, to the right, up and down, one step here, two or three steps there, until she was completely disorientated. At first she thought that she must be above the Valide's hammam; but soon it occurred to her that this upper corridor had most probably been built to parallel the lower corridor, which she knew led past the entrance to the Valide's apartments, and eventually into the Courtyard of the Cariyes.

Then, suddenly without warning, she turned a corner and there was a fork in the way ahead. On one side it twisted steeply downwards to the left. On the other, which curved sharply to the right, it was so narrow that at first Celia was doubtful whether she, or indeed anyone, let alone someone trying to carry a lamp, could squeeze down it at all.

It was very dark now. The only source of light, which had been the moonlight filtering in through the openings in the cupola, was far behind her. Celia squeezed down awkwardly on all fours and rubbed the back of her aching neck. It was no good; she would have to go back. Was it possible that she had been imagining the lamplight after all? She remembered the stories about the *efrits* and ghouls who were said to roam the palace at night, pale and sorrowful as moonlight. Some said that they were the souls of the dead *cariyes*, discarded favourites who had died of a broken heart, or who had been thrown into the Bosphorous and drowned.

No, no. I mustn't think about that now. Celia forced herself to stay calm. The opening to the left-hand pathway was as black as pitch, but when she focused carefully on the right-hand turning she caught something perhaps not quite so black in the distance – a greyish tinge of light.

Celia took a breath and began to make her way down the right-hand corridor. Her bare feet made a shuffling sound against the debris that had collected in the narrow opening. The odour of old wood, and something else at once rank and rotten – bird droppings? a dead rodent? she tried not to think about what her bare feet were treading on – prickled in her nostrils.

The little passageway narrowed, and after a while Celia found that she could barely move forwards in the confined space. With an effort she turned her body sideways. Was this what it had been like for Gulay Haseki, when they put her in the sack? A feeling of panic rose in her throat.

It was then that she saw the hole in the wall. The hole was at exactly her eye-level, but so small that if her face had not been almost pressed up against it, she might well have missed it altogether. This hole, she realised now, was the source of the grey glow of light. From her vague sense of where she might now be, Celia guessed that the hole gave a view over the Courtyard of the Cariyes. She put her eye to the hole and peered through.

At first the light coming from the other side of the wall was so blinding after the darkness of the tiny passageway that Celia could see nothing at all. Gradually her eye adjusted, and when she saw at last where she was she drew back as if she had been stung. Great God! If she had found herself suddenly in the Sultan's own bedchamber she could not have been more appalled. She was not looking out over the Courtyard of the Cariyes at all, but into the very heart of the harem. She was looking directly down into the Valide Sultan's own apartments.

The hole had been bored into one of the tiles, but so high up on the wall that its concealment was almost perfect; even if you knew it was there the hole would be impossible to see from below. Just as well, for what would the penalty be to be caught spying on the Valide? Celia gave a shiver of fear.

The room was just as she remembered it. The tiles on the walls, deep blues, turquoise and white, infused the room with that strange dim green glow, the light of a mermaid's cavern. Although there was no sign of a human presence, a fire burned in the fireplace. Through the hole in the wall Celia could now see the exact spot beside the window where she had sat with the Valide that morning (could it only be three days ago?) looking down at the boats moored in the

219

safe harbour of the Golden Horn, and talking as if she had known her all her life.

Annetta's words came back to her: 'Whatever you do, try not to say too much. She'll use everything you tell her, *capito?*' But when the time came, she had forgotten all about Annetta's warning.

What had she said, what had she told her? Then she remembered. We talked about the ships. She asked me if there was anything that reminded me of the life I had before. And she showed me the ships in the harbour.

So all along the Valide, too, had known about the English ship.

Even now, in the dead of night, the window casements were thrown open. A fur-lined rug lay discarded amongst the cushions, as if someone had recently been sitting there, looking out over the moonlit garden. Did she never sleep, Celia wondered? They watch and they wait, Annetta had said, and it was true. What had Safiye had to do to become Valide? Was there no rest, no respite? Celia could not shake off the impression that there was something almost melancholy about the scene.

Just then there was a movement. If it had not been for the confined space in which she was standing, instinct would have made Celia jerk her head back. As it was, she quickly saw that it was the fur rug that was moving. Cat! Celia watched as the creature uncurled itself from its sleeping place, you wicked creature – what a fright you gave me!

The cat was licking its paws when suddenly it stopped and seemed to be listening to something. And then Celia realised that she could hear that something too. She closed her eyes so that she could listen more intently. Sure enough, there it was again; quite distinctive this time. The sound of someone weeping.

It was not coming from the Valide's room, but from somewhere at the end of the little passageway. Celia left the spy-hole and quickly squeezed her way to the end of the corridor, to where a piece of cloth had been hung up like a makeshift curtain. Cautiously she pulled the material a little to one side, and emerged into what looked very like a cupboard, a tall cupboard this time, in which she could easily stand upright. Its sides were made of wood and there was a piece of open fretwork at the top part. The sound of weeping was very clear now. Standing on tiptoe Celia peered cautiously through the holes into the room beyond. Inside the cupboard it was so cramped she could not

220

move, could hardly breathe; any moment now someone would surely hear her. She was about to turn and make her way back down the tiny corridor when the weeping started again. Something about it – a sound so lonely, so utterly forlorn – made the tears start in her own eyes. Celia hesitated. Idiot! she said to herself, you have no idea who it is – it could be anyone. It's too dangerous, go back! But somehow she found herself on tiptoe again.

The room, which was lit by a single lamp, was of a good size and fitted out, she saw immediately, for a woman of high rank. The tiles on the walls were nearly as fine as those in the Valide Sultan's apartments, decorated with tulips and sprays of carnations. A kaftan of butter-yellow silk, lined with fur, hung from a peg on the wall; furs and embroidered brocades were strewn across cushions. Immediately opposite the cupboard in which she was now standing was a recessed alcove, of a kind usually used for sleeping in. It was from here that the sound of weeping came. No one that unhappy could be dangerous, she decided. Could they? Celia pushed open the cupboard door and stepped out into the room.

At once the weeping stopped. In the alcove a dark form half-rose from the cushions. For a moment there was silence, then a voice whispered: 'Are you a ghost?'

The voice was soft and low, but not a voice that Celia recognised.

'No,' Celia whispered back, 'my name is Kaya Kadin.'

The woman was sitting up now, but it was too dark for Celia to see more than her silhouette.

'Have you brought me something?' Her voice wavered, as if she might start weeping again.

'No,' Celia took another step across the room, 'but I won't hurt you, I promise.'

The room was very warm; there was a strange, acrid smell in the air as if something had been burning.

'They said they'd bring me something, but then they never did . . .' Her voice tailed off. Celia saw the outline of a thin arm as the woman pulled one of the coverlets over her shoulders. 'I'm so cold,' she shivered. 'It's always so cold in here. Put some coals on the brazier, *kadin*.'

'As you wish.' Celia approached the little brazier which stood at the foot of the alcove. She wondered what had been burning on the coals to make the curious smell. 'But it's not cold . . . it's like a hammam in here.'

Celia piled on some fresh coals. The woman shrank back into the shadows.

'Are you sure you're not a ghost?' Her voice was still no more than a whisper.

'Quite sure,' Celia found herself speaking soothingly, as if to a child, 'ghosts and ghouls are only in dreams.'

'Oh, no, no, no, no, no. I've seen them.' The woman made a sudden violent movement that caused Celia to start. 'Let me see you, let me see your face!'

'All right.' Celia picked up a lamp from the floor and held it up. As she did so a beam of light fell across the entrance to the alcove. It was only a brief flash of light, but it was all that was needed. A woman with hollow eyes and the body of an emaciated child stared back at her.

When she first felt the light on her the woman had put up one arm, as if to protect herself. Unsteadily she put it down again, and Celia saw that her face was not a face at all, but a mask, a mosaic of coloured stones stuck to her skin. Her hair, which hung loose about her face, was the colour of ink, black with a sheen to it that was almost blue. Black eyes, heavily outlined with kohl, glimmered in her strange jewelled face. The effect was at once eerie and spectacular, a Byzantine princess rising from her tomb.

'What have they done to you?' Celia dropped to her knees beside her.

'What do you mean? No one's done anything to me,' the woman said plaintively. With exploratory fingers she patted one of her cheeks, feeling its lapidary outline with something like surprise, as if she had forgotten that the stones were there. 'They told me that I'd scratched myself. I don't know . . . I don't remember. But now I don't like to look at myself any more, so I cover myself up.'

She started to scratch again, this time at a patch of skin on her upper arm, where Celia now saw there was an open sore.

'Please, you're hurting yourself.' Celia caught at her arm: it was weightless, hollow as an old bleached bone. How old was she, Celia wondered? Thirty, forty? A hundred? It was impossible to tell.

'Did you bring me something?' The black eyes looked up at Celia anxiously. 'The spiders have come again, they're all over me, *kadin*,' with a little cry, she brushed her hands over her hair, and then the coverlet, 'get them away, get them away!'

'It's all right, there's nothing there.' Celia said, trying to take her hand, but she shook Celia off impatiently.

'No spiders?'

'No, no spiders.' Celia bent towards her. 'May I know your name, *kadin*?' she said, taking the frail hand in hers. 'Who are you?'

'Who am I?' the woman looked up at her pitifully. Behind the glittering mask her eyes were rheumy, like an old woman's. 'Everyone knows who I am.'

'Of course they do,' Celia smiled at her, 'you're the Sultan's favourite, aren't you?' she said gently. 'You are Handan. Handan Kadin.'

The sound of her name brought on a fresh spasm of scratching. When it was over Handan lay back, exhausted, on the pillows. Celia looked around her nervously, conscious suddenly of how long she had been gone.

'I think I must be getting back,' she whispered.

But as she turned to go, Handan caught hold of the edge of Celia's robe.

'How did you know I was here?'

'Gulay Haseki told me about you.'

'Gulay Haseki?' Handan's voice was blank, as if she did not recognise the name at all.

'Yes . . .' Celia hesitated, wondering whether to say anything about the Haseki's fate, then thought better of it. Besides, Handan, in this state of jewelled confinement, probably had little knowledge – and still less care – about the goings on in the harem. Then another thought occurred to Celia. She sat down on the edge of the bed again.

'Gulay Haseki told me something else, or at least she started to tell me. I think you might know about it too, *kadin*. About the Nightingales of Manisa.'

At once Celia noticed a change in her demeanour. Handan looked at her suspiciously.

'Everyone knows about the Nightingales of Manisa . . .' her voice tailed off. Her gaze alighted on a bluebottle that was crawling along the wooden wainscoting.

'You were saying, *kadin* . . .' Celia shook her arm, to try to get her to concentrate again.

'Three slaves were given to the old Sultan by his cousin Humashah. They were all chosen for their beautiful singing voices.'

'Who were they? What were their names?'

But Handan had lost concentration again. Still watching the blue-bottle as it crawled towards her, she shrank back into the shadows.

'Please . . . try to remember who they were.'

'Everyone knows who they were: Safiye Sultan and Hassan Aga, of course.'

'And the third slave?'

'The third slave was called Cariye Mihrimah.'

'Cariye Mihrimah, who's she? I never heard of anyone by that name.'

'She died. The Valide loved her, they say she loved her too much. Loved her like a sister. Oh, the Valide would do anything for her, they said. But she was killed. They put her in a sack and drowned her. That's what they said, anyway. But *I'm* never going to tell anyone,' she leant towards Celia. 'I'm never going to tell *anyone* what I know.'

For a moment there was silence. Then Celia said carefully, 'Shall I ask Gulay Haseki then?'

'Does she know?' Handan sounded surprised.

Celia nodded.

'She knows their secret? That Cariye Mihrimah is still here, in the palace?'

'Yes, *kadin*,' Celia nodded again, more slowly this time, 'I think that's exactly what she knew.'

Safiye, the Valide Sultan, the mother of God's Shadow Upon Earth, came back to the open window casement where she had been sitting. She pulled the sable-lined shawl over her shoulders, and called to Cat, who was sitting licking his paws on the far side of the divan.

It was the dead of night. She tucked one of her bare feet under her, took off the heavy rock-crystal earrings. Rubbing her tender ear-lobes, she sighed luxuriously to herself and breathed in the scent of the gardens beneath her on the cool night air. Beyond them lay the sleeping city, never so beautiful as at night. She could just make out the familiar shapes of the boats and galleys, the black silhouette of the Galata Tower and beyond them the houses and vines of the foreign

224

envoys. The thought of the Englishman still lingered at the edge of her mind: she had enjoyed his conversation, his courtesy – and something else she could not put her finger on. Something – she hardly knew what – about the way he stood. Slim hips, a man's hips.

Had she been rash to arrange to see him again? The thought of him was troubling. In all these years, all the years since she had become Valide, she had never made a mistake. It was not the time to start now. She had seen the way his eyes had lingered on the lattice of her screen . . .

The sable pressed down on her shoulders, heavy as lead.

With a sigh the Valide stretched herself out amongst her silk cushions. There was no denying it, she had more difficulty sleeping these days. It did not trouble her especially. When she was still very young she had trained herself never to need much sleep, an inexpressible advantage in Murad's harem since it gave her time that no one else had: time to think and plan and stay ten paces ahead of everyone else. And when, after more than twenty years of extreme self-discipline, she had finally become what she had always set out to become – the Valide Sultan, the most powerful woman in the Ottoman empire – she found that her old habits were still the best ones.

Solitude had become more soothing to her than sleep. To be alone in the House of Felicity had always been a pleasure rarer than the Sultan's favours, and even now it was a luxury she rarely allowed herself. She thought of the Greek Lady, Nurbanu, and how in the old days she used to chide Safiye for her propensity to seek solitude. For the ordinary *cariyes*, living on top of one another like so many hens in a coop, solitude was out of the question; but for the Sultan's concubines it was unseemly, a question of propriety. As for Safiye herself, the Haseki, she was second in rank only to the Valide Nurbanu herself, and should be attended at all times.

If it had been up to Nurbanu, her attendants would have kept vigil over Safiye even in her sleep. The Valide smiled to herself. If only you could see me now, Greek Lady, she thought, stretching out her hand, turning it so that Nurbanu's emerald glinted faintly on her finger. The ring had a catch on the side, and inside was a small compartment containing a pellet of opium, the same one that had been there more than fifteen years ago now, the day she had taken the ring from

Nurbanu's still-warm finger herself. Oh yes, my lady, Safiye Sultan smiled to herself again, I know all your secrets now.

A faint sound, muffled but distinct, made her glance up. At once she was *en garde*. Instinctively her body tensed and she scanned the room – but there was nothing. The tiles on the walls of her apartments seemed a little blurred these days, but it was the darkness and the shadows that made them so. She closed her eyes and breathed in, feeling round the room again with that sixth sense of hers – her ears, her nose, the skin of her body even – her favourite hunting trick, as she used to tell Cariye Mihrimah in the old days, the one her father had taught her. It never failed. Even the slightest thickening of the air, the breath of a shadow passing beneath a crack under the door, the smell of fear, she could detect them all.

But no, there was nothing. Just Cat.

Safiye lay back again. Even at the worst moments of her life – the day that Murad had finally chosen another, younger concubine, the day they came to take Cariye Mihrimah away – even then she had not been tempted to take the gilded pill, as so many of the other harem women did. Not like Handan, poor foolish Handan, who had allowed another to take her place, who had thrown everything away for its sake.

Safiye snapped the ring shut. There were, after all, other dreams, other pleasures, even now. From beneath one of the cushions she took out a small hand mirror, its ivory casing encrusted with emeralds and rubies, and in the forgiving darkness examined her face carefully. Could it really be that she had grown old? In the darkness she did not look old. And she was not yet fifty. Esther Nasi had taught her well. There was, if she were truthful, a little crepiness on the back of her hands and around her neck now, but she refused to dwell on that. The skin of her face was still pale and unblemished, and so fine it had the creamy texture of gardenia petals. Or that's what Murad used to say when they lay together. In those days she had no need of mirrors, for he had been her mirror. For what was she, his Haseki, if not a reflection in his eyes?

She remembered how, night after night, when she was carrying his child and it was forbidden for him to embrace her, still it was she who would be summoned to his bed. He could have taken other concubines then, they would have allowed it, but – to the consternation of them all – he did not.

226

They were not much more than children themselves then. He was nineteen, she just sixteen when Safiye bore their first child. He would bid her stretch herself out beside him, just for the pleasure of having her there. He would undress her, and then dress her again, but wearing only her jewels this time, and she would lie quite still and quiet, as she knew he liked her to, while he stroked her breasts and the insides of her thighs with his fingertips.

She remembered how he would watch with wonder when the child turned inside her; how she would lie on her side when her belly grew too big for comfort, and the exact feeling of the coverlets – for it had been cold in Manisa in the winter months – the fur prickling against her neck, against the tender skin of her newly swollen breasts. How she would watch him as he ate up her body with his eyes, ravished her with his hungry gaze, until she shivered, and burned, and begged for his love.

Murad, my lion.

Slowly Safiye loosened the braids and tresses so painstakingly dressed by her maidservants until her hair hung down to below her waist. She untied the heavy girdle, ran her fingers up beneath her skirts to the smooth insides of her thighs. Dreamily she pushed her hand higher. There was hair there now, where once – for all those many years when she had been Haseki – there had been smooth skin.

She lay back softly amongst the cushions.

Later a feeling of calm filled her, but also another more troubling sensation: a small shard of memory, like a distant cloud, or a faint half-remembered echo of a childhood song. She did not often think of Murad these days. He had loved her for a long time. For more than ten years in Manisa, and then nearly as many years again in Constantinople, he had kept faith with her, no matter what others had done to force them apart. It was not seemly, they said, for the Sultan to consort with only one concubine, even if she had been raised to the official position of Haseki. His mother Nurbanu, and his sister, Humashah, had searched the empire high and low for the most beautiful slaves to give him – they even sent a special envoy to Esther Nasi, she remembered with amusement, who, incredibly, almost twenty years later was still trading in Scutari, despite her then tremendous age (and being too fat and old to walk, Safiye's informants told her, but quite as rich as a pasha).

For a long time Safiye held out against them. First with her own beauty, but when that was no longer enough, with the help of Little Nightingale and Cariye Mihrimah. For right from the beginning, from their very first months in Manisa, the three of them had all been agreed. Each of them had sworn always to do everything in their power to help the others. And so they had. When fortune favoured one of them, it smiled on them all. Under Safiye's patronage Little Nightingale had risen to become Hassan Aga, the Chief Black Eunuch; and, in the old harem still presided over by the Valide Sultan Nurbanu, Cariye Mihrimah – Safiye could think of her by no other name – had become the harem official second only to the great Harem Stewardess, Janfreda Khatun.

Little Nightingale and Cariye Mihrimah were the first and most important rung in Safiye's formidable network of allegiances, a network that had taken a lifetime to create. Like the huntress she was, Safiye relied on surprise and disguise, and often it was only she who knew who they were – the mutes, the eunuchs, the palace slaves, and above all the harem women she bought at high prices and then freed after only a few years' service, marrying them off advantageously to a grateful pasha or vizier.

But it was the Nightingales alone, Safiye knew, who would do anything she asked, whose loyalty was absolute. For her she knew they would lie, spy, cajole, steal – perhaps even kill. They would do, in short, whatever it took: which in the end was everything.

And so it was that when Safiye could no longer hold the Sultan's interest on her own, it was Little Nightingale who had found the physician for her. And when his handiwork was discovered, it had been Cariye Mirhima – who else? – who took the blame.

Another sound, even fainter than the first, registered somewhere in her consciousness: a small sound like a mouse scuffling in the wainscoting. Safiye Sultan glanced up to the shadowy ceiling and smiled. Very good, my little Judas goat. It's about time we had a resolution to this business, once and for all.

Chapter 25

Istanbul: the present day

It was a Saturday towards the middle of December that was finally fixed on for Elizabeth's trip on Mehmet's boat.

On Haddba's instructions she took a taxi early in the morning to the small dock near the Galata Bridge where it was moored. Mehmet was to meet her there. She rang the mobile phone number that Haddba had given her, and stood shivering on the dock, waiting for him to appear.

'Elizabeth.'

He was taller than she had recollected.

'Hello.'

She half expected him to kiss her hand again, but he did not.

'Well, it looks as though we have chosen a good day for it after all.'

She remembered now how much she had liked his voice.

'Haddba made me bring this,' Elizabeth said, holding out a basket.

'A picnic? Ah, Haddba! She thinks of everything. Here, allow me.'

He took the basket from her. 'You didn't mind getting up so early on a Saturday morning?'

'No, I like it.'

'We think alike then.' He turned to smile at her over his shoulder. 'My uncle used to say that the person who wakes up early skims the cream off the day.'

The boat turned out to be a launch with a small cabin at the front. They set off straight away, along the Golden Horn towards the entrance of the Bosphorous. There was little water traffic at that time of the day. It was cold, but clear; the sky transparent, flecked with pink and gold. On the Sea of Marmara, Elizabeth could see where the tankers had gathered, whole flocks of them, paper cut-out behemoths, painted black and red.

He followed her gaze. 'Do you like them?'

'They're absolutely amazing.'

He seemed amused by her enthusiasm.

'Are you laughing at me?' she said, but she found that she did not mind. Marius, she thought, would have laughed at her, too, and she would have felt diminished by it. But she did not feel diminished; she felt, to her surprise, exhilarated; intoxicated by the strangeness of it all.

'Well, most people would prefer to look at the sailing boats, a beautiful sloop, say, or even one of the big ocean liners that we get here now. But not the . . . how do you say it?' he gave her a teasing look, 'the grotty old tankers.'

'But look at them,' Elizabeth said, 'they're wonderful; so vast and yet there they are just sort of . . . floating. Like clouds, completely weightless, just floating there on the horizon.'

'They're waiting for their turn to make their way up the Bosphorous, to the Black Sea mostly. It's such a very narrow channel they have to navigate. In the old days, when more people lived on houses that fronted directly on to the water, families were known to wake up with half a tanker in their house.'

He took her first up the western shore of the Bosphorous, past palaces and small docks, the smart yachts and cruise liners in the harbour at Bebek. On the water, the roar of the city was muffled. Elizabeth could see shoals of lilac-coloured jellyfish, floating pale and clear like mermaids' hair in the water. She felt completely at ease in his presence. They could talk or not talk with equal comfort.

'You're very thoughtful,' he said after a while.

'I'm trying to imagine what the city used to look like; you know, before—'

'Before what? Before the motor car came along and choked us all to a standstill?'

'Oh no, much before then,' she said. 'I meant in the sixteenth century.'

Although she had not intended to, Elizabeth told him the story of Celia and Paul. She told him everything: about the Levant Company merchants and their marvellous gift to the Sultan, the mechanical organ with its astronomical clocks, and automata of trumpeting angels and singing blackbirds; she told him about the shipwreck and the missing fragment of narrative.

'It's the reason I came to Istanbul in the first place, to try to find it – the missing fragment, I mean.'

Mehmet had listened carefully, without interrupting. Now he said, 'I never thought academia would be so exciting. You make it sound like a piece of detective work.'

'Well, that's exactly what it feels like sometimes,' Elizabeth said. 'I suppose that's why I love it so much – although I know that Haddba thinks I'm absolutely mad to shut myself up with a lot of books all day long.'

A gust of wind rattled the door of the cabin. Elizabeth shivered, and pulled her coat more closely round her shoulders. She made no mention of the other reasons that she had come to Istanbul.

Over the hills on the eastern shores of the Bosphorous a pale winter sun rose at last. Light caught at the roofs of the houses, turning the grey waters a brilliant blue.

'And so? Have you found any clues?'

'So far nothing on Celia. I've applied for permission to visit the State archives, but they keep wanting more and more pieces of paper, letters of recommendation from my supervisor, and I don't know what,' Elizabeth said. 'It's always the same with archives. They want you to tell them exactly which documents you'd like to look at,' she sighed, 'which of course you can't possibly do until you go there and see for yourself what they've got.'

'All very Byzantine.' He gave her a smiling sideways glance. 'So she remains a mystery, your little slave girl?'

'So far. But I just have this feeling, you know . . .' She turned to him.

'What kind of a feeling?'

'Oh well, it's just that the more I think about it, the more I think she did eventually escape – in fact, she must have done.' Elizabeth found that she had put her hand protectively to her stomach. 'Otherwise how would her story ever have come to be written?'

'Why should she have had to escape?' Mehmet said. 'Have you considered that there might be some other far simpler explanation?

People assume that slavery was for life but, from what I learnt at school, I seem to remember that under the Ottoman system it hardly ever was. Slaves were freed all the time, and for all sorts of reasons.'

'Even from the Imperial Harem?'

'Especially from the Imperial Harem. If a woman didn't catch the Sultan's eye, after a few years she was given dowry and then married off to some high-ranking official – the personal slaves of the Valide in particular. It was considered a very meritorious act on her part. Because of their training – and their contacts with the palace – they were extremely highly prized. It's perfectly possible that your Celia Lamprey was one of them.'

'Well, maybe you're right.'

Elizabeth thought of the strange atmosphere she had picked up in the harem that day. Not only in the Valide's apartments, with its double walls, its secret corridors hidden in the wainscoting, but in the warren of tiny rooms, rotting and claustrophobic, belonging to the ordinary rank and file women, that sense of a windowless labyrinth. She was certain now that Celia must at some point have left the palace, but Mehmet's explanation sounded just . . . well, it sounded too easy.

'And if she did leave, then what would have happened to her?' he asked.

'That's what I'm trying to find out.'

'You think she was reunited with her merchant?'

'It's what I'd like to think.'

'Ah!' he smiled again. 'Not only a detective, but a romantic too. Well, if you really want to know what Istanbul looked like in the sixteenth century—' he turned and pointed back down the Bosphorous in the direction from which they had just come, 'then that's the view you want.'

Elizabeth turned and saw the silhouette of the old city massed on the horizon behind her. Now that the sun was up, a glow like golden mist hovered over it. Grey walls spiralled down into the green and black parkland; golden domes and minarets and the spiked tips of cypress trees pushed up into a pale-blue winter sky. And in a strange trick of the light, the whole city seemed to rise up from a dazzling expanse of water, a citadel conjured up by djinns.

✳   ✳   ✳

At around midday they came to Andalou Hisari, the last village on the Asian shore before the Bosphorous opened into the Black Sea. The shores here were thickly wooded. Wisps of morning mist still clung to their dark interiors; men fished from the rocks.

They anchored in the little bay. The water was flat, an opaque green reflecting the trees.

'Come,' he said, 'I'm going to take you for lunch. If we're lucky we might see dolphins here.'

'What about Haddba's picnic?'

'In December? I think not,' he laughed, holding out his hand to her. 'Don't worry, Haddba won't mind.'

He knew a fish restaurant on the front. Although it was out of season, the place was open. A deferential waiter showed them to a table overlooking the water. While they waited for their food to arrive they talked, watched the fishing boats and the gulls, improbably large, bobbing like corks on the water.

He told her about his family, Turkish father, French mother, four brothers; and she about hers, parents in the Oxfordshire village, no siblings, unless you counted Eve, the sister she had never had. They were so concentrated on one another that their conversation seemed to proceed in a kind of shorthand.

'Do you have someone?' he asked. 'Back in England, I mean.'

'I did,' Elizabeth watched a flock of cormorants flying low over the water, 'not now.'

No other explanation seemed necessary. The image came to her of Marius: a Marius who, she realised, had not so much as crossed her mind all day. Now she seemed to see his figure as if on a distant shore, a prancing incubus, waving to her as he receded, getting smaller and smaller, until in a tiny pouf of smoke he was gone.

She turned to Mehmet with a smile. 'You?'

'The same,' he said. 'Or something like that.'

To pass the time he ordered them a plate of fresh almonds. As he spoke to the waiter she studied him carefully. He was not so much a handsome man, she thought, as a vivid physical presence.

'What's your favourite drink?' he asked her.

'Let me guess . . . yours is . . . pineapple juice,' she countered.

'Pineapple juice? Don't be absurd!'

'Well, what it is it then?'

'Vodka. Grey Goose, of course. And you?'

'You'll never guess mine.'

'Bet I will.'

She shook her head. 'I'll give you a million pounds if you do.'

'Champagne.'

'Champagne? Well, I have to admit that does come a very close second, but no.'

The conversation shimmered and spiralled between them on golden threads.

'What is it then?'

'Picnic thermos tea.'

'Picnic thermos tea,' he laughed. 'Well, OK, I guess you'll have to keep your million pounds. But,' he leant back in his chair, 'I bet I can guess what your favourite food is.' He looked at her through narrowed eyes.

'Oh?' she smiled at him, and as he held her gaze she was suddenly and overwhelmingly so erotically possessed that she felt as though she might faint.

'Baklava,' he said, watching her mouth, 'I'd give anything to see you eat baklava again.'

Their food came but Elizabeth did not eat much. Not because she was not hungry, but because she did not want him to guess at her discomposure. She had brushed aside his reference to the baklava as best she could, pretended not to have heard him properly, not to have understood the inference. But now she was afraid to betray herself in other ways. She had suddenly become clumsy. She knew that each time she lifted her fork her hands shook; knew that if she lifted her glass, the water would spill. So he had recognised her, all along. And, of course, somewhere in the back of her mind she had always known that.

Although, on the surface, their conversation continued as before, the whole tenor of the afternoon had changed. The ease that had been between them was gone. Instead it was as if the very air between them, each individual molecule, had become charged. With what? Elizabeth could not – dared not – put a name to it.

I am not ready for this, she kept saying to herself. She knew that he found her suddenly wary; and without apologising treated her with a kind of immaculate but tender courtesy.

'You're cold, Elizabeth.'

'I'm fine.' But she knew that she was shivering.

'I'll get you a glass of wine.'

'No, really . . .'

'Yes. I think you should drink it.'

He made a signal and the wine was brought instantly.

She saw him watching her mouth again as she held the glass up to her lips. He makes me feel like a queen and at the same time something quite . . . other, she thought. With a conscious effort she managed to stop herself shivering. When he leant across the table and touched her mouth it was all she could do to stop herself flinching away, as if he had tried to hit her.

'A hair,' she felt his fingers brush against her lips, 'a hair in your mouth, that's all.'

Her skin felt warm where he had touched her.

'Elizabeth . . .' he began.

'I don't . . . I can't . . .' she started to say.

Suddenly his phone rang. They looked at it for a moment, the BlackBerry lying on the table between them.

'What d'you think?' he said. 'Shall I answer it or not?'

Elizabeth passed her hand over the side of her face. 'Perhaps you'd better.'

He pushed the button. '*Evet?*' She heard him speak in Turkish. And then in English. 'Oh yes, of course, just a minute.'

It was a moment before she realised that he was holding the phone out to her.

'It's for you . . .' His eyes danced at her.

'For me?' Elizabeth took the phone from him. 'Hello . . . oh yes, *hello*! Still in Istanbul, yes. But how . . .? Oh, I see. How good of you . . . really? But that's fantastic news . . . I'll have a look at it straight away. Yes, thank you so much.'

When she rang off they looked at one another.

'Let me guess . . .?'

They were both laughing now.

'Haddba gave her the number.'

'Who was it? Your friend, Eve?'

'No. My supervisor, back in Oxford, Dr Alis. When she couldn't get me on my mobile she rang the guest house and Haddba gave her yours.'

When Elizabeth handed him back the phone he caught hold of her hand and held it. And this time she did not try to draw away.

'Did she have some news for you?'

'Yes.' She lowered her eyes to where he was holding her wrist. 'Some very good news. She thinks she's managed to trace the portrait of Paul Pindar. Do you remember I told you that I found it reproduced in a book?'

'Yes, I remember.'

With her eyes still lowered Elizabeth turned her hand slowly until her palm was uppermost between his fingers.

'The reproduction was so bad that I couldn't see any of the details.'

She watched as he drew his thumb over the delicate skin of her wrist.

'But maybe now . . .' Her voice trailed off. 'Anyway it's all in an email.'

'Do you want to use this?' He indicated his BlackBerry.

'No,' she shook her head slowly, 'it can wait.'

A silence fell between them. She looked up and found him smiling at her, and suddenly they were in clear waters again.

'Well, aren't you going to say something?' he said.

Perhaps it was the wine that made her bold. She leant towards him. 'You've been seducing me,' she said.

'Really?' He picked up both her hands between his, slowly kissed her wrists, then the palms of her hands. 'And I thought it was the other way around.'

Chapter 26

Constantinople: 4 September 1599

Dawn

I t was barely light when Paul set off for his audience with the Valide.

Word had been sent by palace officials that a boat from the Valide Sultan's own household would attend him, but when it came – a small caique rowed by just six slaves – it proved to be not big enough, after all, to take the retinue Paul had so painstakingly assembled. He climbed into the waiting boat on his own, watched in silence by the liveried forms of the other embassy men – the Reverend May, Mr Sharp and Mr Lambeth, John Sanderson's apprentice John Hanger, and Ned Hall the coachman – who then turned and made their way back up towards the Vines of Pera.

The oarsmen rowed silently, not across the Golden Horn to the palace, as Paul had expected, but in the opposite direction altogether, up the Bosphorous, and after only half an hour the boat had left the seven hills of the city behind. Travelling swiftly in the direction of the current they made their way first along the European shore of the waterway. Opposite them, on the eastern shore, Paul could just see the roofs and minarets of Üsküdar, the village where the Sultan bought and sold his horses. There were many houses and mansions here, their gardens and orchards fanning out along the waterfront. The Valide, Paul knew, owned several summer palaces here, so perhaps that was where they were headed, but the little caique showed no sign of crossing the Bosphorous at this point, and neither the boat's captain nor his escort, one of the palace eunuchs, responded to his questions.

Soon they were out of sight of human habitation. After another half hour of silent rowing, the caique at last crossed over to the Asian shore, making its way in the shadow of the woods.

The water here was flat and green, its surface glassy. When Paul trailed his hand over the side it smelt of river water. The trees – chestnut, almond and ash – were tinged with the faintest tarnished gold. A colony of herons, hunched and grey like old men, clustered together in an umbrella pine; and once a flock of cormorants flashed past them, flying low over the water. Paul could see the occasional house on wooden stilts overhanging the water; a few men fished from the rocks. But for the most part a cool and eerie silence permeated the forests.

He shivered. Although it was still early in September and the days were generally warm, a sable-lined cloak had been provided for him along with a supply of cherries and pomegranates in a small basket lined with an embroidered linen cloth. He drew the cloak up over his shoulders.

'How much further?'

The eunuch mute made an incoherent noise in his throat, and then jerked his chin. Paul turned to look. They had reached a small inlet. And there, as if gliding towards them between the trees, a small rose-red building came slowly into view.

Alighting from the caique, Paul was greeted by two more eunuchs who escorted him into a formal garden which gave out directly over the water's edge. Marble channels running with water led through rows of orange and lemon trees; umbrella pines and plane trees made shady pools over the rose beds. There were fountains and a fish pond in which several fat carp floated lazily.

At the very centre of the garden, in the shade of a Judas tree, was a pavilion. Paul had often seen these little pleasure houses – not unlike the newly fashionable banqueting houses in England – but instead of being made from tiles, this one was constructed entirely of glass. Examining it, Paul saw that whoever sat inside the kiosk would be able to see the entire garden, but would not be seen by anyone.

He waited, but nothing happened, and no one came. He was entirely alone in the garden. The two eunuchs were nowhere to be seen. Then, out of the corner of one eye, he became aware of a small movement – a shimmer of something green – but when he turned there was nothing there, and he was alone as before.

Except he was not alone. Coming up the path towards him was a large cat: a white cat, with burning eyes, one green and one blue.

'Hello, puss.'

When Paul leant down to stroke the animal it wrapped its body disdainfully around his legs and stalked on past him. He watched the cat pick its way down to the water's edge, where it sat down with its back to him, staring sphinx-like into the middle distance. 'You like my cat, Paul Pindar Aga?' A voice – *that* voice – beautiful beyond dreams, was speaking to him from inside the glass pavilion.

Paul resisted the urge to spin round. Instead, he removed his hat and stood quite still, his head bowed to his chest.

'Ah, very good, Englishman.' Her laugh was just as he remembered it. '*Va bene.* But it is quite all right. You may turn around now.'

When Paul turned round he found that she was indeed sitting inside the pavilion, although how she had got there without him seeing her he could not tell. A close-woven screen had been let down across the doorway, hiding her from view.

'Come, do not be afraid. You may approach. As you can see, we're quite alone.'

With his eyes still fixed on the ground, Paul walked slowly towards the pavilion.

'So, we meet again, Paul Pindar Aga.' There was a pause. 'I am sorry that there was no room for your colleagues on board my little boat, but it is better this way, I'm sure you'll agree.'

'You do me a great honour, Your Majesty.'

Paul bowed low to the shadow behind the screen.

'Yes?' She sounded amused. 'But I'm sure your ambassador was hoping for . . . how shall I put it? A little more ceremony, perhaps.'

'My ambassador is aware only of the very great honour you do us,' Paul answered her. 'He asks me to tell you that he – indeed, each one of us – wishes to serve you in any way that we can.'

'Well spoken, Paul Pindar Aga! Business first, why not? It does you great credit. We all know you wish to renew the Capitulations – and between ourselves, I don't think you will have too much trouble there, for all de Brèves's generosity to the Grand Vizier. Trade is good for us all, I've told him so myself: our great city has always depended on it. Besides, France and Venice can't expect to keep the rest of you trading under their flag for ever now can they? I hear the

Dutch particularly wish to trade under English protection these days,' she added. 'But all that is really of minor importance. The fact is, we are to be allies now, isn't that so? Your marvellous ship . . . how do you call it?'

'The *Hector*, madam.'

'Ah, yes, the *Hector* . . .' another pause, 'the *Hector* . . . now that was a good idea,' she went on, musingly. 'This marvellous ship is the talk of the city, they tell me. Only a very powerful monarch, the people say, could have sent such a vessel. And by happy chance we find we have a common enemy: Spain. We shall be very useful to one another, don't you think? Even the Spanish would be hard pressed to take on us both.'

'Friendship with your great empire is our Queen's dearest wish.'

'Courteously said, Paul Pindar Aga.'

Paul bowed low again, and as he did so he became aware of a small white foot, its instep high and smooth, peeping from the bottom of the latticed screen. He looked away quickly.

'But the fact is I didn't really bring you here to talk about all that,' Safiye said. 'Tell me, do you know where you are?'

'At your summer palace, madam?' Paul replied.

The jewelled toes of the little foot curled with amusement.

'This little place my summer palace? Look around you, Paul Pindar; surely you don't really think that?'

Paul looked and saw that the little wooden building he had seen on his arrival was really no more than a gate house. Although he had not realised it at first, he was in a simple pleasure garden, clearly designed to be as far removed from the formality and etiquette of the court as possible.

'Madam, there is no palace here, it is true,' he said at last, 'but this garden – I've never seen one like it. A garden most fit for a queen.'

'No, not a queen, Paul Pindar,' the Valide replied. 'A garden for the Haseki, for the Sultan's favourite. The old Sultan, my master the Sultan Murad, gave this garden to me as a gift, many years ago. We used to come here together, to walk by the water and to watch the boats. In the summer, when the nights were warm, it was his favourite place to watch the moon rise. He would have them string lights from the branches of the trees, so that they reflected like stars in the water.'

240

In the distance, at the garden's edge, the Bosphorous danced with sunlight. Paul could see the white cat sniffing speculatively at the water in one of the pools. Beneath the surface the golden carp, unaware of its presence, swam.

'All my life – that is to say, since my master moved his household back here from Manisa;' she went on, 'all that time I have watched the merchant ships sailing to and fro along these waters. I used to wonder if any of them were going back to my country, a dangerous thought for a slave to have.' The beautiful voice caressed his ear. 'And then later, much later, certain things happened. For a time I lost the favour of the Sultan, and this place became my refuge. A place, the only place, where I could sometimes be alone. Until the old Valide Nurbanu stopped it.' Safiye gave a sad sigh. 'It was unseemly, she said, that I – the Sultan's Hasecki – should come here unaccompanied. I must have servants, handmaids, companions. I was forbidden to come here without them.'

The sun had risen over the Asian hills and the garden began to fill with sunlight. Behind the screen a fan undulated slowly. Paul found himself straining to make out the contours of her face. Was there a man alive who would not try to fit a face to that voice, once he had heard it? Was there anyone who could tell him? Her foot was still there. He dragged his fascinated eyes away.

'Do you know why I have brought you here, Englishman?'

'No, madam.'

'Partly, of course, it is because I wished to thank you for the gifts you brought me from your Queen. And to tell you also that your servant – the cook – has been released. A misunderstanding all along, most regrettable. This is what you will tell your ambassador.' Behind the screen he saw the shadowy silhouette shift slightly. 'But also,' she sighed again, but this time it seemed to Paul that it was a sound of pure pleasure, 'well, let's just say it's because I can.'

In the garden now there was not a breath of air. Paul could feel the sun beating, hot now, against his uncovered head. Whatever her real business was with him she seemed in no hurry to set about it; nor he to hear it. He could, he thought, stay in that garden for ever.

'You are fond of gardens, then, Paul Pindar Aga?' she said after a while.

'Yes, very fond. When I was an apprentice, my master – Parvish, his name was – taught me about them; it was amongst the many things I learnt from him.'

'Oh? And what else did he teach you?'

'I learnt about maps, and mathematics, and the seafaring arts. He was a merchant, of course, but a good astronomer, too. And a scholar. There was nothing, I think, that he was not curious about. He collected instruments, all kinds of them: instruments for navigation, mostly, compasses, astrolabes, but he loved all kinds of curiosities, too: clocks and watches, even children's toys, so long as they had a secret mechanism to them. I was only a boy when I was apprenticed to him, but because of him I became fascinated by them too.'

Her instep, he saw, was high and white; the nails polished till they glowed like seashells. On one ankle was a small black tattoo.

'So, you are a scholar too?'

Paul smiled. 'No, just a merchant, madam, plain and simple, and I thank God for it.'

'Come now, there is nothing either plain or simple about the life you lead. You English merchants could soon become kings of the seas, they tell me, and quite as rich. The world grows smaller every day at the prow of your boats. Why even now your Company is planning new trading routes, to the spice islands, to India even. They've never been afraid to take risks. I like that.' She seemed amused. 'Are you surprised I know all this? You shouldn't be. We have skilled intelligencers, Paul Pindar Aga. We know you merchants have both the ear and the tongue of that great lady, your Queen. Why, she even selects her ambassador from amongst your number – quite a scandal, I am told, amongst the other Franks, who think it a great impropriety,' she paused consideringly, 'when really what it speaks of is esteem.

'If I were a young man, just starting out in life, I think I might well have chosen a path like yours. Freedom, adventure, riches . . .' There came the sound of silks rustling together as she leant towards the lattice again. 'Come and work for us, Paul Pindar Aga. The Sultan has always welcomed and honoured men like you, men of intelligence and ambition. You can be part of the greatest empire the world has ever seen. We will find you a handsome house, many slaves, beautiful wives.' She paused once more. 'Especially beautiful wives.'

Paul tried to answer her, but he found, suddenly, that he could not. He put his hand in his pocket and felt for the compendium, felt the familiar smoothness of the metal against his fingers.

'Ah, but you do not speak.' There was disappointment in her voice. 'You seem distracted, Paul Pindar Aga.'

When still he did not reply, she continued, 'But you already have a wife and family perhaps, who are waiting for your return?'

A wild thought came over him. Now here's your chance, take it! Show her, show her Celia's portrait! The compendium burnt into his flesh.

'I had a woman once, Majesty,' he heard the sound of his own voice speak at last. 'She was dear, very, very dear to me.'

'Were you married?'

'We meant to marry, but no.' Paul's heart was racing. In his mind's eye he saw her: her skin, her eyes, the living gold of her hair. The colours in the garden seemed to shimmer and dissolve before his eyes. 'She was the daughter of Parvish's partner, Tom Lamprey, in the days of the old Venice Company. He was a sea captain. If ever there was a fearless man, and an honest one, it was he. Before I joined the Levant Company as a merchant in my own right, for many years I worked as Parvish's factor in Venice. I got to know Tom well. It was his dearest wish that I should marry his daughter.'

'His wish, but not yours?'

'Oh, it was my wish too. The match was suitable in every way . . .'

Show her!

'She didn't wish it, then?'

I can't. I can't risk it.

'I believe she loved me, very much,' he forced himself to say the words, 'quite as much as I loved her, if that were possible. But she . . . was lost.'

'Lost?'

'Lost to me.'

'How so?'

You won't get another chance!

'The Company asked me to accompany Sir Henry here, to Constantinople. And as you know, our mission here has taken rather longer than expected.' Paul hesitated. 'Two years ago she went back to England on her father's boat. It was the last merchantman to sail that year, before the winter storms. But they were too late. There was a great tempest, the ship and everything on it was lost. All our cargo. And Tom and his daughter, too. On the coast of Dalmatia, they say.'

His thumb flicked the catch.

'And her name?'

'Celia, madam,' Paul said. He took his empty hand out of his pocket. 'Her name was Celia.'

Apart from the sound of water, running and trickling in the marble channels, everything was quiet now. No birds sang or rustled in the thick woods which enclosed the garden on either side.

After a few moments Safiye Sultan spoke again.

'Nurbanu, who was the Valide when I first came to Constantinople, taught me everything I know,' she said. 'She was an excellent teacher, just like your master, what was he called?'

'Parvish.'

'There, you see – just like your Parvish. Those early lessons, we never forget them, I think you will agree. Although I think that mine were perhaps rather different from yours.

'Nurbanu knew nothing about maps or mathematics, but she knew a great deal about the world; does that surprise you? You Franks always presume that just because we women are protected by the confines of the harem, we know nothing of what goes on outside. Nothing could be further from the truth. Nurbanu taught me that there are only two things more precious than love: power and loyalty. Never share power: that is what that great lady taught me. And in your servants, value loyalty above all other things.'

There was another silence, slightly longer than the last.

'It is a long time since I have visited this place, Paul Pindar,' she continued after a while, and Paul thought that he could detect the faintest note of melancholy in her voice. 'I was always very fond of the roses here, especially the damask ones. The Sultan had them brought for me all the way from Persia. Imagine it: the caravans brought them packed in ice, all the way across the desert. My roses were more costly than emeralds, he said. I don't think she ever knew that.'

'May I pick one for you?'

'Why, yes . . . yes, pick one, Englishman.'

244

Paul picked a single, half-opened red rose. He held it out and saw the shadowy form hidden behind the screen bend towards him.

'My advice now is, go home, go home to England, Paul Pindar Aga. So long as loyalty is preserved, you shall have your Capitulations.' She was so close to him now, despite the screen, that he could see the jewelled glitter of her dress, could glimpse her hair; could imagine, almost, that he could smell her perfumed breath. 'But keep my rose, Mr Pindar, I think it is only fair – for I find that I have already taken something that belongs to you.'

Chapter 27

Constantinople: 4 September 1599

Day

When Paul arrived back at the embassy later that day the place was in an uproar. Servants, both the embassy's own and those of several Ottoman dignitaries, swarmed at the entrance, which was now guarded by a battalion of janissaries, the plumes in their distinctive tall white caps fluttering in the breeze. Two horses, richly caparisoned with red and blue cloths and jewelled bridles, stamped on the cobbles.

Paul met Thomas Glover in the courtyard.

'About time,' Glover was cramming an enormous plumed hat on to his head, 'we were about to send out a search party.'

'What's this?' Paul indicated the waiting horses. 'My welcome home committee?'

'The Grand Vizier's men. They're with Sir Henry now.'

Paul looked at him with raised eyebrows. 'And you've left him up there on his own?'

'A visit of etiquette, that's all. I'm told they're not here to discuss business, so not too much harm can come of it.'

'I wouldn't bank on it.'

'Don't worry, I'm on my way up there right now.'

'A bit of fog dispersal?'

'You could say that.' Glover grinned. 'I'm to let Sir Henry know the moment you appear. There's good news Paul. Dallam's finished his repairs, and they're just now giving word that Lello can present his credentials at last. I must hurry, before he does anything to make them change their minds.' He shook out his sleeves, slashed to reveal cherry-pink silk linings. 'How do I look?'

'Well, not quite enough spangles for my taste,' Paul gave a weary smile, 'but very pretty all the same,' he said, walking with him to the bottom of the stairs.

'And the Valide?' Glover began, then he stopped and looked curiously at Paul. 'Why, my dear fellow, what is it? You look quite drained.'

'Nothing, I'm just a little sea-sick that's all, those eunuchs can't row straight for all the piastres in the Sultan's treasury.' Attempting another smile, Paul put his hand on Glover's arm. 'Can you stand more good news? We're to have our Capitulations, Thomas. I'll tell you after. Go on, it won't do to leave Sir Henry all on his own.'

Thomas started up the steps.

'Which grinds more slowly do you suppose: the mills of God, or the office of the Grand Vizier?' Paul called after him.

'Ask me another one.' Halfway up the steps to the ambassador's receiving room, Thomas Glover stopped again. 'Oh, and by the by, more good news – if you can call it that,' he called down.

'That villain Carew turned up again this morning, bold as you like. Turns out there was some sort of mistake. The janissaries got the wrong man after all, or some such; couldn't make head or tail of his story,' he shrugged, 'but that's nothing new. If you ask me, a good long spell in irons wouldn't do him any harm at all. Anyway, he's back.'

And with that he disappeared from view.

Once again Paul found Carew sitting on the garden wall.

'So, they finally let you out, did they?'

'Good morning to you, too, Secretary Pindar.'

'Where were you? In the Seven Towers?'

'No, in your friend Jamal's cellar actually. Thanks for the mercy parcels,' Carew replied, not looking up. In one hand he was holding a lemon which he appeared to be examining intently. Behind the shock of unkempt hair his face wore a well-used scowl.

'Well, let's be thankful for something: at least you're wearing your shirt this time.' Paul climbed up on to the wall beside him. 'And it's good afternoon, I believe. Shouldn't you be making yourself useful somewhere?'

Carew took one of the several knives that he was now wearing in a leather harness strapped to his belt and, with the delicacy of a seamstress, made a small incision in the top of the lemon.

'Have a mercy, I'm a condemned man.'

'That was yesterday.'

Carew grunted. 'Seems that Cuthbert Bully Boy has managed to get his finger sewn back on,' he said glumly, 'and I'm to be allowed back in the kitchens after all. To cook syllabubs for Lady Lello – as if she didn't already have quite enough bubs to go round.' With fierce concentration he began to cut the rind away from the fruit in a fine spiral shape. 'Don't laugh.' His eyes glittered. 'I'd rather go back to catching rats in Jamal's cellar.'

'And I know a few people who'd be only too pleased to put you there,' Paul said. When Carew did not reply, he added, 'Lello has let you have your knives back then?'

'As you can see.' Carew held out the spring of lemon peel on the point of his knife. His hands were criss-crossed with cuts and old burns.

'When did Jamal let you go?'

'Early this morning.'

'Did he say why?'

'That old woman, the one dressed all in black – you remember her? Esperanza Malchi. Well, she brought him a message. Seems it's getting to be something of a habit with her.' Carew squinted into the sun. The scar on his cheek showed up very white against his brown skin. 'Turns out she's some kind of carrier pigeon for the Valide. Between them I'd say their information is very good, just as you suspected.' Carew turned to Paul: 'Did you know that Jamal does astrological charts for someone at the palace?'

'I didn't, but it stands to reason. He is a stargazer, after all.'

'Well, I wonder if that's the only thing he does,' Carew said. 'It seems they found who really poisoned the Chief Black Eunuch – that's why they've let me off. A woman in the harem. Did you hear the guns go off last night? That's what they were signalling, Jamal told me.' He cleaned his knife thoughtfully on his sleeve. 'They threw the poor creature into the Bosphorous in a sack.'

'Yes, I heard the guns.' Paul looked down over the Golden Horn; the waters looked sparkling and innocent in the afternoon sun.

248

'You were right about Celia. She's there all right.'

Carew looked at him quizzically. 'How do you know?'

'The Valide told me.'

'*What?*'

'Well, not in so many words. She's too clever for that.'

'How then?'

'Well, it's the most curious thing,' Paul said, frowning. 'But I think that's why she wanted to see me all along. I'm to tell Fog that it's all to do with the embassy gifts, and that she can converse with me because I speak Venetian – that's what everyone will think, including her own people. But it wasn't anything to do with that.

'It wasn't her summer palace that I was taken to, but a little pavilion she has on the Asian shore. She told me that the old Sultan had given it to her, a long time ago when she was still the favourite. A garden on the water.' Paul thought of the colours in the late summer garden, of the shimmer of light; the white foot, its instep arched high like a dancer's. 'One of the most beautiful places I've ever been to, John, like something out of a dream.'

'What did she say?'

'That was it, she didn't really say anything. She talked – we talked – about all sorts of things. About gardens. About the merchant's life. About Parvish and his box of curiosities.' The absurdity of it struck him momentarily. 'Then she said something like: "I find I have taken something that is yours."' Paul reached into a bag that he had been carrying at his side. 'And she gave me this.'

Carew took the sugar ship from Paul. He looked at it dispassionately for a few moments and then handed it back. 'I've just spent two days in a vermin-infested cellar because of this – here, you take it.'

Paul took the little boat and held it up to the sun, until the sails, the spun-sugar ropes and the little caramel-coloured men swirled and gleamed with light.

'You surpassed yourself this time, my friend,' Paul said. 'As I live and breathe it is the *Celia*; Lamprey's merchantman down to the very last piece of rigging.' He put the boat down carefully. 'And there it is, even her name inscribed right here on her side.'

'She can read our English script?'

'Unlikely. But there must be plenty of others who can.'

'What's unlikely is that she thinks this has anything to do with Celia. Why should she make the connection at all?'

'Aren't you forgetting something? Your subtlety – your not-so-subtle-subtlety,' Paul said drily, 'has been at the centre of a harem scandal. The Chief Black Eunuch nearly died. The whole thing seems to have been hushed up very expertly, we don't know why, but we do know that for a time they thought that this had something to do with it.' He put the sugar ship carefully back in the canvas bag. 'Not much escapes her, I'll wager she's three steps ahead of all of us.' Paul's eyes smarted with fatigue. 'Believe me, she has found us out Carew.'

'You're sure?'

'Quite sure.' Paul tugged impatiently at the points at his shoulder and pulled off one of his sleeves. His face looked haggard now, dark shadows pressed beneath his eyes.

'What do you think she'll do?'

'If she were going to do anything she'd have done it by now.'

'Do you think she's told anyone else?'

'If anyone at the Porte knew that there was even a hint of an intrigue surrounding one of the Sultan's women we'd be dead meat.'

'Perhaps this was just a warning.'

'Perhaps.' Paul ran a hand through his hair. 'I don't know quite why, but I get the feeling that this is all part of something else . . . of some larger pattern.'

For a moment the two fell silent. Beneath him Paul could see the waters of the Golden Horn thronging with midday water traffic. On board the *Hector* a sailor climbed high into the rigging; slowly the sun was slipping behind the golden roofs of the Sultan's palace.

'She wants us gone, John. When the *Hector* sails again for England in two days' time we're to be on it.'

Carew, fiddling absently with his knives, nodded silently.

'And I'm going to have to tell the others.'

'What, tell Fog?' Carew looked at him with disgust.

'Are you mad? Of course not. I mean Thomas Glover and the others. Mostly Thomas; he's been here longer and worked harder than any of us for the Company. It looks as if Dallam's finished his repairs at last, and we've just had word that Lello can present his credentials. And when that's over and the *Hector* sails, we sail with her.'

'If you say so.'

'No more trying to get messages to Celia.'

'If you say so.'

'Thank God Jamal refused to help when he did—'

'I give thanks for it every day.'

'So she doesn't know we're here, and what she doesn't know can't ever hurt her.'

'Right.'

Another silence fell between them. Into it floated the plaintive sound of the muezzin's voice calling the faithful to sunset prayers. 'I nearly told her, Carew.'

'Who?'

'The Valide.'

'Christ Almighty, Pindar, and you accuse *me* of taking risks.'

'I came *this* close to showing her Celia's portrait.'

The image came to Paul again. Not of Celia as she appeared to him in the compendium miniature; but Celia like a mermaid, her hair wrapped around her neck, floating, green and gold, in the ocean deep. And now I wonder, why didn't I? he thought to himself in anguish. I had my chance and I didn't take it. I should have thrown myself on her mercy, asked her to take pity on me. Paul gouged the knuckles of his fists into his eyes; rainbows of light exploded in his brain. The one person who could have told me for sure. Sometimes I think it would be better to know, and die, than not to know.

'Can it really be true?' He turned to Carew. 'Celia's risen from the dead, John, hasn't she? Tell me I'm not dreaming.'

'You're not dreaming,' Carew replied.

At that moment a familiar figure in workmen's clothing came into the garden. It was Thomas Dallam, the organ maker. When he saw them he quickened his pace.

'How now, Tom, what news?' Paul climbed down from the wall. 'I hear you are to be congratulated. The Sultan's gift is good as new.'

'Aye.'

Dallam, never a man of many words, stood twisting his hat awkwardly in his hands.

'What can I do for you, Tom?'

'Well, Mr Pindar, sir, it's probably nothing, but—'

'But?'

'Well, that business that we were speaking about the other day—'

'Come, speak out, man.'

Dallam looked from Paul to Carew and back again, as if wondering how to proceed.

'By God, man, if you've blabbed so much as a syllable about it—'

'I found this,' Dallam said bluntly. From inside his doublet he produced a piece of paper. 'I don't know what it is, but I thought you should see it anyway.'

Paul took the piece of paper from him.

'What is it?' Carew went to look over his shoulder. 'Looks like a picture, a drawing of some kind—'

'When did you find it?' Paul said. His face was deathly pale.

'First thing this morning, sir, when I went to make my last check on the organ,' Dallam said. 'I reckon someone must have left it there last night.'

'You're sure about that?'

'Absolutely sure. I always check everything myself, make sure none of our tools are left lying around, that kind of thing.'

'Where was it left?'

'On the organ. It was rolled up, inside one of the angel's trumpets. No one could miss it.'

'You're sure it wasn't one of your men, Bucket or Watson?'

'Quite sure.'

'What's it a picture of?' Carew was still craning over Paul's shoulder. 'It looks like a worm . . . No, an eel more like. An eel with fins . . .'

'Brilliant, Carew. Can't you see?' Paul tried to keep his hand from trembling. 'Dear God, it's a lamprey, John. It's a picture of a lamprey.'

Chapter 28

Constantinople: 4 September 1599

Night

In his observatory in Galata Jamal al-Andalus had worked throughout the night.

As was his custom, he sat in his writing room at the very top of the tower. This room was above the observatory where he kept most of his instruments and books, and where he received the visitors and travelling scholars who occasionally called on him: a secret laboratory seen by no one, not even his own servants. He sat cross-legged on the floor in front of a broad, low table, writing figures in a book. A large star chart, weighted down at all four corners with stones, and tables of astronomical data lay spread out in front of him. For many hours the only sound in the room had been the steady scratching of his pen against the thin vellum. Now and again he looked over, half-expectantly, towards the stairs, but there was no one there.

If there had been someone to observe Jamal, they would have seen that his face in this room looked quite different from the face he showed to the outside world. Was he older, or in fact much younger, than his purported years? They would have found it hard to say. In repose, the playfulness that so animated his features whenever he was in company gave way to something altogether more concentrated. For it was here, in this room, that Jamal's real life took place: a life of the mind, a sinking down so deep into its depths that when he came up for air again it was with the dazzled, almost sightless gaze of a man who has supped with angels.

The table where he sat was as uncluttered and chaste as the mathematical figures he was working on that night. The other side of his secret room, however, told a different story, and was more like an artist's workshop than an astronomer's laboratory. Pestles and mortars; a variety of beakers, funnels and sieves; spots of black ink; pieces of tissue-fine cloth covered in sheets of gold leaf; and glass vials of coloured powders, red and green and blue, ground from a variety of substances: lapis lazuli, malachite, cinnabar, white and red lead, green vitriol, haematite, alum, verdigris and gypsum. A number of small brushes, rulers and quills lay in neat rows. And beside them all, laid out neatly on the floor, was a work in progress: a long shirt, open from the neck downwards like a kaftan. One side was still plain, but the other side was covered, in a hand so small it looked as if it had been worked on by djinns, in talismanic figures.

Jamal took a pair of spectacles from his eyes and rubbed his hand over his face where the metal bow had pinched the bridge of his nose. He fitted them carefully back in their wooden case, and took up two strange-looking instruments from their place on the table in front of him. Then, pushing aside a curtain on the wall, he made his way through a door hidden behind it, and up a small flight of steps and on to the roof.

It was a perfect night. The sky was cloudless, without a breath of wind, and the moon was full. Jamal took an astrolabe from his pocket and began to fit it together, pressing two metal discs into a circular outer shell. First the *tympan*, showing the correct latitude and co-ordinates for Constantinople, and then on top of it an openwork star map covered in spiky curlicues, the *rete*. Making up part of the *rete* was a second smaller disc, the ecliptic circle, on which were marked the twelve signs of the zodiac. When the discs were all secured together and ready, Jamal looked up at the sky, and experienced that same vertiginous stab of wonder that he did every time he came here. The stars blazed in the firmament above him. Some, brighter than the others, winked at him with their unearthly light: Aldebaran, Betelgeuse, Markab, Alioth, Vega. Their very names, he sometimes thought, were like an incantation, as powerful as poetry.

Which of you shall I use tonight, my brothers? Jamal thought to himself. Low on the horizon he spotted the Dog Star. Ah, there you are, Sirius my friend, you will do nicely. With a well-practised movement he held the astrolabe up to his eye by a metal ring at the top, spinning the sighting bar, the *alidade*, on the back of the outside case so that the hole at one end of it was level with his eye.

Then, when he had located Sirius through the hole, and holding the instrument very still, with expert fingers he adjusted the *rete*, turning it delicately round so that one of the thorny pointers, the one that corresponded to Sirius, was correctly aligned.

He took it down and had just begun to take a reading when a voice spoke from behind him.

'No need, Jamal. It's the seventh hour after sunset, just as you requested.'

At first the astronomer did not look up, but said with a smile in his voice, 'Telling the hours by starlight is an enthusiasm I cannot share with many other people.'

'Even the unequal hours, Jamal?'

The astronomer turned round at last, and when he spoke his voice was mild. 'It was not I who made them unequal, my friend.'

A dark figure was standing in the shadows behind him.

'*Al-Salam alaykum*, Jamal al-Andalus.'

Jamal put his hand to his heart and bowed towards the visitor. '*Wa alaykum al-Salam*, Englishman. I was beginning to think you wouldn't come. It is too long since we last had a gazing together.'

'You're right, it's been too long.' Paul stepped out from the shadows and on to the astronomer's roof.

'You wear a grave face, Paul. You weren't stopped on your way here? My friend John Carew is not in trouble again, I trust?' Jamal's black eyes gleamed.

'No. Carew's not in trouble again – not yet anyway.' Paul stood blinking in the moonlight. 'You must forgive me, Jamal. I haven't thanked you yet, for everything you did for him. And for me; for all of us, in fact.'

'But not enough, I fear. That other business, Paul, the girl . . . That day, the last time you were here, I feared you were angry with me. I refused you, and I'm sorry for it—'

'Please, don't,' Paul put his hand up, 'don't say any more, it was wrong of me even to ask.'

They fell silent, looking out at the night.

'And Carew?' Jamal said at last. 'He is quite well?'

'Thank you, yes.'

'I'm guessing that it would take rather more than a few days in a cellar to discompose your Carew too badly.'

'You guess right.'

'And your ambassador, Sir Henry Lello, I hope he didn't take it too badly? Battalions of janissaries banging on your doors?'

'We managed to keep it from Sir Henry until after you let Carew go. No harm done there either. I am told the vizier mentioned it when he came to call on the ambassador this morning – full of apologies for the mistake – so, far from being disgraced, if anything the embassy has made some gains from it all. The mechanical organ is finally repaired, and it's to be presented to the Sultan at last. Tomorrow in fact.'

'So Sir Henry will have his credentials?'

'Yes.'

'All is well, then?'

'Yes, in that respect all is well,' Paul said. He looked around the rooftop terrace. 'You said you had something to show me?'

'Yes. It's something I've been working on these last few months. I wanted you to be the first to see it.'

He held out a curious-looking object, a long narrow cylinder about two feet in length, crudely made of leather, narrow at one end, slightly broader at the other.

'Is this it?' Paul's grave look left him, 'What kind of a fairground toy do you call this?' He took the cylinder from Jamal.

'Ah! So you've seen them too?' Jamal was watching Paul eagerly.

'In a tinker's tray, yes, I believe I have,' Paul said with amusement, 'and in good Mr Pearl's shop in Bishopsgate, where Merchant Parvish used to get his spectacle supplies.'

He held it up, and inspected the instrument at both ends: not one, but three interconnected cylinders, covered in shagreen.

'A child's spyglass, Jamal? A very pretty one, I grant you, but . . . well, I thought you must have discovered the Philosopher's Stone, at least.'

'Now what would I want with the Philosopher's Stone? What nonsense you talk,' Jamal said, taking the cylinder back. 'And as a matter of fact it *was* spectacle lenses that gave me the idea. But this is no child's toy, I can assure you. The outside may look crude, but it is a work not fully realised yet, Paul. The beauty, the craft of it, can come later. Its genius lies in these two simple lenses: here and here.' He pointed to two thick discs of transparent glass held in place at either end of the cylinder. 'This one is a weak convex lens; the other,

256

a strong concave lens. Nothing very special about either of them. But if you put them together like this, with the concave lens nearest the eye . . .' He put one end of the spyglass against his eye, and trained the other up into the sky. 'Well, that's what I've brought you here to see for yourself. Here, it's quite heavy; rest it on this.' He pulled over a wooden stand and helped Paul to balance it on top. See for yourself.'

He stood back while the Englishman drew close and trained the spyglass to his eye.

'I can see nothing,' Paul said after some time, 'only blackness.'

'You must be patient,' Jamal came over and swung the cylinder round so that he could stand behind it, 'it takes time for your eyes to adjust. And it's easier if you decide what you're going to look for.'

'What about the moon? That's big enough.'

'No. This is what I want you to see. Jamal swung the cylinder so that it was pointing high at the luminous band of milky light which rippled across the night sky. Paul took the instrument from him and looked again. He looked for a long time in complete silence. When he finally turned to Jamal again it was with a strange, dazzled look.

'Stars, Jamal, thousands, no, millions of them . . .'

'Millions upon millions, Paul. More stars than we ever thought could possibly exist.'

'It's incredible.'

'My instrument has the power to bring everything closer. The glass lenses, you see. I had the idea just after I took to using spectacles myself, that and a little help from Ibn al-Haytham's work on optics, the *Kitab al-Manazir*,' Jamal said, looking modest. 'When you use them on their own the lenses don't have much strength, but used together, one in front of the other, well, you can see for yourself how powerful they are.'

'Extraordinary.' Paul turned back to the eyepiece again. 'Quite extraordinary. How much closer?'

'I estimate about twenty times closer,' Jamal shrugged, 'perhaps a little more.'

'So the luminous haze we can all see across the night sky is actually made of stars,' Paul repeated, 'millions upon millions of stars,' he put his eye back to the lens, 'it's unbelievable.'

'I've seen many things you wouldn't believe, Paul.'

'The moon?'

'But of course. And Venus. With this instrument I've been able to establish that Venus has phases, just like the moon. I can show them to you.'

Rubbing a hand over his eyes, Paul stepped away from the instrument. He went and stood leaning up against the balustrades of the rooftop, gazing up into the starry firmament.

'I believe that your heretic doctor was quite right in the model he proposes,' Jamal said.

'Nicolaus Copernicus?'

'Oh, yes,' Jamal smiled. 'What I have just shown you proves without question that the universe is infinitely bigger than anyone ever dreamt.'

'And that it is not the sky that is moving at all,' Paul turned to Jamal, 'but us?'

'Why not? What's more I believe that my instrument can help prove it.' The astronomer gave Paul one of his mischievous smiles. 'You Christians, always so stuck in your ways.'

Jamal came and stood next to Paul and for a few moments they contemplated the sky in silence together.

'When I first became an astronomer, many years ago now,' Jamal said after a while, 'my task was about making maps: maps of the sky and of the fixed stars. My job was to predict the motions of the sun, the moon and the planets, and the times of particular events such as eclipses, oppositions, conjunctions, solstices, equinoxes and the rest. To reason why they happened was not supposed to be part of my concern. These events happened, but I was not supposed to look for causes behind these events. But now—' he pointed to the cylinder, 'I find I can't be satisfied with that any more. I have to look for the reasons behind things.'

'And I, I too have to look for the reasons behind things, Jamal,' Paul said. 'I have seen further, tonight, than perhaps any Englishman has ever seen, and yet . . . and yet Jamal, I must be frank with you, there are things right here, right beneath my very nose, that aren't altogether as clear to me as I'd like them to be. Before I go, I need to know, you see.'

'Before you go?'

'She wants me gone, Jamal. The Valide. When the *Hector* sails the day after tomorrow, Carew and I are to be on that ship.'

Jamal looked at Paul sorrowfully. 'And I shall miss you, Paul Pindar Aga, more than I can say.'

'What's this? No surprise? No questions? Aren't you going to ask *why* she wants me gone?'

'I think we both know the answer to that, don't you?'

As he spoke, Jamal pulled the hood of his robe over his head, so that his face was hidden in shadow. Paul had the odd impression that he seemed taller, thinner, suddenly.

'What's the matter, Paul?' Jamal took a step towards him. 'You look at me strangely.'

'Do I?' Instinctively Paul took a step back. 'Perhaps it's one of the things I need to know. What's this really all about? Who are you, Jamal?'

'Don't be absurd, you know who I am. The astronomer, Jamal al-Andalus.'

'But is that all you are?'

'I did not know that metaphysics was one of your interests,' the astronomer said drily.

'I came here the other day to ask for your help, because I knew that you came and went freely to the palace. Neither of us guessed just how freely. That woman who came for you, Esperanza Malchi—'

'Ah, so you found out about her, I wondered if you might.'

'Carew did, he's useful like that. This Malchi woman is one of the Valide's most trusted servants. And the most feared, so my informants tell me. And yet you're on good terms with her—'

'Your *informants* . . .'

'You knew all about the Chief Black Eunuch, and about Carew's sugar ship,' Paul went on. 'You hid Carew here to protect him, then released him again the moment they found the real culprit, all without fuss, without clamour, without so much as the smallest ripple penetrating the palace as far as I can tell, all before the Grand Vizier himself could so much as sneeze.' Paul paused. 'How did you do all that?'

'Well, yes, I must confess, I was rather proud of how smoothly it all went—'

'And then there's all this.' Paul gestured to Jamal's new stargazing instrument. 'Carew was right. You have an extraordinary collection of things here, Jamal. The finest precision instruments that I've ever seen: astrolabes, globes, maps, books. Where did they all come from?'

'Perhaps you'd like to ask your informants that too?' Jamal was no longer smiling. 'You spy on me – and then you have the temerity to think that you'll get me to spy *for* you as well.'

'No, not spy. I just wanted information—'

'Is there a difference?'

'Of course there is.'

'No one at the palace would see it like that. You foreigners are all the same, like children. You always want to know about the things which are *haram*. Don't think that you're the first one who's tried it with me.'

'I'm sorry, but God knows I had good reasons. Surely you can see that?' Paul ran his hand through his hair. 'This is Celia we're talking about, the woman I loved – whom I still love,' there was desperation in Paul's voice now, 'the woman who was going to be my wife. All these years I've thought she was *dead*, Jamal. And then it turns out she's not dead, but living here, right here in Constantinople. All this time, right beneath my very nose.' Paul laid his head in his hands. 'And I have done nothing to help her!'

'Suppose Carew was mistaken?'

'He wasn't mistaken,' Paul thrust a piece of paper at Jamal, 'here, look at this.'

'What is it?'

'It's a picture of a lamprey, a kind of fish like an eel. It's a pun, a play on her name. Dallam found it hidden in the organ.'

Without speaking Jamal handed it back to him.

'What? Have you nothing to say? She knows I'm here, Jamal, I'm sure of it—'

'You still don't understand do you, Englishman? The women's quarters of any man's household, let alone the Sultan's, are *haram*,' Jamal repeated himself slowly, as though to a child, 'that means forbidden, absolutely forbidden, to all other men. Not only by sight, but by word, by thought, even. If your girl Celia Lamprey really is in the House of Felicity as you say, then she belongs to the Sultan now. She does not exist for you any longer. No matter what she was before, she is his slave now; she belongs to him. Nothing – nothing short of a miracle – can change that.'

260

Jamal sighed. 'And I thought you were different, Paul.' He looked down at the shagreen cylinder. 'I thought you came here because you were interested in my work for its own sake.'

'Don't be absurd, you know I did,' Paul said with a look of anguish.

'Yes,' Jamal said, more gently this time, 'I know you did. I looked into my heart and I saw what you really were: an honest man. Even when I knew that things between us were – how shall I phrase it? – not all that they seemed.'

'It's just that I thought I knew you.' Paul rubbed a fist across his forehead. 'And then you seemed like a stranger suddenly.'

'When it is you that is the stranger, Paul.' Jamal looked at him sorrowfully. 'I forget sometimes that that is what you are: a stranger in our land. You must speak, say what it is you have come to tell me with confidence. But first here, come with me,' he put his hand on Paul's arm, 'the night is becoming cold, and you are chilled.'

Jamal took Paul back down to his observatory. A small brazier was burning in one corner and the room was warm. One of Jamal's servants came in, bringing them tiny glasses of hot mint tea.

'You must sit here awhile and get warm again,' Jamal told him. 'And while you drink the tea I will tell you something, something that I hope will explain why I helped Carew.'

'When I was a child, barely ten years old,' Jamal began, 'I was apprenticed to a scribe, one of the palace calligraphers. I was a dextrous and able boy, and I soon learnt my trade, and learnt it well, but I was never satisfied by it.

'Something in my belly made me want more from life than copying words other people had written, even if they were sometimes holy words, suras from the Qu'ran. Next to my master's workshop in the palace was the workshop of another craftsman, a man who made clocks, sundials and instruments of all kinds for the Sultan. I grew fascinated by the things in his workshop, not just because they were things of beauty, but because of what they were used for. I spent all the time that I could with this other master, learning everything that I could persuade him to show me, including the rudiments of arithmetic and geometry, to the amazement of the other craftsmen, and the despair of my real master. Fortunately for me he was a good man, almost like a father to me, and when he realised that he couldn't beat these interests out of me, and that I had a real mathematical ability, somehow he arranged it that I should attend the palace school.

'I was very happy at the school. At last, I had a sense that I was doing the thing that God meant me to do. Soon it became clear that I was a boy with very unusual abilities. Within a few years I had learnt everything that the teachers could show me about mathematics, but I didn't care. I carried on, teaching myself when I had to. All I cared about was numbers, their beauty and their clarity. In the Christian world you think that the universe turns to the music of the spheres, but you see, Paul, I know that the language of the universe, its deepest and most profound music, is numbers.' Jamal sat back with a smile. 'Most of the other boys of my age were only interested in archery, or in horses, and there was I, puzzling over the problems in Euclid!

'When I was thirteen, Sultan Selim died, and his son, Sultan Murad, the present Sultan's father, came to power. He brought with him his old teacher and scholar, Hoja Sa'd al-Din, who took an interest in me. This man, by good fortune, was a friend of the head astronomer Takiuddin. For some years Takiuddin had wished to have a new observatory built in Constantinople. The available astronomical tables had become outdated, and he wanted to compile new ones, based on fresh observations. When he came to the Sultan and the Diwan – the Council of Viziers – with his proposal, Hoja Sa'd al-Din was one of the principal supporters of the project. Takiuddin built his observatory, very near here in the Tophane quarter of Galata, and two years later when it was ready I was accepted there as one of his principal assistants.

'Well, you know what happened,' Jamal sighed. 'That same year, 1577, a great comet appeared in the sky. Takiuddin prepared a prognostication for the Sultan. The comet, he told him, was a harbinger of good tidings, and a sign that the Ottoman armies would win victory in the wars against Persia. He was right, of course. The Persians were defeated – but the Ottoman armies suffered greatly at the same time. Furthermore, a plague struck our city that year, and a number of important officials died, all within a short space of time of one another. Hardly the propitious tidings that my master had predicted.

'My old patron, Hoja Sa'd al-Din, and his ally the Grand Vizier Soqullu Mehmet Pasha, had made some dangerous enemies at court. One of them was the Sheik al-Islam – the principal authority on

Islamic law in Constantinople. This Sheik went to the Sultan and tried to persuade him that it was the observatory itself which was the cause of these evils. To pry into the secrets of nature, he said, could only bring misfortune upon us all. Indeed, empires in which observatories were built, he claimed, were known to suffer speedy dissolution.

'At first the Sultan didn't want to listen to him as he was a man who greatly respected learning, but eventually, after some years, the Sheik and his faction prevailed. A wrecking squad was sent – and, well, you know the rest,' Jamal said sombrely. 'There was no warning, they just burst in on us all one day. The viewing tower, all our instruments, the library, our charts: priceless. Irreparable. Worst of all, our team was dispersed. We were disgraced. Where could we go? What could we do? All our precious work had been destroyed. Most of the other assistants had families they could return to, but I had no one. I came here, to this tower.

'This place, which was still surrounded by fields, was known as the Small Observatory, part of the larger complex, and a little apart from it. It too was wrecked by the Sultan's halberdiers, but not so thoroughly as the larger observatory. There was just enough of it left standing for me to build a makeshift shelter in one part of it. It was from here that I salvaged some of the books, some of the smaller instruments.

'When the people of the town heard that one of the astronomers was still living out here, wild as a hermit, they began to come and see me. Cautiously at first. They were simple people for the most part, with only a very rudimentary idea of what astronomy is about. At first they'd ask me for small things: to interpret their dreams; or to cast horoscopes for them at the birth of a child or when they needed to find a propitious date for a wedding or a circumcision. Gradually their requests became a little more complicated. Sometimes they'd ask for charms, or talismans, for protection against the Evil Eye, against sickness, that kind of thing. And just occasionally . . . something stronger.'

'Sorcery, you mean?'

'Is that what you'd call it?' Jamal looked at Paul quizzically. 'Well, for the most part it was harmless enough. Sometimes it was no more than a few verses from the Qu'ran wrapped up in a little cloth bag. I could still write with a fair calligrapher's hand, remember. As I say, harmless enough stuff. Most of the time.'

'And then?'

'And then one day I had a visit from someone who changed everything: a black eunuch from the palace. His name was Hassan Aga.'

'The Chief Black Eunuch?'

'The very same. Although this was more than twenty years ago, so he wasn't the Chief Black Eunuch then, of course.'

'And he asked you to cast a horoscope for him?'

'Not exactly. He said that there was a very great lady who desired my services, although it was of course a matter of the utmost secrecy. If I could help her, I would be rewarded beyond my wildest dreams. But if I ever divulged the nature of her request,' Jamal gave a rueful smile, 'I would end up a gelded man, just like him.'

'And did you help her?'

'Actually, I refused. A wise man wouldn't normally dare to refuse a request from the palace, but I did. The nature of her request so terrified me that at first I didn't dare – even if I had been able to help her, which I doubted. But between them they worked on me. I could rebuild the tower, they said, they would provide me with new instruments, new books. I could work again, as an independent scholar, pursuing whatever interests I liked, under her patronage this time.'

'A powerful lady.'

'Oh yes.'

'So what did she want you to do?'

'She wanted me to put a spell on the Sultan. A spell to make him unable to lie with any woman other than herself.'

'To make him impotent, you mean?'

'Precisely.'

'Who was this woman?'

'In those days she was the Haseki, the Sultan's favourite. You know her as Safiye Sultan.'

Paul stared at Jamal.

'Did it work?' he said after a few moments.

'Ha!' Jamal gave a sudden shout of laughter. 'My talisman? Of course it worked.' Then, serious again, he added, 'For a while. The Sultan Murad had been faithful to Safiye for nearly twenty years. It was something of a scandal, to tell you the truth. It was common knowledge that he took no other concubines; chose to father his children only by her. But when he came back to Constantinople as Sultan things changed. For a start, his mother Nurbanu was here, and she hated Safiye and was jealous of the power she had over her son. It was she who was instrumental in trying to persuade Murad to take new concubines. She and her daughter İsmihan searched high and low to find the most beautiful slave girls in the empire, but to no avail. Despite the fact that Safiye Sultan was no longer young by then, he had eyes only for her.' Jamal took a sip from the tiny glass of mint tea, replacing it carefully on the table next to him. 'And then, one day,' he went on, 'they found someone. Two women, in fact, a pair of slave girls, beautiful as angels. As soon as she saw them, Safiye knew she was beaten. It was then that she sent for me.'

Jamal took another sip from the glass. 'The talisman I made for her worked for a long time. As hard as he tried the Sultan could honour no one but the Haseki herself. But then they found it.'

'The talisman?'

Jamal nodded. 'One of her handmaids took the blame, so they told me, and was thrown into the Bosphorous for her pains.'

'And Safiye – what happened to her?'

'She took to finding girls for the Sultan herself, each one more beautiful than the next – and in all he fathered nineteen children with them before his death—'

'But she kept his heart for herself?'

'Something like that, I suppose.'

'So that's how you built your tower. All the astrolabes, the globes. Your library.'

'Yes, Safiye Sultan has been as good as her word. A great patroness, and generous, too.'

'And you still work for her sometimes?'

'Over the years –' Jamal nodded slowly, 'from time to time. But until that business recently with Hassan Aga, she had not asked anything of me for many years, even though I go to the palace often to teach at the school. The Valide knew that Carew had nothing to do with the poisoning, and she asked me to help. That's all.

'You should know that I am not the only one she uses, Paul. There are many of us whom the Valide can call on if she needs to. She calls me her physician. When Hassan Aga was poisoned I was called in to help.

I was reluctant then, too.' He shook his head again. 'The man had taken so much poison – he was beyond my help and I think even she knew it. It's God's work that he's still alive, I tell you. That and—'

'And what?'

'Who knows?' Jamal shrugged. 'He must have something very precious to live for. But he's a eunuch, after all, so who knows what that might be?'

When Jamal had finished his story, Paul sat for a moment in silence, looking down at his hands. He felt so weary suddenly he could not speak, could hardly think.

'And what about me, Jamal?' he said, closing his eyes, tilting his head back and resting it against the wall. The bitter taste of defeat, like ashes, slurred his words. 'Am I to have nothing precious to live for?'

'You have everything to live for.' Jamal looked at him with compassion. 'But let me give you some advice. Go home, Paul. The Valide has given you a chance. You won't get another one.'

Dawn was breaking when the two men said goodbye to one another at last.

'Until we meet again, Paul Pindar Aga.'

'Until we meet again.'

They embraced.

'Jamal?'

'My friend?'

'One last favour?'

'Anything,' Jamal smiled, 'what's this?'

'My compendium.'

'Yes, I can see that.'

Jamal stood with Paul's compendium in the palm of his hand.

'Get it to her. Please.'

For what seemed to Paul like a long, long time, the astronomer looked at it, saying nothing.

'It's not a look; it's not a word, not even a thought,' Paul said, 'but she'll understand. At least she'll know I tried.'

'Very well.' Jamal took it from him. 'It's as I've already said, Paul Pindar, there's no *man* on earth who can help you but – perhaps – there's someone else who can.'

266

Chapter 29

Istanbul: the present day

It was not until the morning after her trip up the Bosphorous with Mehmet that Elizabeth was able to open the email from her supervisor, Dr Alis.

My dear Elizabeth,

So glad you're having a productive time in Istanbul. Good news this end: the department have approved your transference from MLitt to DPhil. We can discuss where we go from here when you get back, but in the meantime here's a scan of the portrait you asked for, hope it's clearer than your copy . . .

Without waiting to read the rest of the message, Elizabeth clicked on the attachment. After a few moments a message popped on to the screen: *there is a temporary problem accessing this page, click the refresh button, or please try later.* She clicked on 'refresh', the timer whirled briefly, but still nothing happened.

Damn! She went back to the message, scrolled through until she found where she had left off:

. . . hope it's clearer than your copy. In case you're wondering the object he's holding is called a compendium, a part-mathematical, part-astronomical instrument. If you look carefully you'll see that it is composed of a number of different parts: a nocturnal, a magnetic compass, a table of latitudes and an equinoctial dial. In practice the whole thing would have folded up into the outer brass case, small enough to fit into a pocket (rather like a modern fob watch and chain) but as you can see he is holding it open for the viewer. Rather more unusually, this one seems to have some kind of extra compartment at the bottom, probably for keeping something in: drawing implements, perhaps? What you have to ask yourself is, why did he choose to be painted with it? What's its significance? The Elizabethans loved symbols, codes of this kind. Perhaps the date (just visible in the bottom right hand corner) will give you a clue.

There's a date? Damn this machine! Impatiently Elizabeth tried the attachment again, but the message was the same as before: *click the refresh button, or please try again later.* Why was there always a glitch on these Internet café computers? There was nothing for it, she would have to wait until Monday to try again on one of the university terminals.

When she returned to Haddba's house she found an official-looking brown envelope waiting for her. It had a local postmark and was addressed to Bayan Elizabeth Staveley. Later that night she rang Eve.

'Guess what, my permission to visit the archives has come through at last.'

'About bloody time. What's the latest?'

Elizabeth told her about the portrait of Paul Pindar with the compendium, and Thomas Dallam's diary.

'It's odd, but you know what I keep thinking about?'

'What's that?'

'I keep thinking about Pindar's house. Do you remember me telling you about it before?'

'Mmm, vaguely. It was big, I seem to remember.'

'More than that. Listen, let me read you this – I had a good trawl on Google again the other day, and this is what turned up.' Elizabeth took out her notes. ' "One of the finest specimens of timber-framed domestic architecture in London, constructed about 1600 by a wealthy London merchant Paul Pindar" ', she read. 'The façade of the building turns out to have been rather famous. "A two-storey façade, jointed and carved oak with richly carved panels at the bottom of each bay on the first and second floors. Above this are windows made up of many pieces of glass." '

'Is it still there?'

'No. The house became a public house in 1787, and then was demolished altogether in the 1890s to make way for the extension of what is now Liverpool Street Station. The façade's in the V&A though – one day I'll go and have a look.'

'OK, OK, I get the picture.' Eve seemed exasperated. 'But I don't see how any of this gets you any nearer to finding out what happened to Celia Lamprey.'

'Well, it doesn't – not directly, anyway,' Elizabeth said. 'I started trying to call up images of Pindar's house, and amazingly there are some. Someone has taken the trouble to put something called *Smith's Antiquities of London, 1791* online, and, bingo, there it was – not only the house itself but also the lodge of the original park surrounding the house, which apparently still existed then in a place called Half-Moon Alley. "Persons now living,"' Elizabeth read out the caption, '"remember the mulberry trees and other vestiges of the park near it."'

'So? He had a grand house with a garden. Bishopsgate was just outside the old city walls, and in the late sixteenth century the whole area would still have been largely fields and countryside.'

'But don't you see? It says that the house was built in 1600, that's only the year after the merchants presented the Sultan with the organ. We know Pindar was in Constantinople until at least 1599 because Thomas Dallam mentions him in his diary; he was one of the two secretaries who accompanied the ambassador when he finally went to present his credentials. But the point is that his house wasn't just any old house; it was an enormous great mansion, on a par with those of Thomas Gresham and other great London financiers. But if he were on his own – still a bachelor, with no wife and family – why would he have built something so big?'

'Um, because he was very rich?' Eve said. 'You said so yourself. Pindar was the original merchant banker – what else was he going to do with his money? I thought that was what the Elizabethans were all about: ostentation and extravagance.'

'But that's just it, he wasn't either of those things.' Elizabeth thought of the portrait, the man with his chaste black velvet doublet. 'You make him sound like some awful *nouveau*, when he wasn't anything of the kind. He was a gentleman, a scholar.'

269

'He might have been gay,' Eve countered. 'Oh come on, all those sumptuous interiors!'

'I don't think so,' Elizabeth said, 'a house like that is about the future, about posterity, surely. Something to be handed down to the next generation.'

'He might have married someone else. Have you ever considered that?'

'Of course I have,' Elizabeth pressed the fingers of one hand to her eyes, 'I've considered every possibility there is. But no, he never loved anyone else but her. Celia escaped, I'm sure of it.'

Elizabeth glanced up, and saw through the window of her room the view down over the Golden Horn and towards the palace: a grandstand view of old Constantinople, the very same view that the Levant Company merchants would have seen from their houses in Galata. How strange that she had hardly noticed it when she first arrived. In just a few weeks the whole room had become so familiar to her that she hardly saw it any more, and now for a fraction of a moment she suddenly saw it again as she had then: the bare dipping floorboards, the twin beds, as chaste and neat as a ship's cabin.

Eve was saying something again.

'Sorry, what was that?'

'I said: it's all very well to say that but you've got no evidence.' Eve emphasised the last three words slowly.

'Well there's no need to speak to me as if I were a complete idiot. I can't explain why, but I just *know*,' Elizabeth snapped suddenly. 'And I don't *need* any evidence. Not for this.'

The words were out before she could stop them. For a moment there was silence on the line.

'For a DPhil thesis?' Eve's voice sounded terse. 'I rather think that you do.'

'What I mean is . . .' Elizabeth sighed. 'Oh hell, what do I mean?' she said, almost to herself. 'Have you ever . . . have you ever had the sense that the past is speaking to you?'

There was a pause.

'Not in the deluded way that you seem to think it does.' Eve muttered.

Elizabeth was silenced.

'You sound tired.' Eve said eventually.

270

'It's true . . .' Elizabeth rubbed her hand over her eyes again. 'I haven't been sleeping very well.'

There was another pause.

'Is there something else? Marius hasn't tried to get in touch with you, has he?' Eve said after a while. 'I heard he's telephoned the college a couple of times.'

'Marius?' Elizabeth almost laughed. 'No.'

The image came to her, not of Marius, but of Mehmet. *Delete Marius.* Was it possible that she actually had?

'Well, that's something.'

There was another awkward pause.

'OK then, I'd better go.'

'OK then.'

'Bye.'

'Bye.'

Elizabeth lay on her bed and looked up at the ceiling. What was wrong with her? That was the closest she had ever come to having a row with Eve. She could have told her about Mehmet, but she hadn't – why not? She, who always told Eve everything. She rolled over and picked up her mobile from the bedside table, called up the photographs that she had taken the day before, gazed at his profile, the sculpted nose, what wouldn't she give now to see him in the flesh, to hear his voice. But he was away, had gone to Ankara on business, would be away for two whole days.

Elizabeth turned her phone off and lay back on the bed. In the distance, through the darkness outside her window, she could hear the muezzin calling the faithful to prayer.

She closed her eyes. It was true that she was tired. She had hardly slept last night for thinking about Mehmet. Her sleep, such as it was, had been shallow and feverish. Sometimes she was back in the hammam, that morning when she had imagined his eyes on her naked body. Other times she replayed in her mind that moment when he had taken her hand in the restaurant, felt again the touch of his thumb on the delicate skin of her wrist.

On the return journey they had stood close together, their bodies not touching, but so close that she was aware of his breath against her neck.

'Are you all right?'

'Yes.'

'You're shivering again?'

'No, really . . .'

'Sure?' He reached over to tuck a strand of long hair behind her ear.

'Quite sure.'

'Look, there's something here that I want to show you.'

He had pointed to a row of stately wooden houses overhanging the water on a little bay. 'These are the *yalis* that I was telling you about. See this one here,' he pointed to one of the largest ones, its wooden walls painted russet-brown, 'this is what Haddba wanted me to show you.'

'It's beautiful,' Elizabeth said. 'Who does it belong to?'

'My family.' Mehmet replied. 'One of my great-aunts, my grand-mother's youngest sister, still lives there, but she's away in Europe for the winter.' He looked at her carefully. 'I will bring you here one day. If you like.'

They motored on in silence for a while. The sun, which was low on the horizon now, had gone in behind the clouds. A flock of cormorants flew past them, low on the water.

'Are you afraid?' he asked her.

'No,' she had said.

'That's good.' He turned to her. 'You have nothing to be afraid of, you know that, don't you?'

'Yes,' Elizabeth had nodded. 'I know.'

And so she had dozed on fitfully through the night, thinking about him. There were times when she was not sure whether she was dreaming or awake. At one point in the night she thought she heard her door bang open, the sound of footsteps running suddenly into the room. Elizabeth had sat up with a cry.

The shadow of a young woman – her hair dishevelled, pearls at her neck – stood over her.

She heard a voice – was it her own? – cry out.

Celia?

But there was no one there.

Chapter 30

Constantinople: 5 September 1599

Morning

I t was not until two days after finding Handan that Celia had a chance to speak to Annetta again. She found her friend alone, sitting up amongst her cushions. Although she still looked pale, she was fully dressed, her hair neatly combed and braided.

'You look better.'

'And you look terrible.' Annetta ran her eye critically over Celia, and then enquiringly over her shoulder out into the corridor beyond. 'Where are your women today?'

Celia lowered her eyes. 'The Harem Stewardess said she wanted them for some other job.'

'Does that mean you are no longer *gözde*?' Annetta said, not mincing her words.

'So it would seem.' Celia thought of the Sultan, the heavy pale flesh, the little goatee beard, the hanging jowls. She remembered Hanza's frail form, rising and falling on top of him, and the strange little hiccoughing sounds she had made, like a child trying not to cry. 'And I don't care what you say,' she gripped Annetta's hand suddenly, 'I'm not sorry for it.'

'It's all right.'

'And I expect I'll be back in here with you before long,' Celia looked round her at the little windowless dormitory that Annetta shared with five other *cariye*, 'and I won't be sorry for that, either.'

'We'll stick together,' Annetta squeezed her hand again, 'whatever happens, now more than ever.'

273

'Yes, we must,' Celia looked at her, 'which is why you must tell me what really happened the night that Hassan—'

'*Madonna*, not that again!' Annetta lay back on her cushions, the good humour draining from her face. 'Why can't you just forget about it?'

'Forget about it? You agreed to tell me! "No more secrets," you said, remember? Do you think it's just going to go away all on its own? Well, it's not. If Hassan Aga really did see you there, then you're in as much trouble as I am.' Celia was whispering now. 'Shh! What's that?'

'What? I don't hear anything.'

'Wait a moment.' Celia ran over to the door, glancing quickly down the corridors on each side, and out into the Courtyard of the Cariyes. There was no one in sight. When she came back her face was pale. 'They've been through my things, I'm sure of it. Wherever I go, I can feel them watching me, listening. All the time. Even people I thought I could trust – Gulbahar . . . Hyacinth . . . all of them. You've no idea what it's been like. I don't know who anyone is any more.'

'Why? Because of the sugar ship? But they've proved that had nothing to do with the poisoning . . .'

'Have they? I'm not so sure. I keep thinking about it, Annetta: suppose they've found out about Paul, supposing he's in danger now too?' Celia pressed her hand to her side, to where a pain nagged constantly now. 'Annetta, it's not over yet: the ship had my name on it!' The feeling of breathlessness had started to come over her again. 'Look, we don't have much time. Just tell me what you saw. Believe me, this isn't going to go away by itself.'

'Well, as a matter of fact, I think it *is* our best chance – that we let this whole thing just go away by itself. Which it will, so long as some busybody doesn't go around stirring things up again,' Annetta snapped, glaring at her. 'The fact is, nothing *has* happened.' She sat up again. 'They've found who did it, Hanza or the Haseki, or both of them, who knows, and I'm sorry for it,' she added, half-grudgingly, 'because I know you liked her, the Haseki that is. But if Hassan Aga had seen me there he would have said something by now. You think I haven't thought this through? No one has said anything, and no one is going to – now can we just leave it?'

'You wouldn't say that if you'd been there. It was terrible, Annetta – I was there when they were taken.' Celia held out her wrist. The Haseki's bracelet, little chips of blue and black glass, glittered dully. 'The Chief Black Eunuch was poisoned, and two women are dead because of it. They tied them up in sacks and threw them into the Bosphorous. Imagine it . . .' She fingered the glass beads, feeling their smoothness against her fingers. 'The fact that Hassan Aga hasn't said anything about you might be a good sign, perhaps he didn't see you after all. Or it might mean that he's just waiting for the right moment. Because that's what they do in here, remember? They watch and they wait, you taught me that yourself.'

Annetta rolled over, lay with her back to Celia, trying not to hear her.

'The Haseki was trying to tell me something, but she never got the chance to finish her story,' Celia said, shaking Annetta by the shoulder. 'You think that Esperanza Malchi put the Evil Eye on you – but I don't think she's got anything to do with this. There's someone else involved. The Haseki said as much – someone much more dangerous.'

'In that case, all the more reason for you to leave well alone,' Annetta said, her face still turned towards the wall.

'I can't. Not now.'

There was a long silence.

'You've done it, haven't you?' Annetta said, rolling over at last.

'What?'

'Don't act the innocent with me. You've been to the Aviary Gate, haven't you?'

Celia blinked rapidly, there was no use denying it, certainly not to Annetta. 'No one saw me.'

'You think so?' Annetta closed her eyes despairingly. 'I can't believe I'm hearing this.'

'Then I think there's something else you should hear, too.'

Quickly Celia told her about Handan, and her discoveries of two nights ago. Annetta heard her out in complete silence. When she spoke at last, her voice was an angry hiss.

'What's come over you? *Santa Madonna*, it's not *me* you should be worried about, it's *you* who's really going to be in trouble now.'

'Shh!' Looking round her, Celia put a finger to her lips. 'Come on, think. Cariye Mihrimah. Have you ever heard of anyone by that name?'

'I knew that the Chief Black Eunuch used to be called Little Nightingale. But Cariye Mihrimah? No,' Annetta shook her head. 'I've never heard of anyone called by that name.'

'If we can find out who that person is, well, I think that's the key.'

'The key?'

'The key to everything. To finding out who poisoned the Chief Black Eunuch and who was really behind the death of Gulay Haseki,' Celia said, impatient now. 'The key to why the sugar ship – a subtlety in the shape of my father's boat, with my name on it – has somehow got mixed up in this. It's all connected, I'm sure that's what the Haseki was trying to tell me.'

'But they've found out who did it, it was her all along!' Annetta was almost wailing now. 'What about the horoscope that Hanza found?'

'I've never believed that, have you? Does anyone? Anyone could have planted it. You remember the day we saw Esperanza Malchi deliver something to her apartment? Someone took it in, but I never saw who: did you? I think Gulay knew something like that was going to happen. She said so in as many words to me. She certainly knew she had enemies. Enemies dangerous enough to make her want to give up being Haseki.'

'Oh, so that's what she told you, is it?' Annetta gave Celia a withering look. 'Aren't you forgetting something? Gulay had a *son*. He could be the next Sultan, which means she would have been the next Valide. The stakes don't get higher than that. When the present Sultan came to the throne, all nineteen of his brothers were murdered – don't you remember Cariye Lala's stories? And Gulay knew that unless she won, that's what would have happened to her son too. It still could,' she added grimly.

'I'm not denying that. But I still think it was part of her plan.'

'Has it ever occurred to you that that might have been what she wanted you to think? That she had her own reasons for telling you about the Nightingales?' Annetta shivered, and pulled the coverlet up around her shoulders. 'The more I hear about all this the less I like it.'

'You're wrong,' Celia said. 'You've got to trust me on this. And now – please – will you tell me exactly what you saw?'

276

'Oh, very well, I'll tell you.' Annetta sighed, closing her eyes.

'That night – the same night that you were taken to the Sultan for the first time – I couldn't sleep,' she began. 'I kept thinking about you. Wondering if you were – safe. Wondering,' Annetta gave a ghost of a smile, 'what kind of tricks Cariye Lala had up her sleeve, and whether she was worth the money we paid her.' Annetta's eyelids flickered. 'So much seemed to depend on it, and I knew it might be our only chance to succeed. Scores of girls come through here, and most of them are never even looked at. But you, Celia, you are beautiful and gentle, and you carry yourself like a noblewoman. I knew you would be noticed. Whereas me, well, look at me,' she laughed, 'just a scrawny thing with black hair, that's what the nuns always used to say. No one – far less the Sultan – was ever going to look at me. But I have wits, good sharp wits, and between the two of us – well, two is better than one.

'Anyway that night, as I told you, I couldn't sleep. If you remember, there were very few of us here that night. Apart from the novices, most of the women were still at the Valide's summer palace and were not due to return until the following day. I came down to the bathhouse for some water. It was so quiet. I remember seeing my own shadow in the moonlight and thinking that this was what it must be like to be a ghost.

'It was then that I heard a noise – the murmur of voices speaking very quietly to one another – coming from somewhere inside the Valide's quarters. I wondered if it had something to do with you, so I went over to the door which connects the Courtyard of the Cariyes with her antechambers, so that I could listen better. Then, just as I got there, the door opened violently, and out came Cariye Lala. She was carrying something in her hands: the sugar ship. We both nearly jumped out of our skins – I think it was as much as we could do to stop ourselves from screaming out loud – and for one horrible moment I thought that she was going to send me to the Harem Stewardess, but instead she simply handed me the sugar ship and said that she had been told to take it to the Chief Black Eunuch's room, but that I would do just as well.'

'So that's how it got there? *You* took it! My God, Annetta—' Celia stared at her friend. 'So now there are two people who know where you were that night?'

'Oh, Cariye Lala is harmless enough, everyone knows that.' Annetta clicked her tongue impatiently, 'the question we have to ask is *who* sent *her?*'

'Yes, yes, but one thing at a time.' Celia ran her fingers across her eyes feverishly. 'First tell me what happened when you reached Hassan Aga's room?'

'That's the strange thing, there was no one there,' Annetta said. 'I put the ship down on a tray that had been set out next to his divan, but not before I'd had a good look at it. I'm so sorry, goose, I know I should have told you,' she looked at Celia and swallowed, 'but anyway, after I'd put the subtlety down on the tray I wasn't sure what to do. It occurred to me that perhaps I should wait and tell Hassan Aga what I'd brought him, but no one came,' she glanced at Celia, 'so I thought, here's my chance, I'll have a look around . . .'

'You *what?*' Now it was Celia's turn to look horrified. 'In Hassan Aga's room?'

'Well, you're one to talk.' Lowering her voice, Annetta leant a little closer towards Celia. 'And just listen to this, I did find something – or rather, I *heard* something. I heard the sound of a cat.'

'A cat – what's so extraordinary about that? This place is full of cats.'

'But the sound was coming from *inside* one of the walls. I listened and listened and eventually I traced the sound to behind the tiles on one of the walls, the one immediately opposite his divan. The sound of this poor cat became louder and louder, so I ran my hands up and down the tiles and eventually I found a sort of catch in the wall. I pulled at it, and straight away a whole section of the wall just sprang open before my eyes.'

'A secret door! Another one!'

'Precisely. And inside the door was a cupboard, quite a large one, easily big enough for someone, even a great fat eunuch, to hide inside. And there was the cat—'

'Poor thing!'

'But not just anyone's cat. Imagine! It was the Valide's great white cat, you know the one? With the creepy eyes?'

'Of course I do,' Celia said in amazement, 'but what on earth was Cat doing there?'

'I'm coming to that. When I opened the door the cat shot out of the cupboard – he almost knocked me over he was in such a hurry to get out – and I saw that at the back of the cupboard there was another door.'

'I think I know what you're going to say—'

'Exactly! Behind the second door there I found a secret staircase. Just like the one you found in the Haseki's apartment.'

'So that's why you were so interested in the different entrances to her apartment. Do you think the two might be connected?'

'Of course. That must be how Cat got in there, he must have found a way in through one of the other entranceways, and then got trapped. Anyway, I was still inside the cupboard when I heard the sound of voices coming into the room behind me.' Annetta looked at Celia uncomfortably. 'What could I do? There was no time to get out. I just had time to close the cupboard door, with me inside it this time, before Hassan Aga came in.'

Celia stared at her.

'I know, I know,' Annetta shrugged. 'Don't look at me like that. It was stupid – but then again, maybe not so stupid as it sounds. The old rhinocerous wasn't alone. Oh no, he was with a girl, Cariye Lala's servant girl from the Valide's bathhouse. I could see them both quite clearly though a spy-hole in the back of the door.'

'The girl with the braided hair? I remember her.' Celia said sharply. 'She was helping me to prepare that night. I don't think I've seen her since then.'

'That's because she's dead.'

'Dead?' Celia echoed. 'Her too?'

'Oh, yes.'

'But how?'

'That girl – that innocent-looking young girl – turned out to be the Chief Black Eunuch's very own *culo*.'

'Impossible!'

At the sight of Celia's horrified face, Annetta gave a wry laugh. 'You think that because these eunuchs are gelded man and they can't actually fornicate for real,' Annetta made an eloquent gesture with the fingers of one hand, 'that they have no affections, no desires? Or—' she cocked her head to one side, 'that they cannot satisfy a woman in other ways? Well, if what I saw that night is anything to go by, it is quite to the contrary. She wrinkled up her nose in disgust. 'But of all the unnatural, beastly acts I ever saw—'

'You didn't—'

'Well,' Annetta gave a nonchalant shrug, 'I've told you before, one brothel is very much like another. But it wasn't so much what he did to her, or made her do to him, as all that fawning and cooing and cajoling. *Faugh*!' she shuddered. 'It was enough to make me sick. Do you know, I think he might really have felt something for her, the poor deluded fool. It was all, "my little faun", and "my little flower; here, strip for me, my little song thrush, let me see you naked, let me kiss your little feet, let me suck your little nipples, so soft, so sweet, like tender pink tulips."' Annetta crinkled up her face, imitating the eunuch's curious cracked falsetto voice. 'All that baby talk, *ugh*! That monstrous grizzled old hippopotamus nuzzling all over her, I wanted to burst out of the cupboard right there and then, I tell you, and slap his fat ugly face.'

Celia, still staring at her mutely, looked faint at the thought.

'But as you can see, I didn't.'

'Clearly.'

'And then I saw her reach out and take something from the sugar ship.'

'Snap off a piece of the sugar, you mean?'

'No.' Annetta was frowning. 'I think that there must have been something already hidden inside the ship. In fact, I'm sure of it. I hadn't seen it myself, because it was dark, and in any case I wasn't looking for anything; but she must have known it would be there, because she went straight for it, and put whatever it was in her mouth.'

'And he didn't see her doing it?'

'No. He had turned to get a shawl to put round her shoulders. She waited until his back was turned.'

'And then what?'

'When he was sure she was quite comfortable – and he seemed to *want* to wait on her – imagine it, the Chief Black Eunuch, as if he were a servant girl! Then he tried to kiss her mouth. She didn't want him to, at first. I saw her turn away from him, but he insisted. He pushed her down on to the divan, pinning her underneath him so she couldn't move. I could hear – oh it was too disgusting! – the sound of his wet lips, sort of sucking at her, chewing at her mouth, licking her all over her face like a dog.' Annetta gave a disgusted shudder. 'I couldn't bear to watch any more. So I just sat inside the cupboard with my eyes closed. It wasn't long afterwards that I realised that something was wrong. It was the girl who cried out first – a cry of pain. And I thought, well, I thought he must have done something to her; you know, actually violated her in some way, I don't know how – with his fingers, perhaps, or even a false manhood – oh, believe me,' she said, catching sight of Celia's horrified face, 'I've seen worse than that. But then he cried out too. And then I heard other sounds – and smelt . . . oh my God, you can't imagine what it was like.' Annetta's face was white. 'Vomit everywhere, their own soil, the stench of it! But then it was all over. The girl was dead within a matter of minutes.'

'So you think she put poison in her mouth,' Celia said slowly, 'and when he kissed her, I suppose it poisoned him, too.'

'No, no.' Annetta was vehement. 'I'll wager a thousand ducats or more that she had no idea she had taken poison, far less intended to poison the eunuch. She probably thought it was some kind of love potion . . .'

'Well, she certainly had access to all sorts of things. Cariye Lala has a whole apothecary shop inside that special box of hers. It would have been the easiest thing in the world for her to have taken something from there when no one was looking.'

'But then why go to all the trouble of hiding it inside the sugar ship? In any case, she couldn't possibly have known that I was going to bring it in and put it on that tray . . . oh God!' Annetta put her head in her hands. 'All this is making my head spin. No, no, it's all wrong. Besides, why would she bite the hand that was going to feed her? To be the Chief Black Eunuch's lover – revolting though that sounds to you and me – would have given that girl more power than she can ever have dreamt possible. Almost as much power as the Haseki herself. No, someone else was using her, I'm sure she couldn't have known what she was really doing. Someone else was behind it all, I'm sure of it.'

'Someone who knew that she was going to visit him that night.'

'Perhaps even someone who had sent her there on purpose, who knows?' Annetta shrugged. 'But wait until I tell you what happened next.

'I waited a long, long time – or so it seemed to me – inside that cupboard.' Annetta swallowed nervously at the recollection. 'I was so frightened, you can't imagine it, goose, almost too terrified to move. If anyone had found me there, I knew they would surely think I had had something to do with it. Eventually, after what felt like hours, I plucked up the courage to leave. I was so sure by then both of them must be dead. I opened the door and had just begun to pick my way across the room when I heard more voices, more people coming. So back I went – what else could I do? – back into that blessed cupboard again. And who should come in but the Valide herself, with Gulbahar attending her, and Esperanza Malchi.'

'The Valide? So she knew about it all along. But no one had given an alarm. How on earth did they know?'

'I've no idea, but someone must have tipped them off.' Annetta shook her head. 'At first they just stood at the door, as if they were too frightened to come in. But even so they were so close I could hear them talking, every word. I was sure they would discover me. Once I even made a noise, but thank goodness they thought it was the cat . . .'

'What did they do?' Celia's face was pale.

'The Valide asked: "Are they dead, yet?" Esperanza came into the room to look. She said: "The girl, yes." Then she looked very closely at Hassan Aga, and held a mirror up to his nose. And when it turned out that he was not actually dead, she offered to send for the palace physician, but the Valide said something like, "No, not yet."'

'She refused to help him?'

'Not exactly. It was as if . . .' Annetta screwed her face up in an effort to remember, 'as if she already had another plan. As if she already knew, or at the very least had been expecting something like this to happen.'

For a moment Celia said nothing. 'Do you think she did it?' she whispered eventually. 'The Valide?'

'Well, she could have done, but why would she?' Annetta said. 'The Chief Black Eunuch is one of her principal allies. He's her right hand. The one she's always been able to count on. And besides, if she had done it, do you think she would have rushed to the scene like that? No, she would have stayed well away.' Annetta shook her head. 'No, I think the Valide went there because she was trying to stop it from happening in the first place.'

'You mean she knew what was going to happen?'

282

'I think she had an idea that *something* was going to happen.'

'And ever since she has been protecting the person who did it.'

'Oh, she knows who did it, I'm sure of it,' Annetta nodded. 'You don't know her like I do. Why do you think there's been no real investigation all this time?'

'Well, it's obvious, isn't it?' Celia said, standing up.

'It is?'

'Of course. Who, apart from the Sultan himself, would the Valide ever go this far to protect? The other Nightingales, of course. Well, Little Nightingale clearly didn't poison himself – so it must have been—'

'The third Nightingale?'

'Exactly.'

'Cariye Mihrimah.'

'The one who's supposed to be dead.'

'And if I'm going to find out who Cariye Mihrimah is,' Celia said, 'there's only one person who can help me.'

'Who's that?'

'I'll have to go and see Handan again.'

'That's madness,' Annetta gripped Celia by the arm, 'please, that's absolute madness. You'll get caught – and even if you don't, Handan is half mad, they say. Whatever she tells you, how will you know it's the truth? It's a bad idea, I tell you.'

'I got her to tell me about Cariye Mihrimah, didn't I?'

'Yes, but . . .'

'So perhaps I can get her to tell me the rest. And, besides, I don't think she's mad at all. She's been made weak and ill by the opium – but she's not mad.'

Just then there were voices in the courtyard beneath them. As Celia got to her feet, Annetta caught her arm.

'Please, goose, I'm begging you, don't go.'

'I have to.' Celia bent and kissed her on the cheek, and before Annetta could frighten her into changing her mind she was gone.

Celia made her way down the narrow wooden stairs and into the Courtyard of the Cariyes below. Two old black serving women were sweeping there with brooms made from palm fronds. When they saw Celia they backed away, murmuring respectful greetings. On one of the rooftops a pigeon flapped. Its wings made a sharp retort, ringing like a pistol shot in the drowsy air. Suddenly Celia was reminded of the morning when Annetta had first summoned her to see the Valide. They had stood together, right here, just outside the door to Safiye Sultan's apartments. Could it really be less than a week ago? And that girl, that Celia: Kaya Kadin, the one who was *gözde*. She hardly recognised her.

With a clattering noise one of the servant women dropped the broom she had been carrying, and for the first time Celia looked at them. Were these the same women who had been cleaning in the courtyard then? Annetta had spoken to them sharply, she remembered that, but other than this she had no recollection. Even in the House of Felicity, where everyone lived on top of everyone else, one serving woman looked very much like another. Was that how Cariye Mihrimah had done it? Had herself smuggled back into the harem, disguised as a servant so that no one would recognise her?

On impulse, Celia stopped and turned back towards the two women. When they saw her they bent their heads towards her, bowing respectfully in unison.

'*Kadin*!' Celia was about to move on when she realised that one of the women had called out to her. 'My lady!'

She wore a thin gold chain around her ankle. The other, whose thinning, crinkled hair had more grey in it than her companion's, had a slight cast over one eye. The first old woman with the golden anklet took the other by the hand, and they shuffled slowly towards her.

'Please, my lady . . .'

Now they had her attention they seemed unsure how to proceed.

'Did you want something, *cariye*?' Celia looked at them curiously. 'What's your name?' she asked the one with the gold chain.

'Cariye Tusa.'

'And yours?' she turned to the other.

'Cariye Tata, my lady.'

Still hand in hand, they stared at her wonderingly. Why, they're as helpless as children, Celia thought, and then was struck by a sudden realisation.

'Why, you're sisters, aren't you? Twin sisters.'

'Yes, *kadin*.' Cariye Tusa put her hand protectively on her companion's arm. The second old woman, the one with the damaged eye, gazed straight at Celia. Or rather not at her so much as through her. Celia turned round, looking over her shoulder to see if there was someone there, but the courtyard was empty.

'You,' she said, nodding at the second woman, 'Cariye Tata – do you know who I am?'

The old woman searched for Celia's face with her one good eye. The cornea was blue, the bright blue of a cornflower. Her sister, Cariye Tusa, started to answer for her, but Celia stopped her.

'No, not you, let her answer.'

'I . . . I . . .' In confusion Cariye Tata shook her grizzled head from side to side. She was still staring obliquely over Celia's shoulder with her strange vacant gaze; the gaze of one so old she could see only ghosts in that deserted courtyard. 'You are one of the *kadins*,' she said at last. 'Yes, that's right. I know what I must call you. *Kadin* . . .' She bowed her old head, bobbing it up and down, faster and faster. 'Please, that's what I must call you. If you please, my lady.'

'Please,' Cariye Tusa's old eyes filled with tears, 'please don't, Kaya Kadin. Please forgive my sister, she means no disrespect.'

'Ah, but it is you who must forgive me, *cariye*.' Celia said, and this time her voice was gentle. 'I did not see—' she corrected herself, 'I did not know until now that your sister was blind.'

And at that moment, in her mind's eye Celia saw them suddenly as they must once have been: two little slave girls, black skinned and blue eyed, as well matched as a pair of perfect deep-sea pearls. Everyone has their story: what was theirs, she wondered? How old had they been when they first came here, six, seven? How they must have clung together, two frightened little children so far away from home, as they clung together still, grown old and slow and blind in the service of the Sultan. And as she was wondering all this, Cariye Tusa put out her hand. And Celia saw that she was offering her something, something that she had pulled from her pocket, and which glinted, bright as brass.

'For you, Kaya Kadin.' Her old paw closed over Celia's hand, pushing her fingers down around something smooth and round. 'It's what we came to tell you. One of the *kiras* left this for you.'

Celia opened her fingers. The gilded brass case of Paul's compendium gleamed at her in the sunlight.

'What is it?' Cariye Tusa put her hand on Celia's arm. 'Are you unwell, *kadin*?'

Celia did not reply. She flicked the hidden catch at the base with her finger, the compendium opened and her own face stared out at her.

As Time and Hours passeth Away, so doth the Life of Man Decay,
As Time must be Redemed with Cost,
Bestow it Well and let no Hour be Lost.

And right then and there, before she knew what she was doing, Celia sat down on the doorstep of the bathhouse and wept. She wept and she wept, from some deep well inside her which until now she had never known had been sunk so deep: for Cariye Tata and Cariye Tusa, two old women whom she had never known until that day; she wept for Gulay Haseki, drowned at the bottom of the Bosphorous. But most of all she wept for herself, because she had survived the shipwreck, and for the sailors on the boat, because they had not; and she wept for her dead father, and for her lost love: a love that was never more lost to her, now that she was once again found.

Chapter 31

Istanbul: the present day

The day after her dream Elizabeth stayed in her room most of the day, reading. Late that afternoon, when she came downstairs hoping to send Rashid out for a sandwich, she was surprised to find Haddba waiting for her in the hall.

'Elizabeth, you're here after all . . . I've just rung your room. I'm so glad I've caught you.' Looking inscrutable, Haddba beckoned her to the under-the-stairs cubby hole. 'My dear, you have a visitor.'

'Mehmet?' Elizabeth's heart soared. 'Is he back?'

She was about to turn and run into the sitting room when Haddba put her hand on her arm. 'No my dear, *not* Mehmet—' but before she could finish the sentence Elizabeth heard a familiar voice behind her.

'Hello, Elizabeth.'

She turned round. And there he was, just the same. Faded jeans, leather jacket, come-to-bed eyes. And despite herself she felt a liquid rush of pure desire for him.

'Marius?'

'Hello, beautiful.'

'What are you doing here?' Stupid, stupid question. 'How did you find me?' Even worse. Was it nerves that were making her smile at him?

'I came to find you, baby.' His voice was soft, almost crooning: a voice that in the past had made her submit to almost any humiliation simply in order to hear it again.

'I'm sorry, Marius, but I don't . . .'

But before she could protest any further he had put his arm around her shoulders, was kissing her on the lips.

'You ran away from me,' he whispered.

'Don't—' Elizabeth tried to pull away from him, felt her hip clash awkwardly against his.

What's the matter with him? She could hear Eve's bitter refrain. *He doesn't want you, not really, but he can't seem to let you go.*

'How did you find me?' Looking up at him she gave a small shiver. Was it dread or excitement that she felt? His hair, always dishevelled, had grown even longer, was curling around the collar of his jacket. He was so close she could smell his familiar scent, his hair and skin, the bad-boy smell of cigarettes and dirty sheets; the not unpleasing, slightly sour odour of leather from his jacket.

'I've missed you, baby . . .' he said. Brazen. Not replying to her question. Somehow, Elizabeth found that her arm was round his neck, her fingers laced in his hair. Nearly six whole weeks of forgetting, and for what?

'Shall we go to your room then? We need to talk.' She felt him run his fingers lightly down her back. 'I tried to persuade the concierge here to let me up,' he murmured in her ear, 'but she wasn't having any of it. Who is the old bag anyway?'

Elizabeth became suddenly and acutely aware of Haddba's solid and imperturbable form standing only a few feet away from them.

He trifles with your heart.

Startled, she turned to Haddba. 'What did you say?'

'I said nothing.' Haddba continued to stand there. The screaming impropriety of Marius's behaviour was written so clearly on her face it was like a shower of icy water. Ashamed, Elizabeth pulled away.

'I'm sorry . . . Haddba, this is Marius. Marius, this is my landlady, Haddba.'

Marius put out his hand, but Haddba pointedly made no move to take it. The emeralds on her earrings glinted like a cat's eyes in the soft light. She was looking at him, Elizabeth saw, with an expression that would have flailed alive most ordinary mortals.

'Good day to you,' her words were a clear dismissal.

Outside, even Marius seemed disconcerted.

'God, what a bloody old harridan.' To Elizabeth's mingled disappointment and relief, he did not put his arm around her again, but thrust his hands deep into the pockets of his jacket, walking on up the street slightly ahead of her. 'Do you normally let her boss you around like that? But you do, don't you? Of course you do.'

'Don't speak about her like that, she's a friend.'

'The hotel concierge?'

'She's not a *concierge*.' Elizabeth was almost running now to keep up with him. The air outside was so cold it made her teeth ache.

'Really?' His voice was sour. 'She looks like one.'

Elizabeth suppressed a smile. It was not often that Marius failed to charm a woman – young, old, the middle-aged – no one seemed immune. No wonder he was annoyed.

They walked together for a while in silence, up the steep narrow streets towards Istiklal Caddesi. It was dusk; the sky was filled with livid purple clouds. Skinny cats sheltered in doorways. They passed the *bufes*, tiny slips of stores, where Rashid went to buy tea and newspapers; the old barber shops and pudding houses; the man on the street corner selling roasted chestnuts. How familiar this landscape had become, Elizabeth thought, in just a few weeks.

On the corner there was a ruined house, its doorway nailed up with boards. Marius stopped and pulled her to him suddenly, pressing her up into the niche of the doorway.

His lips hovered just over hers. 'Now can I kiss you?'

He rocked her to him, pulling her by the lapels of her coat.

No! that voice inside her head was still screaming at her, but it was no use. She could feel his breath against her throat, in her hair. With a sigh her eyes closed, her neck and throat arched towards him. He came to find me, was all she could think. How often have I dreamt of this? There was a time when I would have sold my soul for this. But when she kissed him, his tongue felt cold against her lips.

'Christ, it's freezing here.' He pulled away from her at last. 'Can we go somewhere?'

'Yes, I know somewhere.'

She took him to her favourite café on Istiklal Caddesi. It was dark, and so cold Elizabeth was sure she could smell snow in the air. She walked ahead now: up the street selling musical instruments, past the graveyard of the dervish *tekke*, their turbaned headstones sliced with moonlight.

'Where are we exactly?' Marius followed her up the narrow streets.

'We are in Beyoğlu; in the old days it was known as Pera, the area where the foreigners always lived.'

She took a short cut through one of the narrow *pasajs*. It opened up into a kind of half-square, where old men were drinking tea and playing dominoes by the light of a 1930s street lamp. They looked up when they saw Elizabeth. Marius hesitated behind her.

'Are you sure it's safe?'

'Safe?' With a laugh, Elizabeth turned to him with surprise. Was it her imagination, or did he look different all of a sudden? Smaller. Less substantial. 'I suppose it depends what you mean by safe.'

Inside the café it was warm, lit with brass lamps like a Viennese coffee house. The walls were lined with glass and mahogany panelling. Elizabeth ordered tea and cakes. When the waitress had gone, she saw Marius looking at her.

'You look different,' he said at last. No longer amorous; reflective, rather. 'You look beautiful, Elizabeth. Really beautiful.' She had the strange sensation that he was looking at her for the first time.

'Thank you,' she answered simply.

'No really, I mean it.'

Usually Elizabeth would rush in to fill the silence with words; but this time, she thought, she would let him speak first.

'You didn't reply to my texts,' he said after a while.

'No.'

Another silence. He picked up one of the teaspoons on the table and started to drum it against his hand. My God, Elizabeth thought, it can't be. Marius is nervous!

'I've missed you, baby.'

'Have you?'

Had he? He sounded as if he might actually mean it.

'Yes, I have.'

How odd, was all she could think; how very odd to be sitting here with Marius. She was having a conversation, but it seemed to have nothing to do with her. Now that the initial shock of seeing him had worn off, she found she could look at him with composure. Good-looking, unshaven: the sleazy handsomeness of a fairground attendant.

'What do you want, Marius?' Mildly curious. 'What happened to her? The other girl, I mean, the blonde.' But even this thought, this

290

once excoriating thought, no longer seemed to have any power over her.

'Oh, her . . . she meant nothing.'

'No. No, I don't suppose she did.' Elizabeth put her teacup down. Her hand was quite steady. 'So, why *are* you here?' She heard herself with amazement.

'I've come to take you back. Come to take you back with me.'

He trifles with your heart.

Elizabeth heard the words quite clearly. She looked round, half expecting to see someone sitting on the bench next to her. Where did they come from, those words? Once, back in Oxford, she had thought she had heard Eve say them; and then Haddba. But this time there was no one there.

Instead, sitting on the other side of the café, she caught sight of a young woman in a navy coat, long dark hair falling over one shoulder. Elizabeth was struck by how serene the young woman looked and, in the very same instant, saw that it was her own reflection.

'Why are you laughing?' Marius said. 'I said I've come to take you home.' He repeated the words as if he thought she could not have heard him.

'You mean you've come to rescue me?'

'You could put it like that.' He seemed puzzled. 'I don't see why it's so very funny.'

'I'm sorry,' Elizabeth wiped her eyes, 'you're quite right, it's not funny. It's . . . well, sort of sad really.'

In her handbag she heard her phone buzz with a new message. She looked at the screen quickly, and then without saying anything put it back into her bag.

There was another short silence.

'You've met someone,' Marius said at last.

When Elizabeth looked at him again it was with a strange vertiginous sensation, as if she were falling, falling, not downwards, but somehow upwards.

'Yes, I have, as you put it, met someone.' She looked at him with her head slightly to one side.

'But that's not it.'

'Not it?'

'That's not why I'm not coming back with you.'

She stood up, and then, leaning over, kissed him lightly on the cheek. He watched her collect her things together.

'I hope you know what you're doing, Elizabeth,' he called after her. 'Will you be safe?'

'Will I be safe?' she stopped at the door. 'No, it's better than that. Much, much better.' She turned to him: she was walking on air. 'I'll be free.'

Chapter 32

Constantinople: 5 September 1599

Morning

T he two old women let Celia cry. Between them somehow they pulled her out of the courtyard and into the bathhouse, pushing her down behind one of the marble basins, shielding her from the eyes of the other women and harem officials who occasionally passed across the courtyard on their daily round. They said nothing, but took it in turns to stroke her hair, and made strange little clicking noises at her between their teeth.

Eventually Celia had no more tears left to cry. She sat on the marble floor between the two basins and allowed the women to dry her face, and to press cold cloths over her swollen eyes. Her breathing returned to normal, but instead a feeling of fatigue so overwhelming came over her now that she could have lain down on the cold marble floor and slept.

'But I can't stay,' she said, more to herself than to either of them. And in place of fatigue, a creeping sensation of dread came over her at the thought of what she still had to do.

She looked around her, at the fluted marble basins with their golden taps shaped like dolphins, and tried to collect her thoughts. The last time she had been in here to bathe was with Annetta and the Valide's other handmaidens. There had been a conversation, what was it about?

Celia looked at the two old women again, and as she did so a feeling of disquiet began to come over her. She took Cariye Tusa by the hand.

'*Cariye* . . .' Celia said, 'how old are you?'

'I don't know, Kaya Kadin,' the old woman shrugged, 'just old,' she said simply.

A thought – or was it a memory? – was seeping slowly into Celia's mind.

'Do you remember – the old Sultan?'

'Of course we do.'

'We were here before anyone,' her sister said, nodding and smiling with pride. 'The others were all sent to the Palace of Tears, but not us. We served the Harem Stewardess, you see, Janfreda Khatun.'

That name, *Janfreda Khatun*. A memory then. Definitely a memory.

'That's right, everyone left. Everyone. Even the little princes. All nineteen of them. Dead, all dead. How we cried!'

Where had she heard those words before? Celia's heart skipped a beat. And those eyes – not so blue, perhaps, but somehow . . . milky. Where had she seen those eyes before?

'Then you, who are such senior ladies here,' she smiled at them encouragingly, 'perhaps you can help me find someone.' In an effort to keep her voice steady, Celia spoke slowly. Her mouth was dry. 'Will you help me – do you know – Cariye Mihrimah?'

Cariye Tusa shook her head. 'Oh, no, she's gone, long ago. Didn't you know?'

'What are you saying, sister?' Cariye Tata's blind eyes opened wide in surprise. 'I hear her all the time.'

Cariye Tusa turned to her. 'You hear her, sister?' she seemed astonished. 'You never told me.'

'You never asked.' Cariye Tata's face was as innocent as a child's. 'She came back, right here to the bathhouse.'

'Are you sure?' Celia felt tears start in her eyes. 'You're sure it's Cariye Mihrimah?'

'Oh, they don't call her that any more, *kadin*. They've given her her old name back, I don't know why. They call her Lily, or at least that's what Hassan Aga calls her. Lily. Such a pretty name. Only the rest of us don't call her that, we call her Lala.' The old woman gave Celia a radiant smile. 'So that's what we must all call her now, if you please. Cariye Lala.'

Celia ran to the Valide's Courtyard where she found the Haseki's old apartment exactly as she had left it the night before. On the floor lay the broken cup, the single beaded slipper, discarded as before. There was the doorway at the back of the cupboard, and the set of tiny stairs leading to the hidden corridor. At the top she found the second doorway. Quickly she made her way through it into the passageway, inching her way along, past the fork in the way, past the spy-hole into the Valide's apartment, and finally, out of the cupboard door and into Handan's room.

As before it was very warm and close in the room. Despite the richness of the furnishings, the brocades and embroidered hangings, the fur-lined robes hanging from their pegs on the wall, Celia was struck again by the room's unkempt air, the strange, almost feral, feel to it. In one corner was a sandalwood chest. On top of it was a bowl of dead flowers and a gold box encrusted with rock crystal and rubies, crammed with various pieces of jewellery – mostly diamonds and a magnificent aigrette made of an emerald as big as a rock – but even they had a dusty, tarnished look about them: the empty riches of the discarded concubine.

At the sound of her footsteps something in the bed stirred.

'Handan Sultan!' Celia went over and knelt on the floor beside her. 'Don't be afraid; it's me, Kaya.'

A sound, like a tiny sigh, came from the frail form beneath the coverlets.

'Handan Sultan, I think I know who Cariye Mihrimah is,' she said, 'but I need you to tell me if it's true.'

From beneath the jewel-like mask, Handan's kohl-lined eyes stared out at her. They were open, but so glassy that Celia almost doubted whether she was awake at all.

'Handan! Please, can you hear me?' Celia spoke softly in her ear. She shook the skeletal shoulder and as she did so, the coverlet slipped from Handan's shoulder. A terrible smell, at once rank and sweet, like a nest of old mice, hit the back of Celia's throat so powerfully she almost gagged.

'I don't think she can hear you, *kadin*.'

Celia span round so fast she almost knocked the brazier over.

'But you mustn't worry,' said a gentle voice from behind her, 'she's not quite awake, but not quite asleep either. Handan is doing what she does best. Dreaming. Lots and lots of beautiful dreams. Let's not disturb her, shall we?'

'*You*! But we all thought you were—'

'Dead?' Gulay Haseki stepped into the room. 'Well, as you can see, I'm not,' she smiled. In one hand, she held the little jewelled slipper. 'And look, I've found my shoe.' She gave one of her charming, merry laughs. 'You poor child, you look as if you're about to faint! I'm so sorry if I gave you a fright. Do you want to touch me?' She put out her hand coaxingly. 'Make sure I'm not a ghost?'

'Oh, yes!' Celia rushed to take her hand and pressed it to her lips. 'Oh thank God, thank God,' she kissed her fingers, pressed the palm of the Haseki's hand to her cheek. Her skin felt cool to Celia's hot face. 'Oh, I thought they'd . . .' Tears filled Celia's eyes. 'Oh, I thought . . .'

'I know what you thought,' Gulay said. 'I knew that they would try to accuse me. That unfortunate affair with the Chief Black Eunuch was too good an opportunity to pass up. The Valide had a horoscope made, which predicted Hassan Aga's death, and had it planted in my room. Fortunately, I found it, and had it switched, so when they opened it – that day in the Great Chamber, when we were all watching the tumblers – all they found was a recipe for making soap.' She gave a soft chuckle. 'Imagine their faces. Imagine *her* face, the poor little fool.' She drew her hand away from Celia's eager embrace. 'Rather clumsy of them, don't you think? The Valide must be slipping.'

'So it was the Valide, all along.' Celia could hardly speak. 'Oh, I knew it couldn't be you. And what about Hanza?'

'Oh, don't worry about *her*,' Gulay gave one of her merry little laughs, 'she's not coming back from the dead.'

Celia watched her move over to Handan's divan. When she walked it was with an exaggerated undulation of the hips. In the quiet room, the stiff brocade of her dress made a soft susurration. She sat down on the divan, and picked up Handan's hand, feeling her pulse between her fingers. The Haseki looked up at Celia thoughtfully, her head to one side. Her face, with its perfect proportions, was exactly as Celia remembered it: the creamy skin, the soft dark hair and eyes as blue as a winter sky. Diamonds glittered in her ears and had been stitched to her headdress, so many of them it looked as if she had been touched by hoar frost. 'Hanza . . .' the Haseki said softly, almost to herself. 'The little bitch was getting ideas above her station. You know that as well as I do.'

Celia opened her mouth to say something, and then shut it again.

'You should thank everything you hold holy that it wasn't you who was made the messenger,' Gulay added. 'At first, I wasn't at all sure which one of you she'd choose. But then, well, it was obvious to me that it would be Hanza. The ambitious ones are always the easiest to manipulate, the ones who think they can do it all on their own. That was a lesson I learnt very early on.'

A silence now fell between them; a silence like the shrieking of a banshee, so loud Celia wanted to cover her ears to block it out.

'But what about your apartment? They've taken everything away, all your things, they're gone,' she said at last. 'Are you still moving to the old palace?'

At this Gulay gave a laugh of real amusement.

'You really think I'd do that? Leave here, and leave the field open for *her*?' The Haseki's lips narrowed. 'If you really believe that, then you're more of a fool than I thought. No, I'm moving to a new apartment, that's all. I've been staying with the Sultan at the summer palace for the last two days. After all that bother the other evening we all thought it was for the best. Besides, it was becoming a little – draughty – in the old one.'

'All that "bother", is that what you call it?'

In the bed next to her, Handan's frail form stirred. A small sound, like the pitiful mewing of a cat, came from beneath the coverlets. Gulay dropped her hand in disgust.

'*Faugh*! How it stinks these days.'

'Can't you see, she's not well!' Celia was trembling. 'I can't believe the Valide can have done this to her.'

'Hmm . . .' Gulay Haseki put her head to one side thoughtfully, 'well not the Valide, not exactly.'

'What can you mean, *not exactly*? Who then?'

'Well, little Kaya, me of course.' The Haseki fixed Celia with her cerulean gaze. 'It was rather kind of me actually. You see, when her son Prince Ahmet was born she had some problems – women's problems, you know. She was very ill. So they gave her opium, to ease the pain. Well, everyone has their little weakness. They tried everything to stop it, the Valide even had her shut her up in here, poor creature, but somehow,' she sighed, 'her friends always found a way to help her. They always do, you know,' she turned to Celia, fixing her with a steady gaze, 'just like I helped you.'

'You helped me?'

'Of course. As soon as you became *gözde*. I thought to myself: I must help that poor child through her ordeal. So I sent the servant girl with a little drink.'

'Oh!' Celia put a hand to her hot cheeks. 'And I thought it was Cariye Lala who had given me too much opium.'

Gulay laughed again, incredulously this time. 'Well, I'm sorry about that, but I'm afraid it had to be done.' She gave a little shrug. 'Do you know, I really was afraid that he might like you.'

'Well, he didn't,' Celia said in a hollow voice. 'He liked Hanza instead.'

'That scrawny little bag of Bosnian bones?' Gulay said, playing with the rings on her fingers. 'Hanzas come and Hanzas go. I've seen many of them over the years and believe me, she'd never have lasted. A few quick pokes—' she made a crude gesture with her fingers '—and *pouf!* they're gone, back to their cramped little dormitories. Oh, no, I've never worried about the Hanzas.' She turned her blue eyes on Celia again. 'What he likes is softness, sweetness,' she lay back against Handan's cushions so that Celia could see her breasts, white as milk, through the fine lawn creases of her chemise, 'sweet, soft flesh.' The glance she gave Celia was almost lascivious. 'Oh, for goodness' sake, don't look at me like that. We all do what we have to do to save our own skin. Even those who are closest to us. Even your friend Annetta . . .'

'No, she wouldn't!'

'You think so? How charming!' Gulay gave a little shrug. 'Listen, it's what we all do, it's what you're going to do.'

'What do you mean?'

'I mean that you are going to help me destroy the Nightingales of Manisa.'

The Nightingales again. Why did it always come back to them?

'Why are the Nightingales so important?'

'Because if I can destroy them, I can destroy her.'

'Who?'

'Oh who do you think?' Gulay made an impatient sound. 'The Valide, of course.' She sighed as if she were dealing with a particularly stupid child. 'Oh, very well then. I can see I'm going to have to do a little more explaining. Although as a matter of fact, you've already helped me very considerably – more than I ever anticipated.'

'So Annetta was right after all,' Celia said slowly. 'You have been getting me to do your work for you. You didn't know who Cariye Mihrimah was either. So you set me up to find out for you.'

'Well, what would you have done?' Gulay laughed, she sounded almost coaxing again. 'In my position I really couldn't go around asking too many awkward questions. You saw for yourself how the Valide spies on me. I had to find someone, someone – let's say – who was fresh to this way of life; someone a little older, perhaps, than the average *cariye*, and with enough status to move about the palace relatively unimpeded. But most of all someone who had a reason of her own to want to find out. Someone who would stir things up a little . . .'

'But I had no reason at all to want to find out about Cariye Mihrimah,' Celia countered. 'I didn't even know I was looking for her, until—'

'Until?' The Haseki's blue eyes looked almost black in the dim light of Handan's room.

'Until the business about the sugar ship.' Celia sat down on the bed. Her legs were weak and she felt very hot suddenly, and her head was swimming.

'Rather clever of me, hmm? I made sure that you knew that there had been an English embassy. And that it was they who had sent the sugar ship—'

'The one that they said had poisoned Hassan Aga—'

'Otherwise known as Little Nightingale.'

Once again, Celia was silenced.

The Haseki stood up and went over to the brazier. She took some resin from a bowl and, crumbling it between her fingers, threw some lumps on to the burning coals. They burst into flames instantly, and their sweet smell began to permeate the fetid room.

'You're wrong to think that I didn't know who Cariye Mihrimah was. I suspected for a long time that Cariye Lala must be the third Nightingale, but I couldn't prove it absolutely, and I needed to be sure. That insignificant little under-mistress from the bathhouse the intimate of the Valide and the Chief Black Eunuch! It didn't seem possible.

'So I started watching her. I watched her very carefully. On the few occasions when I saw her in the presence of the Valide, neither of them ever gave even the smallest sign that there was a connection between them. But with Hassan Aga it was different. It was at night, there were fewer people around, and their guard was down. For a start, I was able to see them together far more frequently. When he and his eunuch guard escorted me to the Sultan at night, Cariye Lala was often there.

'The first time I just intercepted a look passing between them; but then, over the months, I began to see other things, small but unmistakable gestures, imperceptible to anyone who wasn't looking for them: a smile, a few whispered words, the touch of his hand. So, yes, for some months now I have suspected that she was Cariye Mihrimah, the third Nightingale, but I still had no real evidence.'

'But why did it all have to be such a secret?'

'Because Cariye Mihrimah,' the Haseki said, 'was supposed to be dead.'

'Dead?'

'Yes, like Hanza. Tied up in a sack and thrown to the bottom of the Bosphorous.'

'What had she done?'

'It was in the time of the old Sultan, many years ago now. It was kept very quiet at the time, because Safiye Sultan was involved, but there were plenty of rumours. I first heard them from one of the old eunuchs when I was living in Manisa myself, before any of us came here. They said that the old Valide was plotting against her, trying to lure the Sultan away from her with new concubines. Safiye Sultan was terrified of losing her influence; terrified that the Sultan might prefer another to herself, or worse, perhaps even choose another concubine's son as his successor. They said that she had put a spell on the Sultan, used witchcraft, or worse, black magic, to ensure that he would be unable to love any other woman. But one day she was found out. Perhaps it was one of her own servants who gave her away, who knows? Whatever really happened, in the end it was Cariye Mihrimah who got the blame. She was sentenced to death, but somehow,' the Haseki shrugged, 'she didn't die after all.'

'What happened to her?'

'I don't know. My guess is that they must have bribed the guards, sent her into hiding somewhere, until the old Sultan died. At that point all the women who had been part of his harem were sent to the Eski Saray, the old palace, everyone except for Safiye Sultan, of course, who then became the Valide, presiding over her son's new household.'

And Cariye Tata and Cariye Tusa, Celia thought. But she said nothing.

'In Sultan Mehmet's harem there was no one who knew who she was,' Gulay went on, 'no one who would recognise her. So they brought her back into the household again, changed her name, and no one was any the wiser.'

'But what does any of that matter now?' Gulay crumbled some more resin into the brazier; the tiny red-hot embers hissed and spat. 'It has taken me years. Years of watching and waiting; smiling, smiling and smiling as if I hadn't a care in the world, but finally I have found her weak spot. Just like I found hers . . .' She put her hand into Handan's hair and with one swift movement jerked her head, with its sad vacant eyes, round to face them. The flames, Celia saw, made two tiny sparks in the dark pupils of her eyes.

'Haseki Sultan,' when Celia finally found her tongue, she addressed Gulay formally again, 'Cariye Lala is an old woman now. Why do you want to hurt her?'

'It's not her I'm interested in, you fool. It's the Valide. Don't you see? When the Sultan finds out that she deliberately countered a royal command – that Cariye Mihrimah be killed – it will discredit her so far in his eyes he'll have her banished from here once and for all.'

'You think the Sultan would do that to his own mother?' Celia was disbelieving. 'They say he can't make a move without her advice.'

'The Sultan is fat and weak and idle.' Gulay spoke as if she had tasted something sour. 'At the beginning, when he first became Sultan, four years ago now, he needed her, it's true. But do you really think he likes her meddling ways? She tries to influence everything he does, from which foreign embassies to favour, to whom he should appoint as the next grand vizier. She's even had a secret door made in the council chamber so she can sit in on his audiences. Why, there was even a time when she tried to stop him from making me his Haseki – for some reason she thought I'd be less easy to control than this one—' Gulay said, indicating Handan, 'and that was her biggest mistake.'

So that's what all this is about, Celia thought. She could feel the sweat breaking out on her forehead. Throughout their conversation Gulay had spoken with the same gentle, serene tones that Celia remembered from their first meeting in the garden. But when she turned to her, there was that look again: an expression of pure intelligence, and behind it such a terrifying concentration of will that Celia dropped her gaze as if she had been burnt.

'Nothing is going to stop my son from succeeding as the next Sultan.'

'And so you will be the next Valide.'

'And I will be the Valide.'

For a few moments there was complete silence in the room.

'So you see, little Kaya, in my position there is everything to play for – and everything to lose.' With her jewelled fingers the Haseki smoothed the gauze of her headdress. 'If I lose, well, I risk not only banishment with all the others to the old palace, but the murder of my son. He will be strangled with a bow string, just like the others.' For a moment a shadow seemed to pass over her face. 'I was here – I saw it. Those nineteen little coffins, the women keening for their babies,' for a moment her voice seemed to catch in the back of her throat, 'you can have no idea, Kaya Kadin, no idea at all what it was like.'

Behind her on the bed the frail form of Handan stirred lightly beneath the coverlets.

'The Sultan is weary of his mother's meddling. He's often threatened to send her to the old palace, and this, you mark my words, this could have her banished there for good.'

'And the other two?'

'Powerless without her protection. Perhaps she'll take Hassan Aga with her, but as for Cariye Lala, I don't suppose she'll escape the Bosphorous second time round.'

'But Cariye Lala is old,' Celia said softly. 'Why should she take the blame again for something she didn't do?'

'Oh, but this time she did do something. Don't you see, it was Cariye Lala who poisoned the Chief Black Eunuch?'

But no, no she didn't, Celia wanted to scream out. Instead she said in as calm a voice as she could manage, 'But I thought you told me Hassan Aga was her friend.'

'I think he was more than a friend.' Gulay laughed. 'I have an instinct about these things. Haven't you heard of these under-standings? Innocent little arrangements for the most part, easily crushed, all childish posies and stolen kisses and holding hands, they happen all the time.' Gulay stood up and walked towards the chest; she took up a pair of dusty diamond earrings and held them up to her face. 'Some of them can be very passionate; there are some, so I'm told, that last a whole lifetime.' She dropped the earrings with a careless clatter. 'Which is why I knew she would do something – perhaps even something quite terrible,' Gulay picked out the words with care, 'if she ever found him with someone else.'

'What do you mean?'

'I mean I wanted to flush her out,' she replied, her voice suddenly harsh, 'flush her from her hiding place. Make her do something that would expose her completely.' She picked up the emerald aigrette, testing its spike idly against her finger. 'So I arranged for one of my own serving girls to seduce him. I found the perfect night for it. By coincidence it was the same night that you were chosen – the Valide's doing, by the way – for a visit to the Sultan. If you remember – can you remember anything about that night? – the harem was almost empty; most of the women and eunuchs were was still at the summer palace.

'Anyway, after I had got rid of you, the Sultan and I . . . rested . . . for a little while, and when he was asleep I sent one of the guards to find Cariye Lala for me. I gave her the sugar ship, the same one that had been left by the Sultan's bed, which after our little rest together now by rights belonged to me, and told her to take it to the Chief Black Eunuch's room,' Gulay smiled, 'with my apologies for upset-ting the evening.'

'And you knew that she would find him with the girl.'

'Yes.'

Gulay tossed the emerald aigrette to one side; it landed beside the still-sleeping form of Handan on the divan.

'And – did she?' Celia could feel a trickle of sweat running down her belly. She hoped her voice sounded normal.

303

'Well, of course she did. You know what happened, she poisoned them, poisoned them both. After all, who else would have wanted them dead?'

'But . . .' Celia began, getting to her feet, but the words would not come. In the stifling room her head was swimming.

'In the end, he didn't die of course – but we must be patient, you and I, always patient—'

'You and I?'

'But of course, you and I. One thing you must learn is that things never work out quite as you expect them to.' Gulay seemed to be talking almost to herself. 'The Valide covered it all up this time, but not even *she* can keep protecting her for ever . . .'

'But Cariye Lala . . .' Celia tried again.

'Yes, Cariye Lala.' Gulay's eyes burned. 'Cariye Lala, Cariye Mihrimah – whatever that pitiful, worn-out, withered-up old crone calls herself – the Valide must actually *love* her.' She spat the words out. 'Saving that useless old woman is probably the only mistake she's ever made.' On the Haseki's cheeks two bright spots of red had appeared. 'Well, it's given me my chance at last. I'm going to expose them once and for all, and you are going to help me do it. I'll break her. I'll break her power. And her heart!'

'But Cariye Lala didn't do it.'

'What?'

'Cariye Lala didn't do it,' Celia almost shouted at her. 'Cariye Lala didn't poison the Chief Black Eunuch – you did!'

At once the Haseki's expression changed to cold rage. Her eyes were two narrow slits. 'You're mad.'

'No, not mad at all.'

There was a shocked pause.

'You'll never prove it.'

'I can prove that Cariye Lala didn't do it.'

'I don't believe you.'

'She didn't take the sugar ship to Hassan Aga's room that night. Someone else did.'

Celia took a step backwards, but the Haseki was too quick for her. She grabbed her by the wrist. 'Who?'

'Well, I would be mad if I told you that, wouldn't I?' Celia could feel Gulay's nails biting into her wrist. 'And she saw the girl pick something off the tray on the floor and put it in her mouth – it was never anything to do with the sugar ship—'

'So we know it's a "she" then, that's a start—'

'—you gave it to her, didn't you? Told her it was some kind of aphrodisiac, when really it was poison—'

'Tell me who it was, or I'll kill you too.'

The circle of pain around Celia's wrist burnt into her flesh like a branding iron.

'She died a horrible death, and it's only by a miracle he didn't die too. That was your idea of "flushing out" Cariye Lala was it? Making her see that?'

A terrible wailing sound filled the room. In the corner of her eye Celia saw a flash of green, and all at once a small figure, a naked incubus, all skin and bone, was flying towards them. Another flash. The Haseki dropped Celia's wrist and put her hand to her neck with a cry of pain. The pin of the emerald aigrette was sticking into her neck.

'The little bitch . . . look what she's done!'

In a rage she turned and lashed out at Handan, knocking her flying back on to the bed with no more effort than if she had been swatting a fly. Blood, black as tar, began to trickle from the wound in her neck. 'You'll pay for this!'

The Haseki stepped backwards, one hand raised to strike the now cowering figure of Handan, when all of a sudden Celia saw her freeze. For a moment the Haseki stood there as if petrified, her mouth forming a little 'O' of surprise, and then just as suddenly she pitched forwards, prostrating herself on her knees and rubbing her face in the dust.

'It's too late for that, Gulay,' said a familiar voice.

A panel on the wall where Handan's robes had hung on pegs had opened silently behind them.

'I am very much afraid,' the Valide said, standing on the threshold, 'that you are the one who is going to pay.'

Chapter 33

Constantinople: 6 September 1599

Morning

Safiye, the Valide Sultan, the Mother of God's Shadow Upon Earth, sat in a kiosk in the palace gardens, looking down over the confluence of the Bosphorous and the Golden Horn. A breeze ruffled the surface of the waters with tiny foaming waves, turning them from turquoise to purple to pearl. When it blew in her direction, faint sounds, like the hammering of carpenters, could be heard in the distance.

'They say that the Sultan's gift from the English embassy will be ready for us to see today,' she said to her companion. 'Can you hear them, Kaya Kadin?'

Celia nodded. She too had heard the sounds of the workmen at the Aviary Gate.

'They say it is an organ that plays music by itself, and a clock, too, with the sun and moon, and angels blowing trumpets, all manner of marvels.'

'Will it please the Sultan?'

'Oh yes, he is very fond of clocks.'

'Then the English embassy will find favour?'

'You mean, will they have their Capitulations, the right to trade freely within our lands?' Safiye Sultan shifted slightly on her cushions. 'The French have always claimed that right, and they're not going to give way easily. They say the French ambassador has given the Grand Vizier a present of six thousand chequins not to give in to the English demands . . .' She let the thought hang in the air between them. 'But I wouldn't worry about these English merchants, they are very resourceful, I've always found.' Safiye picked up a crimson damask rose, which had been left by the tray of fruit and sweetmeats at her side, and held it to her nose thoughtfully. 'And they too have friends.'

For a few moments the two women contemplated the view below them, the water and cypress trees. All around the kiosk walls jasmine grew, perfuming the breeze. Celia breathed in the sweet air, with its scent of sea salt and flowers, and for a moment, she could almost believe that her time in the House of Felicity had always been like this, a place of beauty and courtesy, where she had never been afraid. She looked at the Valide, at the creamy courtesan's skin, almost unlined, despite her age; at the Sultan's tribute of turquoise and gold hanging at her ears and around her neck. But for all that there was something strangely *simple* about her, Celia thought. How very still she always sat, her pure profile turned towards the horizon. Always watching, always waiting – for what?

Celia looked down at her hands, wondering how to begin. Was it permissible to ask questions? Was that why she had been brought here? Ever since the incident in Handan's room she had heard nothing, not a hint, not even a whisper, of what was to happen to them all.

'Majesty?' The word was out before she could change her mind.

'Yes, Kaya Kadin?'

Celia took a deep breath.

'The women, Handan and Gulay Haseki, what will become of them?'

'Handan will recover eventually, I'm sure of it. It was a mystery for a long time, even to me, why she was made so ill by the opium. And then we began to suspect that it was Gulay who always found a way to bring her more. That's when I moved Handan to the room above my apartments, the safest place I knew, but even then she found a way, down the old corridors, the ones that have been sealed off since the old Sultan's day.'

'What will happen to her?'

'Gulay? She'll be sent to the old palace, where she can do no more harm.'

'She won't be the Haseki any more?'

'No!' The Valide gave a short laugh. 'She will certainly not be Haseki any more. The Sultan has decided, on my advice, that there is to be no Haseki. After what she did, she was lucky to escape with her life.'

Celia looked around her at the little kiosk with its white marble walls – the very same place where she had sat and talked with Gulay the first time.

'I believed everything she said,' she shook her head in disbelief, 'everything.'

'Don't be angry with yourself. So did many people.'

'How did you know that Gulay knew about the Nightingales of Manisa?'

'Well, in a curious way you told me. Do you remember the day Gulay sent for you? It was then that she began to hint to you about the Nightingales, wasn't it? Don't look so surprised, Hanza reported it to me.'

'I remember, she was one of the servants who brought the fruit.'

'Hanza had very good hearing,' Safiye said drily. 'She didn't know what any of it meant, of course. But on Gulay's part, it was a very bad mistake.'

'So you sent Hanza to . . .' Celia searched for the right word, 'watch Gulay?'

'No, I sent her to watch you.'

'Me?'

'Aren't you forgetting something? You and your friend Annetta were a gift to me from the Haseki in the first place. And from the start you were unusual girls; most of the *kislar* come here when they are very young. I myself was only thirteen. I always wondered what was the real purpose of Gulay's gift; what she might try to use you for. And I was right, wasn't I? It's not so difficult to work it out. When men go hunting in the mountains they often use one animal to trap another . . .'

'So is that what I was? A trap?'

'Something like that,' the Valide gave one of her dazzling smiles, 'but does it matter now? It's all over, Kaya Kadin.'

Still holding the rose between two fingers, she lapsed into reverie, scanning the horizon on the Asian side of the Bosphorous.

'I'm not looking for mountains, if that's what you think,' she said after a while, reading Celia's mind. 'I stopped looking for them long ago. Unless you call that a mountain,' she exclaimed suddenly. 'Look!'

On a terrace far below them two figures came walking slowly through the trees. Although he stooped a little now and walked haltingly, one was the familiar outline of the Chief Black Eunuch; beside him was the much smaller figure of a woman, in the simple dress of a palace servant.

'My Nightingales. That's what they used to call us, you know, when we first became slaves.' Closing her eyes, the Valide stroked the velvety petals of the rose against her cheek. 'Oh! You can't imagine how very, very long ago it all seems now. We could all sing you see . . .' Her voice tailed off.

The hint of sadness in the Valide's voice made Celia brave.

'And what of Cariye Lala? Will she be safe?'

'I have spoken to the Sultan,' was all the Valide said.

And Celia, knowing better than to question her any further, fell silent again.

'She is happy, look at her,' Safiye Sultan said. 'His little Lily, that's what he always called her. *My* little Mihrimah. She may look old to you, but she'll always be little Mihrimah to me. She was so small, so frightened. A frightened child. I told her, I'll always look after you, I'll teach you every hunting trick I know. But in the end it was she who saved me.'

Celia followed her gaze. The two figures paused; they did not speak much, but stood close together, looking out towards the open sea, to the ships sailing like paper cut-outs on the distant horizon.

'Is it true that she loved him?' Celia's words were out before she could stop them.

'Love?' A faint look of puzzlement came over the Valide's face. 'What has love to do with it? Love is for poets, foolish child. With us, it was never about love; it was about survival. She saved him too, you know. Or so he always believed.'

'How?'

'Once, long ago. In the desert.'

'In the desert?'

'Yes. After they gelded him. A long, long time ago.'

The Valide picked some petals from the rose and tossed them swirling into the breeze. 'His Lily. His Lala. His Li.'

And me? What about me? Celia shifted in her seat. Surely, she thought, surely she is going to say what will happen to me? But the

Valide said nothing. Below them the water traffic plied its way between the two shores of the Golden Horn. From the Aviary Gate the sound of hammering had stopped. It seemed very silent now in the still afternoon garden.

At last Celia could bear it no longer.

'These Capitulations—' she began, recklessly.

'What of them?'

'I've heard it said that they are not just trading rights.'

'Oh?'

'That under their terms any Englishman who has been captured is to be released, provided that the purchase price is paid back in full. Is that so?'

'It was so, yes. But you must remember that treaty has not been in operation these last four years, ever since the death of the old Sultan, and has not been renewed yet.'

On board the *Hector*, the merchantman so big it dwarfed all other vessels around it, Celia could just make out tiny figures swarming up the rigging and up the masts; a lone sailor stood high above the others in the crow's-nest.

'I see the English ship is preparing for its voyage home,' the Valide said at last.

'So they tell me,' Celia began, but she found suddenly that she could not go on. 'I'm sorry—' she put her hand to her throat, she could not breathe, could not even swallow, 'I'm sorry, Majesty . . .'

'Come, come, don't be sorry. All shall be well, Kaya Kadin. It has to be this way.' As she spoke the Valide put her hand out to the white cat asleep on the cushions beside her, sinking her fingers deep into his fur. 'When we first met, I remember saying to you that one day you would tell me your story. And now, I believe, is the time. Will you? Will you trust me?'

The weeping girl looked up, and to her surprise she saw that, like her own, Safiye Sultan's eyes were bright with tears. They looked at one another for a long time.

'Yes,' Celia said at last, 'I will.'

Chapter 34

Istanbul: the present day

As Elizabeth left Marius in the café the first flakes of snow had begun to fall at last, and soon the city was carpeted in white. It had become very cold. On the other side of the Galata Bridge the ghostly domes and turrets of the old city glittered in the water. The air was pure, and so icy it almost hurt to breathe.

As before she met Mehmet on the dockside.

'Here, I thought you might like to borrow this,' he said. He put something round her shoulders. It was soft, but so heavy it felt as if it were lined with lead.

She exclaimed, feeling the weight of it. 'What's it made of?'

'Sable.' He saw her expression, held up his hand with an apologetic laugh. 'I know what you're going to say. Don't be alarmed, just think of it as an antique. Which in a way it is, since it used to belong to my grandmother. A rather practical antique. You're going to need it, it's very cold on the water.'

He took her hand, brought it swiftly to his lips. 'You look like a queen,' he said, still holding her hand. He drew her closer; kissed it again, palm upwards this time

'I feel like a queen,' she said.

They looked at one another, smiling.

They set off. The waters of the Bosphorous were like silvered ink. Although there was little traffic at this time of the evening, the occasional small vessel passed them, shining like a firefly.

'When did you get back?'

311

'This afternoon.' He was still holding her hand. 'Was it right to call you? Haddba said you were with someone . . .' He glanced round at her.

'Haddba! I might have know she'd have had a hand in it,' Elizabeth laughed. 'Actually, your text came at a very good moment,' she hesitated, 'and yes I was with someone but—' She wondered what to say about Marius's sudden arrival.

'It's all right, you don't have to explain.'

'No, I'd like to. I hate to think what Haddba told you—'

She remembered with something like shame the way Marius had tried to kiss her, to take her upstairs to her room; and how close she had come to letting him, following behind him like a dog.

'I wouldn't worry. Haddba is completely unshockable. She just thinks that he's no good for you, that's all.'

'He isn't – wasn't,' she corrected herself, 'although I don't know how on earth Haddba thinks she knows that. I've never so much as mentioned him to her.'

'Haddba is a – how do you say it? – a *sorcière*. I've often said so.'

'A sorceress?'

'When it comes to affairs of the heart. I'm joking of course. But she has a kind of genius for these things – hard to explain.' He smiled at her. 'She brought us together, after all.'

A feeling she could not quite describe came over her. A feeling of lightness, of clarity.

'Is that what we are going to have: an affair of the heart?' Addressed to anyone else the words would have sounded stilted, coy almost. But not to him. Despite the heaviness and warmth of the sable-lined coat, she found that she was shivering, but not with cold this time.

'Oh, I think we should,' he said.

They stood, as they had done before, side by side; very close, but not touching. Her desire for him was so strong she was almost fainting.

'I think we already are, don't you?' He turned to look at her. 'My beautiful Elizabeth.'

He had not said that they were going to the *yalı*, the wooden house on the Asian shore of the Bosphorous that he had showed her last time, but she knew that that was where they were heading. When they arrived a man, a caretaker of some kind, was there to hand her out on to the little jetty and take charge of the boat. Behind the house the wind sighed, shivering the snow-laden trees. Elizabeth picked her way carefully across the icy ground, following Mehmet into a kind of antechamber. The house was lit up, warm and bright after the bitter night as though guests were expected, but apart from the manservant, who did not reappear again, there was nobody else around that Elizabeth could see.

'Will you wait for me here? Just for a moment or two?' He kissed her on the mouth. 'There's something I need to do.'

'Yes, I'll wait for you,' she said, but neither of them moved.

He bent his head to kiss her again. She tasted him, smelt him, and a kind of sweetness pierced her whole body.

'I won't be long.'

'No.'

'I promise.'

'Really?'

'Yes, really.'

He was still kissing her, not only her mouth, but her hair, her neck.

'Are you sure?'

Her body was pressed up against his.

'Yes, quite sure.' He ran his hand tenderly over her cheek.

'Mehmet?'

'Yes?' He was staring at her mouth.

'Nothing . . .'

She closed her eyes, felt him trace the outline of her lips, felt him push his finger in between them, parting them with his finger.

'Are you sure? You don't mind me bringing you here? I can wait, you know.' He looked at her in a way that made her heart skip a beat.

'I'm sure. Go,' she said, pulling away at last. 'I'll wait for you.'

Following his instructions, Elizabeth made her way up a staircase and found herself in a gallery, a long thin drawing room which ran the whole length of the house. In the centre, raised up on a platform, was an alcove that jutted out over the waterfront. Cushions covered in heavily brocaded velvets and silks had been arranged around three sides of the alcove in such a way that whoever sat there would have the sensation that they were floating just over the water's edge. Reclining in the centre of the furthest divan seat was a large black cat.

'Well, hello puss.' Elizabeth let the sable-lined coat slide from her shoulders. She went over to the creature and sat down next to it, searching for the sweet spot beneath its jaw. The cat took no notice of her; lay with ostentatiously closed eyes. Only by a faint, reproachful movement in the very tip of its tail did she know it had registered her presence. Outside the window, on the European shore, the lights of the city shone. Elizabeth could see a small boat cruise by, its light shining against the inky blackness.

'If I had this house I would never leave it,' she said, half to herself, half to the cat.

'What would you never leave?' It was Mehmet returning.

'I would never leave this house.'

'Do you like it?'

'Very, very much.'

'I'm glad. The Ottomans built these wooden *yalis* as summer houses, because they were close to the cool of the water.' He came and sat beside her. 'But there were many fires. Because they're made of wood the *yalis* were always burning down. People stopped using them, and many just rotted away. Now they're coming back into fashion again.'

Together they looked out at the city sparkling on the opposite shore. 'It's beautiful in winter here, too, don't you think?'

'Oh yes, wonderful.' Elizabeth replied.

There was a pause.

'I see you've found Milosh.' He watched her stroking the cat.

'Is that what she's called?'

There was another pause.

'There's an angel walking across someone's grave.' She looked round him. 'That's what we say when there's a silence like that.'

'You are pensive?'

'No . . . well, I suppose so,' she said, 'it's just that I've had the strangest, *strangest* day. You can't imagine. And now this—'

She wondered, with a feeling of sudden misgiving, how many other women he had brought to this place, this place which seemed made for the act of seduction.

'And now?'

'And now, well, this seems like the strangest part of all.'

As if he could read what was on her mind he said, 'I can see you have some questions. You can ask me anything, you know.'

'I know I can,' she said. And she realised that, unlike Marius, she could.

He was pulling her towards him, kissing her neck.

'I'd like to ask you how many women you've brought here,' she said, amazing herself with her own boldness. She looked round at the ravishing room. 'But I'm not sure I want to know the answer.'

'The truth is I have brought just one person here before,' he said. He loosened Elizabeth's hair so that it fell like a sheet of dark water over her shoulder.

'Recently?'

'No. That's all in the past.' He was taking off her shoes.

'You mean it's over?'

'The love affair is over, if that's what you mean.' He smiled at her. 'Now she is married to someone else, but still my very great friend.'

'Oh, I see,' Elizabeth said. She tried, and failed, to imagine what it might be like to be friends with Marius.

'You sound surprised.'

'No.' She watched as he unbuttoned her shirt, and then laid out the sable coat for them, the fur uppermost against the cushions.

'Is that what we shall become,' she said lying down, naked now, watching him as he undressed, 'very great friends?'

But I feel something more than friendship, she thought; what is it that I feel? – this feeling of skinlessness. Is it love? she thought, a moment of sudden dread.

'Elizabeth, why are you thinking of the end, when we are just at the beginning?' He kissed the soft skin of her shoulder. 'Let's be lovers first,' he laughed.

Elizabeth laughed too, and pulled herself on top of him, held his arms down over his head. And there it was again: a feeling of extraordinary lightness, of clarity. It occurred to her that she might be, quite simply, happy.

Looking down at him, marvelling, she said, 'Yes, let's.'

Chapter 35

Istanbul: the present day

Inside the Third Courtyard of the Topkapı Palace, Elizabeth waited outside the Director's office for her long-anticipated appointment to visit the palace archives.

'Elizabeth Staveley?' A man in an immaculate brown suit and white shirt opened the door to her.

'Yes.'

'I am Ara Metin, one of the Director's assistants. Please, come in.'

Elizabeth followed him inside.

'Have a seat, please.' The man indicated the chair on the other side of his desk. 'I believe that you have requested permission to consult our archive?'

'Yes, that's right.'

Elizabeth could see that he had her papers in front of him: her application form, the letter of recommendation from her supervisor, Dr Alis.

'It says here that you are interested in the 1599 English mission during the time of our Sultan Mehmet III.' He cast his eye over the form. 'You have also asked to see the organ that was given by the British merchants to the Sultan?'

'Yes. That's correct.'

'And this is for?' He looked benignly at her through his spectacles.

'My thesis. My DPhil thesis.'

'On trading missions to Constantinople?' he pressed her gently.

'Yes.'

Why do I feel like a fraud? Elizabeth shifted uncomfortably on her chair. She remembered Dr Alis's advice: the important thing is to get your foot in the door; if you don't know what to ask for when trying to get access to an archive, just apply to see something – anything – that you know they must have.

'Congratulations,' he gave her a courteous smile, 'you will be a Doctor of Philosophy, then? Dr Staveley.'

'Well, I've got a while to go yet, but one day I hope so.' Elizabeth searched around for something else to say. 'Thank you so much for seeing me at such short notice.'

'It says here that you have only a few days left in Istanbul, is that right?'

'I'm going home for Christmas.'

'In that case, we must give you our express service,' he smiled. 'Especially since this is your second application to us, I believe? Your first was . . . let me see . . .' He shuffled back through the papers.

'I was looking for any information regarding a young English woman,' Elizabeth explained. 'Celia Lamprey. I believe she may have been a slave belonging to Sultan Mehmet – at around about the same time that the English mission arrived here.'

'But you had no luck?'

'No.'

'Well, this is not surprising. Except in the case of the most senior women – the Sultan's mother, for example, or the occasional concubine or powerful harem official – practically no information has come down to us about them. Not even their names, which for the purposes of any records held here would have been different, in any case, from their birth name. Your young woman, Celia Lamprey, would never have been known as that, she would have been given an Ottoman name, probably before she even arrived. But you know this, I think?' Looking at her again over his spectacles he shook his head. 'What is this Western obsession with harems?' she heard him say, half to himself. And then, brisk suddenly, as though the subject embarrassed him. 'Now, let's see if we can be more helpful this time.'

He took another paper from beneath Elizabeth's application file and read it carefully. 'Well, I'm sorry to say,' when he looked up at last his eyes behind his spectacles were sorrowful, 'I'm very sorry to have to say that it doesn't look as though we can help you much this time either.'

'Not at all? Surely there must be something?'

'This note here is from one of my colleagues.' He held up a piece of paper that had been clipped on to Elizabeth's application form. 'She says that there is an official record of the original presentation,' he ran his eye over the note, 'but all it contains is an itemised list. Nothing much, in other words, although I'm sure we can arrange for you to examine it if you so wish. The organ, on the other hand, is no longer in existence. It seems that it was destroyed a long time ago.'

'How long ago is a long time?'

'A very long time,' he smiled. 'In the time of Sultan Ahmet, Mehmet III's son. It seems that, unlike his father, Sultan Ahmet was a very religious man, and he believed that the organ given by the English Queen was – how do you say it? – it had images of human beings on it, which we do not allow in Islam—'

Elizabeth thought of the angels with their trumpets; the bush with the singing blackbirds. 'Idolatrous?'

'Yes, that's the word. Idolatrous.'

'So it was destroyed?'

'I'm afraid so. Not a trace remains of the merchants' gift.' He seemed genuinely disappointed not to have been able to help her.

'I see.' Elizabeth stood up to go. 'Thank you so much for your time.'

'But there is something else, Miss Staveley.'

'Yes?'

'There was one thing that my colleague thought you might be interested to see.'

'Oh?' Elizabeth turned back and saw that he was holding a small object in the palm of his hand. It was wrapped in a little bag made from faded red velvet. 'What is it?'

'It was found with some of the palace accounts relating to the English mission. No one is quite sure how it got there. But there is a definite date for it, apparently: 1599 in the European calendar.'

Elizabeth took the object from him. Through the faded velvet she could feel the solid weight of something metallic lying in the palm of her hand: a round and smooth object, the approximate shape of an old-fashioned pocket watch. With stiff fingers Elizabeth pulled the strings

318

of the bag open, tipping out its contents carefully into the palm of her hand. It was smaller than she had expected, and had the look of something very old. The brass case, delicately chased with flowers and leaves, gave off only the faintest glint, like tarnished sunlight.

'Open it. My colleague believes it is some kind of astronomical instrument,' Ara Metin said.

With her thumb Elizabeth carefully eased the catch at the base. It opened as smoothly as if it had been newly minted to reveal its several component parts. She contemplated it in silence.

'It's called a compendium,' she said softly.

'So you've seen something like it before?' He sounded surprised.

'Only in a picture. A portrait.'

For a few moments all she could do was marvel at its workmanship.

'This is a quadrant.' With her forefinger she pointed to the back of the inner case. 'This a magnetic compass. This an equinoctial sundial. On the back of the lid here – see these engravings? – is a table of latitudes of towns in Europe and the Levant.'

Elizabeth held the compendium up so that it was at eye-level. And sure enough, inside the bottom half of the two outer cases were two hinged lids, held together by tiny catches in the shape of a left and a right hand. 'And at the bottom here, if I am not much mistaken . . .' she glanced across at him, 'may I?'

He nodded, and she eased the catches gently to one side and opened the hidden compartment.

A miniature of a young woman with pale skin and dark eyes gazed out at her. Her hair was reddish gold, pearls hung at her neck and from the lobes of her ears. Over one of her shoulders was some kind of garment, a suggestion of fur in the tiny brush strokes; the other shoulder was bare, the skin snowy, almost blue in its whiteness. In her hand she held a single flower, a red carnation.

Celia? It seemed to Elizabeth that the two of them seemed to stare at one another across the centuries. *Celia, is that you?* And then, just as suddenly, the moment was gone.

'How extraordinary,' Ara Metin was saying at her side, 'did you know this portrait was there?'

Elizabeth shook her head. Four hundred years, was all she could think, four hundred years in the dark.

319

'Would you mind very much if I used your computer for a moment?' She indicated the laptop on the desk.

'Well . . .'

For a moment he looked doubtful, but Elizabeth was insistent. 'Please. It won't take long.'

'Well, really it's the Director's computer, and I'm not sure . . .'

'Does it have an Internet connection?'

'Yes, we have wireless here, of course . . .'

But Elizabeth was already logging on to her email. Her in-box showed that there was one new message, together with an attachment.

Oh Dr Alis! Bless you! Without stopping to read her supervisor's message, she clicked straight on to the attachment, and this time the portrait of Paul Pindar came up immediately on to the screen.

'That's it, look,' Elizabeth pointed to the screen, 'can you see what he's holding?'

'Why, it looks just like it – the same object.' He peered over her shoulder.

'It doesn't just look the same – it *is* the same!' Elizabeth said joyfully. 'The question is, what on earth's it doing here? Could it have been one of the embassy gifts to the Sultan?'

'No,' he shook his head. 'If it were, it would have been listed along with the other gifts, of that I'm absolutely sure. Who was this man anyway?'

'A merchant. His name was Paul Pindar, and he was secretary to the same Levant Company embassy who presented the organ to the Sultan. I believe that this compendium once belonged to him. Look, there's an inscription here that I couldn't read when I looked at the portrait before. It's in Latin.' She read it out. '*Ubi iaces dimidium, iacet pectoris mei.*'

'Can you translate it?'

'I think so, yes.' For a few moments, Elizabeth stared at the words on the screen. 'In English it's something like: where my other half lies, there lies my heart.'

'What does it mean?'

'I'm not sure,' she said slowly. 'Unless –' she picked up the compendium and scrutinised the miniature again. 'Yes, that's it, look!' Holding the miniature up to the image on the screen, she was laughing suddenly. 'I can't believe I couldn't see it before. They're a pair!'

'Do you really think so?' He looked sceptical.

'Yes: look at the way they are positioned. She is facing to the right, holding a carnation in her left hand. He is facing to the left, holding the compendium in his right hand. I couldn't see it before because the reproduction was so bad, but the portrait of Pindar must be a miniature, too. No wonder it was so grainy. It must have been enlarged several times over to fit on to a square page.' Her mind was racing. 'Could they be betrothal portraits, do you think?'

'Is there anything to indicate the date the portraits were painted?'

'You're right, there should be a date on here somewhere, I remember Dr Alis mentioning it.' Elizabeth sat down at the computer again. 'Can I zoom in on this? Ah, yes, there it is.' An enlarged image of the inscription came up on the screen. Elizabeth's face fell. 'But that's impossible!'

In a faint but unequivocal hand the numerals 1601 came into view.

Ara Metin was the first to speak.

'Well, maybe they're not betrothal portraits after all,' he shrugged. 'The portrait of the woman must date from sometime before 1599. So this one of your merchant,' he indicated the screen, 'was painted at least a year after it, possibly more.'

'But how can that be?' Elizabeth picked up the old velvet pouch that the compendium had been kept in, fingering the faded nap. 'You say that this has been here since 1599, and yet he's holding it in his hand in 1601 . . .' Her voice tailed off. 'Well in that case it can't be the same compendium, can it? I wonder how much I can enlarge this . . .' She shifted the focus of the zoom on to the instrument itself. 'Look.' She pointed at the hidden compartment. 'Blown up like this you can see the hidden compartment quite clearly. And, see, there's no miniature inside it. No portrait. It seems I've been quite wrong about all this all along. Quite wrong.' She pushed the chair back from the table and stood up.

'Miss Staveley, are you all right?'

Ara Metin, still hovering at Elizabeth's shoulder, saw that she had turned pale.

'Yes.'

'You look rather faint. Sit down again, please.' He put his hand under her elbow.

'No. Thank you.'

'A glass of water then?'

Elizabeth did not seem to hear him. '*Where my other half lies, there lies my heart*,' she said the words out loud. 'Don't you see? It's very simple: in fact, it means exactly what it says.' She looked at him. 'It's a kind of game; a riddle if you like. This *is* the other half – but not only of the two portraits. I think it means that she was his other half.' She looked down at the portrait of the girl, at her calm eyes, her porcelain skin. 'The other half of his heart, his soul. And she lies *here*. Literally, here in this palace.'

So he had known, she thought, he knew all along that she was here. Had Paul Pindar, like Thomas Dallam, somehow been able to look through the grille in the wall and see her? Elizabeth felt a shiver run down her spine. And what of Celia? All this time she had been imagining her laughing, running and running towards him, across the deserted courtyard. But clearly it had not been like that after all. He knew, and he left her here.

'But I really don't see that you can know for sure . . .' Ara Metin was saying.

'But I think I do,' Elizabeth said with conviction. 'All this time I've been guessing. Guessing and feeling my way along. There was nothing else to go on. But this time I do have evidence.' She gave him a pale smile. 'Look here,' she pointed again to the painted compendium in the portrait, at the bottom half where the miniature of Celia should have been, 'there's no miniature in this one, because he wasn't painted with *this* compendium, because somehow the original had ended up here in the palace – I don't suppose we'll ever know exactly how or why. But there *is* something in its place.'

'I can't see anything, just some engravings on the metal case.' Ara Metin peered over her shoulder at the screen. 'It looks like some kind of fish, or an eel perhaps?'

'The Elizabethans called them lampreys,' she was cradling the brass compendium against her breast, holding the miniature very close to her in the cup of her hand, 'and this is Celia Lamprey, the girl I was telling you about.' To Ara Metin's consternation he saw that Elizabeth was weeping silently. 'The portrait is not a betrothal painting at all. It's a memorial. A memorial to someone who was already dead.'

322

Chapter 36

Constantinople: 6 September 1599

Evening

'Celia!'
         'Annetta!'
'You're back!'

In the Courtyard of the Valide, Annetta put her arms around her friend, hugging her roughly.

'Why, what's wrong? What is this – you're trembling,' Celia laughed.

'I thought . . . when she sent for you like that . . . oh, never mind what I thought!' Annetta hugged her again, more fiercely this time. 'What did she say? Why did she want you? I can't believe she . . .' she peered into Celia's face, put her hand tenderly up to her cheek, 'but, no, here you are, still flesh and blood. You must tell me everything,' she looked around her quickly, 'but not here, come on.'

Annetta pulled Celia into her old apartment. She saw at once that it was empty. Celia's things, her clothes and her few possessions, had been removed. The room already had an expectant feel to it, as though it were already waiting to receive the next occupant.

'So you've already been moved? Where to?'

'I don't know . . .' looking around the empty room Celia seemed momentarily nonplussed, 'they haven't told me anything yet.' Quickly she ran across to the niche above the bed and put her hand inside it. 'Well, at least they didn't find these.' From the hiding place in the wall she took the Haseki's bracelet and another object, something small which she concealed in the palm of her hand.

'Well, I don't think I'll be needing this again.' With one last look Celia flung the bracelet with its tiny little blue and white glass eyes back into the niche again. 'I should have listened to you all along. You were right about Gulay. That time in the Great Chamber when she threw that bracelet at me, I should have realised that she wasn't throwing it at me at all. She meant to hit Cariye Lala – it was a sort of clue, I suppose. She wanted me to start asking questions about her, to stir things up – flush her out, is how she put it – and expose the Valide that way. It was all like a sort of game to her,' Celia said, 'a game of chess.'

'Oh, she was clever, I'll grant you that. Almost a match for the Valide,' Annetta said, 'but not quite.'

Annetta followed Celia's gaze as she looked round at the apartment for the last time. She did not seem either sad or anxious, but rather mysteriously buoyed up, elated almost, by some secret knowledge.

'It's so quiet, don't you think?' Celia went to the doorway and looked out. She gave a little shiver. 'Do you remember the last time we were in here together?' she laughed. 'That time when Esperanza Malchi gave us such a fright?'

'I remember.'

'And now everyone's gone to see the English gift, the marvellous organ that plays tunes by itself – did you know?' Celia said, talking too fast. 'They presented it to the Sultan this afternoon.'

'But you didn't want to go?'

'No—' she gave a small wince, put her hand to her side, to where the pain was a constant now.

'Tell me about the Valide.'

'Oh, she was very kind, you know how she can be . . .' Celia began to pace the room again. She seemed restless, feverish almost.

'Do I?' A tiny seed of suspicion took root in Annetta's mind. 'What's she said to you?'

'Nothing.' Celia did not meet her gaze.

'Then what have you said to her?'

'Why, nothing.'

'You seem . . . different.'

'Do I?'

'Yes.'

As Annetta watched, two bright spots of colour appeared on each of Celia's cheeks.

'Goose?'

Celia did not reply.

'Oh, goose.' Annetta sat down heavily on the divan. 'And you say you've not been told where to go? Now that you are no longer *gözde*?'

'I am to wait here . . .'

'For what?'

'For dusk to fall.'

For one long moment there was absolute silence.

'For dusk to fall? What will happen at dusk?'

Again Celia did not reply. She was looking at the object she had taken from the niche, something round and metallic.

'What will happen at dusk?' Annetta was insistent now.

Celia turned to her, her face luminous. 'The Aviary Gate, Annetta. She says I can see him there, just one last time.'

'She told you that?' Annetta said.

But Celia did not seem to hear her. 'If I could see him, just one last time, see his face, hear his voice, I think I could be happy.' She looked up. 'You see, I know he's here. He sent me this, look.' She pressed the catch and the compendium opened on the palm of her hand.

'Why, it's you!' Annetta looked at the miniature with astonishment.

'It was me. Once upon a time there was a young woman called Celia Lamprey,' Celia looked down at it sadly, 'but I can't remember her, Annetta,' she seemed to struggle to catch her breath, 'she's lost . . . gone.'

'But the Aviary Gate? Surely—'

'I have her blessing.'

'It's a trap, you know it is.'

'But I have to go, you understand that, don't you? I would give anything – *anything* – just to see him one last time. And this is my chance, I have to take it.'

'But you mustn't!' Annetta was frantic now. 'It's a *trap*. She's testing you, can't you see? To see where your loyalty lies. If you go, you'll fail the test . . .'

'But I've already been there, Annetta, I've already been through the Gate. When I was there, the other night, I stood at the threshold and for a moment I could almost remember what it was like to be free.' Celia looked around the windowless room, her eyes unnaturally bright. 'I can't do this any more, Annetta . . . just can't.'

'You can, I'll help you, just like I always have.'

'No.'

'Don't go – don't leave me . . .' Annetta was weeping now. 'If you go there tonight, you won't come back. She won't let you come back. You know that as well as I do!'

But Celia did not answer her. Instead she put her arm around Annetta, kissed her and stroked her dark hair. 'Of course I'm coming back, silly. I'm going to see him, just one more time, the Valide said so,' she said at last, rocking Annetta against her shoulders. 'Now who's being a goose?'

After some moments Celia stood up again and went to the door, looking up into the narrow patch of sky.

'Is it time?'

The late afternoon sky had a pinkish tinge.

'No, we still have time.' Celia came back to sit next to Annetta. From the chain around her neck she took out the key, and sat holding it in her hand. For what seemed like a long while the two kept vigil, sitting together very close, very still, their arms around one another, not moving. Eventually, Celia stood up again. The room had darkened.

'Is it time?'

Celia did not reply. She went to the door and looked out again. Outside the pinkish tinge had faded to grey; overhead a bat swooped. She came back into the room. The pain in her side had gone.

'I love you Annetta,' she whispered, kissing her softly on the cheek.

From her pocket she took out a piece of paper.

'What's this?'

'It's for Paul.' Celia folded the paper and pressed it into Annetta's hand. 'If something—' she started, 'if I don't, will you get it to him? Promise me, Annetta, promise me you'll find a way to get this to him.'

Annetta looked down at the piece of paper in her hand.

'Is it time then?' was all she could say.

'I can't believe it, I can't believe I'm going to see him again, Annetta! Be happy for me.' Joyfully Celia stood at the doorway, poised. 'Promise me you'll do it, Annetta.'

'But you're coming back, remember?' Annetta said, trying to smile.

'Promise me all the same.'

'I promise.'

'And if you break your promise – I'll be back to haunt you, you'll see if I won't,' Celia said.

And with those words she was gone. Laughing and running, laughing and running noiselessly, on her little slippered feet, across the courtyard to the Aviary Gate.

Epilogue

Oxford: the present day

E arly one bitter January morning in the first week of the Hilary term Elizabeth met her supervisor, Dr Alis, on the steps of the Oriental Library. There were traces of slushy snow on the ground and even the golden brick of the Sheldonian Theatre across the road looked grey in the morning half-light.

'Well, *you* certainly look well.' Susan Alis, a small, energetic woman in her mid-sixties, gave Elizabeth a kiss on the cheek. 'Istanbul must have agreed with you.'

'I've split up with Marius, if that's what you mean.' Elizabeth could not help smiling.

'Ha!' Dr Alis gave a triumphant shout. 'So I gather,' she said more gently, pulling Elizabeth to her and kissing her again. Her cheeks gave off a faint, spinsterish smell of old-fashioned face powder. 'But you're glad to be back, all the same?'

'Well, I wouldn't have missed this for the world.'

'You mean our manuscript expert? Yes, it does sound as if they might have to eat their words after all. "Not very interesting" is what they said at first, I seem to remember. But then you know they always say that, especially if it's anything to do with women.' Her small button eyes glittered.

From somewhere close by came the muffled sound of a clock striking the hour. A small fleet of students rode past, the lamps on their bicycles piercing the chilly air.

'That must be nine o'clock,' Dr Alis was stamping her feet inside

328

her snow boots to keep warm, 'come on, let's wait for him inside. It's perishing out here.'

Despite the electric lights it was dark inside the Oriental Library. Elizabeth followed Dr Alis along a linoleum-lined corridor into the Reading Room. The room was the same as she remembered it: a relatively small functional space, long bare wooden tables, open shelves of books all along the walls, banks of drawers with their old-fashioned card indexes; the portrait of Sir Gore Ouseley, bookish and beaky-nosed, gazing down from the wall between the windows.

The Pindar Bequest, twenty leather-bound manuscript volumes in Arabic and Syriac, had been laid out ready for them on a trolley. Elizabeth picked them up one by one, opening each briefly, admiring the beauty of the script inside. From somewhere behind the librarian's desk a telephone rang shrilly.

'So these are they, the Pindar manuscripts?' Dr Alis came to stand beside Elizabeth.

'Paul Pindar was a friend of Thomas Bodley. It seems that he asked him to keep a look-out for books on his travels, and these are the result.'

'When were they acquired?'

'The bequest was made in 1611, although of course the books could be much older.'

'My word, very early then.' Dr Alis picked one up and examined the inside back page. 'And look at the cataloguing numbers, it makes them amongst the first few thousand books in the entire Bodleian. Do we know what they are?'

'Mostly astronomical and medical text books, I believe. I've got a list here of their contents from the old Latin catalogue.' Elizabeth fished in her bag for her notebook.

'Rather an esoteric choice for a merchant, wouldn't you have said?'

'Maybe,' Elizabeth said consideringly, 'but Paul Pindar was a rather unusual man; quite a scholar, by the looks of it, as well as a merchant and an adventurer.'

'He sounds absolutely perfect.' Dr Alis gave a surprisingly raucous laugh. 'Can I have his telephone number?'

She reached into her bag and took out a pair of spectacles with modern oblong-shaped lenses. 'He was a bit of a gadget man as well, your Paul Pindar, I seem to remember, with that beautiful compendium of his. The Elizabethans loved gadgets as well as riddles; and that's what a compendium was you know, the most superb little piece of gadgetry. You could tell the time with it, not just during the day, but also at night, by starlight; find your way with the compass; measure the heights of buildings; any number of different uses. What would he have if he were alive today, I wonder? Not just the humble mobile for him, but the most state-of-the-art BlackBerry, or an iPhone.'

'In that case I don't suppose the humble book would have been enough for him either.'

'Electronic books all the way.'

'And I don't suppose he'd be corresponding with the Chief Librarian either.'

'What? When we now have these fascinating new professors of Cyberspace Studies at the Oxford Internet Institute? Definitely not.'

Elizabeth laughed. Dr Alis's enthusiasm for technology was legendary amongst her much younger colleagues, most of whom, she liked to joke, were still flummoxed by the most basic video recorders.

'And look, here it is, the manuscript that the fragment was hidden inside.'

With excitement Elizabeth picked up one of the volumes. The book was smaller than she remembered it. Bodley Or. 10. She identified the catalogue entry in her notebook.

'Yes, look here it is: *opus astronomicus quaorum prima de sphaera planetarum.*'

The manuscript had been leather bound at a much later date, but when she opened it the pages gave off a faint peppery smell, like the inside of an old sea chest. She examined the sloping black and red hieroglyphs; with one hand ran a finger down the pages, feeling its rough edges, the thick, faintly sticky slub of the paper.

This too, she thought to herself. Four hundred years – the phrase came back to her again. *Four hundred years in the dark.*

'You know it really is amazing that we should still have catalogue entries written in Latin,' Dr Alis was saying, interrupting her reverie.

'I wouldn't worry, we'll soon be able to look at manuscripts like this online, no doubt,' Elizabeth said, 'but it won't be the same, will it?'

'Meaning?' Dr Alis gave her one of her intense bird-like stares.

'Well, I know how I felt when I first found the fragment. How I felt when I first realised I was holding Paul Pindar's compendium in my hand. How I feel now looking at this . . .' Elizabeth glanced down at the book.

'My dear, you always were a hopeless romantic.'

'Am I?' Elizabeth looked up again. 'You know, I don't think so. I think it's because they are—' she searched for the right words, 'human things. They have been handled and written on, breathed over, by others, hundreds of years ago. And it's as if in some strange way they contain the past within them, the stories of the people they once belonged to. This page that I am touching now was once touched by some unknown astronomer who wrote in Syriac . . .' She shrugged. 'Who was he, do you suppose? I don't imagine we'll ever know now; or discover how a Levant Company merchant came to acquire his manuscript.'

'You're quite right. I do agree with you, really. But I also know how arbitrary these things can be. And that we must always be wary, my dear, of reading too much into them.' Dr Alis took the book from her and scrutinised one of the pages. 'Well, we do know that he had very beautiful handwriting,' she said musingly, looking at the black and red script, 'and quite an eye for colour too. And I can tell you something else: whatever the catalogue says, this isn't a text book either, this is more like an astronomer's notebook. Look, some of the pages in here are still blank.'

'So they are.'

Elizabeth saw that there were indeed still some blank pages. On others grids had been drawn in red ink; some were empty, others only half-filled in with strange figures and symbols that she could not interpret; the writing broken off suddenly, as though the scribe had been interrupted in the middle of his work.

'Dr Alis?' a voice said behind them.

'Yes, I am Susan Alis. And you must be our manuscript expert?'

'Richard Omar.' The young man shook her by the hand. 'And it was you who found the fragment?'

'No, alas, I wish I could claim it were. It was Elizabeth, Elizabeth Staveley, my graduate student.'

'Ah,' he turned to Elizabeth, 'then I expect you'll be glad to see this again.'

He took a sealed plastic folder from his briefcase. Between its pages Elizabeth could see the outline of the manuscript fragment, watermark and all.

'That's brilliant, you've brought the original with you. I wasn't sure—' absurdly, her heart leapt in her rib cage, 'may I?'

'Of course,' he handed her the folder, 'it's all right, you can take it out.'

Elizabeth took it out of the folder, and held it tentatively to her nose. 'Oh . . .'

'Is there something wrong?'

'It has no smell.'

'Of course not; it's been treated since you last saw it. Makes it safer to handle.' He smiled at her, showing teeth that were very white against his black skin. 'What did it smell of?' He seemed puzzled.

'Oh, nothing really,' Elizabeth said, feeling foolish, 'you know, just old paper.'

She laid the fragment carefully on the table in front of her: the same frail page, the colour of old tea, its watermark still clearly visible,

Loving Friend . . . You desire to have the whole proceedings of the unfortunate Voyage and shipwreck of the good ship *Celia*, and still yet more unfortunate and tragical history of Celia Lamprey . . .

Elizabeth's eyes skimmed quickly over the familiar words.

The *Celia* set sail from Venice, with a fair wind, on the seventeenth . . .
There arose a great gust of wind out of the north . . .
    And there guard . . . his daughter Celia . . . Dogges, scurvy curtailed skin-clipping Dogges . . . stop stop take me but spare my poor father I beseech you . . . her face as white as death . . .

Elizabeth closed the folder in silence.

'Do you know who she was?'

Richard Omar took a laptop out of the case he had been carrying and began to set it up on one of the tables.

'Celia Lamprey?' Elizabeth put the folder down on the table. 'She was the daughter of a sea captain.'

'Well, I know *that*.' He seemed amused. 'I've read the fragment too, you know. What I mean is, what more do you know about her? I gather you have been doing some research. I always like to know how a story ends, don't you?' He glanced up at her, half-teasing. 'Does the girl get the boy?'

'What makes you think there's a boy?'

'There's always a boy.' He frowned, concentrating as he connected up the wires and plugged them into the power point on the desk. 'What I mean is: she survived the shipwreck, but did she survive the rescue?'

'That's a good question.' Elizabeth looked at him consideringly. 'For a long time I was convinced that Celia Lamprey must have been set free: that somehow she escaped from the harem eventually. How else would we have her narrative, if she didn't write it? It's so very alive, so full of detail – all those details about her dress being so weighted down with water that it was as heavy as lead. Do you think a man would have written that?'

'No, probably not.'

'Well, that's what I thought at first anyway. But now, well, I'm not so sure. I'm pretty sure now that she never did get out. The girl, as you put it, didn't get the boy.'

'But if she didn't write her story, then who did?'

'And why did they write it. That's exactly what I've been trying to find out.'

'Well, I must say, it reads like an eyewitness account to me,' Dr Alis said.

'In that case, if it wasn't Celia, then it must have been someone else who was on board the boat when it was shipwrecked,' Richard said. 'Come on, it's obvious, isn't it? One of the nuns of course.'

'One of the nuns?' Dr Alis laughed.

'I'm serious.'

'You don't think anyone on board a Turkish man-o'-war would have bothered to rescue them, do you? They were probably all just thrown overboard, poor things.'

'What makes you think they were all old? There was at least one young one, if I remember rightly.'

'You're right, and I did wonder about that myself,' Elizabeth said, 'but even if one of them had been taken captive as well as Celia, they would surely all have ended up in different places. The original narrative claimed to tell her whole story. How would any of the nuns have got to know the rest of Celia's tale?'

'Oh well,' he shrugged, seeming to lose interest suddenly, 'you're the historian.'

'Now, Mr Omar,' Dr Alis said, businesslike again, 'what can you tell us about the fragment? I'm surprised, I must say. Usually it's rather hard to get you chaps interested in this kind of thing.'

'Well, you're quite right – I didn't think it was very interesting at first. Most of the work I do is on vellum, on manuscripts that are far older than this. But – luckily for you – the guy who usually works on the early modern stuff is away on leave at the moment, so it got passed on to me. It was the story that intrigued me: a white English girl who ended up a slave at the court of the Great Turk. I didn't even know there were such things as white slaves then.' He turned to Elizabeth. 'And then I noticed something. Something – especially after what you've just told me – that I think you should see for yourself. It'll be easier to explain if I show you.'

He typed something on to the keyboard.

'The first thing we do with manuscripts these days is have them digitally photographed – it's quite straightforward. And this, as you can see, is it.'

An image of the fragment popped on to the screen.

'A good clear secretary hand,' Dr Alis peered at the screen, 'easy to read. Any graduate student could do it. What more can you tell us?'

'Well, the paper is almost certainly Ottoman, although curiously there are very faint impressions of a seal having been used – probably on an outer page which hasn't survived – which is Italian. Venetian, as a matter of fact.'

'Ah, so that's where your nun theory comes from.' Elizabeth turned to Dr Alis. 'You remember, the nuns came from the Convent of Santa Clara in Venice.'

'OK, anything else?'

'Well, the first thing that struck me was how much of the page did *not* have writing on it, look how wide these margins are,' he pointed to the treated original, 'but the thing I was most struck by was the reverse.' He brought a second photograph on to his screen. 'As you can see, it's blank, completely blank.'

'What of it?'

'Paper was valuable in the sixteenth century. Too valuable, on the whole, to leave such large amounts of it unused. As I was telling you, most of the work I've been doing recently is on vellum, on manuscripts that are far older than this. Vellum was so valuable that in medieval times monks developed a technique for washing and then scraping the vellum to erase what was there, and then reusing it, writing something new over the top of the original text.'

'You mean a palimpsest?' Dr Alis said.

'Exactly, a palimpsest. Well now, there's a technology – X-ray fluorescence imaging – that allows us to see through the surface writing, as it were, and read the rubbed-out original below.'

'You don't mean to tell me that you've used X-ray fluorescence imaging on this?' Dr Alis's eyes lit up.

'Not on this, no,' he laughed, 'but it gave me the idea. For this, I used quite a simple bit of software actually, not much more complicated than good old Photoshop,' there was a tiny pause, 'any graduate student could do it.'

'You're quite right. I stand corrected,' Dr Alis said solemnly. 'Now be a good fellow and get on with it – we're on tenterhooks here.'

'Well, I got to wondering about the blank parts of the fragment, and then it occurred to me that perhaps they weren't actually blank at all. Marks made in ink survive pretty well, as you can see; but supposing someone had written in something else, pencil for instance?'

'You mean, it could have rubbed off?' Elizabeth said.

'Exactly. What happens is that over time the pencil markings themselves fade, but the grooves where the lead has dug into the page would still be there. Exactly the kind of thing that I had been working on with the vellum manuscripts. Anyway, there's a relatively easy way to find out, all you have to do is put the paper through different light spectrums, and see if anything shows up. Ultra-violet didn't show up anything, but then I tried infra-red—' He paused, like a magician about to pull a rabbit out of a hat.

'And?'

He adjusted the screen.

'And I got this.'

What seemed to be a ghostly photographic negative of the original picture came up on the screen: white writing on a black page. Elizabeth peered at it.

'I can't see anything different.'

'Not on this side, no. But look what's on the reverse.'

He clicked the keyboard again and brought up the second image and suddenly, where once there had been a blank page there were now definite markings. Frail and spidery, in a hand so tiny Elizabeth could hardly make out the words at all, they glowed in an unearthly blue light, as if written in ectoplasm.

For a few moments they stared at the screen in silence.

'My word . . .' Dr Alis said at last, 'what does it say?'

'I'm not entirely sure . . . it's too small to read.' Elizabeth turned to Richard. 'Can you enlarge it?'

He nodded silently.

'Oh my God—' Elizabeth felt tears start into her eyes.

'What? What is it?'

'It's, well, it looks like a poem.'

'Read it,' Dr Alis said, 'read it to me, Elizabeth.'

So Elizabeth read:

> To my love, farewell –
>
> Whenas I saw you at the gate
> Barred hence from my enslave'd fate
> And knew in that one instant sore
> I would not see you ever more:
> Oh love! How my small heart did break
> And tears course down for thy dear sake!
>
> And now I think me where thou art
> And with what weight of lonely heart,
> And wish me where thou liest, to say
> Perhaps hard fortune will one day
> Relent its cruel division of me:
> My sad heart here, its love with thee . . .

But in the darkest hours of night
When ev'n the moon has lost her sight
And from the dark mosques' tow'rs arise
The heathens' strangest midnight sighs,
I lie awake and hear truth speak:
Thou'rt lost, and never more to seek.

Oh love! Remember me I pray
When to thy eyes the English day
Sheds oft its soft and ruby glow
Upon the gard'n we trod below,
When all the world and time was ours,
Unnumbered in its bliss-thought hours;

Remember me, that on the beach
Of Bosphorous thy name doth teach
Beneath a bough of foreign tree
In whispers to my memory:
Who loves thee still, and ever will,
Though time's long grief my heart doth kill.

The shrill sound of the telephone ringing again at the librarian's desk finally punctuated the silence in the Reading Room. Susan Alis was the first to speak.

'Well, well,' she turned to Richard Omar, 'congratulations, young man, I take it all back, this is a wonderful find, absolutely wonderful.'

Richard bowed his head in acknowledgement. 'I know it's not the missing part of the narrative,' he said to Elizabeth, 'but it looks as though you hit on the right conclusion after all. I'm afraid I don't think the girl got the boy.'

'You knew that all along.'

'Only if the poem was written by Celia Lamprey. Do you think it was?'

'Oh yes,' Elizabeth said, 'I'm sure of it. Although I don't suppose it can ever be proved absolutely. I keep thinking of what you were saying earlier,' she turned to Dr Alis, 'about how arbitrary our knowledge of the past can be. Sometimes it's as if we know *just* enough,' she held her thumb and forefinger up, an inch apart, 'for us

337

to ask ourselves what it is that we *don't* know; what is it that's missing?'

She turned back to the screen again. 'When as I saw you at the gate . . .' What gate? Could she possibly have meant Thomas Dallam's grille? But no, if she had meant a grille she would have said so, surely . . . Elizabeth ran a hand impatiently through her hair.

'So it looks as if she did see him one last time – or was hoping to. But then what happened? I don't suppose we'll ever know for sure.'

'But someone knew.' Thoughtfully, Dr Alis picked up the treated fragment again. 'Whoever wrote the poem – and perhaps it was Celia Lamprey – seems to have known she would never be set free. But maybe someone else was, years later, for all we know, someone – another concubine perhaps – who knew her, and knew her story. Someone who cared about her enough to write it all down – and send it to Paul Pindar, her "Loving Friend".'

'Perhaps Richard's right. Perhaps it was one of the nuns after all.'

'You mean perhaps they survived the shipwreck together?' Dr Alis said. 'Well, that's plausible enough. But then they would both have to have been bought at exactly the same time, by exactly the same slave master. And then sold as concubines into the Seraglio at exactly the same moment. Come on, what are the chances of that?'

'You're right, of course,' Elizabeth said.

'But isn't that what we're dealing with all the time?' Richard was packing his laptop back into its case. 'With chance. With coincidence. The most implausible, apparently arbitrary things happen all the time.' He zipped up his bag. 'After all, what were the chances that you would find the fragment after all these years? Or that I would have found the poem on the back? And consider this: if you had been even a year or two earlier with your discovery we would have missed it altogether. The technology simply didn't exist.'

As they stood up to leave, Elizabeth took the fragment and held it for one last time. 'She bided her time then. Waited for exactly the right moment.'

'What do you mean?' Richard was putting on his coat and scarf.

'Celia. I know you'll say it's fanciful of me,' Elizabeth glanced round at Dr Alis, 'but all the way along I've had the most curious feeling that Celia found me – rather than the other way round. I don't

338

know why.' She handed the folder back to Richard. 'It's silly of me, I know. Here, take it. I shan't be needing it again.'

Dr Alis and Elizabeth said goodbye to Richard Omar on the steps of the library.

When he had gone, Susan Alis sniffed the air. 'Look,' she said, 'it's a beautiful day after all.'

And it was true. The sky was blue, the sun sparkled on the snow.

'And where to now?' Dr Alis gave Elizabeth a sly sideways look.

'Do you mean, am I going back to Istanbul?' Elizabeth laughed. 'Oh yes, I expect so.'

'I meant now, as a matter of fact.'

'I'm meeting Eve; but not till later.' Elizabeth took her arm. 'Can I walk you back to college?'

'By all means.'

For a while they walked together in silence.

'You know, I keep asking myself, what happened, what happened to her in the end?' Elizabeth said thoughtfully as they went along. 'And it's just occurred to me that in some way, well, perhaps this *is* the end of Celia Lamprey's story. With the finding of the fragment, and the compendium – and now the poem. With us, here, piecing her story together—'

'—after four hundred years in the dark.'

'What?' Elizabeth gave a startled laugh. 'What did you just say?'

'I said "after four hundred years in the dark".'

'Yes, that's what I thought you said.'

They stopped and stared at one another.

'How odd,' Dr Alis said, giving Elizabeth a puzzled look. She put her head to one side as though she were listening for something, 'Now whatever made me say that?'

Acknowledgements

I would like to thank Doris Nicholson, at the Oriental Reading Room of the Bodleian Library, for tracking down the Paul Pindar bequest, and for helping me decipher the Syriac and Arabic texts. At the British Museum, Silke Ackermann navigated me through the workings of the astrolabe. I am grateful, too, to Professor Lisa Jardine for her advice about modern research practices, Ziauddin Sardar, Dr Ekmeleddin Ihsanoglu and Professor Owen Gingerich, for conversations about Islamic and Copernican astronomy, to Abdou Filali-Ansari for his advice on Arabic transcriptions, and most especially to John and Dolores Freely, who, when I first started researching this book fourteen years ago, were the most generous and entertaining of guides around Istanbul, past and present. Grateful thanks, too, to John Gilkes, Justine Taylor, Reina Lewis, Charlotte Bloefeld, Melanie Gibson, Maureen Freely, Simon Hussey, Tom Innes, Dr David Mitchell and my agent Gill Coleridge. My affectionate thanks, also, to Lucy Gray and Felice Shoenfeld who valiantly helped to keep my house and family in order during the three years that it took to write this novel.

Finally, I would like to thank A.C. Grayling for his numerous, forensic readings of various drafts of *The Aviary Gate*, and for Celia's poem. And last but not least, everyone at Bloomsbury: especially Mary Morris, Anya Rosenberg and Kathleen Farrar in London; Karen Rinaldi, Gillian Blake and Yelena Gitlin in New York; but most especially my editor Alexandra Pringle, without whose vision and extraordinary powers of diplomacy this novel might never have been written.

A NOTE ON THE AUTHOR

Katie Hickman is the author of five previous books, including two bestselling history books, *Courtesans* and *Daughters of Britannia*. She has written two travel books: *Travels with a Circus*, about her experiences travelling with a Mexican circus, which was shortlisted for the 1993 Thomas Cook Travel Book Award, and *Dreams of the Peaceful Dragon*, about a journey on horseback through the forbidden Himalayan kingdom of Bhutan. She was shortlisted for the Sunday Times Young British Writer of the Year award for her novel *The Quetzal Summer*. Katie Hickman lives in London with her two children and her husband, the philosopher A.C. Grayling.

A NOTE ON THE TYPE

The text of this book is set in Linotype Stempel Garamond, a version of Garamond adapted and first used by the Stempel foundry in 1924. It's one of several versions of Garamond based on the designs of Claude Garamond. It is thought that Garamond based his font on Bembo, cut in 1495 by Francesco Griffo in collaboration with the Italian printer Aldus Manutius. Garamond types were first used in books printed in Paris around 1532. Many of the present-day versions of this type are based on the *Typi Academiae* of Jean Jannon cut in Sedan in 1615.

Claude Garamond was born in Paris in 1480. He learned how to cut type from his father and by the age of fifteen he was able to fashion steel punches the size of a pica with great precision. At the age of sixty he was commissioned by King Francis I to design a Greek alphabet, for this he was given the honourable title of royal type founder. He died in 1561.